The Training Farm

Ultimate Submission

Amity Harris

DEDICATION

For my fans, I'm back.

For my boy, your new journey has just begun. Now, *kneel!*

TABLE OF CONTENTS

PREFACE

When we left Ron, the perfectly trained slave whose story I revealed in *Debbie's Gift*, he learned how to love being trained into the slave-husband that Debbie always wanted him to be. Debbie's experiences with his trainers, the colors, Gold, Red, Blue, Green and Black, and her special relationship with one particular Gold, reminded us through Debbie's journey that all men should be trained into perfect slaves. Sometimes you just need a special place like the Mistress's Training Facility.

Join us as we visit *The Training Farm*, where each Season on the Farm brings 245 males to the Owner's secretive Farm where each undergoes strict training, discipline and proper punishment to become the perfect animal that is part of a male's primal nature. Those who emerge as perfect slaves are returned to their owners to serve or can be purchased by the Owner's friends.

Walk (or gallop!) with the herd through Intake and Processing, where males are stripped of their former lives and get their first taste of conversion into the animals whose characteristics the Farm staff grows inside them. Then join them through Placement with their proper herds where their primal animal instincts are trained into perfection. Spend a Season in their training barns where their primitive reactions to strict training and discipline at the hands of the Farm's superbly-trained female staff are achieved.

Individual training is time-consuming and requires a superb cast of women who work a new herd every Season. Under the watchful eye of the Owner and her hand-picked staff, the new animals perform dazzling feats at First Competition where an audience of Mistresses enjoys their show.

Enjoy *The Training Farm* as the herd makes the ultimate journey into submission.

Chapter 1: Choosing the Farm

The room was crowded but comfortably cool for the hundreds in the audience whose eyes were riveted on the big screen at center stage. As the video flashed on the screen, a voice narrated the scenes that exploded in front of them. That voice, artfully punctuating the scenes, neither yelled nor shouted. In sharp contrast to the eerie images that shifted relentlessly across the screen, her voice was surprisingly calm.

The audience – all men with their eyes transfixed on the video – were carefully screened prior to this final session that was about to determine which of them would be invited to the upcoming Season on the Farm. It would be one of the most unthinkable yet fulfilling journeys and it would change their lives forever, just like it had for so many before. As they stared at the video, oblivious to their surroundings, leather-clad ushers strode the aisles and studied the males' faces. Some were taken aback by what they saw; but the women were really searching for the ones that were truly elevated by the carefully-selected scenes they were watching. The particular eyes they sought were the ones that drank in the images and wore faces that betrayed their arousal. Of course, a few were terribly scared while others were transfixed. Their reactions were studied, evaluated and noted on the staff's tablets.

Finally, the images came to a close and the overhead lights glowed again. The narrator's voice slowed while hundreds of males shifted uncomfortably in the auditorium's chairs. The ushers, moving almost inconspicuously among the crowd, returned quietly to the stage and took their seats behind the speaker. After what seemed like a long pause, her voice started anew.

"Now you've seen what the Farm is. Now you understand that it is your time to choose and you must choose right now."

She waited for the finality of her single-sentence challenge to sink in before continuing.

"You've learned what the day-to-day life is like at the Farm and what the conditions are. You have read and signed the contracts and have seen the reward that may be yours if you complete the Season. There is nothing more for me to add. Before I have you make your decisions, are there any questions?"

She stood elegantly on the stage and seemed so tall to all the eyes that were fixated on her. Her leather pants hugged her thighs tightly and the heels from her boots clicked loudly as she moved across the stage in the silent auditorium. She walked from one end of the wide stage to the other and peered into the audience for any raised hands. Seeing none, she brought the event to its finale with simple instructions.

"There are voting devices in the chair pocket in front of you. Take one out and check the number against the number on your wristband. If they do not match, signal a trainer."

Again, her heels clicked in an unrelenting staccato as she traversed the stage and studied the audience's reaction. With their usual careful preparation, she would have been stunned if any didn't match, but it was always a good idea to check. Confident that they were all in order, she issued a final instruction.

"Press the green button if you wish to continue. Press the red button to leave."

She added, "There will be no repercussions if you choose to leave; however, understand that when you press green, there is no turning back." Waiting only a moment for the finality of their choice to sink in, she concluded. "Choose now." A 30-second countdown clock filled the screen.

Unsteady hands reached out to grasp the smart devices. They hovered over the red and green buttons yet within 25 seconds the main control panel glowed brightly, signaling that every button had been pressed. It was always amusing to her that after such a long series of interviews, questionnaires and one-on-one meetings, the males rarely took more than 25 seconds to seal their own fates. Glancing at the main panel, she watched the numbers flash and smiled broadly at the crowd.

"Congratulations, boys," she said with a lilt of pleasure in her formerly flat voice. "We have only four who have chosen to depart."

With that pronouncement, four ushers made their way toward the males who had just opted out electronically. Taking each by the hand, ushers led them to the door that led directly to the Outtake staff. Those who chosen to leave would be processed out quickly and dispatched to their normal lives. For the males who remained, what happened next would replace what had just been their unfulfilled lives. Their former 'normal' would soon devolve into a hazy dream. What their futures held would evolve into their new reality.

She liked this next part the best.

"Secure the building," she said without fanfare.

Mass movement began. The ushers scurried toward the exits and made sure all the doors were locked. As the audience stared first at the ushers and then at each other, their bewilderment rose and many began to sweat in spite of the cool temperature in auditorium. Within minutes, the speaker on stage declared the room secure. Her ushers took their places in the aisles.

"You leave in a few minutes," the speaker said into her headset. "First, you have to be readied for the long trip."

The males had been informed that they were traveling north and west to a warm and secluded area for the duration of this Season in which they had just agreed to participate. They knew the conditions would be harsh. But each male had his own reasons for seeking this journey.

They knew the conditions were lovely in the summer and barren in the winter yet they had seen video of the huge dome that would shelter them from severe weather. They watched it open and close on the videos they had been required to study. The seclusion as well as the thousand-mile distance both stimulated and frightened them.

At the moment when their decisions had just been sealed, what struck them with full force was that the journey they had merely heard about and seen pictures of was now actually beginning. Everyone knew his life was about to be changed. Each, whether or not he would admit it, was as terrified as much as he was captivated.

The final order was given with the same flat voice they had listened to for the past two hours.

"Strip," she said casually. "Then dress in the outfits handed to you by the ushers. Leave your clothing on the floor; you won't need it again."

Switching off her microphone, she turned to exit the building and leave the chores of corralling the males into the buses that would take them to the airport to her trusted trainers. With barely a look back at the hundreds readying for transport, she made a final comment that a Leader Trainer's mike picked up and boomed throughout the auditorium.

"Issue the cattle prods," she said as she continued walking toward her limo which would whisk her to a private jet that would land at the Farm hours before the new herd arrived. The new Season was unfolding and she wanted to approve the final touches for this Season.

The news of cattle prods seeped into the audience's ears and the trainers grinned at the males' reactions. It wasn't the first time they had seen men reduced to shivering heaps from one of her off-hand comments. It always amused them to see every Season's group's reaction.

From the aisles, they tossed sets of fabric that were held together by loose strings toward each newcomer and waited for the herd to go through the usual shy process of stripping and dressing in their travel outfits. When they finally got to the plane, the women knew they'd compare and see who had won the trainers' pool. Their Season bet was always the same: which usher's group had the most who asked the same question. It was always a single word.

"Everything?" one male was certain to ask.

A smirking trainer greeted that question with the taste of her electric prod every time it was proffered and a shrieking scream was always the result.

Chapter 2: The Flight North

With their clothes in heaps on the auditorium floor, the group was marched in single file down the aisles, around the stage and out the back door where sunlight flooded their eyes. Eight buses generated a thick cloud of diesel exhaust and mingled with the new smell emanating from each man's travel jumpsuit. The trip was long and exhausting. Their outfit was designed to be unrestrictive.

Each was dressed in a drab gray jumpsuit that zipped up the front from either direction. The zipper could be pulled down when they wanted to remove the coverall, or it could be unzipped from bottom-to-top for use when a trainer might want to expose genitals for her training or disciplinary purposes. The crotches sported snaps that were now secured but each male realized that they, too, could be opened for easy access. Having watched videos and studied the Farm's photos sent to their secure account, each male knew that clothing would not be part of his upcoming Season on the Farm. The jumpsuits were temporary. Every male knew all clothing would soon be taken away. Yet for this moment, each was glad for its coverage.

Lines formed as they boarded one bus after another. Finally each newcomer was seated, belted in and his wristband checked against the master list of attendees. With five trainers per bus, the process was completed quickly and efficiently. The Head of Transport gave the signal and the caravan made its way to the airport. If the sun were still shining outside, those inside the bus never knew it. The opaque windows shut out even small glimpses of light. All memories of the life they had chosen to leave for the Season faded away as the bus engines roared onward. Cars passed the procession and invisible faces inside wondered what adventure the parade was headed to yet the faces inside each bus stared blankly at the impervious windows. Although they had been processed and shown what the Season held for them in excruciating detail, not a single bus rider knew where the Farm was going or how exactly the Season would unfold.

The buses rumbled toward a private airport and they entered the tarmac through a special gate. Shutting down their noisy engines just as they had done so many times before, the drivers opened the doors and exited. A van that would return them to the charter bus company was in place right on time. The drivers' job was done and the soon-to-be-empty vehicles would be returned by special drivers hired only for that one trip.

Almost simultaneously on each bus, the identical speech was repeated by that bus's head trainer.

"When I tell you to and not a moment before, proceed in silent single file to the stairs leading to the plane. Take the seat indicated by the staff on board. Buckle your seatbelt and be silent. It will be a long flight." She cocked her head toward the jumpsuit in seat 1A and said simply, "Now."

Uncertain and hesitating, the first seated male rose slowly and climbed on unsteady legs down the bus's steps. He was forced to squint in the bright sunlight as he stepped onto the tarmac and the sun bathed him in a bright glow. Alone on the pavement, he followed another trainer's crooked finger that pointed toward the path to the plane. He climbed the stairs silently. Inside his brain, he offered a silent goodbye to the life he knew and mounted the plane's steps to begin his journey to the Season at the Farm that would change his life forever.

The bus ride had taken only an hour.

Each man in turn exited the bus and formed a snaking line that climbed into the plane. Watching them with trained eyes, the trainers smiled at the men's instinctive self-patting – searching for their wallets, keys and watches that had been left in the auditorium. Cleanup crews had already boxed them up and transported their belongings to the airport. They would be carried as freight deep in the plane's belly as silent witnesses to what and who each of them had once been.

One by one, they wobbled toward the private aircraft. Each managed his way up the stairs and took a seat as indicated by a trainer's pointing finger. The entry process was perfected by practice and took a mere 20 minutes. When the plane was full and their numbers checked one more time against both their armbands and the roster, the group's head trainer initialed the Intake form and handed it to the flight crew chief.

With a comforting clunk, the plane's main door shut and was bolted. Inside the cabin, 245 men sat in fearful silence as the plane taxied toward the runway and readied for takeoff. It would fly them to the north country for another new Season on the Farm. Takeoff was as uneventful as were all prior trips and the plane soon roared north and west, crossing hundreds of miles on a smooth path toward their new futures.

The trainers gathered in a private cabin and shed their street clothes. Donning outfits more suited for the terrain to which they were heading, each woman slipped on new black leather pants, polished but well-worn black boots and finished off her uniform with a leather vest. The vests' bodices were cut so low that even when buttoned, it revealed full breasts that were supported by a built-in shelf that propped their jiggling flesh up high and out from their chests. It seemed their breasts led the way with every step they took. Each plunging neckline allowed their colors to shine through – a single piece of colored fabric that identified their rank on the Farm staff.

The transport crew's breasts sported a lime green strip.

Back in the main cabin, some of the newcomers dozed while others just stared blankly ahead. Although no order had been issued for absolute silence, the travelers were afraid to speak to each other. Each man knew that the one next to him was naked under his lightweight gray jumpsuit and knew his own naked skin abutted his seat mate's save for thin gray fabric. They also realized that with a single motion, any trainer on board could strip their coveralls and expose any part of them for everyone to see. The videos they watched were explicit. They understood that their bodies were merely a tool this Season on the Farm and would be used or abused as their trainers saw fit. There were no limits or safe words. They signed them away in the auditorium when they each pressed the green button.

Each man thought about the promise of a cash award guaranteed for completing the Season. The rules were clear: finish the Season and win money. Whatever else may befall them, they figured at one point or another, all they had to do was finish the Season and the money would be theirs. Even though the agreement included confidentiality clauses and a choice for them to forego the money and choose a new life instead, most of the males allowed thoughts of cash fill their heads. It was easier than imagining what lay ahead on the journey to the prize or what a "new life" meant.

Their thoughts were as jumbled as the clouds through which the plane flew yet none of the males spoke during the long flight. They crossed border after state border and then a nation's boundary as they flew to the secluded north country that was home to the Farm. Although they had been given a general idea of their destination, no one had coordinates specific enough beyond knowing that they were headed to the Canadian wilderness for this Season at the Farm.

Sliding the curtain open between the cabins, the head trainer, now outfitted in black leather from ankles up and with breasts flowing over the vest's opening, spoke to the passengers.

"We land in 30 minutes," she said as the men's eyes riveted on her breasts and the tiny spot of color that poked out from between them. "In 15 minutes, the captain will turn the seatbelt sign on and you will strap yourselves securely." The men seemed to exhale collectively, partly in relief that the long flight would soon be over, yet also in fear of what lay ahead. She left them no time to wonder.

"Unzip the jumpsuits," she said, "from the bottom up."

As if a river's dam was released, the men mumbled and muttered loudly. Her statement was ludicrous. How would they disembark the plane with their bodies exposed like that?

"Now!" she said loudly and fingered the cattle prod on its hook on her leather belt. Reaching toward the hapless passenger seated in 9A, the first seat in the back cabin and the body closest to her, she touched it against his inner thigh.

His screams filled the cabin and one by one, 245 men fumbled for the zippers, opened their thin jumpsuits and buckled their seatbelts against their naked skin as fast as they could. They scurried to obey her order as if she had electrified each of them with that single touch.

> *Make an example of the closest one, she had been taught. The rest will follow out of fear.*

With 245 exposed men buckled into their seats, the trainers walked the aisle and pulled each jumpsuit apart so each chest, midsection, and crotch was open and visible. When the captain clicked the seatbelt sign, the trainers returned to their cabin, seated themselves and sipped champagne from crystal glasses handed to them by the flight crew.

"To another Season on the Farm!" they toasted and enjoyed the cold liquid sliding down their throats.

Chapter 3: Arrival at the Farm

The plane rolled down the runway before finally pulling to a stop. With only rare traffic visiting this particular airport, there was no danger of being spotted by incoming flights. The trainers exited the plane through the front cabin and descended the stairs with an expectant gait. The travel process had gone smoothly and they were eager to turn the passengers over to the Intake staff who were ascending the back stairs in perfect synchronization. The Intake staff sported similar leather pants and low-heeled boots, but their leather vests were markedly different. Their ample breasts were not peeking out from the low neckline; instead, they were fully exposed from their vests with identical open fronts but added snaps that closed tightly at their waists. A single decoration of neon blue fabric split their cleavage. The head of Intake flung the curtain open with an assured motion and studied her herd of passengers.

The men, still exposed and buckled in, stared at her in silence. Like most males are wont to do, they peered first at her breasts and then at her face. Not one man dared meet her eyes. She was the personification of authority; an apparition of determination. In seconds and without saying a word, she pushed 245 men into a state of abject terror. She was the visualization of all their fears coalesced into a single person.

She issued orders rapidly and never paused.

"Unbuckle your seatbelts. Rise row by row starting with 9A," she said while pointing at the luckless passenger inhabiting that seat. "Exit using the front stairs and march through the cabin in a line directly behind me." Turning her back turned to the hapless lot, she jerked her finger over her shoulder to indicate just where 'behind her' was. "Then proceed down the stairs and follow the next set of instructions."

She used her chin to point at seat 9A forcing the inhabitant to rise on unsteady legs. Pausing frequently to figure out what fate had befallen him to have been placed in the most ill-fated seat imaginable, he plodded through the trainer's cabin, continued down the aisle, and headed to the open cabin door. With every step, his flimsy jumpsuit opened more and more, exposing a few more inches of his skin with every stride. By the time he reached the top of the stairs, his gray jumpsuit was flapping in the sudden breeze, anchored only by an inch or so of still-zipped teeth at his neck.

The feeling of exposure made him dizzy. The cool breeze and the jumpsuit fabric felt oddly comforting as it flapped against his skin. Because the zipper reached fully from his crotch to his neck, the open area rendered his torso available to the spring breezes. Held shut only by a few remaining zipper teeth, the former occupant of seat 9A involuntarily grasped at his neck as if to insure it wouldn't fall victim to the wind's seduction.

Almost immediately, he heard someone yell in his direction.

"Hands down!" A woman's voice whipped through the wind. His fingers flew to his sides as his eyes searched for the speaker but he knew in his heart that voice was speaking directly to him.

"March!" she said and seat 9A felt his legs tremble with every syllable she barked at him.

Focusing on the tarmac, which was really a concrete strip at the end of the runway, he saw a group of women gathered in front of a line of utilitarian buses parked in single file near the plane. Resigned to whatever fate had decreed him to be first, he stepped onto the rolling stairs. He was oddly relieved when his foot finally touched solid ground. He turned his puzzled face toward one of the women as if to ask directions.

"Get on the first bus and SIT!" she barked. Her tone was cold; her eyes steely. The tight leather pants sat well on her hips, he managed to notice, but the vest – it was similar but not quite the same as the one worn by the woman on the plane. It fit her well, but her breasts were fully exposed. This vest had a drab gray stripe between her breasts and the waistband sported snaps that closed it tightly. It occurred to him that the color gray on her vest was identical to his jumpsuit and he …

"Move!" she said and she took a menacing step toward him.

That one step was all he needed to gallop toward the first bus. Trotting as quickly as the flapping jumpsuit would allow, when he neared the open door he swore he heard her snicker. His numb legs carried him up the tall steps and he plopped into the first seat in the front row. More and more men fell into position and within a few minutes, the bus was filled with exhausted and naked men.

When the first bus filled, they pointed the next man to deplane toward the second bus in line. His mind reeled and his brain was confused; worse, he didn't know what their pointed fingers meant. But he instinctively followed the men he saw moments ago in front of him and trotted toward the first bus. When he passed the second bus's open door, his ears were greeted with a shrill, "Stop!" command that made his legs halt suddenly in their tracks. One of the women was standing face-to-face with him.

She reached into his open jumpsuit and grabbed his left nipple tightly and dragged him toward the second bus. The effect of her silent action was not lost on the lineup that followed. His loud shriek of pain filled their ears and taught them a fast lesson. Their bodies betrayed a twinge of dread for what just happened. Watching one of their own being pulled up the steps by his nipple left a lasting impression. It was exactly what she intended.

> *Make an example out of the one closest at hand. Make it immediate. The rest will learn the lesson.*

She tossed him into his seat and motioned for the next to sit beside him. The rest of passengers boarding the second bus needed no extra instructions where to sit or how quickly they were expected to move.

One after another, the men exited the plane and were marched to their respective buses for transport to the Farm. After they were buckled in securely, two trainers boarded each bus to oversee the final leg of the long journey. Each was clad in tight leather and each pair of breasts that jutted out from the open vests filled the males' eyes.

However, when each overseer began her welcoming talk, their attention was refocused immediately when they heard her first words.

"We own you now," each bus overseer spoke plainly.

Chapter 4: Evaluating the Herd

The caravan finally slowed and each bus turned into the Farm's long fenced entrance. The men's eyes instinctively focused on the bus's opaque windows in hopes of catching a glimpse of any landmark that might give them a sign of where they were. The entire trip had been carefully planned so that the 245 passengers would never get geographical hints and they simply had no idea where – or when – they were. Time was suspended each Season on the Farm.

With a nod from Yvonne instructing her to take over, Zoe, her new trainer-in-training, took over the disembarking process. Getting them off the bus wasn't as easy as it looked and Zoe needed training in every Farm responsibility. This was her first transport practice and Yvonne, the head of Transport, wanted to make sure she could handle the job.

"Up!" Zoe squeaked and watched the busload of confused men rise. "Face the aisle," she added and almost to her surprise, they complied.

Yvonne watched in amusement as Zoe's breasts jutted out just a bit from her muscular frame. Marching from the rear toward the front of the bus aisle, Zoe finished unzipping the last inch of one jumpsuit after another as the light fabric that still clung to their shoulders flapped down the men's bodies until it rested tenuously around their hips. Not a single man dared reach for the fabric; instead, they stood and waited for their next command.

It came in very short order.

"March!" Zoe said in a stronger voice toward no one in particular. She grabbed the unlucky first-seat inhabitant's nipple in tight fingers and led him toward the door. With every step he took while locked in her grasp, the gray jumpsuit fell farther toward his ankles. Trying desperately not to fall, he walked unsteadily down the steps into bright sunlight that blinded him for a moment. He struggled to blink and focus.

"You! This way!" a stronger voice said and still almost sightless, he turned in the voice's direction and plodded with the gray jumpsuit fluttering downward with every step he took. Tear-filled eyes clouded his way. The unlucky soul provided the Farmhands with the same amusing image they were greeted with during Intake and this same procession was a hallmark of every new Season on the Farm.

The disembarking process always took more time than loading. Given the males' inability to move precisely with the jumpsuits twisted around their ankles and their discomfort at being reduced to a line of naked marchers heading toward an unknown destination growing with each unsteady step, the line moved at a snail's pace. Their destination was the Intake Barn.

The huge building was the first of many at the end of miles-long path that made up the Farm's chilling entrance. With only one entrance door, the procession moved slowly but the Farmhands made certain that the line never stopped. Intake was skilled at taking in 245 males and they perfected the task more and more each Season. The male faces changed, but the continuous line of naked bodies never stopped.

A brightly lit room greeted the group and in quick fashion each man was instructed to a particular spot. The risers they climbed were arranged in a large semi-circle that was dotted with aisles that separated them into smaller groups. The Intake crew arranged them specifically as each Farmhand directed. The process was as speedy for the Farm's young trainees as it was mystifying for the males.

Each Farmhand surveyed the small group of males and led them by their nipples to a designated waiting area. None of the Farmhands or their trainees wondered which area the men were led; it was as if they could size them up with a glance and direct them to the right stable. In short order, the wooden platforms were filled with weary men, many of whom still sported their jumpsuits now hopelessly tangled around their ankles. Several had simply given up and stepped out of them.

With the lights reflecting brightly off their sweaty bodies, a new Farmhand took center stage. Her voice needed no microphone.

"You have arrived at the Farm," she said clearly. "You are about to enter Processing. This procedure will last for the rest of your day. When Processing is finished, you'll be fed, watered and quartered."

"Welcome to the Farm," she finished and stepped off stage.

Four hundred ninety eyes stared at Willa's vest and every man's stare shifted first from the neon blue stripe that started from her waistband and floated upward between her breasts and landed on her huge bosoms that stood almost on their own propelled from the tight bodice that pushed them higher than looked possible. Hers were breasts that would have excited every one of them a mere 24 hours earlier. But now, they could manage only gaping jaws as their tired bodies trembled in growing fear.

A scream penetrated the enormous barn.

Their eyes instinctively turned toward the shriek. The barn's auditorium design was simple and the acoustics superb. The males on the upper risers had an unobstructed view. What they saw erased any interest in Willa's breasts immediately; instead, it focused their attention to a single man, now flopping on the floor, writhing in pain and shrieking uncontrollably. The Farmhand nearest him had touched him lightly with a short metal rod. The gaggle of naked men watched her touch him again and his gut-wrenching screams sickened them.

"Kneel," she said. Her voice filled the otherwise silent room.

He continued rolling and screaming on the wooden platform as those nearby leaned out of his frenzied way. No one in the auditorium moved; there was no offer of help. The men seemed able to breathe.

"Kneel!" she said again after he had ceased flopping like a hooked fish on a dock.

Interrupted only by the sound of his own gasping breaths, he managed himself to wobbly knees. Reaching toward the floor to steady himself, he was soon on all fours with his forgotten gray jumpsuit in a nearby lump. His nakedness wasn't his problem at the moment. His shame was replaced with a greater need: survival.

With all eyes transfixed on the scene unfolding on the lower platform, the Farmhand who sported a neon blue stripe on her vest held the small metal rod in front of the man's face. The sight of it made him whimper.

Every man in the auditorium made the same mental note: whatever that rod was, they needed to stay as far away from it as possible. Whatever it took, whatever he had to do to avoid it; that's what each man silently vowed.

"Crawl," she ordered and touched the rod to his bare ass to propel him. With a howl of agony, he scurried forward and without any additional orders, the rest of the men on his low-level platform hurried behind him on their hands and knees toward wherever their next stop in the Intake Process would be.

Chapter 5: The Farm Way

Intake Processing was special. It required the trainers' careful inspection of the incoming herd. A particular skill needed in bringing a new contingent into the Farm for the Season was one that the Farmhands practiced diligently and tested every Season. Each new animal-in-training was inspected, examined and catalogued meticulously. Not only was the staff well-drilled in every step of Intake Processing, but they also were instructed in the reasons that Processing was one of the Owner's most prized and well-tested systems. The Farm prided itself on safety and unless each newcomer's health and endurance was carefully recorded, their safety could not be assured.

For the Owner, it did not matter that Processing ignored the herd's dignity because their work insured its safety. According to the Owner, who taught it carefully to each of the Farmhands, loss of dignity was an inconsequential price for the males to pay for the greater good of keeping the herd in good shape. Animals' privacy didn't matter where safety was concerned. The farmhands had the Owner's explicit approval to insure herd welfare every day of every Season.

Enduring Processing carried with it one additional benefit that the Owner found critical to herd training. During Processing, the men would cease to think of themselves individuals. Instead, Intake Processing began their season-long progression from man to beast, which is what each one of them signed up for and would be what each one of them would receive. To earn their promised prizes, they would undergo the Farm's proven course to pass or fail on their own merits. Those who failed were returned to their home cities and their former lives. The Owner was interested only in those who succeeded on the Farm. She was proud of the Farm's success rate and the Farmhands were trained in broad training methods to insure success.

What most males didn't realize was that even those who qualified for the financial prize rarely accepted it at Season's end. They yearned for the new lives that only she could grant them. It was a statistic that stood out from the rest all these many Seasons on the Farm and distinguished her herd from the other so-called slave-training facilities she had visited. Only one, the Mistress's Gold enclave in the Pacific Northwest came close to her own Training Farm. The two were close friends and shared many training techniques.

Every training method and tool was tried out prior to the rare expulsion of a male from the Farm mid-Season. The Owner was proud that fewer than five males had ever been banished during any prior Season at the Farm and on each rare instance, the experts she consulted helped improve training so that such a regrettable event was not repeated. It spoke well of her careful Intake procedures and her continual improvement of the Farm experience.

At this point during Intake, most of the exhausted men were filthy from the grueling day. Processing always began and ended with a complete cleaning of each member of the new herd. Tired males were generally more compliant; however, their endurance had to be monitored carefully.

That was Victoria's job.

Each small group was driven from the auditorium to the Processing Center and each Farmhand taught her group to move together. They had been sorted for a reason that would soon become apparent even to them and keeping the small-group packs identifiable within the larger herd was of prime importance. Once they were assembled in a drab holding area of stainless steel walls and a deep-set floor, Victoria raised her voice so it could be heard over the echo that reverberated from the metal walls.

As soon as she began speaking, every eye turned in her direction, save for the staff and trainees, whose eyes never left their charges.

"This is Processing," she said and every ear could hear the capital "P" through her soft British accent. "Here you will be run through a series of examinations so that you are placed correctly in a pack this Season. Your experiences will be the richest imaginable."

Victoria and the Farmhands noted only a few small smiles on some men's faces when they heard the word "richest." As their charges smiled, the women, who knew what would happen next, smirked.

"No talking during Processing. You will follow the hindquarters in front of you when your pack is led to the next station. Not one of you has a question now so there is no need for any to speak. Move quickly through Processing and when you are done, you will be assigned to your barn for the Season."

Victoria inhaled after her practiced announcement as she studied their faces. Just like every other group in all the Seasons she had been on the Farm, this pack was simultaneously eager, scared and worn out. It was one of her favorite sights.

She recited the names of five farmhands quickly in an offhand introduction to their packs as she directed them to five different Intake Processing positions.

"Ursula, your flock goes to Medical," Victoria pointed to the farthest door on the right, "Tara, take yours to Exercise." Victoria pointed to another door.

"Sharon, your group starts in Measurement, and Ronda, take yours to the Fitting Room." Victoria paused and checked her list. "Paula, I want yours in Assessment. That should do it," Victoria said and added in a voice that cut through the stainless steel echo like a knife. "But first ..."

It was one of her favorite teachable moments. The head trainers moved toward their assigned doors but did not direct that the men should follow. Ever-wary of that pain stick, the new herd stood confused in their assigned groups and waited a specific instruction to move.

As the males stood naked and still, torrents of water spewed from nozzles that dotted every wall and the ceiling in the stainless steel room. In a giant group shower, the herd was doused with gallon after gallon of cold water. They heard a voice over a loudspeaker instruct them to strip and step out of any remaining gray jumpsuits and toss them aside. The men hurried to comply yet peeling off drenched cotton fabric was a nearly impossible task. The water continued unabated while the stragglers stripped and when the last laggard was done, Victoria said mercilessly, "That was NOT fast enough."

Water continued to discharge from the ceiling and jets along the walls. Now saturated from the unrelenting flood, they tried in vain to turn away from the cold stinging spray. No matter which way they spun, there was always another jet impaling freezing needles of water against their bodies. The shower didn't care if it hit their backs, chests, ankles, asses or cocks. It just sprayed inexorably and soaked them without stopping.

With a nod to Control who watched every moment of Intake and Processing from behind dark windows, Victoria pressed another button on the wall of her dry enclosure. In seconds, the water added foamy soap that enveloped the herd. Soon they were covered in white suds and their only recourse was to shut their eyes to avoid the soap's sting. The now-blind group never saw the cadre of trainees armed with scrub brushes flood into the chamber and position themselves to start.

Victoria's nod set them in motion.

Their brushes attacked the herd to complete every Farm trainee's virgin training mission: assuring that her small group was clean and its skin sparkled. The trainees, eager to enhance their promotion list chances, were as zealous as they were scrupulous in their attention to each male's crevice and fold. Their stiff brushes flew as the Farm trainees raised arm after arm and scrubbed everywhere her brush could reach. Lifting one leg after another, their brushes scoured a line of groins and sent several plopping to the floor in pain. They pulled cocks up and out and pushed testicles out of the way. No inch of male skin was left untouched.

Finally, Control was satisfied and was ready to move to the next stage of cleaning.

"Hands and knees," a voice overhead said as 245 men struggled to find floor space to crouch down on and obey the faceless voice. Their eyes still pressed closed against the soap's sting, their hands patted the floor blindly to find a few inches so they could assume the just-ordered position. The Farm trainees knew there wasn't enough floor for them all to have private space and comply to the order, but each new herd member struggled to find some floor on which to drop to his hands and knees and avoid the electric prod.

Every Farmhand smirked. They knew that the only way that the herd could obey would be to overlap each other and share what floor there was. They would soon be pressed into a single mass of flesh. This was a teachable moment every Season on the Farm.

It was always amusing watching a new herd press their soapy faces against another's side, arm or ass as they pushed together to find space to touch the floor. The Farmhands smiled as the trainees prodded a few errant males toward the slippery skin of a nearby floor hugger. Victoria loved the Farm's teachable moments. The trainees were instructing the herd that personal space no longer existed for them. Not at the Farm.

The soapy mass of slippery bodies slithered across the stainless steel floor for what would become another amusing video clip provided by the Intake process. While the trainees pushed the stragglers toward the floor, the lead trainers grinned. The young trainees knew they were being evaluated and wasted no time in arranging their pile correctly. Herding their group efficiently was a goal set out for them in their training agenda. No dawdlers were tolerated. Trainees who didn't work quickly enough risked staying at the lowest level in the Farm's pecking order for another Season and not one of them wanted that outcome. Every trainee anticipated the signal Victoria would issue when she was satisfied that they had performed well. Until she issued that signal, their job was not done. With renewed fervor, they worked each of their herds to position them in a way that would please Victoria.

At long last, they heard her signal.

The whirr that greeted them meant that the first Intake task was finished. The trainees understood that their evaluations would include specifics about their herd positioning task yet none had time to worry about that right now. There was more work to be done with the herd. Looking up, they saw rods descend from the ceiling and they stood in silence until the springy cords touched the floor.

The herd, their eyes still shut from fear of soap sting, never saw them coming.

The trainees wasted little time. Each grasped a nearby rod and flexed it into a small curve. Pressing the tip against the first ass within reach, they pressed the green button that propelled a stream of oil against the exposed hole. Pressing the tip deeper and deeper into the lubricated opening, each trainee ignored the grunts and groans that spewed from the men's throats. The goal was to lubricate all the herd's assholes quickly and accurately without dawdling or worse, leaving one unfinished.

The mass of males, still blinded by soap and kneeling in a tight morass of legs, arms, heads and chests, yelped one by one as a rod was pushed relentlessly inside it. The Farmhands – both the Trainers and trainees – were always surprised by the fierce reactions some in the new herd had when a mere two-inch nozzle was forced into their asses. Sometimes they noted which ones had the loudest objections so they could be observed throughout the Season when larger objects were forced in. It was always amusing on the Farm to watch complainers having their asses inserted by whatever the staff saw fit to press inside them at the time.

The music of their grunts increased as one ass after another was filled and oily nozzles were completely inserted. Each member of the herd understood what the noises meant. If his own ass had been violated, then so had all the others. Functionally blind and their asses skewered by a cold rod, some whimpered in humiliation while others grunted in discomfort. A few howled from sheer degradation. The rest tried to breathe and accept their situation stoically. Yet the Farmhands could see each face and they learned from the Owner that male faces never lie. Betraying their innermost humiliation, even the silent ones grimaced in mortification.

> *Males who can't see think that others can't see them, the Owner taught them. Their faces betray them.*

It was a time-consuming process to have 245 anal rods approved one-by-one by the Head Trainer. Once the sudsy trainees stood up for evaluation as ordered, Olivia, the Lead Trainer of trainees, began inspecting each trainee's anal lubrication handiwork. Following Olivia's demonstrations, each trainee spread each pair of her group's asscheeks so her superior could inspect the three Farm standards: the rod's *position*, the *quality of lubrication* and the *depth of insertion*. Once or twice, she adjusted a rod and had her assistant note the reason on her ever-present tablet.

Olivia stepped from group to group and checked every insertion. It wasn't until she reached the final group that she stopped and looked quizzically at a particular trainee.

"What is the meaning of this?" she asked. The young trainee shook visibly at her seriousness of her question.

Olivia was outraged, "Look at this rod!"

Grabbing her trainee by her wet hair, Olivia plunged the young woman's face close up against the man's impaled ass. She held her there until the young woman choked out a reply. The trainers and trainees watched silently. Olivia's strict level of discipline was well known throughout the ranks. Watching her in action taught them all important lessons about safety standards.

"I – I think it's loose," the trainee babbled and Olivia knew that the girl didn't understand the severity of the problem she had potentially caused. She pushed the trainee's face into the male's ass so that her eyes were now only an inch from the misplaced rod.

"It's not JUST loose," she said unsympathetically. "Tell me what's wrong with it!" she demanded even louder.

The trainee was near tears but Olivia was unmoved by her outburst. Emotions had no place on the Farm.

"We do NOT damage the animals!" she hissed into the woman's ear. "You need a lesson," she said calmly.

As her Trainer grasped an unused rod, Olivia's assistant knew all too well what was going to happen next. She yanked the trainee's leather G-string down, spun her to the floor and pulled her asscheeks far apart. Olivia sprayed the woman's splayed hole and drove the rod in with a well-practiced motion. The young girl screamed wildly from deep inside her throat and the eerie sound echoed from the stainless steel walls.

"Was your ass ready for that?" Olivia asked as if no one were watching except the young trainee and herself.

"No, no, Ma'am," the trainee sputtered.

"Didn't I give you specific instructions for tight assholes?" Olivia pressed. "Were you taught what to do if an asshole wasn't stretched properly for penetration?" Her words were showed no pity.

Everyone in the audience knew that Olivia's rhetorical questions had taught the young trainee a valuable lesson. The Farmhands knew what was coming next and they wore their amusement across their lips. Leaving the trainee attached to the rod pushed far up her rectum, Olivia continued her herd inspection until she was satisfied that all 246 rods were positioned correctly. With a nod to her assistant, she proclaimed this part of the Intake up to her standards.

With her assistant tapping on her tablet and sticking close to her side, Olivia exited the room and Victoria pressed a green button on the wall panel to signal Control.

Two hundred and forty five voices plus a single female shrieked as one and filled the chamber with a magnificent bray. The Farmhands smiled as they surveyed the room of gyrating bodies knowing that each one had just received his – or her – first dose of a thorough internal cleansing. Animal enemas made up a process that would be repeated all Season but the virgin experience was one to behold.

Less than a minute later, the Farmhands were satisfied that the first round of cleaning was done. The water jets were turned on to rinse the herd as they knelt on top of each other with their rods still pointing high. Once they were rinsed off, it was time to take them to Herding, the next round of Intake Processing.

Chapter 6: Herding

With the herd's asses oozing remnants of the herbal enema that was the first step in their cleaning, Victoria was ready to turn the group over to their pack Trainers. She knew their bladders were as full as their rectums and each Trainer relished taking their pack to the next Intake station along their Processing journey.

The trainees were ordered to release the rods. Trainers instructed the kneeling males to hold their bowels tightly until they reached the next station. The thought of a bathroom break helped their weary bodies hold onto their asses' contents for just a few moments longer. Each man's face contorted and showed his Farmhand what she already knew. They were struggling. Watching them battle to hold the enemas inside, the Trainers used leather crops to herd their groups into a mass that crawled toward the next Intake session. One after another, each male crawled through the tight door in anticipation of being allowed to perform the simplest bathroom function. By now, that simple human need was an overwhelming demand and consumed their every muscle.

They crawled forward until the crops smacking their asses told them to stop. Still on all fours, they could see the ass in front of them that formed the line of men herded on narrow platforms that fit only their hands and on another, their knees. Afraid to look down as the motor started, they felt the floor move. To their horror, the platforms expanded and the one that held their hands separated from the one on which their knees were pressed. As it spread farther away, their hands were pulled from their knees and each man struggled to hold on, lest he fall into the unknown abyss that had just opened up beneath them.

Their bowels urged them and their bladders screamed. With no bathroom break in sight, the group began to understand what was going to happen. To their horror, they learned exactly what this Intake room's function was. Tears welled up in their eyes and many allowed them to fall down their faces.

Victoria marched to the front and addressed the dangling group.

"On the Farm, animals are fed and watered only as much as needed. We expect you to perform essential bodily functions only when we allow. Learn how you do this on the Farm." She allowed her words to sink in as the Farmhands marched between the rows of herded men.

Victoria said, "You will learn to enjoy it." And she walked away.

Still uncomprehending her full meaning, the men stared into the empty space where Victoria had just stood. Their ears waited for further instructions – and the location of the bathroom. Some began to understand; however, many could not yet conceive that they were to use this place to pee or worse. Not one could will himself to go first. Each man held himself in check with every ounce of his power, lest he soil himself and the cavernous pit below with his own enema-induced defecation. Eventually, some men's bodies gave in to physical demands. They were unable to control themselves and amid a series of cries and whimpers, emptied their bladders and bowels in front of the ever-mindful Control's cameras.

The Farmhands removed their prods from their leather belts just in case one went a little crazy, but they had learned through Seasons of experience that a male's bodily needs will usually be expressed without the help of voltage. They walked the lines and scrutinized each face, anticipating the first telltale discharge to emerge. It only took one, they had learned.

"No, NO!" one screamed and soon all 245 men groaned as they opened their rectums and bladders.

I wonder which one will go first, Tara thought. She hoped it was one from her pack. Of course, she could watch the video later for a play-by-play summary.

Victoria's voice rang from the back of the room. "You have five minutes until we leave!" she threatened, leaving them alone with their Farmhands to learn the Farm way.

Maybe he'll be one of mine, Paula hoped. None of mine have ever been first before.

The shrieking grew soon enough as the men fought to allow the unfathomable to happen. Suddenly, from a far back corner of the room, a voice whimpered, "Please, oh no, oh God, no, please."

Damn, he's one of Ursula's, Sharon complained to herself. Why is one in Ursula's pack always first?

An unmistakable stench permeated the room as did the sound of the group sobbing. At least one man had relieved himself the Farm way and it was up to the other 224 to follow his example. No Lead Trainer would move her pack forward until each and every one of them had learned this Farm rule and was completely empty. Ronda used her prod once or twice to spur her group along. She learned over the Seasons that a small electric shock on an ass that was fighting for control would loosen it up. The desired results were sure to follow and she would have the outcome she demanded.

After ten minutes, the men were mortified but were empty. Liquid and solids fell out of them, staining their legs as torrents were discharged into the empty area below. What the men hadn't counted on was how loose their bowel movements would be after the enemas that were shot into them earlier through the anal rods would generate. Once their anuses opened, they had absolutely no control. Stopping their feces was simply beyond their ability.

Ursula studied her row of budding barnyard animals pump out enough waste to satisfy her. She marched down the aisle and tapped each asscheek with her prod just to make sure each was empty. Her experience from her Seasons on the Farm taught her that even though a male said he was empty, there was always just a little bit more. Lest the herd expel it at an inopportune moment, Ursula preferred that they get it over with in the proper venue. A little sharp pain on a male's asscheeks produced the result she wanted.

Each Trainer followed her lead and the 245 discovered to their horror that their Trainers knew a lot more about their bladders and asses than they did. Soon each ass had tasted the electric prod on a low setting and had emptied itself more and more until enough was expelled to suit their Trainers. Even with the exhaust fans and deodorizing sprays, the room had become unpleasant enough that the trainees were called in to finish and get the herd ready for the next round of Intake Processing.

The floors shifted; the herd was hosed off; and their bodies were lathered and rinsed by cold jets again. Finally the trainees scrubbed them from head to hoof and they were ordered to stand and walk to the next station of their Intake.

Its name filled them with terror when Ursula announced they were headed to Medical Processing.

Chapter 7: Medical

All Farmhands knew the importance of Medical Intake; after all, this was a working Farm and all the animals performed work under the supervision of a Trainer who led their pack. If the animals weren't healthy or couldn't work, then the Farm suffered. There was too much work to be done for any animal to be under par.

Ursula's clean but disheveled group walked unsteadily behind her. She was resplendent in her shiny orange vest designator as she strode confidently to the Intake Center's medical wing. Once they arrived, she announced their itinerary.

"Medical will assess various aspects of your health thoroughly," she said. "You will undergo a series of tests that are follow ups to the ones you had with our physicians before arrival. Your physiological reactions will be evaluated." She allowed her words to sink as some of the men nodded and others appeared terrified of what could happen next.

Ursula continued as the group paid nervous attention.

"The medical team is expertly trained and will extract all the information required. Your cooperation is expected but they know how to deal with reluctance." Ursula nodded to the team in the white lab coats and gave them permission to begin. She walked to the rear of the antiseptic room and sat in a chair that had no other function than for her to use while her pack was examined.

The medical staff pushed the naked group into small clusters and pressed them, five at a time, against a transparent room divider. Instructing them to stand with their feet squarely on top of the consecutively taped Xs, they weaved tight straps around their ankles and buckled them shut. Dozens of electrodes were pasted to various parts of their bodies. Several were glued precisely onto their testicles and shafts. Technicians positioned themselves behind instrument panels and twirled dials and pressed buttons while their monitors glowed.

Ursula's lips curled upward. One technician flipped a red lever. The fun was about to begin.

Within seconds, Ursula, along with the technicians, watched 45 shafts stiffen as the electrical stimulation increased. As monitors recorded various penis responses, cocks rose and bobbed as if waving to nearby penises suffering the same predicament. When a technician twisted a dial, the bobbling cocks softened and lay flaccid against their thighs. A few seconds later, they shrank to humorously miniscule sizes.

The humiliated males tried to stare at their feet rather than meet the eyes of others whose organs had also shrunk into soft little blobs.

"Let's try that again," the technician said and the trainees ran a strap from the clear plastic room divider around all five men's foreheads, forcing their chins up, chests out, and backs perfectly straight.

She moved the dial again and the tiny cocks grew to a pronounced stiff state. Ursula grinned at the technician who, she believed, enjoyed her work a bit too much.

"Good response," she said toward Ursula as she turned the dial and diminished their erections. Dismissing the first five, she focused her attention to the next group. Another technician detached the electrodes and the group, who missed the joy of their erections, winced at their removal. She unhooked the long forehead strap as well as their ankle restraints so the groups could be replaced.

"Let's check the other end," the lead tech announced as a heavy silence fell. Ursula nodded in approval.

"Face the wall," the technician said and the kneeling herd of five stood and rotated in place. She secured their forearms to the plastic wall and then tapped each one's belly until he figured out that she wanted him to rise up to his knees. Once each lifted his ass to a height that pleased her, she secured his ankles in metal locks. Stepping back to examine her handiwork, she smiled briefly and unpacked new electrodes for the next test.

Medical techs knew their job was important and they enjoyed the sight of a row of spread asses on which to minister their work.

Squirting a large glob of get on a long swab, she inserted it with little fanfare into the first rectum in line. With practiced strokes, she rubbed the swab in every direction to insure that the lubrication touched every wrinkle inside the first rectum. Then she then tossed the swab into the trash and after donning new gloves, opened a fresh swab for the next rectum. When each was sufficiently full of gel to meet her standards, she attached leads and inserted one long electrode into each ready anus. A wide suction cup was pressed against each set of asscheeks to hold the probes in place.

Ursula always enjoyed watching the herd's faces pressed against the clear plastic wall. The gel swab usually made most of them grimace in fearful expectation, but the long length of the electrode certainly surprised them every Season. There was so much about the male body that Ursula had learned during Medical Intake that she was always charmed that men didn't understand their own physiology as well as she did.

I hope one of mine pops the gun, Ursula thought as a wicked smile crossed her face.

After checking the suction cups, the technician returned to her monitors and adjusted dials, flipped levers and pressed buttons. Ursula concentrated on their faces through the plastic wall. She knew how quickly the men were betrayed by their own expressions. It didn't take long. It never did.

She loved their grimacing faces that contorted from amazement mixed with anger to agonizing joy. It was always this way, Ursula remembered, when the pack in medical first realized that they no longer controlled their erections or their ejaculations. These five had just come to learn that they could be made to erect on cue. Now they learned that they could be manipulated to ejaculate at Ursula's command. For most men that insight was not only enlightening. It was a frightening realization of who controlled them.

One of them is going to hump the plastic and I bet it will be the chubby blond one, Ursula predicted.

Each cock filled immediately as current generated through the electrode deep inside them. Their faces revealed their humiliation as Ursula watched them tear up when their own penises betrayed them. Understanding that even their cocks were no longer under their own control was always a valuable learning experience for the packs every Season.

The males worried they would spurt very soon and they fought to take back ownership of their organs.

It never works, Ursula had learned, but they always tried. Her Owner taught her to teach her animals well and the reality of cock ownership was a good lesson.

As the medical technician twisted dials, she changed the pressure until they grew ready to explode. Then she turned it down and their hard cocks – and their eagerness – disappeared.

The fat blond boy in the center was the most entertaining.

His hips began to pump, even though his ankles and forearms were locked to the plastic wall. Ursula watched his ass sway first from side to side as if he intended to force himself to ejaculate on his own schedule and not be the instrument of her whim. Both Ursula and the technician shared knowing glances and the latter pushed a button three times.

There's always one, Ursula smiled at its humping hips and look of determination.

Even as he tried to hump and pump against the wall in an effort to orgasm, the technician turned toward Ursula and with her approving nod, allowed him to spurt a tiny bit of pre-ejaculate against the clear divider. His hips could have pumped all day and his ass could have danced for a week but his ejaculation was no longer permitted and he just didn't realize it yet. When he figured out that Ursula and the medical team controlled whether or not he could shoot his wad, abject degradation covered his face. She was sure she saw tears roll down his cheeks.

Ursula watched his eyes shut and his lips press harder against the plastic. She knew that he was well on his way to learning how it would be during his Season on the Farm.

He had learned one of many lessons at that moment.

Every lesson should be a good lesson, Ursula remembered that her Owner taught her and smiled.

They ran more medical tests on the groups of five. The technicians hardened their cocks at various times and then softened them; calculated their bounce threshold and measured their pain reactions to needles pricking their scrotums; clamped their nipples to gauge tightness capacity limits; and finally bound them to measure their cutoff points for circulatory issues important to calibrate their harnesses and collars. The session produced its usual valuable information and was fun for Ursula as the men came just a little closer to understanding what their lives would be like during their Season on the Farm.

When the technicians assured her they were done with her pack and all had passed, Ursula gathered them up with a single command and marched them on weary legs to the Intake Exercise Gym.

Chapter 8: Exercise

Tara's pack of 45 was finishing their exercise evaluation in the gym at the same time Ursula's was ready to enter. Setting her group on their knees to rest, Ursula studied the faces of Tara's pack and smiled. She deduced with a glance that their Exercise Processing was successful. Shifting her view from tear-stained faces to crop-welted asses, all wore the faces of males who had met the Trainer's whip. An expert in how to stimulate her charges to perform to their peak and beyond, Tara was a Farm legend with reluctant males. Ursula had learned a great deal from her during her own training and made sure she passed along Tara's skills to her own trainees.

Tara's males had obviously undergone thorough exercise processing.

When Tara's herd was marched into exercise from watering, she provided them extra stretching prior to beginning their assessments by the exercise techs. Setting the first boy upright on the track that ran around the room's perimeter, she used her new prod to compel him forward. He took two awkward steps and Tara shook her head from side-to-side at his ungraceful movement.

And why had the beast stopped? Apparently, he didn't get it.

Do lessons that everyone understands. Make them clear, Tara remembered. That's the purpose of a lesson, she learned in her own Farm train-the-trainer years, to make sure each understands and learns. Her duty was to get that lesson to them all quickly and efficiently.

She adjusted the electric prod's setting and touched it firmly to the back of its thigh. Yelping loudly, the male danced inelegantly stopped yet *again* after taking only two clumsy steps. He was downright gawky and probably a little bit stupid in his former life, she figured. Tara decided to fix *that* problem immediately.

Wasted time is lost opportunity, she recalled from her own training many Seasons ago. Words waste time, the Owner said.

Adjusting the dial another notch, she pressed the evil instrument against the inside of its flabby thigh. Its piggish squeal was a delightful symphony. Its tiny jump forward was a pleasant by-product of her tool's bite. Tara kept the rod between the male's legs and used it repeatedly to make him dance another step forward again and again. Screaming loudly in a vain effort to escape her torture, she kept pace with him on the track as the lesson began to sink in. Finally the male understood what she demanded: that he was to move forward on his own because she expected him to do that. Complying was the only way she would holster the prod and take it away from the its home in his raging crotch.

Some males take longer to learn than others, she recalled. But they all get it. Eventually. Make the lesson count.

With tears flowing down his red face and primal grunts escaping from his parched throat, the boy ran inelegantly until he reached the end of the first leg of the track. Tara signed as he slowed down. She took one menacing step toward him and he bolted like a frightened colt, turned the corner and kept running all the while crying and grunting until he finished a complete lap around the gym.

Tara turned toward the rest of her pack and relished in their gaping mouths and surprised eyes.

"Run!" she said quietly in their general direction.

Eager to see which had understood the lesson first, Tara watched the group make a split second decision and start running. The littlest one, short and stocky with red-hair and freckles, was first to dash forward. Tara made a mental note to keep an eye on that one.

One after another, the pack jumped onto the track and jogged the room's full edge. By the time the final one joined the runners, the first boy had lapped the room and was gaining on the ones lagging behind. Tara wondered how long it would take for them to figure out what pace they needed to run in order to run successfully as a group. If this collection of newcomers tried to outrun each other, as if first place mattered within herd mentality, her prod would be well used today. Group behavior had always been one of Tara's interests and seeing it in action was instructive for her, even after her many Seasons on the Farm.

> *They are your pack, the Owner told them. They must think like a pack. They must act like a pack before they can become a herd. Only the herd matters.*

Tara mused on that well-learned lesson as she watched them run.

The first lap for a new pack was always the most illuminating. She learned that how the group managed itself during its initial run was a predictor of how they would interact during their long Season on the Farm. It also gave her insight into how she would best use her training skills on their particular idiosyncrasies. Virgin pack runners were a constant source of education for Tara and she used the knowledge she gained in each ensuing Season's training.

As they ran in circles around the room, Tara turned her attention to the technicians.

"They're just about ready," she said while seating herself in the only chair in the room.

The exercise technicians sported open white lab coats over black leather pants and vests that revealed the same red stripe that decorated all medical personnel. They seemed to nod as one and signaled that they were ready. Tara stopped the trotting group with a single word.

"Halt!" she said and counted the seconds until the group froze in their tracks.

Seven seconds, she thought and frowned. We will improve that score.

"You!" the lead technician pointed to one of the panting herd, "Begin counting. Stop when you reach five."

"One!" he called in a strong voice that made Tara's head turn in his direction and another note was tapped on her assistant's ever-present tablet. It was odd to hear a strong voice so far in Intake and Processing because it was the first word that any boy had been ordered to speak since his day began. This one bore her scrutiny and she memorized its face on the spot.

He was probably a jock, Tara mused. They always know how to count off.

"Two!" another chimed in after a moment's hesitation. "Three!" another too-loud voice called. "Four!" yet another said almost shyly. "Five!" a raspy voice called.

"Follow me," the technician said as she turned and walked toward a far corner of the exercise room. The five who just counted off followed her down an aisle and around a corner to the first station of the exercise assessment tests. Ensuing technicians had each next group count off and each took her portion of five panting herd members to another station to begin their evaluation.

Tara relaxed in the chair as the small groups were positioned.

I love this part; she licked her lips in anticipation.

With practiced efficiency, the technicians secured the clusters into position. Each male was wrapped in a chest strap with its rear o-ring attached to the other four males by a single hog-tie strap that radiated five connectors. The lead tech ran a single nylon cord that looped around the base of their balls and tied off the cord on the central o-ring of the hog-tie strap. Their upper torsos were locked together and provided them mere inches of independent movement. Finally, their genitals were tied tightly to the ingenious device Medical Intake built that converted them from separate human beings into a solitary unit of five animal bodies all facing outward.

They couldn't see each other. The group could move but they could do so only in one direction and within the confines of the length of overhead chain that secured the bunch to the ceiling. Tara believed this one test was the most telling predictor of herd behavior that she'd see during the Season. She leaned forward to watch the events unfold.

"Run," the tech said and tapped her electric prod menacingly against her palm.

After seeing her finger the prod, the five boys didn't waste a second trying to run. After each took a single stride, the group was painfully shown that their motion was limited by their hog-tied chest harnesses and tortured by their connected ball straps. Their collapse made the technicians snicker and their cries of pain raised wide smiles from the techs as well as from a bemused Tara.

"Run!" the technician said again and rapped the prod loudly against her palm.

The group remained stock-still because their chest straps prevented them from moving more than a single step in any direction. If they attempted a second step, the tightening of the nylon cord around their scrotal sacs might rip them off. Here was a group of five grown males, each was likely well-educated and had significant business experience and not one of them could figure out how to run when ordered. The technicians' entertained faces greeted them no matter which way they tried to move.

"RUN!" five technicians demanded at their faces simultaneously. Their voices yelled more loudly and each took a prod-tapping step toward each mini-herd that was bound helplessly together.

The males were terrorized by their predicament. Tears welled in their eyes and their shoulders sagged. Unable even to fall to their knees in fear of their ball sacs being ripped from their groins, each group realized they were merely painful pawns in Tara's evil game. When one stepped forward, the others' agonized shrieks pulled him back.

There seemed no way to obey her orders. Tara stood up, glared at each of the groups, and waited to see if any male would be first to figure out a solution. It seemed so obvious to her.

I hope it's that little red-haired one, she thought, or the one with the buttery asscheeks. I can't wait to get my hands on them, she salivated.

"Run!" the technicians shouted loudly all at once and pressed their prods on the inside of the closest thighs that they could reach. Groups of Intake technicians stalked the outside of each bound circle, all screaming loudly at the bound males in demanding cacophony.

The boys' thighs went into spasms when tortured by the prod's evil kiss and those unintentional movements drew the four genital sacs that were attached along with them. Their muscles contracted uncontrollably from the pain and they were unable to form a solution. As they flopped and flailed, their ball sacs' noose tightened. They screamed in agony that reverberated throughout the Processing Gym. The technicians stalked the locked circles and made sure that every thigh was graced by her prod. As they tested their small group reactions and took notes, they kept their eyes on the monitors which they fed constant information that flowed from the telemetry in the chest harnesses.

Male screams now flooded the room and threatened to break through the soundproofing that separated one medical section from the next. Several males were sobbing and others yelped with each kiss of the prod. They begged for mercy when a tech's prod hovered near their skin. They trembled in terror at the thought of another touch on their cocks, sacs and asses. Yet not one had figured out the painfully obvious solution.

It better be soon, Tara fretted, or this is going to be a very long Season.

She saw it out of the corner of her eye, almost outside her well-developed range of perception.

One boy in a group two sub-herds to her right made a move that caught her attention. Tara studied him. A technician moved closer to get Tara a close-up video of the event on her jacket's camera to review later. It was a simple move, one that would have gone unnoticed by less watchful eyes. At the Farm, all eyes were trained to be extra observant to look for the smallest motions that influenced herd behavior.

It was a nothing more than a hip twist. One boy bumped the one to his right with his hip. Tara smiled as the technician seemed relieved. It had taken this group way too long to figure it out.

Three minutes; they endured three full minutes of cock and ball agony, Tara calculated. Not good enough, but that time was definitely fixable.

Tara and the technicians watched the young colt whose hip had nudged his neighbor's and waited to see how long it would take for the second boy to realize what the implication was. Their seemingly unsolvable challenge had just been sorted out, if they would just realize it. At first, he didn't seem to get it and the young colt had to bump his hip a second time.

Surely it won't take a third try, Tara hoped. The Owner taught them that three times is rarely a charm and usually indicates a sub-standard herd.

His second bump was firmer and carried more significance. Staring at the male he was bound to, the second male, who Tara named the 'bumpee,' blinked repeatedly and then, as if a light bulb clicked over his head, jutted his hip leftward and bumped the next in line. As the succession of bumps repeated around the small circle, the colts gyrated into a circle of bumping hips. The next step would be their most difficult so far.

The young pony that started the bump line took a step to his left and pressed his leg against his neighbor's. Given the hip-bumping a few moments ago, the second colt was quicker to respond and pressed his own left leg against the one of the next in line. Soon, the circle of five males had extended their left legs and caught everyone's attention. Their stares managed to force a small grin on the lead tech's face. After sharing her smile with Tara, the two women waited for the cycle to complete its destiny.

In messy unison, they drew their right legs inward. Except for a few grunts by those who couldn't figure out the rhythm, Tara was pleased that the sub-herd succeeded. Those who couldn't manage the teamwork were reminded that their lack of flexibility resulted in everyone's scrotal sacs being bitten by the nylon cord's teeth. The group finally figured out what was required to complete the simple the order they were given: to RUN! With measured steps, they inched along in a circle and felt the teeth of the O-ring in the center of the leather hogtie strap with every step they took.

The males pressed closely up against each other and felt the touch of male flesh against male flesh, for probably the first time in their adult lives. They were happy to press against each other harder and harder – anything to relieve their fear of their balls being strangled and ripped from their bodies.

They finally picked up the pace, much to Tara's relief because she was getting bored with their baby steps. The group managed to walk slowly in a semblance of moving circle. Figuring that they finally understood, an examiner approached the boy dragging the pack forward and pressed the prod at its lowest setting on the tip of his soft cock as if to alert him that coming up with the solution was only the first part of the task.

The rest of the assignment was to run.

A loud squeal flew from his throat and filled the Processing gym. The corps of technicians and trainers knew that prod's lower settings that were used gave the boy an instantaneous warning. When it was placed on an animal cock's tip, it imparted a quick lesson.

And it is always about the lesson.

Force never works as well as quiet lessons, their Owner told them. Farmhands rarely needed to use force, she explained. This success story was another example of her wisdom in action.

After a moment during which the boy collected himself from the prod's work, it seemed like he finally understood it. He stepped up the pace and dragged the four other members harnessed to him to force them to quicken their pace. Urging them silently and with the vision of the prod's recent bite on his cock fresh in all their minds, they obeyed his lead and fell in rhythm to his gait. The group quickly pranced in a circle tethered by a single ceiling chain that kept the group from falling. Even though they achieved a small measure of success, their faces were grim and sullen. Tara knew these males had never been forced to use their survival wits before or follow another's solution and be physically punished if they failed.

Physical pain works quickly, Tara recalled from her Seasons of training. Pain does its best work when they don't expect it. She learned the value of using pain and she always put her lessons into practice. Judicious use of pain in teaching a lesson was a good tool. Tara marveled again at the Owner's wisdom.

After each of the other groups either solved their running problem or merely replicated the one Tara and the technicians had just created, the packs were administered a series of tests that measured their flexibility, tolerance for heat and cold and physiological reactions to exercise. The results were kept as baseline measurements and were recorded in their electronic files. The Farm medical staff kept a close eye on the physical health of everyone on the Farm and especially of the creatures that inhabited it each Season.

Each male was forced into a variety of strenuous positions and each one's muscle tension was calculated so that it could be assigned to the proper training pack this Season. As they were twisted into situations that were, at best, uncomfortable, Tara watched as the technicians stressed each newcomer's body and noted each reaction to and endurance for physical pain. Knowing – and pushing – their pain threshold was a crucial training tool.

The final physical test was the most physically challenging. The technicians began by dunking each harnessed group into an enormous tank of cold water and measuring their bodily reactions. They were then dragged by the overhead chain into the heated room to measure the same effects. Finally the technicians pronounced Exercise Intake finished and Tara rose to lead her pack to the next stop on the Intake process.

When she met Ursula's eyes in the hallway, the two grinned at each other as they led their assigned packs to the next step – Measurement Processing – in which every male's neck, chest, torso and genital fitting would start.

Chapter 9: Measurement

Sharon's group was shepherded into Measurement Processing to begin measuring every inch of their bodies. The data would be calculated in detail so that the stalls, gear, bits, collars, leads and other Farm fittings fit them perfectly no matter which pack they were assigned to or what stall they inhabited.

> *A Season on the Farm was challenging, the Owner constantly taught them, and a Farm animal with improperly fitting gear would neither benefit the Farm nor grow properly from his experience.*

Sharon was a stickler for methodical measurement. She tolerated nothing less than exact data and believed it was better for a male to endure agonizing measurement procedures rather than to suffer through a Season with equipment that didn't fit well. Chafing was not allowed at the Farm.

> *Get measurements right the first time, Sharon recalled from her own training. A proper fit meant the Farm animals worked harder, faster and better.*

The Measurement Processing room required the technicians' full attention, so Sharon's pack was lined up with their heels pressed to a wall dotted with hash marks etched at increasing heights. One by one, a technician planted a straight edge atop each male's head and pressed it firmly into his scalp to record its accurate height. Then each stepped forward and its weight was measured, called across the room loudly so it was heard by everyone and recorded on the ever-present tablets that the Processing technicians carried.

After these two basic measurements were recorded, the Farm's more complex measurements started. This was the set of tasks that always drew Sharon's careful attention. The accuracy of these numbers was vital.

In order to obtain precise measurements and avoid the fidgeting that some animals displayed in early Seasons, each male's wrists were locked into cuffs hoisted well above their heads to stretch them to the tips of their hooves. The techs knew that the best predictive tool for measuring was a fully stretched-out body. They made it impossible for the pack to pull in their stomachs or puff out their chests as males will do if not checked. The measurements that the technicians took were consistently more accurate than when a sub-herd was stretched out on concrete floor, the prior measurement method that was discarded when vertical stretching was tested and proved. Besides, the males on the cold concrete floor always had cock-shrivel issues that interfered with measurement accuracy.

With a quiet whirr the motor started and their wrists were pulled higher, forcing each one to dance on his toes. When each dangled from the ceiling at a height that was to her satisfaction, Sharon nodded approval to begin.

Sturdy flexible measuring tapes calculated every centimeter of the males' frames. Skull width at various points, face length where the gags would go, necks for collar placement, upper and lower arms for cuffs and stall mechanics, every chest measurement imaginable for harnesses, torso and waist for belts and suspension gear, hips and asscheeks for outer wear, thighs and knees for bands, calves and ankles for upside-down suspension, and of course toes and hooves for foot gear were all included in the painstaking process. Every male was measured at least twice and the lead tech performed spot assessments to double-check accuracy. If she noted an inconsistency, she dragged the inaccurate tech to the spot and made her re-measure the male as she oversaw the process. The now-humiliated technician would measure again and again and again to insure accuracy. Until a tech returned perfect measurements routinely, she had no chance to climb the promotion ladder at the Farm. Every Farm hand lusted for the next level so she could at some point in her career on the Farm, move to the Manor House to serve the Owner. The first steps in the measuring stall were part of the process.

Measuring was time-consuming and exhausting. The boys' arms were raised and lowered and twisted into torturous positions for each required set of height, depth and width calculations. Their hind legs were spread violently apart for inseam measurements that were taken with stiff rods jammed into the crevices of their groins for a perfect measurement of inner thigh to heel. Straps around their waists were pulled tightly to force their chests to expand and then left in place to measure how long each could hold his breath. Sharon was always amused by the quiet ones during Measurement. For them, pain was both a punishment and a reward and that peccadillo would soon be revisited upon them during training, discipline and the always-scary punishment sessions.

When the techs pronounced the Measurement Processing done and this sub-herd's results were recorded, Sharon nodded and an electronic whirr filled the room. All the sub-herd heard was the machine-like sound but for Sharon and the seasoned technicians, the whirr indicated that there was a list of instructions that needed to be shared. The seasoned Farm hands enjoyed the mechanical noise begin and watched as their smiles elicited growing anticipation in each of the boys. Sharon read that fear on their faces. Dread, she knew, was a handy training tool.

It didn't help a bit when the steel panel beneath their feet dropped away and only the security of their wrist and forearm locks prevented them from tumbling into the new abyss. A few were too horrified to move; others flailed at their bonds, crazed by the nothingness that appeared suddenly under their hooves.

You can always pick out the fearful ones. There are always a few that can't handle heights and it's to our advantage to know which they are and use that when we need it. Learn their weaknesses and use them.

Sharon's eyes studied the males' flailing arms that tried to find anything to hold onto as the floor drew away and the empty pit stared at the few who weren't too afraid to look down. She saw looks of sheer terror on many of their faces. Farm animal terror was palpable.

The motor's sound grew louder and their dread increased in proportion to the increasing volume. The always-anticipated whimpering began, Sharon noted, as did the first manifestations of gut-wrenching fear. The sound of terror was one of the Farm noises she enjoyed each Season. That special sound was the precise racket that was growing right now among the males in her charge. Her eagerness grew as their shrieks filled her ears.

The males dangled fully by their forearms and wrists with almost 90% of their body weight held by their secure cuffs. Within moments, the winch connected to their calf and ankle restraints and groaned into action by drawing their legs and feet aloft. As designed, all the members of her little pack now dangled from the ceiling by their arms and legs. Only the techs knew why this position was so important for the next measurement.

Sharon could feel the tension in her males' bodies and wondered why they didn't just relax and allow the strong cables to support them? Instead of forcing their heads up, as if there was anything for them to see in Processing Measurement, why not just lay back and give in to the process? The control they were straining to exert in vain amused her every Season and her lips curled at this Season's sight. She enjoyed it because this measurement taught the group their first step in the journey of putting their complete trust in her.

They trust you when you relieve their terror, the Owner taught them. Sharon recalled her own terror in the Green Salon and how the Owner rescued her. She learned to trust her Owner completely and that made her feel safe.

A louder mechanical noise told her and the technicians that it was time for the final measurement positioning. Each tech surveyed her sub-group of five males and made sure that each was dangling exactly as required for the final measurement to be accurate. If this particular measurement was wrong, then the male's Season on the Farm would be more uncomfortable – even horrific – than he could imagine. A little discomfort and a lot of indignity now was a small price to pay for a Season of proper fit.

The chains tightened and their legs were wrenched wide apart. This was the juncture that brought Sharon from her chair to inspect the process more closely.

She was searching for hard cocks.

The few males whose shafts stiffened even when they were terrorized always drew her attention. The number was usually small, no more than four or five in the entire herd, but those whose cocks rose to this occasion were worthy of her making a mental note for use later. There was always fun to be had to with males whose penises betrayed their excitement during tortured suspension.

As the technicians prepared for both external and internal measurements into the clean anuses, Sharon walked cat-like down the long row of hoisted humans in search of the hard cocks she craved. Striding forcefully, her heels clicked on the concrete floor and left no doubt in anyone's ears that she was prowling for visual confirmation of fear-excitement reactions that she would use as training tools. Although all the Farmhands were assertive, it was Sharon's boots that told everyone she was a Pack Leader to be feared. As every Season got underway, males learned fast when under her hand and her prod. Sharon loved training the ones who reacted so well to terror.

With a sudden click, her boots stopped between the eye-level legs of a boy dangling in front of her.

"What's this?" she said loudly and grabbed his thick cock in her leather glove. If it weren't attached to his body, she would have broken it off and waved it over her head to make her point.

Several technicians turned to watch. Her style was unmatched on the Farm and it was a treat to see Sharon work her pack. They were constantly amazed at how quickly she could own a room of 45 men with a single question, especially one that had no answer. Her power both thrilled and entertained them.

"What's THIS?" Sharon's voice rose even as she knew the question would remain unanswered. Without even seeing a face, every tech in the Measurement lab knew that one male was cringing in fear, sweating in terror and was awash with foreboding about what was going to happen to him – and his cock that she gripped so tightly. He had to be beyond exhaustion. His body would predictably stiffen and his muscles contract into spasms from growing terror. She pulled harder as if to break the penis from its groin. He couldn't help his primal reaction and screamed. Sharon ignored his noise and relegated it to the back of her mind. She was on a mission.

"How does a suspended animal get a hard cock?" she asked no one and expected no answer.

Sharon toyed with the cock, playfully yanking and pulling it, slapping it from side to side and eventually pulling it so high that the animal almost spun over in its harness. This male, plus the 44 other pack members who couldn't see what was happening but knew from the screams that whatever was happening should be avoided at all costs, were the only ones in the room that couldn't understand the bigger point she was making.

She jerked the cock in her glove harder to make him give a much more agonized scream to his pain so the others could learn quickly. She knew it was always better when the males learned lessons on the Farm directly from other animals. Sharon loved when the animals screamed their most animalistic sounds as part of training and this was an opportunity to teach that lesson early. The quiet types don't make it on the Farm, Sharon's experience told her, and they were usually weeded out in the early selection process.

I hope he growls, she thought. I love animal growling.

She let the idea dance in her mind. He uttered a magnificent groan that was music to Sharon's ears. The sound of horror was all that 44 pairs of ears heard and it may have been the first time any of them had heard such primal noises from another male. This lesson was one of their first when a single member of their group was selected for personal attention but learning how the male reacted was even more important. During the training of one animal, every other member of Sharon's herd was quietly grateful that his was not the cock that was being torn off a body by a leather glove. Yet every one of them listened and a few showed signs of enjoying the experience. There were always some that did.

She drew the shaft toward the ceiling even more and directed her question again to no one in particular. "Why is this cock so hard?"

By now, the humiliated male stiffened his limbs against his overhead hoist and desperately humped his hips in a futile effort to get away from her grip. Perhaps he realized all his efforts were in vain; perhaps he knew that he could not escape her hold. Yet something inside drove him to flail against the black leather glove that was torturing his fat, juicy cock.

Just when he may have thought there was nothing worse she could do to him, Sharon reached into her bag of experience and drew out the finishing touch.

Oh, this is going to be a hoot, Sharon smiled. It'll make for great video review and discussion at dinner tonight.

She reached grasped his testicles and drooling cock with a gloved hand and pulled up, first to the left and then to the right. Repeating the motion again and again, she made him swing using his genitals as her lever. He was a toy on her string; his cock and balls were merely her handle.

His gut-wrenching growl filled the room and 44 males trembled as they dangled from the hoist.

Nothing replaces experience, Sharon realized.

She let go suddenly and she knew what was going to happen next. So did the technicians as each of them backed away from the dangling male.

Animals pee when they are terrified. These males were no different and this group didn't disappoint. Most of them dribbled pee or sent streams up, down and sideways as they tried to control their embarrassing production. Some tried to force their own pee away from their bodies to escape the foul-smelling pee. The technicians giggled at the their incontinence that Sharon caused by inflicting such primitive fear in them. Then they watched warm urine fall onto the males' own bodies as one more addition to their growing degradation. It was a normal Processing mishap.

"Hose them down," Sharon said happily. "Then we'll start the anal probes."

Taking her seat again in the room's sole chair, she smiled in anticipation of the next step of measurement to begin.

The urine-stained males who still dangled over the open pit felt their smelly skin crawl in terror from her words, 'anal probes.' A few whimpered aloud.

A stream of icy water mixed with soap spewed onto the dangling bodies as the Processing trainees scrubbed them with stiff brushes. The soaping was followed with clear cold water that washed the suds and the stench away. As the water fell into the gaping pit beneath them, some of the males wondered what further horrors could be hidden in the vast void below. But the technicians' scrubbing and icy water rinse jerked their attention back to their painful reality.

What they felt was the trainees' fingers pulling their asscheeks apart and reaching unceremoniously into their dark holes.

One by one, the technicians jammed a wedge-like divider between the herd's asscheeks and sprayed each hole with oil. Finally they inserted a cold rod into each lubricated rectum. The techs were well-practiced and made almost perfect entry although some required two or three insertions before the rods went in deeply enough. Within minutes, the lead tech pronounced the small pack ready.

"Let's begin," she said and each tech tapped her tablet. For a moment the room was bathed in silence. Then the dance began.

All at once, heads shot back or upward, bodies stiffened and went into spasms, arms and legs flailed against the hoist's steel cables and the small herd was jettisoned into pure hell. Their rectums were filled with sensations of being impaled, explored and intruded and they were shocked with anal contractions. Their reactions were purely animalistic; their struggling absolutely visceral.

They were learning the Farm way.

The process took barely five minutes for the techs to check that each anus was filled with a rubbery gel that was now hardening. They knew this was the best way to get the perfect measurement for anal plugs that were to be used throughout the Season. Each male was plugged daily during its Season on the Farm and if the measurements were not exact, their rectums and even their bowels might be irritated by a bad fitting plug. The special gel had been designed for each animal's own good and every technician made sure that every animal on the Farm had a well-fitting plug. The males' shrieks of terror were a small price to pay for a good fit and soon the squealing males would figure that out, too.

Enjoy your work and it shows. I love this part; Sharon thought and licked her lips and silently thanked her Owner.

As the males struggled in terror against the cables' grip and thrashed their hips as if to expel the solidifying gel in their asses, their fervor diminished into exhausted acceptance. One by one, they settled down and relaxed, letting the cables hold them as they dangled over the pit. A few threw their heads back and growled in utter defeat while some still fought against absolute indignity. Sharon noted the percentages of each and saw that they were generally par for the course. Each Season on the Farm seemed to bring a few more strugglers, but not enough to be noteworthy.

She leaned forward in her chair as the lead tech nodded to her team.

The motor began again and threw the bedraggled group into what would be their final fit of frenzy in this part of Intake and Processing.

Each male sported a rod hanging from his ass that was molded solidly in his new rectal mold. As the rectal rods spun and were withdrawn corkscrew-like from their anuses, the technicians grasped the perfect molds that perched on the tip of each rod. They ignored the bellows of protest that greeted the extraction. Profanity pervaded the din as the perfect plugs were unscrewed rectum by rectum and catalogued by the technicians. They're loud this year, Sharon thought.

The Owner always taught her staff that a male who is noisy usually enjoys its Season more than the quiet ones. Like always, the Owner was right again.

After a final spray of warm oil to rinse their violated bowels, the hoist whirred and 45 males returned to upright positions and danced on their toes as they balanced on narrow platforms. The techs watched relief spread across their ashen faces and smiled knowing that they were unaware that one final measurement would soon be taken. Lowering them so they could perch on flat feet, each tech approached a male and slapped its flaccid cock onto a stiff metal ruler to get the final length into their records. The techs called out each length mercilessly aloud to an assistant who dutifully transcribed it on her tablet.

"Five-and-a-half long," one said.

Another, "Only one-and-a-quarter around. Very small."

"Testicles are soft, no palpable masses," she said as she squished his ball sac repeatedly between her palms.

"Very soft almost adolescent," yet another said loudly.

A voice added, "Still a little drool but otherwise short and insignificant."

The technicians called the data out matter-of-factly and loudly as each male winced at the thought of his own cock's attributes being shared for public consumption.

"Such a little one!" one tech called out and all voices hushed. "Three and a quarter," she said solemnly. "Short, that is," she finished to chuckles from the techs.

"I've got a big one!" one said. "Seven and three quarters, SOFT!" she said as Sharon turned to get a better look at one who would surely find his way to the Farm's stud barn.

The final part of Processing Measurement was fun for the technicians and soon each participated to see who could find the longest, the shortest, the lightest, the most retractable and the most exciting measurement: thickness. By the time measurement was completed, the techs were happily sharing lengths and widths as Sharon readied to move her pack to the next area of Intake Processing.

The exhausted group struggled behind her in a tight line with one stomach pressed into the ass of the male in front of him, the collection plodded ahead. Sharon passed Ronda and her pack who had just left the Fitting area and was going to Measurement.

"The record today is seven and three quarters," Sharon gloated as Ronda eyeballed her males to see which of them might be wearing a size big enough to beat this Season's new standard. It was always more fun at dinner when you had the longest male and could wallow in it.

The troupe continued down the hallways with not one male daring to look sideways. Instead, they walked under a heavy cover of humiliation while completely unaware that the next area of Processing would test their resolve even further by pushing them harder than anything else that had happened to them so far during this unimaginable day.

The first day of Processing wore on as the herds learned more and more about the Farm way and headed to Fitting.

Chapter 10: Fitting

Intake Processing was divided into efficient systems that could be visited in almost any order. Of all of them, Measurement and Fitting went hand-in-hand and were usually visited one after another. Without proper measurement, Farm animals would suffer from poor fit during their Season. Yet the craftsmanship in the Fitting Room was one of the most highly regarded of all of Processing's areas of expertise. Ronda was thrilled that a gaggle of male flesh had finally arrived at her station. Fitting was a wonderful way to break males completely into the Farm way and being assigned to Fitting meant that the remaining experiences of this pack in Processing would be done with a group that had already been the most well-indoctrinated in the Farm's more severe ways.

> *Be extremely strict first and always, the Owner advised them. It is easy to loosen your grip but impossible to tighten your hand over your animals.*

Ronda rolled those wise words over and over in her head as she marched her inductees into the just-sterilized room.

The technicians ran Fitting with iron fists and every Farmhand ceded authority to the women in Fitting. Even though all Lead Trainers enjoyed a certain amount of authority, the Fitting Trainers were specific and exact. Fitting required precision. Accuracy was critical.

Ronda seated herself in the Trainer's chair on a platform in the rear of the room and enjoyed the view from her elevated roost. During this part of Processing the herd would certainly entertain her and she enjoyed watching the experience from a tall vantage point.

Each male was unceremoniously hoisted atop two adjoining translucent footprints set several inches apart and recessed into the floor. Their legs were spread wide for easy access for the Fitting techs. With only their ankles showing above and their feet firmly restrained in recessed footprints, straps were locked across their legs that held them immobile. A padded bench in front of them made a waist-high rail and each male was ordered to bend over it. As the bench rose and jammed deeper into each belly, the males felt their calves strain and their thighs groan as they were pushed higher and higher away from their locked feet.

Within moments, their chests and heads dangled as their bolted feet were moved even further apart. Ronda was sure they were about as uncomfortable as they had been since arriving at the Farm. She watched the Fitting trainees carefully. Each technician studied her male's position and manually adjusted the height and spread so their feet, legs, and raised bellies were placed perfectly for Fitting. Only after matching measurements to specifications on their tablets did the techs move toward the males' heads.

A motor's hum raised two curved metal rods toward each tech who locked them around her male's neck. They checked three times to be certain there was adequate breathing room but no chance that their heads might slip during what was always one of the most excruciating processes in all of Intake Processing. Safety was crucial and only after the males' positions were evaluated by their superiors could the trainee techs initiate the next step in the Fitting process that required such tight restraint.

The technicians began the well-practiced steps of Fitting. Each boy's hand was wrapped in a leather strap which extended from each side of the rail. After tying them carefully, the boys' arms were pulled away and Victoria, the head of Processing designated by her neon blue vest marker, inspected the circle to review every technician's work again. At one point, she stopped and tapped her tablet to raise one padded bench a couple of millimeters higher; another stop saw her spread a male's legs slightly farther apart. She tested every arm for flexibility before nodding to Ronda. Fitting was about to begin.

I love it when they look like cows in stalls in the barn, Ronda thought as her lips curled upward.

"The first fitting is for lower restraints, cuffs, and leg irons," she said as the technicians scurried to arrange the tools needed for the lower part of Fitting.

In short order, different widths and weights of leather and metal were wrapped around the males' legs and ankles, then adjusted and measured. Widths were recorded, chafe levels calculated, padding applied and adjusted and finally, buckles were marked for the leather workers to create perfectly fitting leg wear for this pack to wear.

The techs moved their attention upward as Victoria announced, "Get the thigh spreaders in place and remember that they will stretch during the Season."

Her remark made the technicians recall their most recent retraining exercise when at least three males' thighs – albeit after significant exercise – had increased their spread by almost three millimeters during a single Season. Their thigh spreaders no longer fit properly and the resulting chafing annoyed the Owner who discovered it during one of her unannounced herd inspections. The culpable techs were reprimanded and reduced in rank by stripping their red designators from their chests and worse, were forced to wear the offending thigh spreaders as discipline for several days. Even though their punishment was amusing to the Farmhands, no one really wanted ill-fitting equipment on a herd at the Farm. Victoria drove that point home viciously during those techs' two-day punishment.

All the techs remembered their comrades' hobbling around the lab while wearing the poorly fitting thigh spreaders but were still required by the Owner to perform their duties. Even encumbered by badly fitting thigh spreaders that left them exposed to whatever punishment the Lead technician wished to use to remind them of their fitting failure that endangered the Owner's prized herd. The women's asses were not off limits; their asscheeks glistened from frequent whippings. None of the techs in Fitting wanted to be punished and retrained like those two had endured so they all dove into the task with zealous accuracy.

Fitting steps were divided into insertion, expansion, evaluation, more expansion, and finally, a single width recorded on their tablets. The techs knew that the herd always sang a special primal song during Fitting and all of them were eager to hear it again. The women began their work in earnest.

A metal rod was placed between the males' taut thighs and compressed air expanded it just enough that it stayed in place between their legs and didn't fall when they let go. Then they expanded it with puffs of air millimeter by millimeter until soft groans indicated the Fitting Song was starting. The techs knew that the pack's initial groans meant mere discomfort and not real pain, except for those few short legged males that the techs jokingly referred to as 'penguins.'

More and more puffs of compressed air were forced into the rods that pressed their legs apart wider and wider. The rods' expansion was unrelenting but measured and slow. The males' groans grew into a song of abject pain.

I love that song, Ronda remembered warmly. She recalled her own song that she sang to her Owner during her Lead Trainer fitting so many Seasons ago.

Once the technicians were certain that the males' grunts were coming from real agony and not simple pain, their experienced listening skills alerted them that the perfect stretch width had been achieved. Recording the exact measurement that each male could achieve on their tablets, they retracted the rods bit by bit and waited for Victoria to signal that the next task in Fitting was to begin.

Victoria's management style was brilliant. She was known to jumble the order of Fitting just to test her team's resistance to detouring from what they knew was correct procedure. Not one of them wanted to be the tech with the wrong tool at the wrong time, so they followed her every command and anticipated out-of-the-ordinary orders.

"Chest harnesses," she said as the technicians turned to their workstations to retrieve the proper tools. Rawhide was their tool of choice for this stage in Fitting.

There is something magical about rawhide, Ronda believed.

The aroma of rawhide always made her feel giddy but its greatest property was how it stretched and shrank. On the Farm, each pack needed tight harnesses for work and the working animals required harnesses that adjusted to the weather and the other unexpected conditions they would encounter each Season. Rawhide made Rhonda smile.

A one-inch wide strip of undyed rawhide was secured around each male's chest. The techs made sure it covered all the males' nipples. They were trained to ensure each male's chest was measured both at its widest and narrowest points so that the harnesses could be cut, sewn and fit to perfection. Raw, bleeding skin from a chafing harness was unacceptable on the Farm. Any animal sporting chafe marks would be reported and its Fitting tech brought to Victoria immediately. Victoria's punishment for an ill-fitting harness was severe. Every tech had seen her dole out punishment at least once and it was painful to watch and worse to experience. Punishment was both tortuous and shameful. An ill-fitting harness resulted in the technician's being stripped of her vest and colors and forced to wear a rawhide breast cover instead that opened only to display her nipples that Victoria often decorated with biting clips. Worse, she removed the clips from time to time and massaged the tech's nipples to elicit screams that the corps of trainees was forced to witness.

She released them only when the tech had screamed herself into enough of a frenzy that Victoria deemed a suitable lesson. That image burned itself into every trainee's brain and taking perfect Fitting measurements took on heightened importance.

As the women wrapped more inch-wide rawhide strips around the narrowest part of each chest, Victoria lowered the padded stools on which the pack was perched so that the males were now suspended mainly by their arms and chin rests while they teetered on squatting legs and bouncing asses. Their quadriceps screamed and their asscheeks trembled as they endured Victoria's demanding 90-degree bend. But she knew that as egotistical as males are – and most of those who were sent to the Farm started out that way – they still tried to suck in their stomachs when the Fitting techs stood back to review their twisted bodies. It made the techs giggle to watch them fight gravity and years of carefree nutrition.

> *They are so self-centered and conceited, Ronda observed as once again, they chose to suck their guts to show themselves off to her. Who did they think they were impressing?*

Pack behavior during Processing always amused her. She shared a slight grin with Victoria.

Once the rawhide strips were in place and the distance between them was measured and recorded, the technicians soaked the strips with ice-cold water that spewed from handy hoses. The rawhide soaked up the liquid and the rawhide darkened into a chocolate brown hue. When the strips sopped up enough to drip onto the floor, the technicians sprayed the next male in line until all were thoroughly soaked. Just to be sure, they soaked them again with another cold stream. Rawhide could be surprisingly thirsty.

Victoria was satisfied and nodded that it was time to dry the strips.

I love it when rawhide shrinks, Ronda smiled.

Heat lamps and quiet fans blew warm air toward the soaked rawhide that circled each chest. The Fitting techs adjusted the fans' so they blew hotter and hotter air directly on the wet rawhide. As the strips dried, the techs began flipping the pack so the bands dried from all directions. Fitting perfected a system to rotate the herds for complete drying and at the same time, bounce them to force off any errant drops of water. The unmistakable sound of a motor rumbled as the pack bounced and flipped upward. Their legs were still spread wide apart. Their necks were still secured in head bars. Their unrestrained backs sagged from gravity's incessant pull. The wet rawhide was now exposed directly to the heat lamps as the hot breeze sucked out the final dampness. In short order, they were now completely dry.

Farm Fitting had begun in earnest.

The techs worked the rawhide repeatedly, first wetting and then drying it so that it expanded and contracted. They stretched and pulled, wet it again and dried it and watched the band retract on each repetition. They ignored the pack's groans that came from their pleading lungs and waited to hear real cries of anguish – the gasping suck of oxygen deprivation – before they tapped exact measurements on their tablets. Leather workers would use these statistics to create beautiful harnesses with perfectly-fitting chains so their data represented the absolutely tightest allowable measurements. They needed to be perfect.

The animal harnesses on the Farm were exquisite. Each upper rawhide band used pure silver buckles and the set of two strips were connected by polished chains. The lower strip would certainly visit both water and heat during a Season on the Farm and could not be allowed to stretch or shrink out of size and make it difficult for an animal to breathe. Getting as close as possible to that critical point was the harness's goal; going beyond it was unacceptable.

Animal nipples were important to everyone on the Farm and covering an animal's nipples was an important step in the Fitting process. Unveiling them was part of the pack trainees' training and was also designed to fill the Owner's ritual of inspecting her animals at random times.

"We're ready," Victoria said after she was satisfied that every chest harness was measured perfectly. "Let's move on to gags and bits."

She loved watching gags and bits close up. Ronda walked around the bound males whose asses now dangled above the stools for a better look.

Victoria raised the padded benches to lift the males' chests so they were ready for gag and bit fitting. The pack's chin rests dropped and each jaw was forced open, first with simple verbal instructions and then by slapping the faces of the few hold-outs. Victoria trained her technicians exactly where to slap animals to achieve a fast open mouth. For Fitting, the desired result of a well-placed slap was not chastisement; instead, it was a straightforward command for an animal to open its jaws on demand. Farmhands knew there was a difference in technique between just applying discipline and making a demand. During each Season, every staff member had to understand and accomplish the subtle difference so each animal reacted quickly to every command. Face slapping was a skill used to achieve specific Farm purposes.

Rhonda enjoyed watching the techs slap flat palms onto stunned animal faces. Slaps that were delivered solidly were the most effective because they didn't give the recipient time to think – only to respond. She remembered her own training: *slap-release-pry*. She relished the sound of each slap-and-release followed by a pry-bar inserted quickly between their jaws before an animal realized exactly what had happened. The goal was usually achieved with a quick downward press and voila! The animal's jaws opened. The technique was both aggressive and delicate and gave her a chill every Season.

With all jaws now hanging open, the males tried unsuccessfully to anticipate what would befall them now. The techs knew the Fitting song of primal screams would soon begin, they worked quickly on this part of Fitting. The males could not possibly imagine what would happen to them next.

I wonder which ones will be the gaggers, Ronda thought. There are always gaggers.

The first step in fitting gags and bits was determining exactly how wide each mouth could be spread without causing damage. The herd's dental team had signed detailed clearances for the technicians and jaw problems were not going to be a problem for this Season's herd. The techs sighed with relief as they rechecked the dental charts: not a jaw restriction in this lot. Without waiting a moment longer than necessary, each tech inserted a rubber bar horizontally between each set of teeth and then forced it back while tugging her male's chin down and forward. To finish, they pushed the rubber stops in as far as they would go.

Each tech's goal was to position the rubber bar deep in the animal's mouth without damaging its bite. The Owner was specific about not injuring her herd and no tech wanted to risk a mistake during bit fitting. Intake training brought a lot of pressure on the techs to get it right or suffer the consequences.

Another carefully-placed slap shut each male's jaw and selected technicians moved down the line and repeated the process. With forty-five jaws now stuffed with three-quarter inch rubber rods, the room fell silent. Techs used the quiet time to measure depth, spread and drooling for a full 10 minutes before slapping their faces one at a time to remove the rods and review the bite marks. Each bit was custom fit; each gag was meticulously created. The indentations from animals' teeth were a crucial part of Fitting.

A loud clank at one end of the room drew everyone's attention. Ronda, followed quickly by Victoria, moved toward the source of the noise. Their boots clicked on the metal floor. Their Seasons of experience told them what happened before they even looked. Ronda had been trained in Farm interrogation and situations like this allowed her to choose the style she would use to achieve the results she wanted.

She launched into a well-practiced routine.

"WHAT is the meaning of THIS?" she said. Her elevated voice echoed throughout the Fitting lab.

The technician was flustered and stood in front of a tethered male whose dangling lower jaw had just let its rubber bit fall noisily to the floor. Unsure whether or not to pick it up, the young tech stood nervously under Ronda's masterful stare.

"I asked a question," Ronda spat toward the trembling technician.

Her voice quivered as she tried to respond. "It opened its mouth," she began tenuously, "and the bit fell out."

Ronda's voice was filled with derision. "Did you tell him to open his mouth and drop the bit?" Everyone in the Fitting lab knew the right answer, but Ronda's demeanor insisted that only the single tech reply.

"No, Ma'am, I did NOT!" she said through welling tears.

"Then why did it open its mouth?" Ronda asked, leading this poor trainer to water to see if she were smart enough to drink.

The woman's hesitation was barely noticeable except to the well-trained eyes of the Pack Leader and Fitting Overseer. Ronda knew she could use that moment of indecision to her advantage.

Isolate the poor behavior and correct it immediately.
That was the Farm way.

"It did so without an order," the technician said. She drew up the remnants of her courage and added, "This animal was disobedient during Fitting."

Ah, Ronda thought, this one has promise. She saw the problem and placed the responsibility exactly where it belonged – on the animal. Ronda made a mental note to discuss the tech with her superior and see where she might fit on the promotion list. She obviously had good training.

"What is your solution?" Ronda's questions were unrelenting. "Do we delay every other fitting until this one's bit is refitted?"

The technician answered confidently. "Its fitting can proceed while it is disciplined. Would you help me do that?"

Ronda's eyes drank in her answer. It was perfect.

"Of course," Ronda said and waited for the younger woman to begin the disobedient animal's discipline.

It takes courage to tell a Trainer of my level what to do, Ronda thought. Let's see if she has more inside her.

"Please stand behind the animal's hindquarters as I use Level Four correction," the young woman said as she slapped its face and inserted a new rubber fitting bit. She ignored its squawks of protest even as Ronda fingered her electric prod. As the technician inserted the bit firmly between the animal's jaws, Ronda set the power on her prod and pressed the metal tip between the male's wide-open asscheeks. When she tapped the silver button with her thumb, its bit helped to mute the scream that filled the room.

Process Four, Ronda thought. An old one but still a good one. I like this one. I want her in my training group.

"Name?" Ronda asked.

"Hailey, ma'am," she said with proper deference.

Ronda's made a note of Hailey's name and planned to put in a request to have her placed with Ronda's pack next Season. Both women ignored the growling male as its ass twitched from repeated shocks from Ronda's prod that darted in the space between his asscheeks and taught it how quality discipline was applied on the Farm.

Satisfied with the trainee's results, Rhonda turned her attention back to the pack's next step. It was time to move to the final and most complicated part of Intake fitting.

All animals – no matter which pack they were assigned to – required leads. Whether they were for a cock or neck, every animal was tethered by a quality rope, leather or chain leash. The cock leashes needed the most precise fitting. This task created a memorable Fitting finale and Victoria was eager to begin.

"Cock leads," she said gleefully as technicians once again scurried to gather all the tools for the Fitting finale. As their asses dangled and the muscles in their stretched legs screamed, each animal trembled with fear of exactly what would happen next.

They're always thinking about their asses, she laughed. They ought to worry about their precious cocks and balls!

When the techs approached the tethered pack with short rawhide strips dangling from their fingers, the usual pack moaning began. As the wet strips were wrapped and stretched tightly behind their balls, the groaning grew louder. As the group was flipped over and the fans and heat blew against the wet rawhide and it shrank, screaming poured out of their throats. As they were flipped over and the padded stools fell away, cocks and balls hung from their groins and the process of wet rawhide drying – and being soaked only to dry more tightly around their genitals – converted the Fitting song into a full symphony.

When the rawhide bands bit into dozens of scrotal sacs and were again doused with cold water, the animals' screams turned into sobs and when the bands were heated and shrunk again to achieve a perfect fit, the pack fell into total hysteria. Finally, a rawhide condom was pulled tightly over their soft shafts and the technicians turned up the voltage so it coursed through the rawhide penis covers. At that moment, 45 cocks erected simultaneously. Cold water soaked them and the animals' organs shrank. Hot breezes dried them and an electric jolt shot them up. Again and again and again.

Forty five males who were shackled like cows in their stalls suffered through the rawhide agony that shrank the hide millimeter by millimeter and bit deeper into their tortured balls and cocks. Their voices turned into a cacophony of primal animal grunts, echoed throughout the Fitting lab.

The pack bordered on panic and their confusion was profound. Rhonda was sure she knew what they were thinking: this didn't happen to men like me!

Faces always betray fear, the Owner taught Ronda during her first Season. Ronda studied the terror on their faces and was thankful for the Owner's wisdom.

"Once more, just to be sure," Victoria said. This was the moment these animals were to learn that they were *not* men on the Farm. This is when they took a huge step toward understanding they were the animals that the Owner knew they were.

The technicians hurried to their consoles and gradually increased the voltage. Forty-five cocks stood up again and gyrated in vain against the rawhide's tightening bite.

"Again!" the Lead Tech said as Rhonda grinned.

I love it when they enjoy their work, she marveled.

Cock after cock dutifully engorged and then struggled against the confines of the rawhide pouches that had shrunk and choked their cocks and balls. Excruciating screams greeted Ronda's ears and Victoria smiled at her. They both nodded and instructed the technicians to reduce the power a little.

Yanking off the rawhide was as much fun to watch as applying it because the animals shrieked in agony when each technician turned her attention toward each of them. They flapped their arms in the air trying to comfort the tortured genitals they couldn't reach. The sight was amusing and it reminded Ronda that a new Season on the Farm had truly begun.

What had arrived as men now realized they were just a herd on the Farm this Season.

"Where to next?" Victoria asked.

Ronda grinned and said, "Assessment."

Victoria smiled and every technician on her team snickered.

Chapter 11: Assessment

The packs passed each other silently through the corridors of Processing as the Trainers traded knowing grins. The males hoofed in single file behind their Pack Leaders. As the packs traded places, not one animal could force itself to look another in the eyes to warn them of the horrors awaiting them in the upcoming hell they faced. They had no words that could detail the degradation and pain they had just endured. But the looks on their faces told much of the story.

Paula's pack headed for Assessment.

As the line entered the cavernous chamber, Paula winked at the Lead Tech, who she had personally nominated for this position. Paula knew how hard it was to get a promotion to Lead anywhere in Processing, but being awarded Assessment was an important accomplishment. Paula was pleased that her influence made the difference and wondered how her first day would go.

"Marla, congratulations!" Paula's voice was filled with joy for the Lead's achievement. The Owner parceled out promotions only after a thorough review and several unannounced inspections, so Paula knew the woman's ability, as well as her confidence, helped her net one of the Farm's highest and most responsible positions.

"Thank you," she said with genuine pleasure. "I'm glad your pack is my first to assess. I'm going to be especially careful with them. After all, they're yours, Paula." She grinned and Paula returned it with her own smile. They both knew this would be a very special Assessment session and they were in the mood for wherever this session might go.

Every Intake procedure was important, but Assessment was special. Their training was thorough and in addition to skill and technique, the Owner insisted that every Trainer, technician and trainee was schooled in the the theory behind the Farm's Processing and Intake procedures – merely going through practice sessions wasn't enough. Bringing new animals to the Farm each Season was complicated and it was critical that everyone understood the meaning of even the smallest essentials.

Assessment was an arena where essentials mattered the most.

Assessment testing was complex. The objective was easy enough: animals were assessed to determine which barn they would be assigned and which herd or flock or gaggle or drove or pack they would be grouped with for the Season. The testing procedures had been worked out with experts, therapists and counselors so that each animal would be placed in the best group for it to develop. Each had to be placed properly to make the most out of every Season on the Farm.

Placing animals in the right barn was the single most important assessment made each Season.

The Owner knew that males tended to gravitate into comfortable groups in their previous lives. Working with the testers and teaching the technicians, she organized a battery of analyses that predicted almost perfectly which sort of animal each new pack member had hidden inside its soul. Then she knew which barn would suit it best from its existing skills, body type, personality, fears and unrealized desires. That was another of the Owner's teachings: most males don't know what was best for themselves and they needed Assessment so they were placed correctly and reached their full potential.

After all her Seasons on the Farm, Paula agreed with the Owner. She had seen only one animal placed incorrectly during her nine Seasons. The Owner's ability to sort males using her own insight along with the test results was uncanny.

The line stopped at the first rung of a concentric maze that ran upward like a spiral staircase. Each level sported small cubicles and each animal was led in and seated on a stool, one to a cubicle. The naked males seemed grateful for the opportunity to sit on an actual chair. More importantly, they seemed to no longer be conscious of their nakedness.

Marla surveyed the circular maze of males and pronounced it satisfactory.

"Begin," she said through a small microphone propped on the red fabric slash that split her full breasts. Paula saw her bosom propped smugly above the vest's cut out front and admired their rich brown nipples. She knew that every animal faced a set of technicians' breasts poking out from their black leather vests and the parade of breasts tantalized every male throughout Assessment. There was a purpose to even the smallest technique used on the Farm.

Techs jogged to their posts and 45 trainees faced 45 naked males that were perched atop high stools. Their legs dangling, the males seemed taken aback at that much female flesh so close to their faces. They inhaled the female scent that permeated their nostrils and shifted uncomfortably in their seats from the intensity of each woman's presence. Their giddiness was multiplied after enduring the agonizing day of that had worn them down to their raw primal emotions. Each male breathed deeply, as if to inhale the moment's bliss.

As if on cue, the technicians started the assessments. First they strapped goggles over the males' eyes and after moving levers and adjusting settings, they wrapped a nylon strap around every set of cock and balls that protruded from them. They finished setup with a tight tug on the Velcro strap that tightened the package. Male mouths fell open as the pain from the sheathing rose through them. Without pausing, the technicians tightened the goggles so they would cover the males' eyes and block any light from intruding the darkness. Headphones were applied using suction cups to cover their ears so no outside sounds would interfere with Assessment. When they were confident their work had been done correctly, each tech pressed a button on her tablet and waited for the next order.

"Thirty four seconds," Marla said to no one in particular and noted it on her tablet.

"Begin streaming the opening images," Marla said to Control as Paula nestled into a comfortable chair. She held a set of goggles loosely in front of her eyes and cupped one earphone against her right ear.

The streaming images flashed in the their goggles in rapid succession. First came ordinary Farm images that included the barns, sties, grazing area, watering holes and the Competition Dome.

Always start with something that centers them, before you twist their reality so it becomes what you want them to know, the Owner taught. Paula appreciated that lesson when she watched the first few seconds of Assessment images.

The images shifted suddenly. The males were no longer seeing Farm scenes; instead, they were watching males like themselves hitched to plows, caged in corrals and run in circles as their leads were tugged by Farmhands. Males were eating from troughs, drinking from waterholes, running in harnesses and herded together under a rider's loud whip. When the crack filled their earphones, all 45 males trembled.

Paula wondered if any in the pack noticed that the woman perched regally on the horse was actually Paula outfitted in dress leathers. No matter, she sighed. They'd find out soon enough.

Techs studied their tablets as one scene faded into another and another. Their autonomic responses were recorded and would be displayed for later review. The techs knew that each animal had its own proclivities and their job was to match them with that barn. The animals' inclinations had to be assessed in order to gain maximum benefit for each one's Season on the Farm.

The scenes they saw in their goggles changed again. This series floated by in longer increments. First, they viewed a flock of chickens and they saw males dressed in fine feathered costumes pecking around the grounds for bits of food scattered by a Farmhand from her bucket filled with coarse meal. Watching them peck for food was repugnant to some but oddly enticing to others – all of which was evidenced by their physiological responses. Whether their interest was in the male's clothing, pecking on the ground or the food bits would be calculated later. Right now, the techs recorded the males whose cocks or balls registered proper curiosity.

The next scene drew everyone's focus. The milking barn was revealed in full glory. Rows of cows locked in stalls paraded across their goggles and soon the audio started. The males were forced to watch cows locked in head braces crawl on all fours and later rest on straw beds. The video stream flipped to the milking barn in which the cows' udders were hooked up to a suction machine. The audio ran through the cows' shrieks of pain and then morphed into sudden shouts of delight. The juxtaposition of noises was quickly replaced by yet another Farm scene.

An immense pasture filled with green grass crept into their goggles. Males had been stripped of clothing and were adorned with neck and cock harnesses and they ran wild in the field until they caught other males whose gear consisted of leather belts with two dangling leather slings that split their asscheeks. Once a male was caught, the scene showed in graphic detail and with loud audio what really took place in that pasture.

> *Paula smiled. The Stud Farm always gets to them. Paula loved her Seasons as Pack Leader at the stud farm because the animals were given the chance to do what they secretly longed for and could never admit, not even to themselves.*

Gasps rumbled through Assessment when the males recognized exactly might happen to them in the green pasture.

The streaming images shifted again and again. More Farm scenes were shown with grunting and gasping audio and the males, even though they had been fully indoctrinated prior to signing their contracts for the Season, seemed to understand exactly how their Season would unfold. In addition to their horror, their genital responses betrayed their hidden lust.

> *I wonder which one will be awarded to the Stud Farm, she thought. Only the best ones got to enjoy the Owner's special plans for them.*

Scenes rolled by incessantly. Perched on their stools, a few males lost their balance and had to be repositioned on their roosts by a tech's strong hands. They were learning the Farm way, the way of life that was to become their new reality.

Paula waited eagerly for the finale. That scene and the special audio accompanying it was a wonderful way to end the Assessment phase of Intake and Processing. She peeked into her own goggles and smirked. It was about time for the big finish.

All 45 males' goggles displayed the same scene with loud audio that shook their senses and elicited intense physical reactions. The punishment barn, a simple fact of Farm life, unfolded in front of their eyes and were pressed into their ears.

> *One of them is going to cry, Paula predicted. If a few pee in fear, so much the better.*

Although the Owner preferred the term *discipline*, this particular barn was known on the Farm as the *punishment* barn so she allowed the word to be part of the Farmhands' vocabulary. Training animals is hard work, Paula learned from her own training, and in order to bring lessons home quickly, strict animal discipline was required. Correcting animals was sometimes more efficient than repeated training. Group punishment was rarely the Farm way, she had been taught, and recalled the Owner's words.

Isolate the offender. Educate it. Return it to the pack.
The rest of the herd will learn from the right example.

Paula recognized how valid that wisdom was. When a punished animal was returned to its pack, it presented a living example of why it was better to comply with a Trainer's instructions than to resist or worse, fight the inevitable. In some of these animals' former worlds, resistance was an admirable trait, even "manly." But on the Farm, group behavior was the goal. Every animal, no matter what its former lifestyle, was expected to perform as part of its pack and then as part of the entire herd. No one animal inhabited a higher rung than another and none could be promoted above another. That was not the Farm way.

The animals were to become a single herd.

The punishment barn images continued relentlessly and the audio pounded into their ears. Several recoiled from the animals' shrieks of pain, groans of anguish and moans of agony. What happened at the punishment barn became clear to the new herd and the technicians were attentive to penile reactions. Some animals learned better through punishment than through training and those had to be sorted out quickly. The techs had been trained to inspect how penises moved and danced during the finale.

Just as Paula began to remove her goggles, she noticed that a new feature had been added to the Assessment video.

This must be why Marla got the promotion, she guessed. This piece is probably going to be great.

She put her goggles on and listened to the new audio feed. What she saw and heard amused her and made it even clearer to her that the Owner had once again chosen wisely by appointing Marla to her new position.

The new section showed the animals how watering worked.

Watering was an issue that the Farm had worked to handle more and more efficiently, but it was also a chore that had frequent trouble spots. Keeping the animals well fed on a strict diet high in protein, also required lots carbs, plenty of vitamins, minerals and suitable water. Dietary was assigned this critical task. The Owner would not allow animals to be fed poorly and refusing to eat was not acceptable. Meager eating disrupted the Farm's health. Feeding time on the Farm was a ritual in which all the Farmhands and trainees received detailed schooling and repeated practical instruction.

However, feeding brought along with it the necessity of watering the herd. Providing them time and place to empty their bladders and bowels was scheduled and their success was monitored. This simple act of physiology turned into one of the Farm's most often studied practices and every aspect of watering was broken down and analyzed. Alternatives were proposed and tried and rejected before the current process was adopted.

Farm animals never used toilets, sinks or showers. Instead, urination and defecation were studied and a proper facility was designed and built to meet those goals. The Owner knew that each herd, flock and gaggle would have emergencies or unscheduled watering needs. She consulted engineers, architects, plumbers and medical personnel to set up the best situation for her animals that mirrored the Farm way.

There were consequences to feeding and Marla was proactive by introducing them with this addition to the Assessment finale.

The watering facility's details filled their goggles and the sounds of animals using it filled their ears. The pack was astonished at what they saw. Even though they had been subjected to one session of group watering during Intake, they may have wrongly assumed it was a one-time event. They would learn not to assume, Paula predicted, when this video was done.

Watering had a unique design. Animals crawled in through a small door, took their places on platforms wide enough to hold only their hands and another for their knees and were locked into place. The set of platforms tilted and the group's watering was done with the help of gravity and a novel Farm plumbing innovation. The animals' cock rings were leashed to a lever that pointed them properly so the angle of the platforms' tilt forced the contents to fall straight down. It was quick and unpretentious.

Some trainees called it piss and shit, but the Owner preferred the more elegant term, watering.

When the group was finished and their bladders and bowels emptied, the trainees scrubbed them inside and out as water jets spewed cold water all over them. The platforms rotated so that every inch of their bodies was finally cleansed. To their credit, the trainees learned how to cope with the stench as well as the tilting platforms to perform their jobs quickly.

After the animals were inspected by their Pack Leaders, they were released and crawled out on a narrow platform to be returned to their stall, barn, pen or coop.

> *Paul thought it was clever to show them watering in the Assessment video. I bet the meters flew off the scales, she guessed.*

The technicians removed the pack's goggles and earphones and then unlocked the cock and testicle straps. The males were still perched on their stools but now filled with dread. They didn't move a muscle until they heard Marla's voice.

"Stand," she said, "and march single file down the ramp to meet your Pack Leader. Intake and Processing is complete."

Paula watched her weary group gather at the base of the spiral platform and she walked them silently through the long hallways toward a door whose title was simply *Feeding*.

She smiled at the thought of meeting up with the rest of the packs which was the time she could finally cede control of the processed pack and hand it over to Admission who would have them for the rest of the evening. After dinner, the staff's first group debriefing would take place at the Manor House. The Owner would watch and listen to her staff but the herd would not meet her yet. That was always a special time, Paula thought as she pinched her own nipples so they would jut out from her chest as a sign of accomplishment.

She was ravenous.

Chapter 12: Feeding

The Owner taught her Farmhands that keeping the animals in an sanitary environment was the best way to insure that they would be healthy, productive and in top shape for the Season's events. The Farm way was grueling and there was nothing worse than having the ranks reduced by sick – or worse – injured animals. Besides, the Owner always insisted that a clean animal was a happy one.

After all their Seasons on the Farm, the staff learned that the Owner was not only right but also had solid reasons for her policies. The Farmhands hoped that they would one day understand all of it half as well as she did. The Farm ways seemed natural to her but they had to struggle with each new understanding until it became part of their reality. They learned new ways to view their duties through the eyes of their Owner each Season and they cherished the insight they gained from her.

Once the herd had completed Processing, the Trainers were so exhausted that rest and watering were scheduled for the animals to give the Trainers a much-needed break. During every Season, the red-striped Processing vests were replaced by the silver stripes of Transport as the herd was moved from Processing to the next stage of Intake simply known as Admission.

A few males seemed to recognize the familiar voice as it filled the cold assembly room.

"Each of you will drink a full bottle of water," Yvonne, who ran Transport, said sternly as trainees handed the herd plastic jugs. "Then you will drink another. Don't drink too fast. Don't drink too slowly. You will be told when the first bottle is to be empty and you will be given another." Yvonne paused as the trainees saw to it that every male was holding a bottle and started drinking.

"Drink the first bottle standing up," Yvonne said. Given that the huge room had no chairs, the herd did not question her order.

And then the room filled with silence. For the first time since they entered Processing, they were given no direct orders. They were left alone, not led down hallways or gathered into assessment rooms or moved from one lab to another or stressed, prodded and poked by women in white coats covering leather vests. It was their first moment of silence since their arrival at the Farm. For a few minutes, each male stood quietly in a few moments for which each was more grateful than he had been for anything else in what seemed like an extraordinarily long time. They grew nervous and restless as they waited for the next instruction.

Males who had so recently been in charge of hundreds or even thousands of others, men who just that morning were captains of their own fates, men who never before looked at a woman for direction, all waited in silence to be told what to do. They were becoming a herd that no longer recognized their individuality and didn't fight their nakedness.

Yvonne broke the silence at the moment she saw that the majority were teetering on the edge of yearning for control and suffering with no direction. She watched their physical reactions to the terrifying thought that they were alone without a Trainer instructing them what to do. She was almost gentle with them.

"Your bottles are being refilled," she said as the trainees collected the empty plastic jugs and encouraged some stragglers to drain each one. Everyone from the trainees to the Farmhands, to the Pack Leaders and even to the lead Trail Bosses, had been trained to check for possible watering and feeding problems with the animals at the beginning of each Season.

When she was sure the bottles had been collected and the naked group was holding onto their collective emotional edge, she gave them a single instruction.

"Sit," Yvonne said.

Without hesitation, every male plunked its ass on the cold metal floor and seemed grateful to be told what to do.

Yvonne said, "Now you eat. You will eat sufficient calories and proteins for the next chores." She watched in amusement as the men winced. Her Seasons on the Farm allowed her to predict their thoughts.

Planned? Planned? There's more planned? She could hear their despair as if they were screaming a giant NO! out loud and she smiled.

Moans emerged from the seated group but Yvonne ignored their whimpering and continued. "You are fed – and you *will* eat – enough calories, carbohydrates, protein and vitamins so you are strong and fit. Work on the Farm is hard and feeding time is scheduled." Their faces contorted as they heard their meals referred to as 'feeding time,' and their brows furled when they listened to her description of what they would eat.

"There are no courses," she explained, "and there are no seconds. You eat exactly what you are fed. You eat quickly. We check your feedbag so you eat it all." She allowed her words to sink in before she added a final remark. "Those who do not comply are sent for discipline."

The room full of naked bodies shuddered at the word 'discipline' and they knew that 'discipline was something that should be avoided at all costs. Eating, after all, was something that they were eager to do and avoiding it seemed to make no sense. Figuring that this was one task that they could do easily during their Season on the Farm, the males seemed eager to taste their first real food of the day.

"Feedbags," Yvonne said as the trainees ran to fulfill the command. Her lime green swatch sparkled from between her breasts and accentuated her smile.

One herd member's mouth after another was locked into a trough that was strapped around the its head and buckled in the back. A second strap ran vertically across each head and the techs snapped them closed. Only their eyes and noses were visible and the males looked from one to another in horror when they understood what feeding time really meant.

As Processing Team Leader, Victoria coordinated feeding to make sure that the Season's Processing ended satisfactorily. Her neon blue rank twinkled in the lights and she patrolled the mass of naked flesh. Finally, she was satisfied that each feedbag was secure. She nodded to Yvonne who in turn ordered the trainees to begin.

"You are now feeling the shields retract. Eat your food now," Yvonne said. She studied their faces as lukewarm paste was pressed toward their mouths by a simple air pressure system. "Eat it all. We know when you are done."

Shutting off her microphone with a toggle near her vest's green sash, Yvonne noted that the herd was silent. In seconds, the familiar sounds of muffled choking rose from under the feedbags and a few moments after that melody started, gags and grunts filled the room.

There are gaggers every Season, Yvonne recalled, as she prepared for the vomiters.

Of course, the Farmhands knew they would have to train the animals how to eat properly so the trainees had been shown how to look for signals and be ready with buckets to catch spills. They also knew that the likelihood of any male spitting out its gruel later was impossible. After all, they hadn't been fed all day and the water they drank merely replenished their sweat. Even if they gagged for a while, the critical nutrition had already been delivered.

With feedbags locked tightly around their mouths, all the herd could do was bend their necks backward and let gravity slide the paste toward their lips. Some were simply hungry and rose to their knees to get the paste to slide to their lips faster while others bent their faces down in useless defiance. Yvonne watched Victoria survey the process and spoke only when she nodded toward a small group to address those who weren't eating quickly enough.

"Lift your head," Yvonne said. "Then tilt it back and let food slide to your lips. Lower your head and swallow. Then repeat the process."

Every Season, the same thing, Yvonne laughed silently.
You have to teach them how to eat.

What the Farmhands were watching for was not who managed the feeding process and who did not; rather, their eyes were focused on the animals that accepted their feedbags and noted those who fought against them. There were always a few who needed correction but the staff's goal was to make sure all animals learned to eat from the feedbags and were properly nourished. There was no arguing that rule on the Farm. There would be no exceptions for any animal nor would there be alternative food. It was a Farm rule: during feeding time, all the animals ate.

A few animals caught the techs' eyes. Because these Farmhands would take them to the final step of Intake, they were especially interested in potential problems that might be lurking in the herd. The Farmhands were experienced and no failure to eat slipped by them. Even though their nails were manicured, their hands knew the value of rough work and they held a tight rein on the creatures in their charge.

"Lift your head and tilt it back!" Yvonne said more loudly and waited till all had complied. Then she added, "Hold that position."

The males obeyed and some pressed their lips shut to ward off the press of pasty gruel through their lips. Techs knew that those who fought against their new diets eventually came around – once they came to terms with their new circumstances – and some reached that goal well before others. Yvonne was interested in how long it took to get 245 males on their knees, heads tilted back, feedbags pointed upward and the remnants of rations pressing against their lips. The techs' tablets glowed when a feedbag was emptied but their interest was focused more on the ones that were not.

It was then that she told the trainees to bring the second round of water. That bottle of water would have a big impact on how well feeding would work this Season on the Farm.

Techs carried nozzles with short hoses and connected them to a feedbag's tip. Once the hoses were locked in place, the animals felt cool water seep into the food compartment and move the paste faster toward their lips. It was at that moment that each trainee unsnapped a small covering on the feedbag and pinned it completely over the herd's noses. With a small tap, each tech snapped it shut and the males' faces were wholly encased in their feedbags. None could breathe until water pushed the paste fully into their mouths.

There was no escape from eating and each member of the herd realized it at the same time.

One by one the animals were resigned to the inevitability of how feeding worked on the Farm. Each parted his lips to suck the now-watery paste so it could gulp air when its quota of food had been consumed. It was odorless and tasteless, the kind of high-nutrition paste that satisfied their physical needs.

Yvonne noticed a few red dots on her monitor. Some feedbags weren't quite empty.

They will all finish every drop, the Owner instructed.
There are no exceptions.

One by one, the techs removed their nose coverings except for those who had unfinished food. Jutting her breasts toward the kneeling animal's face, Zoe knew it would open its mouth rather than stop breathing so she pressed her breasts closer to its eyes and laughed when the startled beast opened its mouth. The pressure allowed the last drops of paste to slide inside. It swallowed and then gagged.

The rest of the trainees followed Zoe's lead and in a few seconds, all feedbags were empty. Marla knew that appointing Zoe as her lead trainee had been a good move.

First Feeding was finished. More water washed through the feedbags and Yvonne and Marla noted that the animals endured a productive first group feeding. Yvonne smiled and Victoria, true to form, tapped notes into her tablet in what everyone knew would become a set of recommendations on how to improve Feeding. That was the Farm way – continuous improvement. And it made for great video and talk at dinner.

The new animals, still kneeling with their feedbags tilted up and waiting for an order to move, grew restless on the cold metal floor. It was time to sort the herd into packs and assign them to the Farmhands who would handle the next part of Intake. Yvonne spouted off names and made the assignments with easy precision.

"Remove the feedbags. Your next step is separating into groups for Shearing. Wipe your faces and look at your hands."

All 245 males wiped their mouths with dirty fingers and stared at dye-stained palms. The colors were vivid and mired with bits of leftover feeding. When they looked up, they saw five senior Farmhands, each clad in now-familiar black leather pants, work boots and sporting the most revealing vests they had seen so far on the Farm. The vests were completely open except for a single clasp across the colorful bands that kept them closed. Their presence filled the males with respect as well as with dread. Each member of the herd knew better than to focus on their rich bosoms yet each was unable to withdraw its eyes from the glorious sight.

"Go to the Trail Boss displaying your color," Yvonne ordered the group. "Greens – go with Nadia and orange – you're assigned to Ursula. The silvers – you go with Paula and the ones with brown – follow Rhonda. Last – the reds. You stay with Tara."

After surveying her tablet, Yvonne concluded loudly, "It's time to drive the herd to Shearing."

Chapter 13: Shearing

The weather was seasonal in the north country where the Farm remained private and secure. Some Seasons brought a harsher climate with frigid winters with biting winds and deep snow. Seasons were the main reason the Owner had built a domed stadium for all-season outdoor training and Competitions that called for wide open fields with plenty of running space. Events that took place under the dome were often spirited and were always primal. By the time certain Farm events were scheduled, the herds had been so well trained that they were always energetic. They made good use of the ample acreage during Farm training and Competitions.

After many Seasons of consultations with specialists, advice from medical teams and her own preferences, the Owner made sure that every Farm animal was sheared regularly. The herd, having studied the videos and signed agreements, knew that grooming would be part of their training on the Farm. What they had not been informed of prior to their arrival was the manner or frequency that shearing took place. It was time for the new herd to experience how Shearing worked on the Farm.

The Owner's animals were sheared to their bare skin. Unless she found a particular animal's fur to be especially attractive, it was a Farm rule to shear the herds near the end of Intake. Given the occasional newcomer tantrum and other childish resistance associated with the procedure, this stage of Intake was performed under strict supervision. Each member of the herd was immobilized first to make sure no animals were hurt through silly resistance.

The herd lined up in single file and was grouped by cock band color. Then they were led at a slow jog toward the Shearing room.

The deliberate jog was designed especially for the herds at this precise time in Processing. Having been fully bound, prodded, bent, hoisted, tied, lifted, lowered and manipulated during each phase of Intake, the Owner knew that her animals needed to keep their legs toned. The Trail Bosses, identified by their vest colors and sashes, ran at the front of their packs and on occasion, dropped alongside to make sure the group stayed together. The hoof beats of the line of naked animals jogging silently was the only noise heard in the long hallway toward shearing. Trainers were tuned in to herd noise and listened for huffing and puffing that showed their stamina for this physical exertion.

"Faster," Ursula, with her orange colors flying and firm breasts bouncing, demanded of a straggler.

"Together," Paula barked at one that had left too much distance behind the asscheeks of the runner in front of it. As the animal struggled to quicken its pace, she ran alongside him with her silver colors and her breasts flapping. She grabbed its cock and yanked the flabbergasted animal forward. It took only a few steps before its bobbing cock and dancing balls brushed against the naked asscheeks of the runner ahead of it.

Each Trail Boss made certain her pack ran as a single unit. Tight groups of animals jogged down a long hallway, turned and continued their pace with borrowed energy they struggled to find. Cocks bounced faster and faster, testicles hopped with each step and heavy breathing filled the hallways with the music of raw instinct and the heady fragrance of sweat.

Suddenly, the unmistakable sound of a Trail Boss's hand slapping an animal's asscheek filled the hallway. One runner had slowed and the pack's Trail Boss communicated with him with a taste of Farm correction. The pack ran forward with each member struggling harder to keep its cock slapping against the ass in front of it because none of them wanted to taste the humiliating discipline they had just heard. The Trail Bosses' boots clapped on the floor and were greeted with the softer plopping of the herds' bare feet.

Finally, the line's pace slowed.

The Trail Bosses retook their places at the head of their packs and began to slow them down. As the distance between packs narrowed, they slowed even more. Finally the packs crushed against each other with sweaty animal hide touching one another as they crowded outside a large double doorway. Every animal noticed that the doors had no handles and they realized that they could go in but there was no way for them even to consider getting out. What they didn't yet know was that the Owner had a penchant for juxtaposing certain clues just to make them wonder and be gripped by fear. She fed their dread like a chef unveiling a sumptuous meal course by course.

This was one of those times.

Ursula, the Trail Boss who took up first position in front of the mass of animal flesh, punched a string of numbers into the keypad and her full palm on the touchscreen. Two big doors swung open and Nadia, the Trail Boss with a neon green waistband burning in stark contrast to her tanned breasts, stepped inside, then turned to address the herd.

"March single file into Shearing. Every animal in the herd will take a place on the wheel. Step lively." Nadia spun on her heel and looked into the brightly lit Shearing pen.

Tell them once and expect compliance. If they don't comply, you did not instruct them properly.

Ursula was the first Trail Boss to lead her pack inside. She seized the first handy cock and pulled it forward while indicating with a single finger that the next cock in line should follow. The line of 245 males began running behind the Trail Boss who was still holding a cock and dragging it behind her. Ursula ran faster and the animal sped up to ease the pain of her fierce grip. The sound of animal feet slapping against the pure white tile floor was enough to fill the gaping room with a roar.

When the herd's speed was acceptable, Nadia nodded at Ursula and the cock in her grip was yanked in a new direction that forced the animal's body to follow. Behind it, 244 other animals fell in line and chased toward an unknown goal. By now, nothing mattered to the herd other than following Ursula and avoiding any on-the-spot discipline like they had witnessed earlier during this very long day.

The packs were run into a wide circle by the lead animal's cock. They were led to the edge of a series of inlaid tile circles, took their places and within seconds, they were all running in a tight pack on a black tile sphere. The lead Trail Boss again slowed the group by jerking the cock in her hand downward, and each Trail Boss took a nearby bouncing penis or set of testicles and crushed them to slow down the animals behind it. The males understood immediately and reduced their speed.

At last, Nadia said, "Stop!"

The herd came to a sudden halt and the Trail Bosses needed to whip only two or three animals' asses to stop the line.

In only one day at the Farm, Nadia assessed with a smile, you can train males to become the animals they are supposed to be.

"Face outward!" she said loudly. "Stretch your arms out." Nadia thought about saying 'paws,' but thought it was just a little too soon for that particular noun. It was only the herd's first day at the Farm.

With their arms reaching out and their bodies absolutely still and waiting silently for the next instruction, the packs finally showed effective herd behavior. Nadia lifted her chin toward the back of the room and Shearing techs trotted to the green circle just outside the black one on which the packs were arranged. Wearing tight leather shorts and matching vests with white sashes, the

Shearing trainees' oiled breasts sparkled from the overhead lights' bright glow. Their vests were cut so deeply that there was only enough leather to form armholes and then clasp at the waist. The Owner liked the bare-breasted look for both the newest trainees' and the Intake Processing experience.

Each trainee had five males in her shearing cluster. The room's silence was broken by the now-familiar whirr of an electric motor that lowered steel cables holding 245 pair of sturdy leather restraints from the ceiling. The trainees wasted no time in securing each animal's wrists and forearms in the restraints and then jerked the cable once to indicate to Control that her restraints were complete. The process took no more than ten minutes and Nadia watched with an eagle eye for any errant shackling.

The trainees stepped backward to allow Nadia to examine their work. After a careful inspection, she returned to the green ring and the trainees resumed their positions close to their animals. The whirring began again and the herd's arms were drawn straight up and back toward the center of the ceiling. With the danger of falling very real, the animals tried to grasp the only support they could find on the steel cable that gripped their wrists and forearms. Some trembled with panic; others shook with terror.

Precisely during the height of their awkward imbalance was when the whirr grew louder. As the motor pulled them up and they were lifted from the temporary safety of the black circle, 245 new animals were suspended exactly 36 inches above the tile floor. Grabbing silver clippers, the trainees sheared hair from the unending circle of legs that hung directly in front of them.

They worked in silence and the Shearing trainees moved from one leg to the next and shaved each calf smooth. After approving the smooth bare skin with their fingers, they touched one area or another before moving to the next leg in line. When they had completed their group, each trainee tapped her tablet and one particularly tall animal was lowered 12 inches so its upper leg was within reach. The process continued quietly as tufts of hair cascaded to the tile floor.

Lowering the animals a few more inches, the techs buzzed every speck of chest and underarm hair, continued to complete the upper arms and forearms and indicated that they were done by stepping back from the dangling line. Each felt the bare skin on each male many times to insure its smoothness. Nadia ordered the trainees to their positions and issued the command for the next step in Shearing.

The dreaded whirr started again and the herd was hoisted even higher. As they hung, Nadia glanced toward Control and nodded for the leg harnesses to be lowered so their ankles could be locked. Only then did the trainees lower their arms.

Nadia checked every one thoroughly before nodding one more time toward the anonymous technicians in the control room.

The herd's world turned upside down as the wrist restraints fell away and 245 males were flipped and hung from their ankles and calves. Not one tip of a finger was allowed to touch the floor and their shrieks of disorientation filled the Shearing room. Naked and screaming males dangled as far as the Shearing techs could see. The Trail Bosses took a look at the herd's disorientation and agreed it made them of the more amusing packs they had seen. Even though they knew they couldn't be dropped on the floor, in their panic their hands slapped the air trying to find something to hold onto. They knew there was nothing there but they reached out anyway.

The trainees approached the hanging animals and sheared a set of legs, arms and asscheeks. Then they raised each one up by its head to make sure all back and neck hair was removed cleanly. Piles of curly clumps of hair floated toward the gleaming white tile as the Shearing techs shaved their males completely.

Technicians adjusted the dangling animals so that each trainee could reach every leg, ass, back and neck. With a nod to Control, Nadia had them spread the males' legs wide apart. Donning gloves, the trainees lathered acrid oil onto the inner thighs, testicles, groins and between the asscheeks of the whimpering animals who were still dangling from the Shearing ceiling. The smell was pungent and its intention unmistakable. The trainees' hands were as merciless as they were thorough. Not an inch of genital skin escaped the creamy oil's bite.

As the concoction did its work, the hoist raised the herd a few feet higher until their heads were level with the trainees' hands. There was only one more task to complete for Shearing.

The Trail Bosses stepped closer to watch the herd's reaction.

I love this part, Nadia thought. I wonder which one will cry first.

Every trainee grasped a handful of hair on the closest head and ran the clippers firmly against the animal's scalp. Huge tufts of hair fell to the tile floor and the animals, with their backs to the trainees, could now see one another clearly.

Their horrified eyes drank in the results of the women's work as they witnessed what was happening to those who had gone before them. They trembled in terror from what was happening to the rest of the pack and one by one began to shake. One by one, they understood their fate.

More and more hair tumbled to the floor as the unshorn males struggled uselessly against the steel cables' grip. They wasted energy that for no purpose but their effort always made the Trail Bosses snicker. The idea of escape amused them as much as it did Nadia and the other Farmhands, including the trainees, who struggled not to laugh out loud.

The process was inexorable. Once a male was completely bald, the trainee moved to the next and began shearing anew.

Protests were hurled from their lips but landed on uninterested ears. The Trail Bosses were served cold drinks as Shearing continued unabated and as they sipped, they mocked male after male, especially those who struggled. They smirked at the males' profanity and wondered if they really thought that cursing would help them retain their head hair. No matter what they did or how long they resisted, that hair was going to wind up on the floor. Why did they fight against it, the women wondered?

Training males takes time, Nadia remembered from her Owner's instruction. They've already forgotten about punishment, she sighed. Maybe a reminder was in order.

Sliding her electric prod from the neon green waistband on her leather vest, Nadia stood behind one noisy beast and touched the tip to its greasy cock. It screamed in rage as it tried to kick its way free from the steel cable that secured the animal several feet above the tile floor. Figuring that it just didn't get it yet, she pressed the tip more firmly into one of its testicles and its agonized screech filled every cubic inch of Shearing.

The pack learned a valuable lesson from the on-the-spot punishment and Shearing continued quickly in eerie silence. Nadia told the noisy animal's trainee to make sure that the corrected animal was the last of the herd to be shorn. It would be better off seeing every shearing before undergoing its own.

Anticipation is an effective teacher, the Owner taught them repeatedly. Make them tremble while you do nothing but make them wait.

Great gobs of head hair covered the floor and the shearers were ready for the last animal's special experience. Nadia grabbed the clippers from the trainee and walked inside the tight circle so that it could see her face and appreciate her breasts. She wanted this particular animal to understand how much she would enjoy his shearing and understand that protestations were useless. Taking one handful of hair after another and shaving its head completely, she threw the clippers carelessly onto the floor and spoke directly into its face. She smiled and said, "Much ado about nothing."

Hot tears fell from its eyes as the animal watched her grin at its helplessness.

"Join me in Control," Nadia said to the other Trail Bosses when she was finished. She had the trainee pick up her discarded clippers as the Trail Bosses followed Nadia to the control room. She tossed a final comment over her shoulder to her trainees.

"Strip," she said.

Certain Farm traditions made the staff remember their own training and appreciate their current senior status. Stripping the new trainees for messy jobs was an effective method of making the new hands mindful of their lowly status and making sure untidy jobs were done with the least impact to their newly issued leathers. The new trainees, however, rarely saw it that way and stared at Nadia with confused stares.

"Now," she said quietly. As the young staff continued staring at her in disbelief, the other Trail Bosses and Pack Leaders took a single menacing step toward the immobile group. Through a few tears, they began to comply and Nadia and her coworkers shifted their gazes from the leather and fabric sashes that were falling to the floor and focused on the trainees' supple breasts, bellies and shaved lips.

> *Not a bad-looking lot, Nadia thought. Make them obey first, the Owner taught. Understanding 'why' isn't important for trainees. In her Green Salon, the Owner used the same techniques even on her senior staff and strict obedience made for a well-run Farm.*

The senior staff gathered up the trainees' leather shorts and vests and the new trainees stood humiliated in their stark nakedness before being ordered to begin Shearing's final task. Taking care of their leathers during the messy finale of Shearing was one of the Trail Bosses' responsibilities and they enjoyed inspecting their girls' bodies to chat later about which ones sported superior qualities. But that was after-dinner conversation and senior staff had a job to finish first.

Chrome nozzles attached to clear tubes descended from the ceiling and the trainees each grasped one. Standing behind the circle of upside-down and spread-eagle males, the trainees aimed their hoses and shot frigid streams of water on the dangling herd's cocks, ball, asscheeks and groin flesh, then finished wetting them with a flourish of icy water aimed right between their red-hot asscheeks.

Wait for it, Nadia thought from her observation post in the control room. Just wait for it. It always happens right about now.

At first, there was stunned silence. Suddenly, in a moment repeated every Season that always amused Nadia and the other Trail Bosses, hysteria overtook the herd. As the trainees moved from one dangling animal to another and shot another ruthless stream of icy water directly on each one's newly hairless and very sensitive skin, each animal bounced from its tethers from the force of the hose as well as from its useless attempts to evade the inevitable. Soon the entire hanging circle of animals was performing the Shearing dance from the power of the spray and recoiling from the trainees' brushes that scrubbed every inch of their hide. Their frenzied gyrations made the next one in line recoil one by one and soon the entire herd was fully engaged in the seasonal Shearing dance.

What a picture, the Trail Bosses smiled as they predicted this clip would be a highlight during tonight's dinner. Shearing's finish was always a special moment of every new Season on the Farm. They felt privileged to participate and enjoyed the naked, soapy trainees cleansing the new herd.

The Shearing dance seemed to go on forever. Twenty minutes after skin balm had been sprayed onto abused shorn skin and the last wisps of hair were washed down the drain, 425 absolutely hairless animals were lowered to the wet tile floor and were finally unshackled. As they fell into lumps on the unforgiving tile, several rolled up into balls and fretted uselessly as if they could hide from the reality that was theirs for the rest of the Season.

"Up!" Nadia said from Control's speaker and the weary group struggled first to their knees and then to their feet. "You will run to the barns and rest so the herd will be fresh in the morning."

The Trail Bosses walked happily into the Shearing chamber and oversaw the herd separate into small groups sorted by color behind their assigned trainees. Without a word, the bald, naked, shorn and oiled animals ran obediently behind naked trainees down the long hallways and around corners into the remnants of daylight toward the barns that would be their homes for the Season.

In the Manor House, dinner was almost ready.

Chapter 14: In the Manor House

From experiences during the Seasons on the Farm, the Farm's physical layout had been perfected by a team of architects, landscape designers, engineers and subcontractors of various expertise whose job was to create a unique community that captured the essence of rural Farm conditions mixed with edge-pushing design. The landscape was pristine and the acreage seemed limitless. The Owner's single theme for the blueprint of what the Farm would become was wrapped up in a single word.

Community.

She insisted in all planning meetings that every expert would incorporate the other's needs and requirements into a total design of form and function. No building would be constructed unless she was convinced that all the supporting services for it were in place. Expansion was always in her thoughts; connectivity and communication were primary challenges; feasibility and accessibility were guiding principles; and most important, the Manor House would be the center from which the entire Farm radiated, like spokes from the hub of a wheel. She gave them huge acreage and generous funding; she demanded perfection in return.

It didn't hurt that some of her contractors were Farm trained.

As plans progressed, she watched hawk-like to make sure that both the simplest and the most complicated details were accounted for and interacted seamlessly. One example all the Farm hands could retell was the Farm's fluid transportation system, now under the supervision of Yvonne and her bus-transport lead, Willa. Transporting animals – and even staff – on the Farm would be only by horse, pony-boy and electric cart. The roads and paths had to accommodate those modes of transportation yet the service areas required larger vehicles. The paved area, the Owner insisted, had to be shielded from the inhabited locations. Nothing could disrupt the herd's mental or visual image of the Farm, she reminded all the workers repeatedly. This was to be a very special community.

In addition, the far North Country's weather posed the problem of limiting outdoor training when it was very cold but Competitions continued even in the Farm's coldest seasons. After several designs, she chose an area for a stadium with a retractable dome that provided heated space for her outdoor spectacles. Every Season on the Farm saw various Competitions among the packs but ended with a special week-long finale that was her Spectacle. The domed stadium had to be built to serve as the venue for that event. Several technical innovations were needed to construct the dome yet in all the Seasons the Farm had trained herds, it still retained the simple name, "Dome." When she wanted to use it, she instructed the staff to 'ready the dome,' even though the structure was much more than the simple name implied.

Each training barn, maintenance building, Control center and punishment area was created to reflect her Farm's concept of community. With a network of underground tunnels, access for the Farmhands to all areas of the property was quick and easy and remained shielded from both inclement weather and curious eyes. The technicians, Trail Bosses, Pack Leaders and the rest of the farmhands and staff appreciated the ease with which they could appear in any location and observe unseen. From the moving walkways to the electric carts, the staff's ability to emerge almost immediately at the Owner's beck and call helped keep the Farm running smoothly at all times in all Seasons.

The hub of the Farm was the Manor House. Home to the Owner as well as central control for the Farm's complex technology, the Manor House had to meet a complex series of requirements and serve countless functions. It was only after a great deal of planning, exploring new technologies and laying new communication groundwork that the Owner selected the shape of the main structure. If form follows function, then the long arms of the Manor House with a central round set of personal quarters and salons gave her and her staff exactly what she wanted: she became the center of the Farm community.

She needed to see everything about the Farm, especially when the animals were in Season. At the center of one of the Manor House's round rooms was the core, the command post from which all technology was controlled. Monitors surveyed every acre of the Farm and displayed different angles in rapid succession except when she wanted to focus on a particular event. In that case, cameras afforded an abundance of angles from which any single event could be viewed.

The main setup was duplicated on remote servers off-site and in case failure could be restored within an hour. Continuity, the Owner remarked, was the fulcrum of community.

Each animal barn was equipped with noise and motion detectors, all of which triggered alarms. The command core consisted of a communications center from which instant text, voice and video were transmitted to all Farmhands via barely noticeable earpieces and concealed monitors from replies could be sent immediately. No situation, accident, amusing event or standard Farm chore could escape the Owner's observation or measuring for quality. Everything was recorded and reviewed. Episodes were often replayed for Farmhand instruction or enjoyment of the Owner and her central staff.

Surrounding the command core was the first of a series of concentric circles that served as living spaces. Because she and everyone else on the Farm worked and lived there, all rooms were designed to be multi-functional. The first ring housed working areas including several kitchens for different functions, leather closets and leather sewing rooms, training studios as well as worker prep areas. The larger concentric ring that ran the perimeter of the Manor House was designed as the Owner's living suite and included a huge dining hall, smaller private dining areas, an expansive media room, resplendent bathrooms and multifunctional meeting areas. Each room had a simple name that spoke specifically to its purpose.

The Farmhands were accustomed to her nomenclature. Some rooms were welcoming while others maintained an eerie sense of mystery even to experienced Farmhands. Staff members wanted to be invited to the staff dining area, known as the Blue Room, a warm and cozy meeting room with a fabulous view of the dome. However, staff were filled with fear if the Owner called you to her 'Gray Studio,' because that meant that you were the subject of one of her trials or assessments. Even though passing the Owner's strenuous tests might result in a highly-desirable promotion, the experience itself was infamous for the personal ordeal inflicted on the Farmhand who had to endure it.

It never mattered what level you had risen to on the Farm. When the Owner tested you, status never mattered. You were simply an piece in her chess game and you were too insignificant on the chessboard to understand her strategy.

The community was famous for its view of the Farm's heavenly land on earth. Each part of the living space around the Owner's outer ring was adorned with floor-to-ceiling walls of curved windows that presented a magnificent view of the Farm. By moving from space to space, a different perspective greeted the viewer's eyes, and if you were lucky enough to be invited by the Owner for a private session, you might be treated to a walk around the stone breezeway that circled the entire Manor House. Very few Farmhands were allowed that tour; in fact, the Owner used that space for her own privacy and took only an occasional pet with her when she meditated there. Even when she chose to punish one of her hands, she could enjoy the view.

The Manor House usually kept several house pets. The Owner adored having personal pets each Season and selected them from time to time to stay an extra Season as her own toy. Being offered a second Season to stay in the Manor House was one of the thrilling ends to Competition and Spectacle that the Farmhands were privileged to witness. When the Owner interacted directly with the herd or when she took a liking to a particular animal, the Farmhand who managed it was rightfully proud that one of her own pack pleased the Owner. The Owner's reward for that particular Farmhand was known to be lavish and the Farmhands scrutinized their packs to try to speculate which one might please the Owner. That one always received extra intense on-the-spot instruction all Season. They also endured very firm on-the-spot punishment. You could tell which the special ones were from their usually bright-red welted asscheeks and fearful expressions.

When that potential pet was identified by a Trail Boss, it was trained to be showcased in many of the Season's Competitions. Although the Owner didn't choose a new pet every Season, she was always on the lookout for one that caught her fancy. The Farmhands busied themselves insuring that potential pet material was highlighted during regular training and special events with adorned cocks, decorated testicles and a variety of eye-catching plugs that extended from their developed asscheeks. They presented a possible pet for the Owner's attention whenever they could. The animals never knew why their cocks were impaled with steel rods or feathers and horsetails hung from their asses, but the staff noticed them immediately and trained those particular animals mercilessly.

Other than a few pets, the Owner never allowed pack animals in the Manor House. The Farm staff was female and each woman had explicit responsibilities for cooking, cleaning, organizing, attending to construction, overseeing leather workers, training to handle the communications technology and, at those times that the Owner specifically desired it, performing personal services for her. She had several women who were assigned to her personal needs. But she always auditioned new private assistants and her inner staff was sometimes selected for special assignments outside the Manor House. She liked meeting new staff as trainees if they had the talent and skills to care for her and farmhands that were allowed to touch her. Those staff members could not mingle with those that interacted directly animals.

Only one Manor worker was allowed to disturb the Owner or contact her outside of normal Farm hours. Leda, the Owner's handpicked chief assistant, had been with her for almost a decade. She had the critical skill that Owner described as the 'ability to read my mind and act on it.' The Farmhands always sought Leda's favor and went to her with all their personal as well as routine Farm needs. Leda was the key to the Owner; if Leda did not approve of a hand, she was habitually moved down the promotion list or demoted to animal training. There was no grievance system on the Farm.

As a result, Leda knew everything about everyone on the Farm. She had leeway to inflict staff retraining and inflict on-the-spot discipline and her personal prod was designed for special vaginal insertion. No farmhand who had experienced Leda's discipline was able to sit during dinner that same week.

Intake day was always special for the Farm, especially in the Manor House. There were times scheduled during every Season so the entire Farm staff could join together for dinner in the opulent "Teal Room," the largest dining room in the Manor House, but none was as filled with as much anticipation and excitement as dinner on the first night of Intake. The pack was terrified and overwhelmed; every Season the exhausting first Intake day was filled with new stories for the Farm hands to share and the best ones were watched over and over on video. The tales the women told were of gloating over new animals' penis measurements, silly performance during Processing and reactions to the feedbags, plus, of course, the tales of the crybabies, whiners and moaners. It seemed that everything happening on the first day was worthy of retelling over a long and leisurely dinner. It was a night when no one had to be on her best behavior; in fact, the Owner set that tone years ago and kept up the tradition that First Night was causal and amenable to sharing the Farmhands' problems as well as their tiny delights and larger successes.

Celebrate small joys. Share setbacks and overcome challenges. They will become your community and they will love being owned.

First Night dinner in the Teal Room was one of the Farmhands' most anticipated events of the Season. When the bell rang just after the herd had been put to sleep in their large dormitory, the only night they would sleep together during their Season, the

Farmhands spirited themselves to the Manor House and were ushered to the Teal Room for dinner while the lowliest trainees babysat the herd. The women were seated at assigned places and offered their first glass of Pinot Noir. They would each be served the limit of two small glasses before the Owner arrived. Her entrance at First Night Dinner was a seminal moment every Season.

Chapter 15: First Dinner

A single gong sounded and the Farm staff knew exactly what it meant.

Tired from First Day Intake but relishing the thought of the First Night Dinner, each Pack Leader finished securing her pack onto its mattress to ready them to turn over to the trainees. The herd's first night required all hands – and especially trainees – to be certain that each ankle strap was secured to each thin metal mattress rail. Trainees attended to ankle padlocks while the Pack Leaders and Trail Bosses latched short cables to the rails. When the herd was secured, Victoria, who earned her status as Processing's Trail Boss after years of training whose breasts were now split by a neon blue vest band, stalked one long dorm aisle while Olivia, Head of Trainees and with cleavage decorated regally in purple, inspected another. As part of their herd inspection, they marched up the remaining aisles and checked every animal. The entire cadre of trainees studied their movements with trepidation. An errant ankle strap would result in unpleasant consequences for the derelict trainee and worse, would delay the staff's dinner. But the Farm was a community and until each had performed her chore perfectly, no one was seated to eat.

The inspection of the herd was fastidious and even more important to the young trainees, was judged satisfactory. Victoria nodded to Olivia who returned her approval, and she gave the herd its final instruction for the evening.

"Lights out," Olivia said, "and you are locked down for the night. You have no needs so you will ask for nothing. Those whose bladders cannot make it through the night will use the nearby cans."

The women smirked at the herd's grimaces as they obediently gazed at the floor where stainless steel relief cans were arranged. No one wanted to use the can but someone always had to and the herd, nestled so close together in their small bunks, was forced to listen as one small bladder after another splashed its contents into the pee can. When that audiotape was played during the morning briefing, the Farmhands always noted who the user was and how the animals reacted to bladder emptying. The morning briefing tapes were very helpful to the Farmhands in planning the day's activities and deciding on which on-the-spot training or discipline was required. Humiliating hints about who filled a can during the night or who groaned while emptying their bowels were dropped carefully by the Farm hands so the herd could hear every word. That reinforced in the herd that it had no privacy on the Farm. It didn't take many nights before the animals learned that every single bodily function was monitored and recorded, including their peeing and defecating.

> *Remove inhibitions, the Owner taught. They will be easier to train to use the outdoor shit hole and once they submit to that order, your ownership is further secured. No trainer could order an animal to the shit hole, the Owner decided, unless she had been ordered to use it herself by the Owner. Training was personal on the Farm.*

With 245 animals fastened to their mini-bunks in what was to be their only night of sleep in anything akin to a bed, the Farmhands left and the dormitory lights were extinguished. Some of the exhausted herd drifted into fitful sleep while others lay motionless as they reviewed the events of this remarkable day. Those assigned to keep an eye on the sleeping herd were the new trainees, but the entire group was monitored carefully via closed circuit by Control. It was one of the Owner's favorite video clips to watch the dorm during First Night. She smiled as the night cameras and microphones presented her a firsthand look at the new herd at the end of First Day. Even though she had observed Intake and Processing in spot checks, first night's sleep always piqued her interest.

She was looking for crybabies and whiners because they amused her. Every Season brought new ones and their bedtime behavior was where they usually let loose of their pent-up fear and ever-present dread. An occasional panic attack wasn't unusual and the Farm was prepared. As she watched First Night in the dormitory to no one's surprise, the Owner scanned the new crop for potential pets. As the staff, second-year trainees and Trail Bosses marched to the Manor House for dinner, she had Control's lead tech spotlight each new entrant so she should scrutinize its hairless body until she instructed that she wanted to see the next one. And down the line her review went, checking out one shackled body after another, noting which she would follow electronically during the Season. Occasionally she instructed Leda to write down an animal's tag number.

Leda's tablet was always at her side.

In the main control room, Katrina made notes on her own tablet of which males attracted the Owner's lingering look and made a list of those animals she might spotlight in this Season's events. That was her silent communication with her Owner – Katrina understood how to find the ones the Owner might like without being given a set of particulars. She took it upon herself to make montages of the ones that might interest her Owner that first night and throughout the Season and presented the videos to the Owner when she scheduled review. The higher-level staff had mastered the art of reading her mind yet their real skill was acting on that knowledge to make their Owner happy.

Back in the dorm, a trainee witnessed an animal's paw hidden from camera view. She notified Victoria, who marched to its location and soundlessly planted her hand over the animal's paw and squeezed mightily.

The stunned roar proved what she knew: it had touched itself and Victoria crushed its balls and cock like a sponge.

"Not in my dorm," Victoria roared and in a single motion cupped the moaning animals waist, dragged its legs to the floor and whipped its hairless ass until she felt that the lesson had been learned. She plunked the animal unceremoniously back into its bunk and stomped away.

> *Punishment should be fast, make the point and be a learning experience, her Owner taught. This animal learned that the Farm owned its paws, cock and balls quickly and efficiently. That made a good lesson and she was sure the rest of the herd had just learned it as well.*

The second clang of Farm's gong told everyone that the staff was accounted for and in their places. The herd was attended to by the trainees under the supervision of the Lead Processing Coordinator and Victoria took the final Intake responsibility seriously. As the trainees' attention shifted from animal to animal and their moans and groans were interpreted by Victoria so they would understand what the noises meant, they learned important lessons of how the herd reacted to physical and emotional stress. First Night was a once-a-Season event and Victoria was careful to make it an educational experience for her trainees. She would drink her wine privately with her Owner later and relate tidbits of tantalizing insight that made both of their glasses of wine taste much sweeter.

After that special moment with her Owner and staff had relieved the trainees, Victoria gathered her new trainees on the floor of the Blue Room for their first formal review. It was a grand ending to an exceptionally busy day and the trainees interspersed their scrutiny of the herd with dreams of the reality of meeting the Owner and learning at her feet.

Kitchen staff encouraged the farmhands and second-year trainees to take their assigned seats in the pecking order at the table that was integral to the Farm way. The Owner, who always sat in the center of the table's long side, surrounded herself with the Trail Bosses first, then the Pack Leaders and then seated the lower-level trainers and Processing staff outward from her. One of the most coveted perks of being a higher level staff member was First Night dinner seating near the Owner.

The table was awash in black leather interspersed with flashes of bold colors across the staff's vest waistbands and between their breasts that were plumped up by the vests' cutouts. Every woman's breasts were cupped by the leather bodice and each level of exposure grew more magnificent as they traveled higher up the ranks. With more responsibility came greater breast display and the highest levels who were seated closest to the Owner's still empty chair had their chests framed by tight vest bodices as their jutting nipples stood proudly and more important, absolutely available for the Owner to enjoy.

The fragrance of their black leather pants and boot leather treatments permeated the dining room as the group passed the time waiting for their Owner's entry with small talk, sharing events of the day and enjoying anecdotes of particular herd member's antics.

"Did you see that one in Shearing?" Nadia asked and the room turned its attention to her. "I mean, I thought he was going to start bawling when I got near its head. He was whimpering, 'No, my hair!' and I couldn't stop giggling." The other women nodded. They had all experienced Shearing meltdowns.

"The redhead?" Sharon from Measurement asked. "Did you see what the redhead did in Measurement?"

A few heads nodded but one asked, "I was busy in Assessment. What did it do?"

"Oh my," Sharon began. "Its measurement was on the small side, only about five and a half full and it argued! I mean it argued!! He swore its cock was bigger than that!" She paused for a moment and added, "He said, 'I know my own dick. I measure it all the time!'" Her voice trailed off as the women broke into gales of laughter.

"Did you watch Feeding?" Olivia's asked the group. Because feeding was a full-herd activity and funny episodes abounded, many heads turned toward Olivia. Might they have missed something?

"This pair, their hands were traveling south," she started to retell the story and held everyone's attention at a hint of masturbation among the herd.

"NO!" Marla exclaimed. "They tried to touch themselves? Which ones?" The idea of masturbators was unacceptable to the Farmhands and was not allowed at the Farm. Potential masturbators were scrutinized regularly and monitored closely. They received repeated on-the-spot correction that usually involved noisy cock slapping or ball crushing. The whole staff was intrigued with Olivia's story.

"Let's see if Katrina can bring it up from Control," Marla suggested and a Manor House staffer sent a tablet message to communications to set up the replay.

In a few seconds, the monitors that dotted the staff dining area flickered and a replay of that Feeding moment began. Suddenly, the camera zoomed in on two feedbags with faces that were fully covered by their harnesses and then traveled down toward their genitals where their hands were most certainly touching two hardening cocks.

"Unacceptable!" Olivia said firmly. "Every one of you will inspect your pack repeatedly for signs. You have been trained in what to do with these miscreants." Olivia's voice wasn't asking; rather, she stated a cold reality and every trainer understood immediately what would happen to a masturbating animal on the Farm.

"Let's make sure about that," a voice said as all heads snapped toward their Owner. The Owner's entrance always dazzled them and this Season's First Night dinner was no exception.

Each woman rose to attention with her feet planted shoulder-width apart and hands clasped by their wrists behind her back. Lead Trainers and Trail Bosses knew how to pull their shoulders back and display their breasts proudly and have them available for the Owner's inspection. Any woman whose shoulders drooped a mere inch was straightened painfully by the Manor House staff who patrolled the group.

She started with Olivia, the overseer of the entire herd.

"What do we do with masturbators?" the Owner asked as her fingers took Olivia's large brown nipples and caressed them into two rigid bumps. She squeezed them slightly in silent communication with her most senior Farmhand. As her fingers enjoyed fondling her two willing breasts, Olivia repeated the often-heard rule.

"Masturbators are sent for punishment," she began as the fingers danced across her nipples and challenged her composure. "They are subject to daily assessment and..."

"That's enough," the Owner interrupted and Olivia's lips stopped talking. As the Owner moved down the line, Olivia's lips curled up slightly. Being the senior staff member had its rewards and the Owner's touch and attention were the two highest on the list.

Strolling toward Willa, the Owner's fingers lifted her breasts by her nipples and pulled her up to her toes. A small 'uhhh' escaped from her tight lips and the Owner's eyes moved to her face. The look she wore was one of intensity mired in deference and touched the Owner with its sincerity. As their eyes lingered, she pulled the woman's breasts up higher and tighter.

"And?" the Owner asked.

Willa, even at her high level as the head Farmhand in charge of transporting herds, struggled to recall the question. Her training shined when she finally replied, "Semen measurement. They are ejaculated and semen is measured against a baseline."

As the Owner loosened her grip, Willa remained on happy toes and looked through the wall of windows toward the lighted Farm and sighed softly. The Owner moved to the next trainer and cupped her breasts. Pulling the woman toward her by her full bosom, she asked a single question.

"And if his semen level is low?" Continuing to pull the woman toward her, she waited for a response.

The now off-balance trainer gazed into her Owner's eyes and luxuriated in her close presence. She responded, "They are locked down." Smiling, the Owner released her and moved to the next trainer, took her nipples in firm fingers and pulled them downward until Tara was forced to bend over yet manage to lift her face toward her Owner to await her question.

"What is the lockdown process?" she asked and Tara grimaced as a stronger tension pulled at her breasts.

"The offender's shaft and testicles are pressed into a mold," she began with a slightly quivering voice that made her Owner grin. "The mold is sealed except for the tip where a ..."

The Owner let go and stepped to the next trainer and Tara's voice ceased immediately. Taking Sharon's breasts and twirling them in circles by their stiff nipples, she watched the woman's eyes glaze over but interrupted her reverie with a question.

"How long does the animal wear the mold?" she inquired. No matter what else, the Owner insisted on constant education for her staff.

As her breasts were jiggled in the Owner's finger dance, Sharon inhaled and replied. "Until it is cured," she responded. "It is cured when the semen count is normal and the animal understands that masturbation or touching of any sort is not tolerated on the Farm."

"Good girls," the Owner said and moved down the line, touching every pair of breasts in greeting to her staff for the new Season. Only after every woman's breasts were acknowledged by the Owner's fingers, did she take her seat.

"Be seated," she said to the staff who immediately sat down at the huge table and locked their eyes on the Owner for the traditional seasonal invocation. Holding her glass of wine aloft, the staff raised their own and she spoke.

"Let this Season be better than the last wonderful Season and let us learn new ways to create a better and stronger herd." The women sipped and the Owner added a new line for this Season.

"I need a house pet," she said. "My dog is leaving at the end of this Season."

Her words shocked the group into silence and filled them with both fear and exhilaration.

"The farmhand in this room who brings me the one I select shall be rewarded." As the servers brought her salad, the cadre of trainers, Trail Bosses and technicians gulped air in anticipation of this Season's exciting challenge.

When the delicious dinner and First Night conversation wound down, the trainers looked forward to retiring to their own quarters for rest. They anticipated an early morning for the Season's first day. The Owner added a few comments to what had been a memorable First Night, more memorable than any of them could recall in recent Seasons. A new pet! She was looking for a replacement!

"Get some rest," she said, "I'll see Willa and Yvonne in my Green Studio after the herd is transported to training tomorrow."

Every woman snapped to attention at the mention of the Green Studio and both Willa and Yvonne trembled, clattered their coffee cups and betrayed their fear. Being invited to any of the Owner's studios was ominous enough; however, the Green Studio was reputed to be the most intense location of her sessions. Many of those seated at the table had not yet been invited to any studio; in fact, some were relieved to have never experienced the Owner's acute and brutal training procedures. Even though a trip to her studio was the only way to advance in the Farm's staff pecking order, the process was frightening and carried a reputation for radical – and sometimes experimental – training methods.

The corps rose as the Owner stood and exited to her chambers with Leda matching her every step as the staff stood at attention.

They were left alone at the table when Manor House personnel instructed them that First Night dinner was over and they were to return to their quarters. The stunned group required a few seconds to regroup mentally and they began walking toward one of the Manor House's double doors to travel the short distance to their own lodgings and get some much-needed sleep. Only Yvonne and Willa lingered, their eyes gripping each other in an effort for reassurance where there was none to give.

Yvonne raised one eyebrow and Willa responded.

"I have no idea either," she said simply.

The two women exited together for the slow walk to their quarters and a night of what was sure to be fitful sleep.

Chapter 16: The Green Studio

As head of transport, Yvonne's most important job on the first day of the Season after Intake and Processing was to move the corral from their mini-bunks to the work area where they would be assigned their First Day learning to perform Farm chores. The chores were important in determining the final grouping of the herd and deciding which barns they would occupy for the Season. Yvonne's task was merely moving them to chores; the decision-making was left to the Trail Bosses and Farmhands whose function it was to queue up the herd into subgroups and assign their Season's barn.

Dividing the herd was one of the Season's most anticipated events.

Yvonne walked into the bunkhouse and flipped on all the lights as she sounded the bell to signal first light. Most of the herd was asleep, some managed a few hours of rest and others had just dropped off after a fitful night. Her training taught her that animals respond badly to sudden awakening and she used their discomfort to her advantage.

"Unlock them," she said to her trainees as 245 ankles were released from their bunks. "Stand up," she ordered the sleepy herd without sympathy for their condition.

Her eyes inspected every pack member to make sure that they rose quickly and responded to her instructions. When she caught a glimpse of a slow-mover, she nodded to the trainee stationed nearby and gave permission for that trainee to strike the errant herd member's asscheeks solidly with a rattan cane. Trainees were not issued electric prods until they passed extensive training and testing but rattan had a reputation for rapid effectiveness and was pretty safe. It usually took only one well-placed stroke but two were not unheard of, especially on the first morning of the Season.

After at least five were whipped on-the-spot into acceptable positions, Yvonne herded them quickly outdoors. She led the straggling group toward the watering shed. Even though there were indoor routes available, she routinely herded them outside in seasonable weather, especially on First morning. The idea of being naked outdoors in pre-dawn light was especially helpful to forming a good collective mindset.

It was their first trip to Watering since Intake and Yvonne expected there to be a reticent few requiring individual attention.

> *Show them all what is expected by disciplining just one, she had been taught. The others will see its mistake and learn from it. Always choose the biggest one as an example on First Day.*

The Watering Shed was a nondescript but solid structure with multiple entrances and exits. The herd was divided into arbitrary groups and each entered via a different door. Once inside, bright lights reflected from the stainless steel walls and floor and many in the herd squinted just to be able to negotiate the slender path. The aisles were narrow and by now many had learned to anticipate floors that would shift at unexpected times.

"Kneel on the pads," she instructed and all 245 knelt on rubber-covered squishy foam kneepads. "Grip the handles," she said and the herd reached forward to grab rubber-covered handles that worked like bicycle handlebars. "Lock them in," she said and nodded to the trainees.

At her command, the trainees attached wrist and ankle restraints on the pack member's legs and when they were approved, added metal casings that locked over each penis. The penis covers encased a few early morning erections but completely covered many more soft dangling organs. The familiar electric motor whirr greeted the herd as the platforms tilted, the kneepads separated and they gripped the handlebars for so as not to fall. Only a few noticed that the floor beneath them had dropped away.

"Adjust the rings," Yvonne said and each penis, encased in a metal sleeve, pointed directly down from their bodies.

"Urinate," Yvonne said and the pack stared open mouthed at her and each face contorted in utter disbelief. Peeing on command was a new instruction for them. "Now," she said ominously.

Some hard-headed strays always refused the command while others struggled to gain enough composure to release their own bladders. A few complied quickly but Yvonne's experience told her that another few would likely resist. She would overcome even the most reluctant ones as fast as possible to teach the herd that her commands were to be obeyed immediately. And the herd would learn this morning that pride had no place on the Farm. She nodded to the control room who released a stream of warm water directly on their hands. Urination usually followed quickly and when she was satisfied with the output, she turned her attention to the next Watering task. Muffled shrieks of humiliation were herd beneath the sound of the flow of the herd's morning pee.

Teach them they have no control and they will learn who does. Own each penis first and the ass second. The rest of the bodies and minds follows.

"This is standard morning elimination," she said as the trainees scurried to insert lubricated hoses into each hanging anus. The herd's groans filled the Watering Shed but as usual, Yvonne ignored them. "Now," she said and 245 anuses were filled with a solution carefully designed to cause two required results.

When she was assured that each member of the herd had been filled to capacity and the hoses were replaced by plugs, she instructed the trainees to replace the hoses and insert them into the sterilization slots for their next use. Then she waited for what she knew would soon happen.

Animal by animal, each member of the herd felt its sphincter struggle to expel its contents. Humiliated moans bounced off the stainless steel walls and ass after ass grunted in degradation. Some were pushing and forcing, trying to push out the anal plugs and let more from their bowels while realizing they were ineffective in their efforts to allow their contents to empty.

That's when the trainees ran down the line and pulled plug after plug from the dangling asses.

She waited for what she knew would begin in moments and only when she heard the first sounds of emptying bowels did Yvonne check off another Watering task from her list. And the herd learned they would empty their asses only when Yvonne allowed it but they would do that whenever she commanded them. One of the the Farm's goals had just been achieved this Season. The second would follow shortly.

> *Almost nothing is as precious to them as their asses, her Owner taught. Stimulate them and let them empty only when you command it – and always when you command it. Owning their asses is easy and it moves you forward on the path to total control.*

"Hose them off then scrub them down," Yvonne said to her trainees.

In a scene reminiscent of yesterday's Intake, the herd was hosed inside and out with cool water then soaped and scrubbed with stiff brushes. A final cold rinse was designed not to miss an inch of skin – inside or out – was inserted into anuses without introduction. The trainees shot stinging streams at and inside the herd and listened to a chorus of mortified anguish rise from deep within their guts. Once they were clean enough to meet her standards, Yvonne had the floor brought back up and level and the trainees finally unlocked the clean and dripping herd.

It was time for Yvonne's second Watering goal to be realized.

The herd was ordered to their hooves and the second and secret result of the anal enemas began. One by one and in rapid succession, the herd felt their bowels tingle. It took only two drops of the Owner's new herbs to be inserted with their daily bowel treatments to make the herd understand everything they needed to know about who owned them on the Farm. Their asses soon were on fire.

But Yvonne wanted to learn more about their reactions to this new herb. She knew that some could no longer stand upright when the drops' effect started and she studied the group to predict who would allow a herd member to fall and which would support one of their own. It took a herd member with future potential to risk on-the-spot correction but do the right thing for a fellow pack member. Those were the ones that Katrina focused on when taping the morning watering and it was those incidents that were replayed for the Owner, who adored watching First Day watering, when the herd was moved to the work area. Yvonne studied them and watched at least a dozen males fall to the stainless steel floor while trembling uncontrollably.

How long would it take this Season for one member of the Season's herd to take the risk?

She watched one male's face because she thought she saw a glimmer of compassion. Would the animal act on that impulse? Did it have the courage to risk having its own ass flogged in front of the herd? Was this an animal with enough courage that might please the Owner?

It happened, like it did every Season, quickly and quietly. A big male, whose swollen shaft looked to be at least seven inches without even being completely hard, lifted the smaller animal that fell behind him to its feet and held its paw to steady it. Looking toward the camera, Yvonne pointed in his direction, to make sure Katrina was recording this event. She needn't have worried but the staff was trained to assist Control at all times, especially when it came to getting good video. Pointing him out to Control was natural to Yvonne; however, her imminent reporting to the Green

Studio after Watering still filled her mind as she watched one or two other animals likewise lift a fallen cohort to its hooves.

Even with their own bowels burning and churning, three males exhibited potential quality Farm material and Yvonne took note of their actions. It was almost time to march them to the work area at which time she faced her own appointment in the Green Studio so she was trying to get them moved efficiently. Both the herd and Yvonne were apprehensive but for very different reasons.

The summer sun would dry them but the Owner insisted that newly-sheared males were oiled so that their skin, especially in sensitive areas, did not blemish or itch. As the herd was marched toward the Watering Shed's exits, trainees sprayed a fine mist on each one's body. The nozzles were designed to cover large areas or when adjusted, directed at hard-to-reach folds of skin. Spreading their legs and lifting their genitals, the trainees were careful to oil the herd completely and slather the oil all around with their hands.

When they stepped into the early morning rising sun, each member of the herd sparkled from its oiling. Yvonne loved the glow. It was one more sign of a new Season on the Farm.

"Follow!" Yvonne said simply as she led the herd in a trot toward Feeding. She ran them gently at first and then faster and faster for the entire half-mile. Then she handed over the watered herd to the Feeding staff.

"They're yours," she said to Nadia who received the herd and then transferred them to the trainees who were at the end-of-course training to become Feeders. "I will be in the Green Studio," she said and turned on her thick boot heel. Her breasts bobbed and her lime green waistband flew behind her in the breeze as she jogged toward the Manor House. Yvonne ran to her command appearance for her Owner but couldn't drive away her fear. On the other side of the Farm where the ponies were readying for their work, Willa did the same thing. Two women jogged and worried as they ran with bouncing breasts and flying colors toward the Manor House.

They arrived at the Trainer's Entrance almost simultaneously. Both glowed from sweat and both tried to find some strength in each other.

Trainers, no matter what level they had risen to, knew that being called to the Owner's Green Studio required that you enter through the Trainers' double doors, report to the Manor House staff person who was expecting you and be ushered to the studio for whatever was on the Owner's agenda for you that day. Knowing that process never made reporting easier or the trainers less anxious.

One thing that Yvonne and Willa recognized was that the house staff was completely in charge of all trainers once they stepped into the Manor House. There was no pecking order; the lowliest kitchen staffer could give orders to trainers once they were in the house with full expectation that they would obey. The Manor House staff excelled at commanding trainers. Their ability to order trainers to do almost anything made up the best gossip Yvonne and Willa had heard since they arrived on the Farm. It was the only means to learn what happened in the Owner's studios. The rest was mystery. No trainer who had experienced the studio ever discussed it with the Trail Bosses, trainers or especially the trainees.

Willa opened the heavy doors and stepped inside with Yvonne close on her heels.

The vestibule was empty, save for a large wooden armoire whose size overwhelmed the tiny hallway. Within moments, they heard a voice issue the first instruction.

"Strip your leathers," the voice said and both Willa and Yvonne were surprised to see that it belonged to one of last night's dinner servers. The server, dressed only in tight leather shorts and flat boots, pointed to the large armoire to indicate they should store their leathers in it. Being ordered to strip leathers was demeaning enough for any trainer, but receiving that command from a mere server was doubly humiliating. Both Yvonne and Willa felt the heat rise in their faces.

Both women hung their leathers carefully in the closet and stood in the chilly vestibule completely naked. Their toes curled against the cold marble floor. Their bodies were hard and hairless; their demeanor struggled to remain proud in their nakedness.

A second instruction was given.

"Follow," the server said as she turned and trotted along the curved hallways that eventually would lead to the Green Studio. Willa and Yvonne followed her closely as they traversed winding hallways dotted with closed doors. The trainers knew they were being watched and were careful to run proudly while holding their shoulders high and forcing their breasts to jut out as far in front of them as they could manage.

> *Pride, the Owner said repeatedly, was found in a woman's stance. If her breasts led the way, then you knew she was filled with her own power, no matter what she did – or did not – wear.*

The two trotting trainers understood that they had to teach their trainees the value of pride and posture as the new girls adjusted to their new wardrobes of leather shorts and boots. Because no woman's breasts were allowed to be covered on the Farm, the staff's open vests and colors were outward symbols of their pride. As the trainers were promoted and received the waistband and color of their new rank, they had to learn to press their shoulders back and their breasts in front of them. Wearing a vest, even one that didn't cover their breasts, distinguished them from the youngest trainees and staff forced to work with naked bosoms. The Trainers' vests propped their breasts up even higher with each level they achieved. Yvonne fondly recalled her first promotion that allowed her to wear her first vest. Her wistful reverie was interrupted by the server's next order.

"This is the Green Studio," she said and walked away. They were alone and outside the studio's door in the vacant hallway.

Each Trainer looked questioningly at the other. Should they go in? Should they wait for a command? Should they knock? Neither had an answer and for a few awkward moments, they stood uncertain just outside the door. It was Yvonne who decided to try the handle and discover what fate held in store for her. Better to be proactive, she thought.

A blast of frigid air greeted her entry into the Green Studio. Her nipples stiffened and for that moment, Yvonne was alone with her anticipation and trepidation. Willa entered behind her and the two naked women stood just inside the door. They shivered in the cold air.

Leda entered from a side door.

"The Owner will enter in a moment when I'm sure you are ready," Leda said. "Greet her properly when she arrives. Then she will tell you what her plans are and you will no longer be confused." Allowing her words to sink in, Leda watched the women tremble before she completed her assigned task.

"This is your Green Studio time," she said in an effort to comfort them but also leave them filled with concern. "Anticipate nothing, expect nothing, and plan for nothing. Be yourselves and remember *all* your training." After an almost indiscernible pause, she asked, "Do you have any questions?"

By now, the only thing Willa and Yvonne wanted was for whatever was going to happen to start so they could figure out why they had been commanded to be there. Neither of them longed for their Green studio experience to be over; rather, they were eager to get started. The trainers were chosen with that in mind, the Owner always said.

It's the journey, not the goal, Yvonne recalled vividly.

"Then that's all," Leda said and she exited through the same side door.

It was either seconds or minutes that passed before the Owner walked in and without glancing at her Trainers, sat in the studio's only chair. Both Yvonne and Willa flew to be in front of her, dropped to their knees and pushed their shoulders back as far as they could while reaching for their ankles behind them. One thing each every trainee learned and practiced over and over was how to greet the Owner in rare command appearances. Yvonne had performed this greeting once before but she was certain this was Willa's virgin experience. Especially in the Green Studio.

She must be scared to death, Yvonne imagined about the younger Trainer. She knew from an earlier experience that the Owner had her reasons and the Trainers could never predict them.

Her suspicions were confirmed when she stole a glance at Willa and saw her shudder.

The Owner observed them for a few moments before taking their nipples in her fingers to finally recognize their presence. Yvonne felt a hard pinch bite her rock-hard nipples and she shivered when the Owner's grip dug in harder. Time meant nothing in the Studio; the only thing Yvonne knew was the pressure on her nipples sent her to a comfortable place where her mind felt free. Being greeted by the Owner was every Trainer's dream, even though its reality was often painful. Having the Owner touch you was your reward. This much attention from the Owner carried with it lot more – but as yet unknown – meaning for the two women.

One of her hands dropped Yvonne's breast and grabbed Willa's as Owner greeted each one individually. Yet Yvonne wondered why her own breasts were greeted first with both of the Owner's hands while Willa received only secondary attention with just one of her hands. Trying desperately to dispel assuming anything as Leda had just warned them, Yvonne closed her eyes, tried to push her anxiety away and allow her body to enjoy the elation that the Owner's touch had rewarded her.

Suddenly, their nipples were released and both kneeling women's concentration focused on their Owner.

"My Farm has a new need," the Owner said, "and our new venue requires a new lead trainer. Yvonne, you have served the

Farm faithfully for many Seasons and I want that new leader trainer to be you. Willa, you are currently Willa's assistant and therefore next in line for Yvonne's Lead Trainer position."

Her explanation revealed why they had been summoned and both women were overcome with a mixture of humility and pride. Yvonne recalled Leda's warning, "Anticipate nothing, expect nothing and plan for nothing." Out of the corner of her eye, she saw Willa smile and push her breasts out even farther but Yvonne knew in her heart that this command performance in the Green Studio was not a simple promotion ceremony. Everyone on the Farm knew that promotions carried along with them individual testing in the Green Studio that involved both personal and skill tests. It required everything you knew. It tested everything you were.

"Testing can begin if you are interested in these new positions," the Owner said with a knowing smile. Both women nodded furiously and proved their Seasons of training where they learned that staff, no matter what level, never spoke to the Owner unless she asked a direct question. In all Yvonne's Seasons, none had been asked of her. "I'll take that as a yes," the Owner said with a grin.

The Owner's Green Studio tests were designed with her understanding that a new venture on the Farm could be difficult and a lead trainer assigned to a new type of training would have to undergo considerable skill training and build up new techniques to deal with a new pack as well as with new administrative tasks. It required good Farm sense, innovative talent and personal flexibility. Not every trainer could muster all that and some were just not suited to new things; in fact, it upset some trainers to have to learn new procedures and enter training that had no prior established rules. Some preferred to carry on and grow existing techniques while a select few were eager to try to develop new ones. The Owner agreed with Leda's suggestion that Yvonne could achieve the new Farm goals, but it was Willa that concerned them both. Were they moving her up too fast?

Yvonne's body posture remained remarkable. Given the fear and excitement that created the tension that the Owner liked to brew in her Farmhands, Yvonne's aching back and tightly stretched thighs didn't fail her. She neither flinched nor showed any discomfort. Hairless, smooth and gleaming, her posture was a picture-perfect Lead Trainer and the Owner, who expected her staff to perform perfectly at all times, turned to Willa and compared the two splayed women's comportment. They were similar to an untrained eye, yet there was a marked difference that she noticed immediately.

Willa's shoulders had slumped a fraction of an inch. Hardly noticeable, but the Owner saw it. Willa was missing that beautiful arch in her back that the Owner enjoyed seeing her women display. As she inspected the younger woman with her own lips turning downward barely perceptibly, Leda watched from Control and tapped a note on her tablet. She touched Katrina's shoulder to make sure she had the camera focused on Willa – and what in her body posture had just displeased their Owner. "Got it," Katrina said and Leda stared at the monitor to see just what it was that dissatisfied her Owner. The control room's all-seeing lenses were focused on all Farm events, even those in the Owner's studios unless the Owner specifically instructed them not to record a particular session.

> *Something's wrong with her body. It's got to be upper torso, that's what she's staring at, Katrina thought as she stared into her monitor and kept a keen eye on her Owner's face.*

Leda's eyes also studied the monitor and Katrina angled a few more cameras to record the Green Studio test for later review.

"Testing does not have to be excruciating or even agonizing," the Owner's voice was crisp and clear. "Testing will grow to whatever level you are capable of enduring."

With that comment, the Owner ordered the two women to their feet and put a hand on each of their shoulders. Her firm grip drew them closer together with their noses merely two inches apart.

Each could smell the other's fragrance and both greedily inhaled their Owner's scent. Yvonne felt her own senses threaten to spill over and challenge her body posture while Willa seemed to be transported into a heady emotional state.

"It is not the Farm way to force any Trainer or farmhand to move beyond her strengths," the Owner said as both women shuddered under her strict grip. "Because we are moving into a new area, I need to know how you both will react to our new events and challenges." She allowed her words to sink in so both women understood what the goal of their test was and could begin to prepare mentally to meet whatever challenge she forced upon them.

The Owner added, "I have been known to push your limits." She felt both women's bodies tremble but their fear didn't subtract from her satisfaction.

"She's going to use the forms," Leda predicted and Katrina nodded. "It's got to be the forms."

Every applicant for a Farm position who was invited to a second interview was required to fill out a battery of forms and was tested thoroughly by psychologists and doctors before she was allowed to move ahead in the application process. The Owner was adamant that no women with fragile emotional conditions that had the potential to interfere with any Season's business would be invited to stay on the Farm in any role. The forms were difficult to complete – they were long, took a lot of thought and required a lot of personal introspection.

Every applicant, no matter for what position, was required to respond to a multi-day series of closed and open-ended questions. After their answers were evaluated, the candidate met with the psychologist and every response was explored. Those who made it through the process had a complete psychological profile on file and the Owner, when she decided to add a new Farmhand or promote one, referred to those appraisals to assess their strengths and weaknesses. She wanted to know which of her women could architect new training, evaluate progress and devise fresh processes. And who could not.

Leda joked that the Owner knew the staff better than they knew themselves and on more than one occasion, the Owner used those forms' information to stretch her women farther than they believed they could perform.

> *Stretching a staff member is empowering, the Owner always reminded them. Whether I stretch you or your do it by yourself, it doesn't matter. You must stretch to grow.*

Both Leda and Katrina tingled with the memories of their own Green Suite testing. Yvonne and Willa shivered as they realized their innermost strengths and weaknesses were fair game for the Owner's test.

"A new Lead Trainer requires absolute support from her staff," the Owner said, "and that absolute support shows itself in many ways. Some is practiced; some comes from personal loyalty." She scrutinized their faces for reactions and noticed that Willa's lips were drawn in an almost painfully straight line. Yvonne appeared a bit more relaxed, but that would soon change.

"Structured personal time is a reward for a Farmhand," she continued. "A lower-level trainer is required to provide services to a Lead Trainer. You," she grabbed Willa's shoulder tighter and forced it into spasms, "will demonstrate how well you can service your new superior in her structured personal time."

With that, the Owner let go of both women and seated herself to evaluate Willa's potential. Hoping that the young woman would figure out the goal and begin the process quickly, she observed with a keen eye as the two women stood nipple to nipple and breathed in successive gulps of air.

"That hasn't been done in so many Seasons!" Leda said excitedly to Katrina, whose fingers were busy setting up camera angles. "She studied that chart, and I bet she's got a low score in personal performance," she guessed.

"I'd guess she's got performance anxiety," Katrina added, never looking away from her monitors.

"Oh my," Leda mused aloud. "This could be great video, if you're right."

In Control, both women's eyes returned to the monitors and surveyed the scene that still hadn't changed. Willa stood immobile while Yvonne's breathing had sped up a little. Both of their bodies trembled every now and then but there was no discernible movement in the room. Clearly, the Owner's instructions had not been internalized and Leda wondered how long she would wait before reissuing her order.

She had been known to wait a very long time. And she didn't like saying things twice.

Say it once. Say it with authority. Mean what you say. And expect them to perform. Those four short commands were drilled into every trainer by their Owner.

The Owner sat quietly in her chair and sipped hot tea. With her leather-clad legs crossed and red lips pursed, she never moved her eyes from the two stock-still women who were either too petrified or unsure of what to do next. Her steely eyes never moved from them and Yvonne felt her glare pierce her perspiring skin. Yet she dared not turn her head to see the look that she knew was trained directly on her.

Afraid that the Owner would unleash her wrath on both women from their failure to perform quickly enough, Yvonne tried silently to cajole Willa into action. After all, her command had been for the lower staff member to service her superior, and that left Yvonne in the peculiar position of waiting for her inferior to begin. Waiting wasn't something that Yvonne was used to; in fact, she despised having to wait for anyone else's timing. She was used to being in charge and leading the way was her style.

Willa needed help and Yvonne's body displayed an increasing sense of control that was noticeable in the cool air of the Green Studio. Both Katrina and Leda saw it; the latter took in a gulp of air that indicated something important was about to happen. With their eyes focused on Yvonne's new authoritative stance, no one in Control noticed the Owner's lips curl upward for an instant.

> *Do it! Do it! Katrina cheered silently for Yvonne to start. The Owner had told them that when faced with new situations for which you had no practice, then do something – do anything. Take a risk. You can sort it all out later.*

Yvonne's movement was clear to everyone except Willa. That lack of recognition had to be repaired and Yvonne was just the trainer to do it.

Grabbing a large chunk of the younger woman's hair in her fist, Yvonne dragged Willa to her knees and pressed her face to her own hairless mons. Willa dropped to her knees awkwardly and felt her head being pushed toward her superior's sex. With continuing pressure from Yvonne's grip on her hair, she forced Willa's mouth and nose between her musky lips. Silently, Willa finally discovered Yvonne's meaning from somewhere deep inside her and the younger woman obediently licked Yvonne's mons with more and more gusto as if a light bulb had just clicked over her head. She finally uncovered the intention of the Owner's command. Willa then threw all of her effort into lavishing pleasure on her superior's thighs, calves, ankles and feet. With her body now splayed flat on the floor, she slithered inch by inch to ram her tongue deep between Yvonne's toes. Then she lifted her head as far as possible to see Yvonne spread-eagle in front of her. As she learned from her training, Willa used only her tongue, lips, and teeth to perform her duty.

When Yvonne started groaning with pleasure, she tapped the licking woman's head. Willa rose to her knees, spread them apart, and crept toward Yvonne's leg so that she might press it between her own thighs hoping that action would please her superior. Her mouth continued upward on Yvonne's body as her thighs nestled around her calf. Willa never felt her hips hump in her dance of giving pleasure nor did she recognize the start of sensual waves in her thighs and vagina as she pressed her spread lips against the shin that might also hold her own secret delight.

When Willa's mouth reached Yvonne's glistening pussy, she added her hands to her servicing. Cupping Yvonne's drenched lips with enthusiastic fingers, Willa first caressed and then spread the soft labia apart and studied the engorged clitoris that greeted her. Tasting it may satisfy the Owner, but Willa shivered as she approached the culmination of the Owner's command. For a moment, she wondered what she would look like; what others might say of her abysmally subservient position and the assignment she was about to fulfill. What would she look like if she succumbed to having an orgasm while servicing a kneeling, perspiring and aroused superior?

It was that single moment's hesitation that caught the Owner's eye and made her replace her cup firmly on the table. The clank of china against table resounded loudly in the control room.

Katrina gasped as she focused other cameras to take in what discipline she believed was about to unfold. Even Leda, who was used to every movement her Owner made, inhaled deeply at the sound of the china cup landing on the table. There was no mistaking that the Owner was displeased. Both knew their Owner would level that dissatisfaction directly on the person who had caused it. She was well-known for that – for never punishing an innocent person yet disciplining the guilty party swiftly, directly and mercilessly.

Her reprimand would soon fall on Willa and the poor trainee, Katrina thought, didn't even know it was coming.

Her mouth is still buried in that pussy, sucking that clitoris and licking with all her might. She has no idea of what's about to happen to her.

The only question was exactly how the Owner would levy the discipline.

Don't punish, they learned over and over during every Season's training. Discipline the offender and fix the behavior.

First the Owner placed both of her hands on the chair's arms and she pushed herself up. Then she planted both boots solidly on the floor and walked a few steps to position herself behind Willa's upraised ass. With her face buried deeply inside Yvonne's dripping pussy as she serviced Yvonne's sex, Willa never felt the Owner approach her from behind.

Ten manicured fingers grabbed two huge handfuls of Willa's long hair and jerked her head up from her Lead Trainer's pussy. Her eyes popped open in surprise and a muffled, "Whaaaa?" escaped from her wet mouth.

What Willa's eyes witnessed when they finally focused sent spasms of fear through her body.

The Owner's lips drew into a tight line that both Leda and Katrina recalled with horror from their own testing. The Owner's face projected terror in any Farmhand pitiful enough to earned the experience. By the time Yvonne pulled herself together enough to concentrate on what interrupted her delightful service from Willa, she also trembled with apprehension and confusion.

What did I do wrong? Yvonne worried but stood ramrod straight with her legs shoulder-width apart. She tried to ignore the drops of excitement that cascaded down her inner thighs.

Ten strong fingers pulled Willa's head back more and more until the girl finally moaned aloud. Dropping her hands to her ankles for support, Willa found herself locked in a torturous backbend. Her poignant gasps were recorded by Control's cameras and would be replayed many times for review. With Willa whimpering like a child who was caught with her fingers in her mother's purse, the Owner maintained her body in that dreadful position. Then she diverted her glance from Willa's tears toward Yvonne's uncomprehending face.

"Who do you think will get it first?" Katrina asked Leda, whose eyes were focused on the monitor. "Which one will she discipline?" Katrina repeated with a touch of anxiety in her voice as Leda remained voiceless, her eyes focused on the monitors.

Never discipline the innocent if they had been taught and the fault is not theirs. But always use swift behavior-altering methods on the guilty. Inaction is worse than wrong action because incorrect behaviors can be fixed, the Owner instructed.

Taking a step forward, the Owner jammed Willa's now fully-extended head and neck between her own leather boots and changed her focus to a tenderer part of her body. Between the anguish of her physical pain and her inability to understand, Willa's nipples stood up straight and pointed directly at the ceiling.

They were ready targets.

The Owner grabbed both of Willa's stiff dark-brown nipples in her fingernails and in a single motion stood up straight with the woman's breasts still in her grip. A guttural scream escaped from Willa's throat and landed directly between the Owner's legs before it penetrated the room. The wretched sound forced Katrina's fingers to struggle to balance the audio. With Willa's nipples stretched mercilessly in her hands, the Owner stared at Yvonne without betraying her reasons for the disciplinary interruption in their testing.

She waited and watched as she continued torturing the woman's breasts. She never stopped penetrating Yvonne's thoughts with her unbending stare.

Make the moment last silently, Leda remembered from her training and only then make your point with actions, not words.

Finally, the Owner stated the obvious in a voice that broke the overpowering silence in the room that was punctuated only by Willa's gasps and groans.

"NO ONE hesitates when I issue an order," the Owner said.

Yvonne's mind realized her own failure of leadership by not forcing Willa to act sooner yet Willa, even in her distress, was ashamed of her own inaction to serve her superior quickly and without hesitation. The two women, both suffering pangs of failure, were given one more command.

The real test is just starting, Katrina noted, as she adjusted camera angles. All of that was a diversion. Katrina smiled at the Owner's crafty plan.

"Discipline her," the Owner ordered Yvonne.

Leda grinned as Katrina adjusted dials, lenses and focus so she could catch it all on video.

Returning to her seat as if nothing had just happened, the Owner waited for her direct order to be carried out and sipped her tea.

Chapter 17: Trainer Discipline

Her rigid training evident, Yvonne leapt into performance at her Owner's command. She knew that her progress through the promotion ladder hinged on her actions right now. She didn't waste time trying to understand Willa's initial hesitation and she did not worry about how the girl would take to being disciplined by another trainer.

Acts and deeds endure, she was taught by her Owner.
Words are superfluous.

A soft whirr opened a cabinet set neatly on a turntable in the studio that was filled with leather, plastic and metal disciplinary tools. Leda smirked and nodded at Katrina as they watched the Owner observe the interaction between her Farmhands.

After surveying the contents, Yvonne grabbed a rattan cane, one of her favorite discipline tools for its simplicity, and pushed Willa's face to the floor and whisked the cane cleanly across her ass. Willa's yelp was captured nicely on the video and the scene would make a wonderful dessert addition for the lead trainers' dinner discussion.

Grabbing Willa's dark hair in a fist, Yvonne dragged her up and kicked her legs apart with a well-practiced move. Now on all fours with her ass displayed high and wide, Willa finally understood out her plight and realized that Yvonne was all business. She understood from her own training that pleading would get her nowhere and struggled to control her reactions. But her voice betrayed her.

Willa screamed as the rattan cane whipped back and forth across her supple asscheeks. Red welts puffed up as Yvonne concentrated on one thing: correcting the girl's poor behavior.

The Owner noted that Yvonne's technique was well-practiced and professional. The blows landing on the girl's upraised ass were perfectly placed and did not cut her skin. When one of the animals in the herd needed to be whipped, the Trainers were taught to administer a beating without harming the animal's hide. A trainer who cut a Farm animal was always sent for retraining which always included a personal whipping that was remarkably similar to the what Yvonne was inflicting on Willa's reddening ass right now. Katrina's tapes of this Green Studio event would become an invaluable source for advanced trainer education.

Her discipline session only took a minute, but to Willa it seemed like hours.

The Owner stared at Yvonne as she replaced the cane in the cabinet on the turntable. After all her Seasons on the Farm, the Owner learned not to predict her staff's actions; instead, she watched and listened and evaluated what they did. Only after they completed their disciplinary session did she ever offer counsel, and that was usually done in private or during small group meals where the tapes could be reviewed and analyzed.

There was one exception to that policy.

What happened in the Green Studio was never discussed outside the room. The events that took place in her private space were intense and personal. It was a strict rule that the Green Studio's proceedings, similar to those that unfolded in the Blue Studio, were always kept only for the Owner's eyes and a selected few of her top staff. Occasional edited shots were included in staff training tapes, but never what led up to or came after the actual episode.

Yvonne circled her moaning subordinate before embarking on the next phase of her discipline.

Good, good, Leda thought. Always make them wait and anticipate. Make them wonder. Make them afraid. Own every ounce of their attention.

Yvonne took the frightened woman's nipples in a hard grip. Yanking upward, she raised Willa to her knees and smashed her face directly against her own vaginal lips. Pushing her mouth deep inside, she instructed the woman as if she were a schoolgirl.

"Service me now!" Yvonne's tone was no nonsense yet her demeanor was calm. As if she were ordering nothing more unusual than a meal in a restaurant, she spoke to Willa in a self-confident tone. Her simple phrases brought a smile to the Owner's lips as she watched a master of discipline perform.

Yvonne's assertive manner melded with the Owner's majesty. As the kneeling woman parted Yvonne's lower lips with her mouth and began to service her superior, Yvonne instructed her every step of the way.

"Suck," she said. "Then lick. In that order."

Willa's face was completely immersed in Yvonne's pussy, but it was apparent to Control that she was enjoying this portion of the discipline. After a few moments, Yvonne instructed Willa again.

"Point the tongue!" Yvonne's words were issued in an instructional staccato that pleased the Owner's ear. Then she added, "Use your teeth."

Willa's dark hair bobbed up and down in silent response. She leaned in and pulled back, then leaned in again when Yvonne forced her head deeper into her task. Pushing her to hump her pussy repeatedly with her face, Yvonne was all business. Slowly, as Willa's efforts appeared to achieve the desired effect, Yvonne relaxed. Willa's gasps of air were interspersed with Yvonne's soft moans of delight.

Suddenly, a grunt shot out of Yvonne's mouth as her body stiffened. She yanked a handful of Willa's hair again. The pain in her scalp caused the kneeling woman to cry in surprise, but Yvonne overrode her complaint with her own.

"You think you're going to bite me?" she said directly into Willa's eyes. "Obviously, you need more discipline!"

Oh, this is going to be good, Katrina thought as she adjusted the monitors for a close up. Using teeth to bite would surely result in renewed discipline that Yvonne could administer so well.

Yvonne was immersed in her role and seemed to be writing the script on the fly. Grabbing bits and pieces of her training and setting them into this new chapter of her Green Studio experience, Yvonne glowed as each step in the discipline process emerged.

More discipline? Katrina wondered. That was certainly a new one. The Owner encouraged her Farmhands to recognize when a new technique was used and to catalog it for future reference.

"This is what happens to animals that bite!" Yvonne said loudly as she stepped toward the Owner's rack of tools while holding Willa's black hair in her fist. In response, the younger woman grunted loudly with each step Yvonne took. Reaching for a large rubber bit, she shoved the gag inside Willa's mouth and locked it behind her head. Her jaws were forced wide apart and she could scream only in muffled agony.

With the gag secured, Yvonne pulled Willa's hair again and dragged her face between her legs for another round of instructional and service. She ordered Willa to continue where she left off and muffled whimpers greeted her order. The Owner's lips curled up slightly at Yvonne's splendid display as she dragged the woman's face against her pussy lips repeatedly and used it as a masturbation tool.

Taking a deep breath, Yvonne took the woman's face in her hands and drew it up to her eye level.

"What did you learn?" she asked between Willa's gulps of air.

Both Katrina and Leda stared at each other in surprise at Yvonne's question. *What did you learn?* was the question every trainer had demanded of them at every step in their progress climbing the ladder at the Farm. It was incredible to them that she could insert that unanswerable question in as perfect a spot as this one. Katrina sighed softly in admiration.

She's got it, Leda predicted. We're going to have a promotion ceremony.

"That will do," the Owner said in a controlled voice. "Release her and come to me."

Yvonne threw the woman's head backward just hard enough to create some space between their bodies and then unbuckled the gag. Handing the rubber bit to Willa, she told her to clean it and replace it in the Owner's collection. Then she spun on her heel to walk two steps to the Owner's chair and kneel gracefully in front of her.

Katrina shut off the cameras. This part was never recorded.

Massaging Yvonne's nipples gently in her fingers, the Owner lifted the kneeling woman toward her and held her face with her piercing gaze.

"You pleased me," the Owner said tenderly as joyful tears fell from Yvonne's eyes. "You are both dismissed for now. There is work for you to do on the Farm."

The two women left the Green Studio through the door that a server silently opened. The Owner added a parting comment.

"Join us at the Lead Trainers' table tonight, Yvonne. You have passed my test."

Yvonne exited the room almost unable to carry the weight of the smile she wore. "As for you," the Owner asked as she made Willa face her, "What did you learn?"

With the cameras turned off in the Green Studio, Katrina and Leda were left to wonder what was causing Willa's screams and how long her discipline and in the Green Studio would last.

Chapter 18: The Herd's First Day

The herd was fitted with feedbags and positioned in even rows in the Feeding Barn. The pointed end of each bag was attached to an overhead feeding hose and each member of the herd knew it would be force-fed if it refused to eat. A click from Control opened the tubes and each animal tilted its head backward and sucked the paste. It was quite simple, Nadia thought, as she observed her ponies feeding on the far side of the room.

Marla, who would spend the rest of the day handling the database entries for Processing, watched the herd suck its breakfast at her command. Ensuring that each member of the herd ate properly was a task that had been assigned to the Assessment Division, and Marla, as lead, always oversaw first day Feeding. Even with their experience yesterday, Marla knew there would be a gagger or two in the herd that required special attention.

You can see it in their eyes, Marla thought. Their eyes betray them, they always do. Her Owner had taught her to look in their eyes and ignore cocks, balls and asses. Their eyes – that's where you understood your animals.

Concentrating on their faces, she watched the monitors to make sure the food had been drained from the feedbags. "Ten minutes," she warned them as a reminder that feeding time was almost up and their next assignment was approaching. A few tilted their leads to drain the final drops and avoid discipline, but Marla focused on those who seemed to be perplexed or worse, defiant.

At the twelve minute mark, she turned her attention to the monitors.

"Zoe," she said to the young trainee, "fix number 54."

Zoe scurried to 54's position and cracked her rattan cane across its asscheeks. The animal's yelp drew its lips apart so the rest of the nutrients slid down its throat. She watched the animal cough and gag and when she was confident that the entire breakfast had been eaten, she crossed her arms behind her back and pointed her breasts almost directly at Marla while waiting for her next order.

"Number 201," Marla said and Zoe trotted to that position. Readying her cane, she watched it see her approach and it quickly lifted and tilted its head. Satisfied that her presence was enough to encourage the animal to perform, Zoe jutted her breasts out again as she stood at attention beside 201.

"Zoe," Marla's voice was harsher this time. "Look at the monitor."

Chagrined to be admonished in front of the feeding herd, Zoe's eyes darted to the control room where she learned that 201 had merely lifted his chin, but not sucked down the contents. Vexed at his attempt to fool her and mortified that it happened in front of the entire corps of trainees; Zoe glared directly into 201's eyes.

> The eyes, Zoe recalled, the eyes always betray them. Focus on the eyes, she had been taught. Actions work, she learned. Words are useless. Changed behavior is the goal.

Her chin rose up to model the behavior she wanted.

She saw fear fill 201's eyes and dread wash over its body. With 244 other males satisfactorily fed, this one was holding up the herd's First Day work. This one was hers to break and her success – or failure – was on display.

Her fingers fingered the handle of the rattan cane. His eyes did not miss the movement; the question was whether he comprehended its meaning. Perhaps he might be one who could endure a caning without ever parting his lips. The grunters were well-known for that trick.

Zoe's considered her next move. Too afraid to glance at Marla, the young trainee struggled to decide the best course of action. Every trainee was now focused on her and Zoe felt the glare of their anticipation smother her.

Action is better than inaction, she had been taught. Do something, even the wrong thing, and sort it out later. Take control and own your animals.

Her hand flew toward 201's bald head and she wrenched its head back as its mouth snapped open reflexively inside his feedbag. A glance at the control panel affirmed what Zoe knew; the beast had been fed. Goal accomplished, she stood at attention and waited for Marla's next command.

"Remove the feedbags," and every trainee began unlocking row after row of clasps.

"The herd will trot to First Day chores," she said to her captive audience. "Remain on the path or risk cutting flesh," she smiled evilly as the herd's attention turned to the huge doors that opened to reveal the North Country's morning light. Marla nodded at Josie, who began a medium-paced trot on the path that led to the Farm's outdoor training area. Trainees caned a few reluctant asscheeks to move the herd along at a proper pace and eliminate gaps in the formation.

Trainees fell in line with the pace, keeping their position on the left-most edge of the path as they chatted loudly about which of the herd's red asses were most attractive. With the trainers' leather boots smacking the ground, the bare-footed animals' feet slapped the path noisily as the group moved forward. A few more asses tasted the trainees' canes as stragglers were forced to keep up. Yvonne's rule of transport was that a herd traveled together.

The morning sun shined brightly on their sweating hide as they were paced by Josie's lead. At times, she slowed down and at other times, sped up. The herd had to learn to work in unison and how to keep perfect distance between bouncing asscheeks. Bunching up was not acceptable and was fixed with a few swats of rattan canes.

The herd jogged in the crisp morning air and felt their testicles bounce with every step. The Trainers watched the line of bouncing cocks and balls while smiling when a particularly low-hung set amused them. Soft penises bobbed and some of the short ones looked like tiny wands peeking out of a soft sac of balls. The longer ones walloped their Owner's thighs and the sound of cock slapping against flesh was the herd's theme song.

Zoe caught the attention of a trainee jogging several meters behind her. "Look!" she hissed at Irena, "That shaft is whacking its belly!"

Irena's eyes scoured the running herd as her face drew into a mocking smile. "Good call," she congratulated Zoe. "You think they'll put it out to stud?"

The two women shared a secret joke while the humiliated runner tried to focus on jogging and the distance between itself and the jiggling asscheeks in front of its own bobbing organs.

"Maybe I should hook that shaft to my waistband," Zoe teased. "Wonder if it could keep up with me?" she joked.

The long-shafted runner fought back tears of embarrassment while enduring having its private parts mocked in public as if they were nothing more than an appendage attached to him. The women continued to discuss the long cock as if the wearer couldn't hear and they laughed. For its part, the runner tried to ignore their comments, but there was no way to avoid hearing them.

"Wait till that one finds out what we will use the big cocks for," Zoe said ominously.

Irena added, "Or when it meets the elastrator, if it winds up in the bull pen."

Continuing to laugh at jokes that were directed at his own bouncing cock, long shaft continued forward as the herd struggled to concentrate and not stare at what had just been pointed out as the largest penis in the hard. Their looks were surreptitious. They didn't want any incident that would refocus the trainees' attention on themselves. Grunting, running and trying desperately to remain anonymous in the crowd, the line moved forward toward the First Day chores.

The trainees were unrelenting in their torment of the new herd.

"That set of cheeks!" Zoe said and lifted her rattan cane to tap a buttery set bouncing in front of her. "Those are cheeks that would look scrumptious with a tail, don't you think?"

"I see it with a long hairy plug," Irena laughed. "Or maybe jammed and filled?"

The question wasn't lost on the jiggling ass that sprung up and down in front of them. As the runner tried to move faster and add distance between its vulnerable asscheeks and the trainees behind him, Zoe reached out and flicked the chubby flesh with her cane. Its wearer grunted.

"Stay in your place!" she ordered and its legs slowed just a bit at her command.

A mass of 245 dancing cocks, jiggling balls and bouncing asses surged forward in the cold morning air until Josie slowed and the herd reduced their speed to a fast walk for the final stretch.

"Don't want 'em huffing and puffing when we get there," Irena said as the asscheeks and cocks and balls bobbed under the morning sun. "Josie likes them ready for assignments," she added.

Trainees loved their First Day interaction with the herd. The animals invariably learned how to work as a functioning group, even if that meant discipline and in some cases, punishment. A rarity on the Farm, punishment had a lasting effect on the recipient as well as on the herd and neither Zoe nor Irena could recall a Season in which punishment hadn't been issued to at least one animal during the First Day.

Punishment, even though rare, served many Farm purposes. Zoe remembered the reasons she had been taught to assign at least one punishment for a herd member on First Day. She could recite the rules by heart:

> *Punish when discipline isn't enough.*
> *Punish when an animal needs a physical reminder.*
> *Punish when verbal responses are unacceptable.*
> *Punish when an animal is stubborn.*
> *Punish when a Farm rule is broken.*
> *Punish only when it is the best choice.*

Not every trainee had witnessed a Lead Trainer or Trail Boss issue First Day punishment, but every one of them had seen the face of a herd member who returned from a punishment session. Their red puffy eyes were the first giveaway. Sometimes, it was the welts adorning their asscheeks that was the clue. Occasionally, the red stripes on the soles of their feet were visible when they hobbled pack to their pack. No matter what method a trainer used, every male returning from punishment was better behaved.

"Ready?" Josie asked the trainees as the herd drew to a standstill.

"Yes!" Yvonne called cheerfully to the welcoming glances of the Lead Trainers there to meet them.

It was then that Zoe noticed Willa and saw an eerie look burned into her face. The trainees knew that both Willa and Yvonne had been summoned to the Owner's Green Studio that morning but this was the first time that Zoe had ever seen anyone post-studio. Willa's face wasn't a pretty sight.

Taking her place in the secondary line of trainers who gave her respectful distance, Willa focused on the herd and concentrated on them while she struggled to excise the memories that filled her brain. Sometime this morning, Zoe predicted silently, an animal was going to feel her wrath.

What they say about the studio must be true, Zoe thought. That's why they don't say anything.

As the herd grouped itself into a tight cluster under the prodding of the trainees' whips, all 245 animals were pressed against each other, with hardly enough room to breathe. Zoe watched the trainers press the herd against each other's flesh. With their arms now intertwined and balls and cocks pressed against asses and into hips, their fingers were forced to touch anonymous thighs and testicles. The trainees eliminated the personal space that the herd desperately wanted. It was a Farm rule: in order to act like a herd, they first had to cede their individuality completely. A single mass of flesh under the warm sun was a First Day lesson in proper herd behavior.

That's what First Day was all about. And that's what the trainees were going to learn under the strict direction of the Lead Trainers who were off to the side hugging and welcoming this Season's newest Trail Boss.

Chapter 19: Herds And Packs

Sipping her second cup of tea that morning, the Owner sat in her small salon and watched Farm events through floor-to-ceiling glass. She studied the flat landscape sandwiched between mountain peaks. From her perspective, the Farm seemed to have been dropped into the valley and all roads and paths radiated from her the Manor House and connected it to fields, sheds, barns and training centers. First Day for a new herd always made her reflect, an act she was convinced was her essence of greater understanding. From that understanding came her power.

The slight elevation on which the Manor House's foundation was built gave her a unique view of everything that happened on the Farm. Katrina's artful camera work afforded her the vantage to see every corral and barn. Each event that took place on the Farm was replayed until she was satisfied that she understood it. At this moment, her eyes and her thoughts focused on the First Day field.

First Day was a once-a-season event. Trail Bosses divvied up the herd and it would be her first glimpse of the quality of this Season's packs. First Day was always chock full of practical information about this Season's animals. No two herds were ever alike.

She tapped her tablet and the monitors in the studio activated.

The staff knew to leave her alone as she took her first look. The Owner was keenly aware that within each pack there would be a variety of flesh, talent, skill and potential. Her staff's absence at this moment was intentional; in fact, although everyone wanted to watch the Owner take her first look, they all knew to leave her alone with her observations and thoughts. She would discover exactly what she wanted to find by herself. Then she would tell the staff which ones she wanted to review later.

The monitors sprang to life. From five angles, the Owner had control over what she saw and Katrina zoomed in on what captured her attention. It was rare that the Owner had to tell Katrina where to focus or which camera to put on the widest screen. She knew her Owner's interests and she sent her the exact scenes that engaged her.

The herd was in stage one. All bunched together, their touching skin seemed misplaced against the expansive field. Her eyes scanned their faces as Katrina zoomed in on the scene.

She tapped the tablet and the audio began.

"Step to the right," Yvonne said and the herd struggled to move a single step. Several animals tripped over each other and at least three were down. The Owner shook her head from side to side.

> *First Day, she laughed. Some always go down on First Day.*

"One step to the left," Yvonne said and the herd pressed against each other while trying to move in comedic choreography. This time two more were down.

"Step forward," she said and the herd struggled to move a few inches toward her.

From her vantage, the Owner switched the main monitor to the overhead camera and watched the group's sloppy movements from above. She saw a few of them fall and then watched as their heads popped up to form a complete herd again.

"Step forward," Yvonne said, and true to form, the herd was a confused mass as they had mistakenly assumed that she would demand a step backward this time. Smiling at the number of animals' asses now flat on the grass, she waited for Yvonne to teach them how to be a herd.

"NEVER anticipate!" Yvonne said as the mangled arms and legs sorted themselves out. "Follow orders. Don't TRY to predict. You follow orders and carry out my commands. Nothing else."

"Repeat after me," Yvonne spoke like a schoolmarm in a boys' boarding school. "I will never assume!"

The grumbling noises of response were imprecise and the Owner sat back to watch Yvonne's lesson unfold.

"Again!" Yvonne yelled. "I will never assume!"

The chorus of voices returned the sentence a little louder this time. Knowing she would issue that same command at least five more times, the Owner turned her attention to the trainees who were gathered in a line behind the herd. Although without specific tasks to perform at this stage, their presence behind the huddle of asscheeks reminded the animals that they were observed at all times. The Owner studied the trainees' faces to evaluate which ones understand their purpose.

Several pairs of trainee eyes wandered and the Owner's tap on her tablet told Katrina to freeze that frame for review. Although most eyes were focused on the herd's asscheeks, Katrina knew that she would enlarge that frame for the trainee breakfast tomorrow so the Owner could point out which trainees had been upgraded on the initial promotion list and which were not. Desperate for the vests that would barely touch their naked breasts, the trainees were disciplined by their trainers when their faults were pointed out with color glossy photographs. The Owner enjoyed those evaluations.

Yvonne's order changed. "Repeat after me," she directed, "Animals do not assume."

Shocked silence filled the herd when they heard but could not accept the new noun she used to identify them. Loss of the "I" in her sentence provoked bitter unhappiness in the herd. Progress was slow on First Day, the Owner knew, but it was always steady. Yvonne had a firm hand; she was certain that this herd, like all those before it in previous Seasons, would mature.

It took Yvonne almost the full hour to corral the herd into acceptable herd behavior. It was a skill she would use many times on First Day as the animals continued their growth into a unified herd. As soon as their group conformity was culled, it would be time to break them up into packs.

Pack assignments always captured the Owner's attention. Using all the data from Intake and Processing, the herd was sorted into small groups that would be taken to their homes on the Farm this Season. Victoria was painstaking crunching data gained during Processing. She compiled and interpreted results before she made her recommendations to the Pack Leaders. Then Ursula, Sharon, Tara, Rhonda and Paula, this Season's Pack Leaders, discussed the reports over late-night café mocha. One of the Owner's favorite moments was when the pack assignments were made and presented to her for approval. Only then were the Season's packs announced. Small group dynamics was one of her passions. Her Pack Leaders had been selected carefully this Season.

The Owner studied the monitors.

The Lead Trainers circled around the herd as the trainees scurried to fill the gaps. Each trainee knew who her Lead was for the Season and they formed a tight ring of authority around the herd. Like trapped animals, the males' eyes betrayed their fear.

The Trail Bosses approached and each Lead Trainer stepped aside to usher her superior through. As the naked bald males recognized the Intake and Processing staff, many trembled while others shuddered violently.

The closed circle of Trail Bosses wore black leather boots, tight leather pants, leather vests dotted with colors that pushed their breasts up in a symbol of defiant authority, drove panic into the herd's souls. Penises dangled limp between unmoving legs and bald heads bowed as the Trail Bosses stalked their prey. Each grasped an electric prod in one hand and a tablet showing the numbers of their herd numbers in the other.

It was time to take their packs to the barns, their home for the Season.

The Owner said a single name. "Ursula," she said. Katrina positioned a close-up on the main monitor. The other Trail Bosses dotted the smaller monitors surrounding it.

All of the animals' eyes recognized the woman who had taken them to Medical Intake and not one of them forgot the horror of those events. Her stature and assertive attitude made her the most fearsome Trail Boss on the Farm. The Owner delighted in observing the new crop react to her presence in the clear light of day.

Ursula always sorted the packs. She was the one who had given them their numbers and she would give them their new identities.

Chapter 20: Branding The Herd

Numbering the herd was a part of Intake and Processing that left the herd completely changed. If any one moment was the definition of losing human identity and becoming a member of a larger herd, it was herd branding that accomplished it with life-changing results.

Every herd was identified and permanently marked. Because certain herd members required special feeding or medication, it was crucial that each was perpetually identified with an individual identifier for the Season – and for the rest of its life, even when they left the Farm.

Branding the animals was a time-honored spectacle and was often replayed at dinners for deeper training. Branding was the herd's most memorable incident during any Season on the Farm and it was First Day's most important procedure. After Seasons of experience, the Owner knew that the best way to brand the herd was to make it quick and let them absorb the torture as a herd. It was always simpler that way.

No matter how carefully done and practiced, the branding process was always excruciating for the herd.

> *Inflict pain so they appreciate the honor they're receiving, but no more pain than is required, she instructed her staff. Some pain is necessary and good. Learn the different kinds of pain and when to use each.*

Branding was a First Day chore. It was always done in an open field where the herd could scream and the air would carry their voices into the hills where they would fade into the landscape. The Owner had no problem with collective herd horror and their expression of necessary pain. Horror could be screamed; hatred voiced; pain endured and total emasculation completed within the single act of First Day branding. And now, it was time.

The Owner leaned into her largest monitor yet kept an eye on each smaller one that focused on the most entertaining animal's reaction when it realized what branding on the Farm meant.

It was also better to do them all at once, she learned. Some herd members could not be to calmed down after they witnessed a fellow herd member's branding. That's why 245 unique branding irons were being heated in well-placed fire pits surrounding the herd. The numbers were counted and matched carefully so herds were never mixed up. After the animals were moved into smaller groups called packs that were identified as the result of Intake and Processing, they would then be branded as a group to bring them closer together and to get the chore accomplished quickly.

Ursula called out the packs and trainees sorted animals into small groups. All that data, the Owner thought, and it took only a minute to identify the like-minded animals.

There was only one satisfactory place to brand a Farm animal, the Owner knew. And it took every Trail Boss, Trainer, Pack Leader, staff member and trainee to do it well and quickly.

All the ranks moved in as Ursula called out, "Get them ready to be branded."

The women moved the herd of crawling males and turned their backsides toward the center of the ring to allow them to face out and see the Farm's beautiful landscape. The herd dropped to the grass and gathered into small circles as Ursula had assigned them. A thick rope was wrapped around each hoof and the trainees drove a stake into the ground through each knot. Within minutes, the entire herd was bolted to the Farm's dirt floor with wide spaces between the packs.

The animals faced each other on their hands and knees. Their asscheeks pointed to the center of the ring where the fire pits were ablaze and glowing irons poked out from center of the fire.

Watching the annual sight of dangling genitalia in front of the fire, the Owner tapped her tablet to zoom in.

Ursula's voice rose above the fire pits' crackling.

"One to an animal," she said loudly.

Each staff member picked up a glowing iron and staked out her prey. Identifications were checked carefully and each farmhand was presented a spray bottle containing ice water mixed with anesthetic. After spraying the concoction thoroughly under every scrotum, they each gripped their brand firmly and impaled the blazing iron against an animal's exposed perineum, counted aloud and withdrew the fiery iron. Staff members quickly sprayed ice-cold anesthetic on the dangling genitalia of the now-branded herd.

The smell of burnt flesh filled their nostrils; the sound of utter torture filled their ears.

Allow them to suffer. Aloud. Together. The Owner told the Farm staff the same thing each Season. It helps the herd to bond.

Of all the Intake and Processing chores, branding was the one completed with the least fanfare but caused the strongest lifelong memories that were now seared into each animal's brain. Not one animal left the Farm without the vivid recollection of branding.

Ursula allowed the herd to scream for several minutes and then she began moving the group to its feet.

"Let's see them each other," Ursula said to the 245 members of the permanently-identified herd. "Lift."

Through their tears, each animal dropped one paw to its agonized testicles and lifted them, enduring the burning with gritted teeth and poorly-muffled grunts. Engraved forever on the bottom of their scrotal sacs was an identification code that at this very moment, they were learning to present to any woman on the Farm who demanded to see it. The males rarely understood why the brands had been burned into them, but Josie quickly commented that many things happened on the Farm and in the Farm way and they were better off not worrying about important Farm matters.

"Don't worry your pretty little bald heads about it," she said sarcastically.

The Owner smiled as they lifted their sacs and held them up for Ursula's inspection. She knew that her Trail Boss would have their codes memorized as fast as she could see them. Her head trainee would also learn them by heart but the list that every Trail Boss always kept at her side on her tablet was a powerful daily challenge.

As for the herd, it was as if they understood a little more deeply that they were now merely identified herd members and no longer men from another world. That was one impact of the Farm's brand. So was the pain.

Ursula charged through the group and demanded that those whose codes she called out line up directly behind her. The Owner loved the herding process as the males responded through their individual agony to her sorting. No one on the Farm ever used a male's name during the Season. The testicle codes were now their only identities.

"Forty-eight!" she said and a male, still holding his sack, hobbled toward her. Unsure of where to stand or what to do, the animal stood silently and held its scrotum high as if to prove to Ursula that he was indeed animal #48 and reporting as ordered. The hilarity of its confusion amused the Owner. Katrina noticed her smile and zoomed in on his tear-stained face. Ignoring its suffering, Ursula called the next number.

"One eighty seven," she said and a second herd member shuffled toward her, its sac also held in its paw. Ursula smiled knowing that there were two suffering pack members lined up behind her, both holding their testicles and too terrified to move. The Owner smiled at the change she saw growing in the herd. One at a time, they were learning this part of the Farm way.

Ursula continued calling numbers until her list was finished and then Tara stepped up to gather her flock. She called numbers and the process continued as the herd was sorted and the animals stood in a testicle-holding cluster. Each was both terrified and mortified under the bright sun in the training field. The Owner nodded. First Day had now truly begun.

Surrounded by the trainees assigned to the packs and each pack to a Trail Boss, the animals were ordered to drop their sacs and concentrate on the instructions they were about to receive. The Trail Bosses spoke quietly to their packs and with all groups receiving instructions simultaneously, it was deliberately difficult for any herd member to understand all the words its Trail Boss said. The noise was an incomprehensible symphony set up intentionally to determine if anyone would ask – or worse, expect – repetition of an instruction.

"Sharon," the Owner said into the microphone and Sharon's pack was projected to the main screen.

> *This is going to be intense. Sharon always is, Katrina thought silently as she pressed buttons on her console to focus on Sharon's pack and bring it to her Owner's main monitor.*

Sharon's long hair was tied up in a bun which the Owner was convinced she did in a futile effort to make her appear taller. One day, she predicted, Sharon would understand that her height was neither an asset nor a liability. She would understand that the Farm's women had it within themselves to command attention merely by walking into a room. She watched as Sharon bounced on her boots, as if to talk above the pack's bald heads.

"We will run to the barn," Sharon finished her instructions. "You'll be quartered there for the Season.

One member of her pack moaned softly.

Eliminate bad behavior as soon as it starts, Sharon recalled from her training. Make an example out of the first miscreant and you won't have to deal with that behavior from your pack for the rest of the Season.

Her boots plodded noisily on the outdoor field as Sharon stepped toward the moaner. Her electric prod kissed the animal's still-burning scrotum for an instant and the touch elicited a howl of anguish heard frequently after branding. Its forelocks reached to protect its testicles but Sharon, anticipating the movement, touched the prod again, this time to an asscheek. By now, its hands were flying back and forth, trying vainly to protect its agonized cock and ass. It was a delightful game of whackamole that Sharon enjoyed playing.

With one hand reaching for its agonized asscheek and the other seeking to protect its scrotum, Sharon pressed her prod against random spots on the animal's body. Its hands were unable to keep up with her torture and finally it fell to the ground and writhed in crazed pain as she continued to find new spots to torment. It flopped like a fish out of water and every Trail Boss stopped her pack to force them to see what could lie in store for each of them. More importantly, each animal needed to understand the discipline that was being applied.

The message was burned into their brains. Some averted their eyes so as not to have to view the suffering; others stared in disbelief as the tortured animal floundered on the Farm's grassy field. Everyone's ears drank in its wailing yet not one stepped forward to interfere. The lesson, observed in excruciating detail by the Owner, had been learned.

Sharon reattached her prod to her belt and called out happily, "Let's run!" She began jogging toward the barns as if nothing unusual had happened yet every member of her pack as well as those in the other four packs wore looks of shock as they followed toward their quarters for the Season in a neatly spaced and unthinking line.

Chapter 21: Trainee Luncheon

First Day luncheon was for trainees as the Owner began her assessment of their potential for both for this Season as well as for upcoming Seasons on the Farm. Each trainee came to the Farm as a bundle of promise and excitement; the Owner was always in the market for the seeds of a future Lead Trainer or Trail Boss as the needs of the Farm grew every Season. Some trainees were repeaters who did not impress her quite enough and she undertook their progress as her personal mission during a repeat trial Season.

When the lunch bell rang and the herd was packed off to the feeding area for their final feeding as a group before they were separated into season-long packs, the trainees jogged toward the Manor House for their private luncheon with their Owner. For some of them, it would be their first personal interaction with her since their arrival and the beginning of the Season's work. For others, it was a repeat performance that held the promise of a promotion path. For all of them, it was always an exceptional experience.

Trainees were trained how to greet their Owner by their Lead Trainers. They knew that this special luncheon was their opportunity to display their new skills to her. As they jogged toward the Manor House, they chatted and shared their enthusiasm and fears about the first meeting. Some of the repeaters urged the newcomers to be sure to make use of the two rules they had learned from their Lead Trainers: perfect body position and special speech procedures.

Get into position quickly, they were taught. Say nothing unless you are asked a direct question.

As they approached the big doors that identified the trainer and trainees' entrance, the young women slowed their pace to catch their breath. No one wanted to enter the Manor House with sweat dripping down her body. Each trainee checked her breasts for dust from the fields and if she found any, tried to brush it away. Clad only in the trainees' official outfit of leather shorts and black work boots, they were reminded of the rule they had accepted when they joined the Farm staff.

Stand tall. Be proud. Shoulders back. Chest forward. She owns your body. Give it to her proudly.

Each of the groups slowed to a walk and the Owner watched them pull their shoulders back and jut their breasts forward. Her smile was all the approval they would get and she nodded to the staff to allow them to enter.

As the line marched into the Manor House through the big doors, they felt a blast of cold air. Many appreciated the air conditioning as the outdoor temperature was steadily rising, yet most of them did not recognize that it was designed to stiffen their nipples. Dozens of pairs of thick, rich brown nipples stood in silent greeting to their Owner. Once the entire corps of trainees was inside the Manor House, they were instructed about the details that luncheon with the Owner included.

A young server, clad in a black leather bikini panty and matching thigh-high stiletto boots, addressed the group.

"You are at Luncheon," she said, "and the Owner will join you in due time. Take a seat at the table – any seat is fine." Her next comment was delivered with the hint of a smile. "Trainees have no rank," she finished. "Where you sit doesn't matter."

But she wasn't done putting them in their place yet.

"Fold your leathers on the floor on top of your number," she said and turned away.

Their faces showed their surprise at the order to strip their leathers. Leathers identified Farm staff and were awarded only after passing strenuous assessment. To the new trainees, shedding their leathers felt like shedding their skin. Complete nakedness was new to them; it was one of the Trainee Luncheon's lasting surprises and one that their Lead Trainers had neglected to mention.

"Now!" she said again and each woman peeled off her boots and shorts, folded and placed them neatly atop their corresponding number stenciled on the floor. They could only imagine how many trainees had folded their precious leathers on those numbers during prior Seasons.

Katrina focused the cameras toward the particularly shy ones and Leda pointed out a few bodies that the Owner might be interested in viewing close up. The images she watched on her monitors in her Blue Salon pleased the Owner. Inspecting the girls was one of her favorite moments of the Trainee Luncheon.

"I'm already on it," Leda said to Katrina as she exited the communications center.

The trainees followed the server toward the large dining room as their naked feet slapped against the wood floor. Upon entering they stood awkwardly in small groups, too afraid even to whisper to one another. Leda's loud entry caught the trainees' eyes focused on her black vest that pushed her breasts up the highest they had ever seen and clearly identified her as the Owner's personal assistant. Her forceful demeanor added to their unease. She surveyed them for at least a full minute before she said a word.

"Welcome to the Manor House," she began. "The Owner will join you in due time. I will get you ready for Luncheon."

Her words penetrated every ear and each trainee wondered what 'getting ready' entailed. They didn't have to wait long.

"Repeaters here," Leda pointed to her left, "and new ones here." As she pointed, the trainees separated themselves into two groups to the areas she indicated.

"Repeaters, position!" she ordered and 15 girls fell to their knees and grabbed their spread ankles. Leda marched up and down the line and adjusted positions here and there to show off highlights of some special bodies for the Owner's perusal. Shoulders were pushed back, heads raised, chins prodded, ankle grips tightened, breasts lifted, labia spread, bellies sucked in and nipples tweaked for color. At last the group seemed to please Leda. She focused her attention on the new set of trainees.

"Look at them," Leda said to the new staff members. "Study their positions. See their posture, shoulders and raised chins. Absorb how open they are for their Owner and learn from them."

The new trainees stared at the repeaters who were straining to hold their perfect positions. But that intense concentration wasn't enough to satisfy Leda.

"Move! Get close to them!" she said. "Examine every one of them. Touch their nipples and feel the hardness. Try to pull their fingers. See how tightly they grip? Hop to it," she finished as the gaggle of newcomers spread out to inspect the repeaters' and learn. No one wanted to be a repeater.

Leda grinned as the young trainees at first hesitated to touch the repeaters' nipples or palpate their shoulders. The Owner paid close attention to their behavior and Katrina zoomed in where she was sure the Owner's interests would be focused. Assertiveness, out-of-the-box thinking and showing power to authority were some of the attributes the Owner looked for potential in permanent staff. When she found one or even two of those attributes in the newcomers, it predicted a decent crop.

She observed them by focusing on the trainees who were still checking out the kneeling repeaters. Leda noted a movement here or there that caught her eye. Positioning herself near the trainee and using her own body language to encourage Katrina to focus her camera angle, she examined one or another girl's behavior close-up. Not only did a particular girl tap a repeater's chin, but she also pushed it upward slightly. That simple gesture spoke volumes about the girl's assertiveness and Leda wanted to be sure it had been caught on video. Tapping her trainee number into her tablet, she nodded to a technician who would later associate it with the name given to each trainee by the Farm.

Still surveying the new staff inspecting the repeaters, Leda caught a trainee whose fingers pinched a kneeler's nipples tightly. Pointing her out so Katrina could display her on the Owner's monitor, Leda watched as the girl pulled the repeater's big brown nipples upward and forced the repeater to raise her hips slightly from the floor. Nodding again to the technician, Leda tasked her with finding the girl's name and noting it for the Owner.

Two potentials in this class, Leda thought. Not bad for a new group.

The Owner's attention was focused on another interaction farther down the line and for the moment hidden from Leda's view. One trainee that captured the Owner's fancy had also been the first of her group to walk behind the kneelers while the rest of the group remained in front. That action caused Katrina to move her to center screen so the Owner would have a clear view. The Owner studied the screen and noticed as the girl took a handful of the repeater's hair and pulled it backward as if to straighten – and correct – her posture. The Owner leaned in toward the monitor and tapped her control panel to tell Katrina to zoom in.

How far would she go this early in the Season, the Owner wondered? Assertive behavior is one thing; aggressive or sadistic actions were unacceptable from trainees. The fine line that distinguished the two was defined solely by the Owner who knew it as soon as she saw it. Katrina zeroed in on the kneeler's hair and the trainee's face to create a graphic that provided exactly what the Owner wanted to see.

Use discipline only until the desired behavior is achieved, the girls were taught in training. Do not discipline for any other reason or any other length of time except to produce the behavior you want.

The Owner was curious as she counted silently.

One.

The trainee pulled the kneeler's hair and generated a look of surprise on the repeater's face.

Two.

Responding to her firm tug, the repeater pressed her head backward and jutted her naked breasts forward even farther.

Three.

With her hair still in the trainee's grip, the repeater didn't understand what was required of her. Shifting once or twice, she repositioned herself until she thought she was properly displayed.

Four.

The trainee's almost unnoticeable upward hand movement still filled with the kneeler's hair lifted the girl off her haunches and drew her torso higher from the floor. The strain in her quadriceps must be excruciating, Katrina thought, but to her credit, the girl's grip held the repeater firmly in place.

Five.

Her body was screaming for mercy but the trainee, still standing behind her; never noticed the agony on her face.

Six.

The Owner had seen enough. Sadism was unacceptable on the Farm and this trainee had just earned a swift session of her own discipline. She tapped her tablet and demanded the trainee's name. Katrina buzzed Leda so she would put an end to the conduct that had offended the Owner, and Leda was seasoned enough to know just how to handle it.

Stepping behind the errant girl, Leda wrapped her arms around the trainee's chest from behind and pinched her nipples firmly in her fingers.

"Trainees, position," she instructed as the flock of new staff members hurried to their designated spots to splay their legs, grab their ankles, press their bosoms out and raise their heads in anticipation of the Owner's entrance. Everyone, that is, except the trainee whose nipples were agonized by Leda's unflinching grip.

"Don't move a muscle," she hissed into the girl's ear.

The Owner's rapid entrance alerted every staff member, from the servers to the staff ranks to her personal assistant that something was amiss. Usually she entered quietly and absorbed the attention focused on her by her underlings. Marching in with her boots generating a loud percussion on the hardwood floors was a clear signal that she was displeased. The entire Manor House staff froze in place in fear.

Her eyes stared at the group of trainees; she noted coldly that all displayed satisfactorily. Only those kneeling did not understand that the purpose of the Trainee Luncheon had very little to do with proper greetings or personal interaction with the Owner. This episode was repeated every Season and was the real reason they had been run to the Manor House, stripped of their leathers and permitted to interact with each other. They were there to be evaluated by the Owner. That was the Farm way.

The Owner walked toward Leda, whose fingers continued their near-death grip on the trainee's nipples. Standing behind the Head Trainer and soon-to-be disciplined trainee, she took one of the girl's nipples from Leda and pressed it between her own fingers. With the Owner now squeezing pitilessly, the trainee grunted in a vain effort to suppress the gurgling scream threatening to escape from her lips. Leda followed her Owner's lead and increased her grip on her nipple. In just those few seconds, the trainee approached delirium yet was still gripping the repeater's hair in her fist. She still didn't get it.

"Not a muscle," Leda hissed into her ear again.

The noise that rose from deep inside the trainee was horrific but not unusual during any Season's Trainee Luncheon. Each of the newcomers had to learn the Farm way and understand the consequences of their actions. Moreover they had to learn firsthand what would happen if they displeased their Owner. Lessons on the Farm were swift and intense. They were never forgotten.

> *Make an example of just one, Leda recalled from her Owner's wise words, and the others will learn. Discipline must be quick and to the point. Achieve the behavior you want and the lesson has been learned.*

Finally, the Owner demanded answers from the trainee. "Why did you pull her hair?" her tone was cold and clear.

The trainee, bent backwards from the nipple torture but held upright by the strength of two sets of fingers clutching her nipples, grunted what may have been a response but was clearly not up to her Owner's expectations. She tried to form words but her nipple agony overtook her. She couldn't speak and the sheer magnitude of her effort captured the attention of every trainee and the repeaters. The episode was captured perfectly by Katrina on several cameras in the communications room. She would certainly include it for later staff discussion.

"Why did you pull her hair?" the Owner repeated, her voice flat and ominous.

Every staff member knew that she would repeat this question until she received the response she wanted. The errant trainee owned the burden of discovering what the proper response was and the Owner had all the time she wanted to enforce this lesson. No one was going anywhere. Hardly anyone was breathing.

The trainee shuddered in self-inflicted agony, yet the two pairs of fingers never loosened their grip. If anything, they gripped more tightly.

"WHY did you pull her hair?" the Owner demanded again, this time in a voice that everyone in the room knew demanded an immediate answer.

Tears ran down her face, and the trainee knew that only a proper response would alleviate her suffering. Her voice started and halted; her words were unplanned.

> *Do not speak unless you are asked a direct question and then answer quickly, simply and completely. She had been reminded only that morning but she had not yet learned the lesson.*

"I ... I wanted her to ..." her voice quivered, "to show respect."

Her nipple still between her Owner's fingers, the Owner chortled at the ridiculous response. "Really?" she asked rhetorically. "Respect to WHOM?" She stood in silence, her absolute grip unyielding as she waited for a proper response.

"I was wrong," the trainee wailed.

"Non-responsive!" the Owner hissed into her ear. "And you were more than wrong. You were inexcusably sadistic!" She threw the girl to the ground by her nipple and glanced at Leda before issuing her final order to this particular trainee.

"Punishment," the Owner said coolly as Leda handed the girl to the Manor House staff for the Season's first trainee punishment processing.

Drinking in a cleansing breath of cool air, the Owner exhaled the anger that rose inside her and allowed it to escape into the room so she could enjoy the calm that replaced it and soothed her thoughts. Standing in front of her kneeling trainees and repeaters, she surveyed them and saw quickly that their legs were stressed from their strained positions yet their faces bore the indelible marks of those who had learned something important only moments ago.

Training is only as good as the behavior it produces, she thought. Let's see how they perform after this lesson.

"We're here for Luncheon," she said aloud. "Shall we sit down?" There was an inviting lilt in her voice.

Several trainees struggled to their feet and flexed their legs to relieve the stiffness. They recalled the server's earlier instructions to sit anywhere and also her admonition that they had no rank during Luncheon. Walking slowly around the huge table to find an empty seat, the servers handed out tiny doilies to place under their naked bottoms so that they would not stain the chairs. It was then that so many of them realized how silky wet their pussies had become by witnessing the trainee's discipline and imagining her punishment.

The Owner issued one last instruction after Leda delivered a short message to her tablet with only two names on it.

"Hailey, Georgia," she read their names as two surprised faces turned toward her. "Sit on either side of me. I'm famished," she said as Luncheon's first course was served.

As usual, the food was as delicious as it was plentiful and the Owner enjoyed every bite.

Chapter 22: Cow Barn

Ursula ran her pack along the paths toward a huge barn that stood stately near the southern perimeter of the Farm. The pack, winded from their morning run and with their scrotums still stinging from the morning's branding, fell into place in front of a huge door that whirred open from an unseen electronic command. As they caught their collective breath, Ursula saw the light turn green and ordered them inside the barn. Her trainees, just returning from the Trainee Luncheon, were waiting for her arrival with the Cow Pack.

The inner entrance began with a long mirrored hallway. The packs' eyes needed a few moments to adjust from the brilliant outdoor midday sunshine to the darkened interior so they could focus on their reflections in the mirrors. Several cows had difficulty understanding what they saw in the mirror. It sank into their brains slowly that what stared back at them was what they had become in a few short days. They hadn't been allowed to see a mirror since they arrived at the Farm except for a few memorable moments after Shearing.

Their first view of their own hairless bodies always upset the Cows and amused the year's Trail Boss and her trainees. Ursula counted slowly to herself. She knew what was coming.

Horrified shrieks flew out of the pack's throats and filled the inner entrance. Cries of distress, moans of agony, whimpers of misery and wails of humiliation echoed throughout the room as each naked and hairless cow finally understood that all their shorn and naked cow pack compatriots looked frighteningly alike. Identities had been ripped away. Naked bald bodies straggled in front of the mirrors and stared aghast at their reflections.

It always works, Ursula smiled. A picture – especially of themselves – is worth a thousand words.

Allowing them to linger a little more and take in the full extent of their reflections, Ursula glanced at the control room and received the nod she anticipated so she could move the Cows into the central barn area that now been assigned as their home for the Season. Having drawn the Cow Barn this Season, Ursula recalled special moments vividly from three Seasons ago when she last trained the cows. That pack was an ornery bunch and vexed her on a few occasions before she finally managed to get them under control and working as a unified herd completing their training and chores. They had disgraced themselves by losing the First Competition through their failure to bind together as a team. She sent eight pack members for Punishment that Season and that was just too many to meet her standards. Not this year, she vowed. They would behave.

Shaking her head to push the memory away, she moved the Cows inside with a single command.

"Trot," she said above the din of their groaning. "Hooves on your number."

Another set of doors opened electronically and taught the pack that the doors opened and closed only when their Trail Boss wanted them to. Once moved inside, they realized they would be granted egress only at the whim of this woman wearing bright orange fabric that stuck out from between two amazing breasts that were forced up and out by her leather vest. Ursula saw that one or two were on the verge of panic and she pointed them out to the trainees as a precaution.

The barn's interior was an open room and the floor was marked with numbered spots that corresponded to each of the Cow's new brands. Several Cows had to lift their sacs again and try to read their own numbers, yet their view was obscured by their own useless testicles. Unsure of what to do, they stood motionless until a trainee approached them.

"What is your number?" each trainee asked each Cow in what would become a season-long repeated question. Every herd member MUST know its brand, the trainees understood, because it was now their season-long identity. It was who they had become.

Dropping each Cow deeper into degradation, trainees forced them to lift their testicles so the young women could view the hidden tagging.

"Higher," one said to a Cow on the verge of tears. "Lift it higher." It never mattered why a woman insisted or demanded, the Cows learned. They were to obey every command.

Red-faced and teary-eyed, the Cow lifted its aching cock and testicles higher so the stretched sac re-burned the memory of its branding into its brain. The trainee, skilled in reinforcing the Farm's lessons, took her time in reading the number.

"A bit higher," she said.

Full of shame that exuded from every pore on its hide, the Cow tugged its handful of genitals even higher and pointed its hips in her direction. For her part, the trainee was efficient in performing her training agenda. Turning her head to offer an offhand comment to another nearby trainee, she said, "These floppy balls make this one hard to read. See if you can figure it out."

The cow's body was now fully encased in its mortification as the second young woman approached and attempted to read the brand. Naked and shorn and standing for all to see in the barn's open space, the cow continued to pull up its testicles while the two women consulted on what the number might be.

"Looks like a 35," one said.

"No, that's 85," the other said with a slight smile.

The cow stood motionless and ready to explode from embarrassment as they debated the brand. They chatted as if the cow weren't standing there with its legs spread and balls in its hand. Finally, they agreed.

"That's 85, we agree," the first trainee said and the cow trotted away to find its numbered stall in the barn. It had become a number that the cow would never forget, no more than it would forget that the brand had become its new name.

The herd of cows scurried about searching for their numbers on the floor while others lifted their sacs for one woman or another to inspect for proper identification. Ursula surveyed the scene playing out in all corners of the barn and watched the cows' faces when they required a trainee to read their numbers. She observed some hesitation and occasional reluctance, but she also saw a few cows trotting rapidly toward a trainee for assistance. It was good to watch proper behavior develop and Ursula was sure some of the better trainee-cow interaction would make the after-dinner highlights.

The herd was soon in their proper places. Each naked cow stood long-sufferingly on his number and waited for the next command. Ursula grinned as they waited in frustrated silence.

Striding through the group, she stopped at one handy set of asscheeks. Ursula slapped them hard in the Trail Boss's proper way of welcoming a cow to her barn. "Number?" she asked loudly.

As if the animal had been thrust onto a concert stage and suffered from numbing stage fright, the cow stammered its response. Ursula frowned as it looked at its hooves that partially covered his number. Swatting the asscheeks harder this time, she demanded, "Number!"

With the cow's forlorn eyes struggling to see the number that his hooves had been forced to cover, it was filled with tangible shame. Its front hoof ventured toward its scrotum and the cow lifted it diffidently toward her, as if presenting a cherished cock, balls and scrotum to her an offering. Gripping its testicles in its hoof's fingers, Ursula culminated the lesson.

"This is how you present," she said as she cupped her fingers around the hand that offered its organs and yanked the whole sac up. The moo of agony it released reverberated from the barn's walls but her fingers never released their grip. Instead, she spoke to the entire group as its flesh filled her fist.

"Memorize your number," she warned them. "Those cows who cannot respond with their number immediately upon request will taste Farm Discipline."

She felt the cow's fingers flex within her grip. Not a bit surprised, she recognized the behavior almost immediately and already had the proper response ready.

Any cow that tries to grip its cock and balls when its Trainer is inspecting them is trying to hide them, she had been taught.

"Trainees," she called to the room, "come immediately and watch this."

Trotting quickly with boot heels clapping on the barn floor, the Cow Barn trainees ran toward Ursula and noticed the corners of her mouth rise. They were eager to learn what Ursula already knew but they were still trying to guess. The best way to rise in the ranks or even hope for a Trail Boss position was to go through every new experience possible on the Farm. The trainees were eager students, hungry for opportunities to learn.

"Cows like these are betrayed by their penises and balls," she said to the women as she ignored the rest of the naked cows that remained stuck on their numbers. "Watch this cock," she finished.

"Drop it!" she commanded toward the trembling cow.

The trainees gasped as they saw the cock fill and point up. Animals' cocks were studied in training but this was the first time the trainees had seen an one that dared to erect in the Cow Barn. They had been taught lessons on how to deal with the situation and this would be the first real-life experience for most of them. Some were so excited that they were licking their lips unconsciously.

Stiff cocks only cause misbehavior, they had all been taught. Nip that behavior early and the rest of the herd will not duplicate the mistake.

"What do we do with a hard cock?" Ursula asked her trainees as if dismembering the shaft psychologically from its wearer. "What is the proper treatment of an engorged cock?" she posed the question to the trainees.

"Strike it once, hard, near the tip," a trainee said.

Ursula considered her textbook response and nodded. "That is one effective method. What's another?" she asked, hoping for a more inventive reply.

A second trainee ventured, "The prod. But that's usually held out for repeat offenses."

Ursula nodded. Using a prod on a cock was a last resort that would be used only when traditional methods weren't successful.

Discipline cows to get desired behavior. Do not over-discipline but punish if the behavior threatens herd unity.

Ursula hoped the girls would offer out of-the-box possibilities to use for first-level discipline and in turn, make sure that the herd would drink in the consequences for their misdeeds and learn from them. She didn't have to wait long. The next trainee's reply had a weighty impact on the herd.

"What if we cage the cock?" she asked. Then she added a second question. "Maybe we should milk it dry first?"

Trainees' heads bobbed up and down at both of her suggestions and Ursula was certain that the approval was aimed more at the girl's second idea. The trainees would be eager to milk their first real-life cock and learn how to use that discipline technique firsthand. Milking a stiff cock dry was a well-seasoned method of control and if the trainees were to learn satisfactory milking techniques, this seemed as good a time as any. Milking was an art and one that Ursula's expertise was well-known on the Farm. Glancing at the control room, Ursula nodded almost imperceptibly as techs' fingers flew over their keyboards and started the milking machines.

"A good and proper suggestion," Ursula said as she watched the idea's originator grin with pride. "I will milk this one while the rest of the herd is settling in."

The group of trainees was excited but Ursula's matter-of-fact tone reminded them to remember that the Farm way was always cool and professional. Trainees needed to learn that discipline was applied only to achieve a behavioral change or demonstrate a technique for educational purposes. The trembling cow whose body would serve as the Season's first educational tool for the trainee's hands-on instruction began whimpering at Ursula's next directive.

"You," she pointed to the trainee whose suggestion they were going to use, "hook it up to the milking machine." The trainee's hand reached for the cock and pulled it, along with the cow who wore it, behind her as she walked toward the complex machinery humming in the back of the barn.

"The rest of you," Ursula pointed at the remainder of the trainees, "settle the pack in and secure each one. When that task is done well, you may join us at the milking machines."

Each trainee dragged her cow and merrily flung each one into its stall. Pushing each one forward, the cows were locked into padded metal bars that fit crisply around their heads and necks. After locking the upper restraints, the trainees bolted the retractable ankle restraints around their hooves and then raised the belly bar to the perfect height for each cow so they would not have to carry any weight on their necks. Finally, the cows' forelocks were sheathed in leather mittens so they could not hurt themselves or touch anything that no longer belonged to them, like the cocks, balls and scrotums that were now owned by the Farm.

Finally, the pack was secure. The barn was filled with animals who would shortly know themselves as the Season's cows. The whirr of the conveyor belt began behind them to catch and carry away what would eventually be their defecation.

Wait till the first one goes and the rest realize this barn has no watering stations, Ursula laughed to herself. The aroma of the cow barn was always memorable.

Ursula spoke into the headset that was designed for the barn. "Control, the pack is secure for the duration of this training session. Monitor movement and vitals and report to me as needed. Notify me immediately of any potential cow defecation on the belt. We should be only two or three hours," she finished.

The pack heard every single word. A bolt of understanding shot through all the cows at the same time. Two or three hours? Defecation on the belt? They were to remain in this ludicrous cow-like position in the stalls with their heads locked and their asses spread and their feet bolted and their hands covered for two to three hours?

"Alert Processing," Ursula continued talking to control in a bland tone as the cows squirmed in discomfort. "Inform them that the cow pack is available for that duration." Calculating mentally, she added, "And give Comm a heads-up."

Several sets of asscheeks quivered after hearing Ursula's final barn-wide comment delivered via a headset that was built for both group and individual communication and changed merely by her flick of a button. Bolted down and secured with a conveyor belt to move their sphincter contents along, every part of their bodies was fair game and they knew that the technicians from Processing would show them no mercy. Their asscheeks were splayed for the use of whoever walked by, metal bars imprisoned their heads, a conveyor belt waiting their defecation and their bellies rammed against a posture bar, the cows were overwhelmed with their situation. Several were emotionally overcome with the inevitability of their incarceration and a few moaned aloud. The sound was picked up by control and sent back to their ears after bouncing it off the barn walls. The resulting noise was unmistakable.

Their collective moans sounded exactly like a herd of cows mooing.

Ursula turned her attention to the trainees who were almost salivating while waiting for her to start the milking presentation. She smiled at the eager group and took the semi-hard shaft in one hand. As she instructed the group, she waved the cock to punctuate her points. The cow attached to it squirmed and extended its body trying to keep up with her rapid motions until a pained grunt escaped his muzzle.

"Just a moment," Ursula said to no one in particular as one trainee figured it out and hustled to the equipment area for tools. She then ran back to the group at full speed so as not to miss any part of the session. "Install it," she told the lucky trainee.

Never ask them to perform, Ursula knew. They must learn to anticipate and use their initiative to move the process forward. Make note of those trainees and develop them.

The girl was excited to participate in the first milking and she positioned herself perfectly. Her breasts were only an inch or two away from the cow's face when she commanded it to part its jaw. As the cow performed as instructed, saliva dripped toward the barn floor. Slapping its muzzle once, she ordered the animal to drop his lower jaw and widen the opening. It performed as instructed; however, moans of fear rose from deep inside.

"Get it in quickly and accurately," Ursula said, "so we don't have to listen to it anymore."

Pressing the rubber bit between its teeth, the trainee pushed the bit in deeper until the cow's mouth was spread satisfactorily. She wound the leather straps around its face and forehead and locked it into place. Finally, she drew the reins behind its neck and handed them respectfully to her Trail Boss.

Ursula looped the reins over a nearby hook, tethered the cow upright and continued her lesson.

"Milking a male is like milking a cow," she began. "Make sure the fore udder is held tightly by the condom catheter, the teat is secure and then start the motor. That's all there is to it." She waited for questions but none were proffered.

Continuing with the demonstration, she said, "Remember, when the udder's contents are emptied, you must be sure to reset the suction pump for the next milking."

A question came from a trainee. She asked, "What's the optimal number of milkings per cow in a session?"

"Good question," Ursula said. "Most cows will need tighter restraints after the third or fourth. I've gone as high as ten, but that was a special case. Use your best judgment and milk the cow until its mooing stops and you are sure it's empty and the lesson has been learned." She waited for those important instructions to be memorized and now in each trainee's skillset. Then she added, "Remember, the purpose of discipline is to cause proper behavior. You are the judge and jury for that on the Farm."

Each trainee smiled at the 'judge and jury' remark and as a group was eager to embark on their first milking using the an actual cow in the Barn. Ursula slipped into training mode with experienced voice and hand mannerisms. First she would cut that excitement short to educate the young women further into a serious lesson of the Farm way. The Milking Barn was more than simply home to the cows; it was the trainees' home as well for this Season on the Farm.

With the cow's bit still tethered to the wall, Ursula warned the trainees about safety.

"It'll kick when you turn on the rectal pump," she said. "I always make sure that its hooves are fastened down like this." She stopped instructing and unfolded the two leather straps that protruded from the machine's base. She had the girls close in and observe the intricate process.

"These aren't just any tethers," she said. "They are constructed from bull hide and the studs that attach them to the machine are particularly strong. See the three wraps?" She waited as each trainee inspected the leather.

"First buckle, then lock," she instructed. "I want you to try all 20 adjustment holes for best positioning. Make sure the fit is tight but not too tight and don't make it loose. That will damage the hide." She added, "We do not damage the animals on the Farm."

The trainees nodded with each safety instruction. "Here's how you determine if it's tight enough." She dropped her finger in the loop between the leather band and the cow's ankle. "You shouldn't be able to slip your finger in easily. Now you try it."

Each girl in turn slipped her finger between the leather band and cow's ankle to feel the tension for herself that Ursula said was the right amount. This process of feeling, Ursula remembered, had been very instructive for her so many Seasons ago.

"Girls, the cow is now tethered by bit and hoof," she said. "For the first milking, it doesn't require to be tethered at the waist as well, but you must observe carefully on each ensuing round to make sure it isn't bucking too hard or in a way that might hurt itself." She allowed her words to sink in and added, "I've seen them wrench a back or tear a muscle. That is unacceptable."

The girls nodded again, drinking in all of Ursula's instructions as if they were sitting at the feet of a scholar whose sage wisdom was theirs to absorb. Not one of her words fell on deaf ears. Even the tethered cow seemed to listen with curious interest.

"Let's get started." Ursula stood up and stood in front of the machine's control panel. "After the milking underway, you'll each choose a cow to milk and we'll make sure you have it carefully under your belts." Ursula smirked at her intentional joke and the trainees grinned back at her. It was their goal to earn their vests, replete with waistband belts and colors. This training session was the first step in their progress to that goal.

"Look at this," Ursula said and held the most important attachment aloft so all could see. "This is the condom catheter that holds the entire fore udder and teat so that the milking machine is most effective. Study the fore udder and feel for the veins; in fact, touch them and feel them. Get to know each part. Unless you recognize all states of a cow's udder, you won't have the background you need to be that judge and jury."

The trainees focused on the tethered cow and hand after hand reached in to manipulate the teat that hung embarrassingly stiff from its lower torso. Fingers lifted and pulled it, palms wrapped around it, nails stroked against it, forearms tapped it – all in an effort to help the trainees understand the teat and udder's various physical states up close and impersonally.

Ursula commented, "I'm sure you've noticed that it stiffened, didn't you?" She added for clarity, "Milking a stiff udder accomplishes two desirable outcomes. First, it makes the process take less time. And second," she paused for impact, "it makes for a much louder experience."

The girls nodded as Ursula grasped the thick udder and lubricated it expertly before slipping the stiff rubber condom catheter on it. With a single motion, the udder was wrapped up and Ursula buckled the leather straps through the cow's crotch and around its girth before locking the leather bands together.

"Let's get the rectal probe inserted," Ursula said as she stepped toward the cow's rear flank. "Do you remember the training video?"

The girls nodded. Who could forget that lesson? The close-up footage showed at least ten rectal insertions and the girls learned more anal anatomy than they knew existed. They could see – and later they would feel – the prostate gland, urethral threads and manipulate sphincter control. Later, their fingers explored a variety of stand-in artificial cows until each could insert the milking probe carefully and successfully. This would be their first real cow.

"Ready the probes," Ursula said.

With glee and anticipation mixed together, each girl stepped to positions behind her cow. In an almost single motion, each donned gloves, squirted lubricant on their fingers and explored the cows' anuses for problems or blockages. One by one, they completed the initial inspection and awaited their next order.

"Insert the probes," Ursula said as her eyes moved around the barn. A cow's moo could be easily translated by an experienced Trail Boss as either bad pain or simple discomfort and Ursula was trained to hear the differences between the sounds. She listened for problems and studied the group's work as the girls fumbled with their first live probe insertion. By the clock, it took fifteen minutes for the herd to be completely inserted. Ursula had to intervene only twice for minor issues. She remembered her first live probe insertion with fondness and hoped this group of trainees would recall theirs under her with the same lovely memory.

Every cow's anus was checked by the technicians who read their internal temperatures from the probes. When the green light shined, the Trail Boss was ready to move ahead with the first milking of the Season. She loved group cow milking.

"We are fine to move ahead," Ursula said and she seemed pleased. Lock your machinery and line up here to observe." The girls did as instructed and surrounded her. Ursula pointed to the still tethered cow and began the final steps of milking training.

She tested her group. "What have you forgotten?" she asked.

The trainees studied the cow and the machinery and searched for a forgotten task. Walking around it, they checked it from every angle and surveyed the belts, locks and tethers. Things seemed to be in place, but something had to be missing or Ursula would never have posed the question. Suddenly, a voice called from the group.

"Its hooves are loose," a voice said.

"Come here," Ursula said and the trainee walked toward her. "You're right. Its front hooves are not secured and the cow could hurt itself when the machinery is started. Good girl." She smiled at the beaming trainee and said, "You take care of it."

Without hesitation, the exuberant trainee found the last two dangling leather straps attached to the machine and artfully bound its front hooves behind him. With Ursula's nod of approval, the cow was ready to be milked.

"Now go and tether your own cow's hooves," she said. They scurried to their charges and finished the task with happy anticipation.

Ursula gave the example cow one last glance and noted that its current tethering faced it toward the barn full of cows, each of which had a cow's-eye view of its milking. Although the primary goal of this discipline was an educational experience for the trainees, Ursula was amenable to providing a memorable example for the rest of the cows in the herd.

> *Discipline just one, she had been taught, and all the animals will learn. Make sure your discipline is to the point and memorable. It will last.*

"Step back and find a good position to observe," she said and the trainees spread out in a full circle around her example cow.

As she tapped the controls, Ursula reinforced every step out loud so the trainees could understand the mechanics.

"First, engage the suction. There are several levels of suction and I prefer to start virgin cows at a low level so they are not milked too quickly. The dial is set at 'one.'" Every trainee made a mental note to start suction at level one.

The cow's teeth suddenly clamped down hard on the rubber bit that split his jaws.

"After the suction is started, the next step is to add some squeeze to the catheter. I'm turning this dial to 'slow' so that the cow gets used to the feeling." Ursula adjusted the dial as the trainees noted mentally to engage squeezing after suction.

The cow's hips shot forward and then relaxed before they shot forward again.

"Note the effect of squeezing," Ursula pointed out. "The reaction can be described as humping." The trainees nodded and Ursula continued. "At the slow level, the animal might even think it's enjoying it. To counteract that feeling, I'm beginning the probe's work while upping the squeezing to 'medium' and turning the suction to level two. Watch what happens."

The trainees' eyes concentrated on the cow as it became fully engaged in the process. Its hips were gyrating and thrust forward and backward as its teeth were firmly compressed on the rubber bit. Given the short tethers, the cow humped in a single spot and performed what was called the Farm's milking dance.

"Cows learn better when they are mooing," Ursula said. "To force the moo reaction, adjust the squeeze dial to 'high' and set suction to at least four or five." She watched as the girls memorized the numerical settings and simultaneously focused on the cow that was now vibrating repeatedly to the rhythm of the milking machine.

"Listen for it," Ursula warned.

It started slowly but soon grew to a level that filled the barn with the sounds of agony punctuated with macabre delight. The cow wailed its song that was picked up by the control room and reissued through the barn as a repeated mooing sound. The cow's ears drank it in and as the trainees smiled at Ursula's skill. The cows in their stalls whimpered in fright. Even though they could see the example cow screaming, what they heard was the distinctive sound of a male in agony.

"How long do we allow that to continue?" a trainee asked.

"Good question," Ursula said. "When the cow is fully milked, the sound will change dramatically and that's when you will know. That is the time to stop the movement and begin your internal work."

Ursula adjusted the controls and both the suction and squeezing ceased as the cow's torso calmed. Within moments, a new feeling invaded its body and the mooing began even louder this time.

"Listen!" Ursula commanded. "The probe is massaging the prostate and pressuring the tubes. Do you hear that?"

The girls nodded ferociously. The cow bit on the rubber between its teeth and barely moaned. "Please...please... stop!" the cow slurped from behind its bit. Ursula smiled at her first milking memory and knew that this experience would become the new memory in the girls' virgin milking recollection.

"What's happening is that it will be milked dry but the body won't feel any ejaculation. Watch and listen closely. We're about there."

The girls peered at the clear catheter covering the cock as the anal probe worked its magic in silence.

"Listen as I raise the levels and conclude this lesson," Ursula said. Her fingers turned dials and snapped switches as she described every adjustment to the eager trainees.

"Increase the suction but lower the squeeze," Ursula said. "Then alternate the process. Discipline is enforced when the cow cannot predict what will happen next. That's a very important element of all of this for you to remember – no expected rhythm," she said.

As she adjusted the settings, the cow first shuddered and trembled, then screamed and mooed, jumped up and down the slight distance its ankle tethers would allow, vibrated and quivered before finally settling into an eerie and dejected quiet. The trainees watched every movement and received a complete lesson highlighting their Trail Boss's skill as well as in the art of milking.

"See?" Ursula asked. "The cow is milked without orgasm. Ejaculation is separated from any sexual overtones immediately and completely." The girls nodded.

"What's more," she said, "if this was punishment instead of just discipline, we would continue the squeeze and suction alternation and then you would hear the what we call the 'moo heard round the Farm." Laughing at her own joke, Ursula allowed the trainees to giggle with her.

> *There is nothing comparable to hands-on experience, the Owner taught the Trail Bosses over dessert every Season.*

"Girls," Ursula reminded them, "always check the output."

With that cue, she instructed one of the trainees to check the monitors and report the cow's output to the group, and in turn, to the entire barn of cows whose faces showed wore both astonishment and disbelief. The trainee scampered to the control panel and called in a loud voice, "About half an ounce," she advised her Trail Boss.

> *Reinforce. Take every opportunity to reinforce.*

"Only half an ounce?" Ursula asked rhetorically with a smirk that could be seen throughout the barn as the weary cow dangled from its bit. "What a sorry excuse for a demo," she finished and turned back to her smiling girls.

"This is the Milking Barn," she recapped for their eager ears. "We milk the herd daily. Get your cow and practice on it." Ursula smiled as not one trainee hesitated in rushing into the stalls to find a cow that interested her. She watched as they spread asscheeks and peered inside, felt udders for fullness and spread jaws to determine what size bit to use. Ursula grinned at the control room and knew that this eager inspection would certainly be the focus of a dessert video this Season on the Farm.

Ursula studied her girls' choices. Selection of cows was a commentary on the trainees' likes and dislikes as well as the level of challenge they would set out for themselves. Given the selections, Ursula was confident that her group of trainees was near top quality.

She nodded to Control and smiled as the cows in the barn breathed in relief that they were left tethered in their stalls as the girls focused on the only some of them.

"You're next," she warned them as each ass trembled. "Today is milking day."

Chapter 23: The Bull Pen

Tara was pleased to draw the Bull Pen this Season and she intended to make the most of every moment. Her trainees crowded around her as she instructed them on Bull Pen procedures according to the Farm way. After the select pack of bulls was corralled into the pen, they were led deliberately through the mirrored entrance so they could see themselves in multiple reflections and get past their initial self-horror. Finally, they were assigned to their stalls by branded number and Tara brought the girls to the barn's southern perimeter to begin this Season's training.

The Bull Pen was one of the Owner's most well-appointed barns. The herd members that were chosen for the Bull Pen had been assessed by Marla and her team as sporting some of the largest and choicest genitals in the herd. Once a bull was assigned to Tara's pen this Season, every other farmhand could be observed checking out their packages whenever the packs joined for group activities. Being the Bull Pen's Trail Boss was a plum assignment for anyone on any Season on the Farm. Tara intended to make the most of her selection and prove worthy of the confidence shown by her Owner.

The bulls' individual personalities were less important than their measurements, so Tara figured she would have her hands full with setting up this pack's discipline. Just like every other Season, the bulls were never informed why they were selected, but hint after hint was dropped. Once in a while, a bull would figure it out. Tara recalled watching a typical male sense of undeserved pride engulf the few who understood the reasoning. Their size was consistently showcased during competitions and the bulls were frequent winners, due in large part to their attitudes. And the bulls were the only pack eligible for consideration for the biggest of the special Season-ending prizes.

Prizes, though, could wait. The first goal Tara set for the bulls was to mold the select pack into a cohesive unit.

"Line them up," Tara said to the trainees as the girls scampered about silently and with their rattan canes stinging well-shaped asscheeks to form the line. Trainees were instructed that using as few words as possible was the best training rule, especially with the hormone-laden bulls. When the pack was brought into a proper line, Tara positioned a trainee behind each one and walked the beefy line to begin this Season's formal training.

"Lift that one," Tara pointed to the first trainee and not at the bull. Circling her arm from behind around the bull's hips, the girl grabbed its beefy and just-branded scrotal sac and raised it uncomfortably high. Tara smiled as she read its number. "172," she said to no one in particular. Trainees already had their bulls' brand numbers memorized. Tara's voicing the number had no particular goal except to train the bulls to expect – and respect – every touch from their betters.

Continuing the identification process with the remainder of the bulls, Tara had each ball sac lifted higher and higher as she read the numbers aloud. Her goal was not so much to insure that the appropriate bulls were present and accounted for in her pack but to create a lineup of stretched scrotums, each in the tight grip of a young trainee. This experience was her goal.

"Our first job in the Bull Pen is to evaluate their stud potential," Tara said to her trainees. "If they are to be sent to the stud pen, then we have to ascertain their real size in all of a cock's states. We don't want to damage any of the cows, ponies or chickens when they go to stud," she said with a smile as her pack gained a glimpse into what the Season would hold in store.

"I want to know not just the size," she said, "but also duration, speed and completion rates."

Her words burned a fiery brand on the bulls' thoughts and several winced when they imagined being used as stud for the other animals. The moment that thought penetrated their brains, their faces sported a sort of horrid insight that Tara recognized and relished. Even after they wailed their way through the mirror walk and took in the sight of themselves shorn, bald and naked, the next step in training was designed to enlighten them as to their proper function on the Farm. They would be mere cocks – penises – nothing more, to be used at their Trail Boss' discretion for whichever of the animals she chose.

A few whimpers escaped their lips.

"Muzzles and bits," Tara ordered and each trainee dropped her handful of bull sac and scurried to find the muzzle and bit specifically built for each bull during Assessment.

"This time it's on real bulls," Tara said. "It'll be different from the mannequins and models you trained with. Get the bit in place, slide it over the muzzle and buckle it. After I inspect it, you can lock it. You've got thirty seconds," she said.

Trainees' fingers flew to the muzzles and bits. Each girl forced the bull's jaws apart and inserted the bit that filled the space between its teeth. Drawing the leather straps around its ears and behind its head, they buckled the bits in place while simultaneously reaching for the muzzles. Time was their enemy and installing their animal's headgear was this moment's challenge. It had to be done right – and fast.

The well-designed muzzles fit nicely around their chins and cheeks, the flaps rose over their eyes cleanly and slid into place properly. Tara silently complimented the fitting team again on their products as the trainees completed attaching the bulls' headgear.

"Not bad," she said. "That took about 40 seconds. We'll improve that time," she said.

As Tara inspected the line again, she tugged each bull's headgear to make sure of a proper fit and assured herself that all the attachments were in place and the tension had been adjusted correctly.

Tara instructed the bulls to get down on all fours on the barn floor and then said to her trainees, "Take the reins."

This training procedure was challenging every Season on the Farm for both the trainees and the bulls. It demanded that the animals fall to all fours, and that was a command that was usually met with initial resistance, especially on first day. However, the order to the girls to 'take the reins' was a clear instruction that they were eager to complete. Tara was measuring not only the bulls' acquiescence, but also her trainees' ability to take control of any bull that was reticent to follow a specific order.

> *Nip reluctant behavior in the bud, she learned, and each day will show proper progress. Whether it comes from an animal or a reluctant trainee, fix it quickly.*

Some of the bulls struggled to get into the required position yet others remained unsure, or worse, defiant. Tara waited a minute for her girls to move the process along themselves and several met that test with flying colors. She watched as each girl positioned her bull but she paid most careful attention to each trainee's technique. Brutality was uncalled for and Tara watched intently to see which could muster the command skills needed to fulfill her directive without injuring an animal. The time for brutality would come soon enough and a cohesive pack of bulls was her first goal.

One trainee's bull was reluctant to bend its knees, so she used a single stroke of her cane to buckle them from behind as she guided its girth toward the ground. Tara approved of forceful strokes to change a bull's position and nodded approval to the trainee who just modeled good skill. A second trainee's animal was on his knees but was refusing to put its hands on the floor. Tara watched the trainee grab a nipple and drag the animal downward until it was in the position Tara wanted. Out of the ten bulls in the pen, nine had been handled efficiently and Tara nodded at the control room to be certain that the tenth's efforts were taped for later small-group training.

She had the feeling, born of Seasons of experience, that this one would need special discipline. There was always one on First Day.

Standing in front of the defiant bull, Tara stayed silent as she watched the trainee use her cane, knees and hands to try to arrange it in the proper position. Every effort she made was met with an increasingly higher degree of resistance and the trainee knew that she was not yet authorized to use an equally higher level of force on an animal. Raising apologetic eyes toward her Trail Boss, the trainee seemed to be at a loss as to what to do next. Tara allowed her to wallow in her contrite stance for several minutes before intervening.

> *Make sure they understand the problem completely before fixing it, Tara learned. And make sure they have the skills to do it themselves later.*

"We have an ornery bull, do we?" Tara asked rhetorically as the trainee nodded with defeated eyes. "I will fix that," she said, "but I want to teach you how to cope with it in the future. Let's learn some new techniques, shall we?"

The trainee nodded, understanding that none of her Trail Boss's questions called for a response.

Tara assessed the girl's attitude first. After all, the purpose of First Day was twofold. Initially, the animals had to learn to live in their packs and obey pack behavior. But more important, the second goal was for the trainees to learn how to control their animals in order to achieve the first goal. Tara believed every errant behavior by an animal, especially a bull, was a learning opportunity for a trainee. She approached each situation with contagious instructional zeal that infused her trainees' experiences with the joy of their work. This session would be no exception.

"Let's state the obvious," Tara said congenially. "You want the bull on his hands and knees. Is that the goal?"

The trainee nodded a little less mournfully this time.

"And the techniques you applied aren't working?" she asked.

The girl nodded again but this time with a hint of a slight smile on her face.

"Well," Tara said, "we *could* use the prod. Electric shock works wonders every time. But you aren't yet authorized for that, are you? I wonder if there isn't a method to be tried before that one."

Standing quietly and tapping her boot against the barn floor, Tara waited for her trainee to respond.

Wait for it, she had been taught. Give them time to understand that they already know the answer. Make them say aloud what they already know in their heads.

After several seconds of uncomfortable silence while the trainee's eyes darted around the platform searching among her fellow trainees for an answer, Tara watched her finally focus on a set of tools that the Intake team had put together for use on this Season's bulls.

Watch for the moment when they get it and understand. It's a wonderful moment for a trainee and the Trail Boss.

Tara waited for the girl to walk the few feet to the tools and choose the right one for this job.

With her mind focused on solving the task, the trainee dropped the bull's sac and moved to the tools. After locating her bull's number on its specially-designed device, she reached into the set of tools and emerged with the lone object that brought a smile to Tara's lips. After turning the handle to ensure it was completely charged, she strode behind her bull and looked at her Trail Boss for permission to begin.

A small nod later and the trainee's hands began a thoroughly-trained process. Just this time, it was being done on a live bull.

After pulling the bull's asscheeks apart, the girl pressed the long clear rod against its anus and pressed the tip to squirt a small amount of Farm Oil into its hole. Tara studied its face as the bull's eyes widened and jaw bit down on its muzzle. From her vantage, Tara focused on the bull's reactions as the trainee continued her efforts. When the rod was inserted a few inches, Tara knew she could judge the approximate depth from how wide the bull's eyes shot open. From the back, she measured it from the remainder of the rod that extended from its ass. She smiled at its humiliated expression and knew that the bull had no notion of what would happen next during this discipline and to complete breaking its defiance.

After squirting a bit more oil from the rod in the bull's ass, the trainee pressed the rod in several more inches with a single well-rehearsed thrust. Tara nodded and silently commended both Fitting and Measurement for their precise work. The rod's length fit the bull's ass perfectly and she was sure there was not a fraction of an inch still extending into daylight.

The bull bellowed in surprise. The trainee managed a smile.

Tara knew that the process was only half finished. Gathering her trainees to observe this exercise from a better vantage, Tara nodded one more time to the trainee and issued her approval to continue. Each trainee knew what was about to happen, but none had seen it done yet with a live bull. The group's anticipation grew as the nine kneeling bulls held their positions in fear of what nefarious activity was unfolding at the end of their line.

They didn't have to wait long. The trainee pressed a button and the bull screamed from the depths of its gut in a growl that reached all corners of the barn's ceiling, where the control room staff made sure it reverberated off the barn walls and echoed back into the offender's ears. Bull bellow was the Farm's symphony of discipline that every animal had to hear on First Day. Its resistance would always be overcome; its reticence conquered; and its defeat assured. That was the Farm way.

The bull's body went into repeated spasms as it dropped to its knees, shrieking and bucking. The trainee allowed its rhythmic humping to continue until the animal realized that it hadn't yet positioned its front hooves on the barn floor as initially instructed.

Unable to think clearly with the spasms of pain coursing through its body, the bull screamed repeatedly before falling to the floor with a thud. Much to Tara's approval, the trainee switched off the rod and extracted it from the animal's anus artfully.

The bull was now on all fours and the trainee held its reins. Mission accomplished. With a successful lesson performed for both the trainees and the bulls, Tara moved immediately to the next task.

Never dwell, she was taught. Discipline, achieve the goal, and move on.

"I want them hard," the Trail Boss said simply.

As studs, bulls' genital elongation and degree of erection would often be required by the trainers, Trail Bosses and on occasion, the trainees. Learning how to create a stiff shaft on demand was a critical goal of bull training. First Day was the perfect time to learn this procedure. Tara watched her trainees straddle the bulls, bend low, and touch their unfettered breasts to the bulls' backs. Sometimes, just their naked dangling nipples were enough to harden even the defiant ones.

As she walked up and down the platform, Tara's focused on each bull's drooping shaft. Her nod to the control room started the timers. This baseline statistic would be used as part of an evaluative measurement against which their future success would be judged. As the girls pressed their breasts against the bulls' shoulders and backs, their hands circled the bulls' hips and grasped their still floppy cocks between their fingers. The trainees had been taught that tugging and pulling rarely achieved a hard cock, but they were also cautioned against traditional male masturbation techniques. The bulls were never allowed to enjoy or complete this experience; rather, they were to be conditioned solely to respond to the order to erect, and as their training progressed, to harden at merely a trainer's look. Staying on the right side of the fine line between a hard cock and accidental ejaculation absorbed all of Tara's concentration at this moment.

"In order to achieve a stiff cock, the animal's shaft has to be manipulated," Tara's voice was strong as she shared her Seasons of experience with her students. "Circle two fingers behind the ball sac and squeeze." She waited for them to lean in and comply. Then she added, "Now circle two fingers of your the other hand at the base of the shaft."

Her voice was instructive. "Very slowly, move the shaft circle toward the tip. Do not touch the tip. I'll count to five. Do not reach the end until I reach five."

The girls shifted their weight to gain better grips and waited for the countdown.

"One," Tara said as she walked the line and peered under the bulls' bellies to see the trainees' fingers in action.

"Two," she said as she gripped one trainee's fingers and pressed them more tightly behind the sac.

"Three and breathe," she told them as the girls drank in cool air, realizing that Tara knew they had been holding their collective breaths. A few giggled and one snickered. Tara drew their attention back to their work with a single word.

"Four," she said loudly and ran her own fingers along the tips of several cocks to determine if any shafts were dripping or worse, were too engorged at this point of the exercise.

"Five," she said and added quickly, "Let GO! Get your face underneath and check your bull's cock."

The trainees scrambled off their bulls' backs and climbed under their bellies to view the cocks and assess their success rate. Using little metal rulers that dangled from a loop on their leather shorts, the trainees measured each cock and used the attached flexible ruler to measure circumference. Memorizing the results, they scrambled back to the tablets and recorded the data.

Tara studied her tablet that updated with their measurements.

"This one," she pointed to the second bull in line, "measures only six and a half. Certainly you can do better than that." As she flipped to the next screen, a small moan escaped the mortified bull's lips.

"Ah," she exclaimed happily and pointed at the fourth bull, "its cock measures seven and a quarter. That's a fine result for First Day." The bull sighed with relief and embarrassment as its most personal numbers were called aloud in the barn.

"What's this?" Tara asked with rhetorical concern. "Do we have a soft cock in the Bull Pen?" Stomping her boots on the barn floor as she strode toward the eighth bull, Tara reached under its belly to ascertain the lack of length for herself. "That appears to be an accurate and unfortunate measurement," she added. Your bull is unresponsive because we know it can get bigger than this puny result or it would never have been assigned to the Bull Pen." Her comment to the trainee holding his reins was really directed to everyone.

"What do we do with unresponsive cocks?" The question hung awaiting an answer and each trainee struggled to come up with the perfect response before speaking. Tara waited for them to recall their training on the bull mannequins and was rewarded with a single voice that replied correctly.

"We train bull cocks to erect using an electrical stimulator," the voice said. All the trainees had been taught that bulls respond quickly to direct electrical stimulation.

"Excellent," Tara said approvingly and drew a smile from her bright trainee. Turning her attention to the eighth bull's trainee, Tara instructed her to visit the tool set and to select the stimulator with the bull's number etched on it. Watching her other girls' faces fall in dismay, she said, "All of you! Go get your stimulators. We'll do this together and learn to perform the task properly."

A good group is happy when they're working together.
It was an old Farm lesson and it was still a useful one.

Grins spread ear-to-ear as the girls assembled their tools. Tara stood in front of the eighth bull's muzzle and spoke into its fear-stricken face.

"You might not enjoy this," she said and smiled, "but that shaft *will* respond. I've never had a bull fail First Day training by not having a hard cock for my use." Watching his eyes fill with tears as she discussed its cock's lackluster performance as if it were merely a toy for her to do with as she pleased, Tara petted its head in an offhand manner that reinforced its lowly status in the Bull Pen. "Every bull gets hard when I want it to," Tara threatened evilly.

The trainees donned latex gloves and prepared the simulators for use on their bulls. Almost merry with anticipation, the snap of gloves resounded throughout the barn. Each bull would come to learn the sound of gloves snapping onto trainees' hands and what it meant. Some tried to grit their teeth but the rubber bits prevented that as well. A few easy-to-ignore bull grunts greeted the trainees' return.

"Let's remind you how this works," Tara said to her girls. "First, make sure your bull is sufficiently lubricated. Second, insert the stimulator while feeling with your fingers for the appropriate angle so you don't nick anything important. Third, wait for my command before you turn it on."

Watching the eager group of trainees, Tara asked the most important question of their training.

"How much lubrication is enough?" she asked them all.

"There is never too much lube," they replied in singsong unison.

"Get started," she said as she walked the line again and greeted each bull's grimacing face with a wicked smile as her red sash fluttered with each step.

The trainees lathered lubrication between the bulls' asscheeks, dipping their fingers deeper inside repeatedly to spread the juicy gel deep into each anus. When satisfied there was enough to start, they finally inserted one finger deep inside to find their bull's exact angle of perfect penetration. As they forced another finger in after another, Tara listened to the sweet sound of bull bellowing that boomed throughout the barn. Control enjoyed taping the bellowing and returned it loudly. Even when the animals ceased moaning, their recorded noise was played and replayed in a growing crescendo. It was exciting background music for the girls' bull training.

Studying her trainees, Tara was confident they had each found the perfect path into the bulls' insides. "Insert the stimulators," she said clearly, but do not turn them on until instructed."

As the girls worked the long devices into their bulls' anuses, the animals' faces contorted first in pain and then in abject humiliation. Not only had their cocks been measured aloud for length, but now their rectums were open targets for these women to explore. Their moaning increased and Control played it back to them again and again. Animal bellow was a welcome sound in the bull barn. As Tara stepped down the back of the line, she watched each trainee proudly display her bull's anus with the long stimulator sticking out as if in a pack salute to Tara's authority.

"Turn them on," she said after inspecting each stimulator's position.

As if the walls of the barn had come crashing down, the bulls issued a simultaneous roar of agony as the stimulators began their task. A single shot of low current flew through them and landed directly on their prostates which, in turn, caused every shaft to engorge and become very thick. Yet not one bull felt the beginning of orgasm. The sight was delightful every Season and Tara loved watching the bulls salute her with their roar.

"Tighten the reins so I can inspect the cocks," Tara said.

The bulls were pulled up to their knees. Every cock was thick and erect, standing up as if greeting her, and a few dripped from the tip. "Very good, girls," she commented. "Measure and record the results on your tablets and let Control know if you've got an especially big one," she said.

"Mine is eight!" a trainee yellowed almost deliriously. Tara glanced her way and hated to burst her bubble by telling her she was certain there was a longer one in the pack.

"I've got eight and a half," another called out.

"Eight and three quarters!" a third shouted joyfully.

For their part, the bulls, now kneeling on their haunches with their reins gripped tightly by the trainees, suffered the ignominy of having their penises put on display for very loud comparison. Some simply shut their eyes as if to make their humiliation go away while others allowed mortified tears to fall down their muzzles and seep onto their chins. One or two were trying without success to will their errant erections down.

That last behavior was never tolerated on the Farm. A cock belonged to the Owner, no matter who wore it during the Season. It was obviously time for another important First Day lesson.

"Bulls 165 and 342 are softening," Tara said. "What is the correct procedure to harden them again?"

Again, the girls thought for a few moments before one of them replied. "Change the stimulation to smaller doses but with higher frequency," she said.

"Good girl," Tara replied. "Girls, make the necessary stimulator adjustments and wait for my signal."

The trainees adjusted the stimulators' settings as they had been taught repeatedly in training. Tara watched their eagerness and made sure she checked every stimulator carefully before she allowed the current to be turned on.

Never damage a bull's cock, she had learned. Bull cocks were used on the Farm almost daily and there was no time for a cock – or its bull – to be unavailable for stud.

"Turn them on," Tara said.

Almost immediately, all ten bulls' throats released a tortured scream of pain. Every cock grew resplendent in its glory and when the stimulation lessened momentarily, they cried out in agony. Soon, Tara increased the stimulation from her master control and another jolt was sent directly into its target. Dwindling measurements of cock height and width were improved immediately. One by one, the bulls realized that their organs would dance to Tara's specifications and there was nothing they could do to prevent it.

"Again!" Tara said.

The bulls' shrieks filled the barn a second time and were sent back to them by Control as an auditory memory of their lesson. Shock filled their faces as they continued to learn First Day's lesson and Tara watched them carefully. The process of education for the trainees always produced a concomitant effect on the animals. It was particularly intense in the Bull Pen because bigger cocks brought raging hormones with them, and Tara was thrilled to have this assignment this Season. She always loved training the Bulls and her joy over cock control made her almost giddy.

"Again!" she said even more happily.

By now, the bulls' cocks were ready to burst, but Tara knew that no cock would ejaculate unless she ordered that specific stimulator setting. Prostate glands were wonderful little tools to be used and Tara taught that lesson to her trainees. The cocks' alternating hardening and softening was completely in her control and little by little, she knew that her power over their organs trickled into the bulls' brains and became their new understanding of what this Season on the Farm would be like. Of course, no animal should be overworked on First Day, so Tara issued a challenge to her trainees.

"What happens if I increase the charge?" she asked.

All the trainees responded in unison. "Every cock would burst!" they replied happily.

"Remove the stimulators," Tara said the trainees dutifully shut them off. "Put them into sterilization," she reminded them.

"Down on all fours," she said over her shoulder toward the bulls as she busied herself with entering her findings on her tablet and then overseeing the cleaning process. To her satisfaction, every bull assumed the all-fours position and waited silently between heaving sobs for the next command. First Day in the Bull Pen was becoming a huge success.

"Line up on either side of me," Tara said and the trainees fell into a perfect line. All the women stared directly into the bulls' weary eyes. "Get them into their stalls and hooked up to the regulators so they are ready for afternoon training." Her voice was clear and cold. "Perhaps we'll get some use out of them tonight. I hear that the cows are being stretched and we might just enjoy a little stud play later."

The girls squealed in delight as they took each bull's reins and secured them in their stalls. Strapping the regulators around the now-flaccid organs so that any cock movement would be detected and reported, they left the bulls in the barn to the sweet replay of their bellowing as they followed Tara to the training room to plan the afternoon's events.

Not one bull even thought about wanting to have an erection without Tara's order for the rest of the afternoon.

Chapter 24: The Pony Corral

No one wore Farm leathers quite like Sharon. Even though she was not selected to work as Trail Boss in the Pony Corral every Season, the Owner was delighted when Sharon's name was suggested this Season. She decided that the ponies were to be in Sharon's hands for the Season and looked forward to several interesting escapades. She usually didn't have enough time to observe all of First Day training until Katrina had sorted out the interesting events and displayed them on her bank of monitors. But having Sharon lead the Pony Corral made her more eager to watch highlights of First Day.

The Intake and Processing teams were always diligent in assigning the new animals into groups; however, as a rule, the ponies were evaluated several times before being assigned to that particular herd. There was something special about being in pony training on the Farm and Sharon seemed to have visceral understanding of the exceptional qualities needed by Farm ponies. In fact, she could routinely draw more skill out of a pony than anyone else might even anticipate and produced more from every pony than could be predicted.

The ponies in Sharon's corral always performed exceptionally. They developed into proud and feisty – but always obedient – animals. They trotted her stringent line. They knew their place, excelled during their Season and at the Season's end very often stood in line to sign up for another Farm Season.

The psychological and physical makeups of ponies were special. The Owner reminded her staff to scour the database and evaluate them during pre-acceptance face-to-face interviews to discover the applicants who loved the outdoors, jogged or ran long distances routinely, got along well with others and had strong enough backs to hold their riders. In addition, there was an intense psychological component of being a pony on her Farm that the Owner always looked for in every application.

It was simple. She demanded passion from her ponies.

Sharon surveyed her pack and assembled her girls for First Day training. She rarely found a reason to delay beginning in earnest; in fact, her training ran long and hard even on First Day. The electric prod that always hung from her leathers solved even the most reluctant herd members' problems and brought about quick attitude adjustments when and where they were needed. Only the Pony Corral trainees were issued governed electrical prods on First Day so that their use was recorded. Until they were better experienced, their prods' electrical charge was limited but still very effective.

Breaking a pack of wild ponies was Sharon's delight.

The pack stood in a loose line in the corral and Sharon observed their sagging shoulders with an audible sigh of dismay. First Day lessons always started with stance and in short order every pony would become a proud Farm animal worthy of being ridden by one of her trainees. Her technique was as powerful as it was brief.

"Stand UP!" she said to the sloppy group. The ponies shook their shoulders and attempted to comply but their results were too slipshod for Sharon's expectations.

"Shoulders BACK!" she said loudly and a few more complied, but their shoddy demeanor merited instant correction. Her boots raised clouds of dust as she tromped across the corral's dirt floor toward them. Sharon strode toward the first pony in line and demanded that it report its number to her. The embarrassed pony with downcast eyes silently sought a trainee to lift his sac and read its identification but Sharon's voice was louder this time. "Don't move!" she cautioned her girls. Unsure of what to do now, the pony hung its head in shame.

"You!" she turned to the next pony in line, "Lift its sac so I can see its brand."

Her demand astonished the second pony as well as the rest of the pack but a quick shot of pain from Sharon's prod touched its shoulder and spurred it to grasp the forgetful pony's scrotum and lift it high. Tersely, Sharon said, "Fourteen! Memorize that!" and moved to the next pony in line. She knew her command would be obeyed and that pony would never again forget its branded number.

"Number!" she demanded and as the prod approached the third pony's stifle, it grasped its neighbor's ball sac and yanked it up so Sharon could call out its number as well. And so she went down the line, each pony lifting another's genitals to comply with her order that no longer needed to be spoken. Her point had been made swiftly and the ponies were now much more desensitized to touching one another's testicles. Every trainee watched the process and made a mental note as to how to break down touch shyness among ponies by using Sharon's well-seasoned methods.

Use as few words as possible. Make them understand what you want from your actions so you need fewer words. Authority is projected from within.

"Stand UP!" she said again and all 25 ponies stood straight and tall, their chests pushed out and their bellies sucked in. Sharon turned her back on the now-proper lineup and spoke to the trainees behind her.

"Bits and reins," she said and the trainees ran to the tack room to obtain the required items. Each pony's custom-fit bit, throatlatch, headpiece and noseband were attached to beautiful leather reins that would be used all Season for training. Every pony had two sets: one for everyday training and a nicer set for shows. Today was a training day and the trainers fingered the thick leather almost lovingly as they returned to their line.

"Each of you is to assigned a pony based on your height and weight and the pony's physical capabilities," Sharon said. "Larger and taller trainees will choose huskier ponies. Stand behind your chosen pony and I'll evaluate your selections. Hop to it!" Sharon stared at the trainees who flew to lineup of ponies and palpated their forearms, hocks, near legs and fetlocks, opened their muzzles to assess bit strength, and flexed their shoulders, elbows and knees to decide if they could carry their weight. In a few minutes, every trainee stood behind a steed and waited for their Trail Boss' approval.

Sharon walked down the line and performed her own inspection of the ponies' girth and power. Lifting and dropping each trainee's breasts and bellies while assessing the trainee's weight and height, Sharon's hands inspected every inch of the ponies and trainees. Finally, she unzipped the trainees' leather shorts and pulled each pair down to the girl's knees. Humiliated to be naked in front of the animals, the girls were chagrinned by the nakedness she inflicted on them so casually.

"My girls and their ponies must be a single unit, working as a single body," Sharon explained coolly. "Except for Competition or shows, you must feel every one of their muscles work as they must feel your thighs press and pull them into position. You will work naked this Season," she said. The stunned trainees reluctantly stepped out of their shorts. One or two pony cocks stiffened when they saw the naked trainees and as soon as one tasted the kiss of the Trail Boss' prod, the others quickly learned that stiff cocks were not allowed. Only Sharon could order them to have one.

Except for Sharon, the entire corral was now naked and the Owner smiled at the scene on her monitors. She loved the Pony Barn and Sharon's training would continue to delight her all afternoon.

"Get the ponies in a circle facing out, and stand in front of your pony," Sharon said. Then she added, "Ponies get on your knees."

When her commands were carried out, Sharon walked in a tight circle around them and pressed each trainee forward so that every set of the girls' glistening labia were almost touching each pony's nostrils. Unable to breathe without inhaling a woman's scent, the ponies were issued their most difficult order so far.

"Learn your rider's smell, and be able to recognize her with your eyes shut," Sharon said.

The ponies slowly began sniffing the women's vaginas that touched their noses and tried to memorize their aromas somewhere in an unused part of their brains. Their nostrils flared each time they inhaled as their heads filled with the trainees' sweet musk. As the girls stood naked and were examined by their pony's noses, Sharon used her short crop to spread the women's legs further apart.

"Get your nose INSIDE!" she said loudly as she pushed the ponies snouts deeper between the women's legs and made them inhale again. The trainees allowed the ponies' snouts to enter; after all, they knew that Sharon was somewhere behind them with a prod and none of them wanted to taste her ire in the corral in front of the animals.

"Now taste them," Sharon ordered as the trainees trembled from this new and unforeseen embarrassment. As Sharon walked the inner circle again, one or two reluctant ponies tasted the prod's kiss on their asscheeks. The shock made them press their faces deeper between the trainees' lips and lick more deeply between the trainees' legs as they tried to learn their trainer's unique flavor. A few trainees whimpered from indignity as the licking and tasting continued for several minutes until Sharon was satisfied.

"Girls, face me," Sharon said evenly as the trainees spun away from their pony's dripping lips. As she walked the circle and made eye contact with each of her girls, she grabbed each trainee by her nipples and pushed her into her pony's face. Everyone in the Pony Corral knew what the next order would be. Sharon made them wait before issuing it.

Make them anticipate even when they know what is going to happen. They should never assume they know your next command. Keep them at the peak of anticipation.

"Spread your legs," she instructed the trainees. "Ponies, taste."

Her staccato command filled the corral as the ponies extended their tongues and drove them deep inside the trainees' asscheeks. Too humiliated to move and unable to even imagine objecting, the girls allowed the animals' tongues to enter deep inside their asscheeks. She watched as some girls spread their legs farther, bent slightly or used their hands to spread their cheeks farther apart. Sharon smiled at their expressions of mutual distaste.

"Learn that a pony is just an animal trained to respond," Sharon said. "It is no more or no less than that and its training must be complete. My ponies are the Farm pack that win Competitions. My ponies are studded out to entertain other animals as a reward for performance excellence. Whenever they are in the corral, they are in training. We never stop training. We have no training limits in this corral."

She walked as she talked and circled the entire group as she explained her corral rules.

The trainees began to recognize the Pony Corral's uniqueness. For their part, the ponies' alarm at what their Season on the Farm would entail increased dramatically when they heard her say 'studded out' and the 'no limits' warning. They were not simply humiliated; they were reduced to whimpering objects filled with abject terror.

In less than 20 minutes into the Season, Sharon had achieved her primary goal. Real training could now begin.

"First, we run them," she said and issued each trainee a single tail whip. After hours of practice during the off season, each trainee had passed a competency test and was certified by Processing to use the whip. There was never a reason to damage the ponies, Sharon knew, but proper whipping was a big part of the Farm way of training in the Pony Corral.

"In a circle," Sharon said. "Maintain proper spacing between them and pay attention to the pace. Not too fast," she said.

Sharon leaned against the corral fence and watched the trainees exercise the ponies. On her own monitors, the Owner also observed the process, searching for exceptional ponies or trainers who might be candidates for her own enjoyment. An occasional pony found its way into the Owner's prize corral for a Season if it exemplified the stance and gait she wanted.

Later in the corral, the ponies knelt in a circle waiting for every command to be issued. They had learned how to avoid a taste of the prod or the new flavor of the whips that were cracking merrily above their heads.

"Up!" a trainee said with a hint of hesitation in her voice. Nonetheless, 25 ponies rose on their hooves.

"Spread apart," another trainee instructed and the ponies separated themselves from one another as they formed a loose ring around the corral's rail.

"Jog in place," a third trainee ordered and 25 ponies raised and lowered their legs while smashing their bare hooves into the dirt in the stationary drill.

Sharon observed her girls readying the ponies to begin their training for the Season. So far, she was pleased with her underlings' work and even though they were still smarting from their own nakedness, they appeared to have risen above their humiliation and performed the training almost to the level that she required in the corral.

"Take the reins," Sharon said to her girls.

Each trainee grasped her pony's long leather reins and pulled each forward by the bit that split its jaws. It didn't take long for them to figure out what Sharon had in mind, and one by one, they ran alongside their ponies trying to form a grand circle in the corral. With the trainees' naked breasts jumping up and down while the ponies' cocks bobbed with each step, the naked group grew into a shining sweaty procession that captured Sharon's attention.

In the Manor House, the Owner bent closer to her main monitor. Knowing that her Owner's interest would grow, Katrina zoomed in on one trainee-and-pony pair after another so that the Owner could observe each of the 25 duos as they jogged around the corral's perimeter. First Day training always tested Katrina's ability to predict which ponies would intrigue her Owner and she had to be sure to capture the special ones in repeated close-up shots.

Sharon stepped to the center of the ring, raised her whip and issued a single instruction.

"Faster!" she said and cracked the whip expertly against the pony's asscheeks that were closest to her. The visible red welt it left would be a suitable reminder for that pony that it had gained the Trail Boss' attention on First Day. In the future, a pony would learn to wear its Trail Boss's mark proudly. But on First Day, it was merely a big red mark on the pony's backside and a first reminder of pony discipline training.

The faster pace challenged the pack to keep up and maintain a well-spaced ring at the same time. A few trainees were not leading their ponies to Sharon's satisfaction so she raised her whip again and this time landed it directly on the asscheeks of a slow trainer. Her yelp of surprise from the stinging pain greeted Sharon's stroke but the lesson was clearly understood. The girl picked up her pace and dragged her pony by its bit to the proper speed. The proper speed, she learned, was whatever her Trail Boss wanted at the moment.

One after another, Sharon alternated between whipping the asses of trainees and ponies so that every pair of cheeks wore her red welt. At trainee dinner, Sharon knew, everyone would recognize which trainees were assigned to the Pony Corral by their tender asses and reluctance to be seated. She smiled at the thought and hoped that Katrina would provide a few minutes of that recording for Trail Boss' dessert discussion. Sharon loved watching the tapes of her trainees' discipline almost as much as when they were forced to strip their leathers for the entire working Season in the Pony Corral. It was no wonder that the Owner usually found promotion-worthy material among Sharon's trainees.

"Faster!" she said and the pairs galloped around the corral. The midday sun poured down on naked skin and sweat poured off trainee and pony alike. Sharon continued the run even faster and after several more minutes, finally halted the herd.

"Jog in place," she told the ponies. "Trainees, sit on the ground around me."

As the ponies performed what would become the routine step-in-place for their Trail Boss and lifted their legs one after another in the training dance, the exhausted trainees plopped to the brown dirt that immediately stuck to their sweaty skin. Huffing and puffing, they waited in silence for Sharon to address them.

> *Keep them waiting. Then wait one moment longer.*
> *Then you will always have their attention whenever*
> *you speak.*

Finally, she looked down at them.

"Now you know what it feels like to be a pony in my herd," she said as some trainees nodded and others simply sat in quiet understanding. "You cannot command without knowing what it means to serve." Allowing her words to sink in, Sharon noticed a few more heads nodding in appreciation for the insight she had just given them.

"There will be times you will be treated like the ponies," she warned, "and eventually you will learn to become their superiors. But you and your pony must develop an intimate knowledge of each other. It must react to your thoughts; it must respond to your slightest physical shift. Likewise," Sharon drew a deep breath to indicate the importance of her next words, "you must feel your pony's abilities intimately and work to expand them. I will push your animal's limits and you must know without doubt where its real limits lie."

The girls nodded in unison at the sense of her words.

"Finally," Sharon said, "you will learn how to break a pony without breaking its spirit. That is your challenge. That is your goal. Nothing less is acceptable."

Expand horizons every day. Never break them.

After a few minutes of silence, Sharon ordered the trainees to take the ponies into the barn so they could be hosed off, scrubbed down and returned to the corral for the next training session.

In front of her bank of monitors, the Owner nodded in approval of Sharon's First Day training accomplishments. She sipped tea as Katrina engaged the barn monitors so their hosing and scrubbing could be displayed for her pleasure.

Chapter 25: The Coops

Not every animal on the Farm was to be a hard-working commodity. A Season on the Farm required a special pack that adorned the Chicken Coop. The Coop was where the Owner housed the animals who would fulfill the Farm's esthetic requirements. Each of the Farm's potential chickens and a few roosters had been screened prior to its admission because once settled in the Coop, they would perform special functions and they had to be predisposed and well suited for the task. Rhonda smiled broadly when she was given the chickens this Season to train. Chickens were fun.

As she led her flock into the Coop and marched them by the full-length mirrors, Rhonda knew from experience that the chickens' personalities would cause their cry of self-recognition to resound through their new home in a louder series of wails than the other packs. In her Seasons of experience, Rhonda knew that the chickens were more sensitive to personal appearance; in fact, some of them could have been called almost prissy in their former lives. Men who stood in front of mirrors and slicked their hair back; men who used too many skin treatments and men who fussed too much about their appearances.

They were the Farm's chickens and their new style was completely controlled by Rhonda's expertise.

This Season would be no exception. Rhonda listened to them cluck their displeasure at seeing the stream of naked and featherless bodies pass by the mirrors. They began to realize they were looking at new incarnations of themselves and were horrified at how they appeared. She watched them recognize that they were no longer individuals with hair to fix or clothing to adjust; rather, they were a single flock of birds that were under her auspices for the Season. What they would become was totally up to Rhonda. What they would do, how they would dress, when they served the other herds were all within her power. Accustomed to dressing up in frills and lace when they thought no one was looking during their former lives, the chickens had to understand that their peccadilloes for pretty things would now entertain the Farm staff and at times other packs in the herd. What they didn't yet even have an inkling of yet is that they would provide some very special services as well.

She lined them up in single file in the Coop's central aisle. As she marched through the lineup of featherless fowl, Rhonda inspected each one long and hard. Nothing was spared her scrutiny and nothing evaded her examination. The chickens were often bisexual before they arrived on the Farm, even if they hadn't yet admitted it to themselves yet. But some of chicken neophytes were merely bi-curious. This year's flock was no different any other Season and their identification numbers were clear indicators of which of Rhonda's chickens fit into specific flock categories.

"Sit on your rumps," she said as the chickens struggled to plop their asscheeks on the narrow aisle's floor. "Bend your shanks up and press your toes next to your hips," she said to the struggling group.

She watched as they wrestled with gravity and the small space to position their hindquarters as she directed. Some held onto their ankles for support while others flattened their hands against the narrow floor for balance.

"This is roosting," she said flatly to teach them all the new term. "When the roosting bell rings, get into this position." She watched their faces try to comprehend what the roosting bell was and what the function of this uncomfortable and off-balance position meant for them this Season. A few looked like they would topple over if she brushed against them and Rhonda took an extra moment to enjoy their physical and mental discomfort.

Keep them off-balance both physically and mentally.
Comfort is contradictory to training.

"Girls," Rhonda said as she glanced at her group of trainees, "it's time to get them identified and assigned to their roosts." The trainees straightened their shoulders and jutted out their breasts as they waited for the Trail Boss' instruction to begin.

"Now," Rhonda said over her shoulder as she glanced at the control room's dark window to remind them that filming should be focused on the next tasks.

The trainees moved toward the roosting chickens and easily grabbed each ball sac to determine both the chicken's identification number as well as each chicken's sexual orientation. For several Seasons, the Owner and Coop Trail Boss discussed the relative merits of assigning the chickens into roosts based on similar orientations or mixing them up throughout the nests. Each idea had advantages and through Seasons of experimenting, they had devised a system that worked well for the Farm's needs from its chickens.

They decided that no chicken would have a permanent roost during a single Season. Its nest would be assigned daily so that no relationships were developed or touching one another were committed by chickens whose bent might be a problem with inappropriate interactions. When it was time for the chickens to be serviced by a rooster, the nests would be rearranged. Given that chickens had responsibilities for the sexual relief and emotional feeding of other Farm animals and were often used by the packs for relief or just for experimenting with Assessment's new research, the Owner ensured that the chickens would have no relationships with each other.

It was better for the Farm when the chickens learned that their functions were arbitrary. The chickens were the Farm's toys and were used by the animals as the Owner saw fit. It took a special and highly skilled Trail Boss to develop responsive chickens in a single Season.

The trainees busied themselves checking their birds' ID numbers and dragged them by their scrotums through the various levels of nests in the coop's risers. Once they were assigned to their nests for today, the trainees turned their attention to their Trail Boss who stood near the five that were left over. As indicated by their identification numbers, these were to be the roosters whose were the cocks that would service the flock. They were never housed too closely to the fledgling birds.

"Bring them here," Rhonda called to her girls across the coop.

The five remaining members of the flock were marched in single file by their sacs to their Season's home. Once they reached the rear of the Coop and the gates were opened, the trainees settled them into their roosts and Rhonda approached the small group.

"You are Farm roosters," she informed the group who tried to understand what she meant from their incomprehensible title, "and you will service my chickens whenever I tell you to do so. In the meantime…" she let her words fade away as she lifted a gleaming metal bar and wrapped the it around one rooster's neck and snapped the lock shut.

Perched on its hocks, the new rooster squealed in dismay at the heavy and very tight collar.

"You will be locked up when you are not in training or servicing the Farm animals," Rhonda finished. They gasped almost as one as they finally figured out what this Season on the Farm held in store for them.

Turning toward the wall of nests, she informed the flock in a loud voice that sang through the metal rooster gates that their Season on the Farm could be understood as one single task. They were there to service the other animals. As their eyes flew open in shock, she ordered her trainees to begin training.

The girls were well practiced. First they unlocked each nest's gates and inspected the costumes in the wardrobe area. A large portion of chicken training centered on making the flock look sexually alluring for the packs. Farm staff had learned that the male animals would respond more quickly to pretty chickens. Their outfits would clearly identify their roles – which chickens would be used for physical comfort and which would be trained to provide sexual relief. During the Season, the chickens' role was specifically to satisfy the packs' needs and their training made them understand how to excite and attract specified packs. They would learn to strut throughout the Farm's barns and sties where the Farm animals were housed and provide instant release for those animals whose training or special performance called for sexual relief. Chickens were never leashed; in fact, they rarely stepped outside the safety of their coop's perimeter without a trainer or Trail Boss to protect them. Farm animals could be very greedy right before relief sessions while others simply needed some feathered cuddling to overcome anxiety or help them sleep.

One by one, the trainees outfitted their chickens with wigs, frilly lace, open panties, garter belts, and sheer stockings to create clearly identifiable chickens that were a vital part of Farm life. All beasts need food to eat and water to drink for health but physical sexual relief worked wonders to improve the herd's attitude. The Owner understood all of her animals' needs and the chickens took on an increasingly important role every Season. Each day, they were dressed in unique outfits so that no chicken could be identified by its wardrobe and build up a following among the animals in the herds. The Owner didn't want any one chicken's prowess to exhaust it before she was ready to use it at Competition.

After an hour of preparation, Rhonda inspected her flock.

"Stand them up," she ordered the trainees. "Take them to the yard."

In single line, the nicely-adorned chickens stepped hesitantly one behind the other as they made their way from the safety of the coop's walls into the bright sunlight and toward an uncertain future. As Rhonda stood in the doorway and smiled approvingly at each trainee's efforts, the chickens were left standing by themselves in the fenced pen. All they could do was stare at each other and explore the confines of their fenced-in area.

The low fence that circled the perimeter of the yard seemed to afford neither protection nor security. Each chicken figured it could easily lift its toes and step over the low railings. The flock seemed almost cocky at the idea of freedom that seemed to be theirs. Smiles of possibility dotted their beaks as Rhonda addressed her trainees.

"Girls, attach the collars," she said.

Each trainee grabbed a leather strap dangling from a carabineer on her shorts and adjusted it behind each chicken's ball sac before tightening the straps and locking the whole contraption in place. After Rhonda inspected each for width and tightness, she pointed to the green field beyond the low fence and offered the chickens a chance to walk the Farm.

"Take a short walk," she said, "and when roosting bell rings, scurry to your nest and roost." She watched as their faces seemed to show the joy of their growing trust in her. Then she added, "Go now." Her voice was soft and reassuring. Rhonda had years of experience with chickens and their peccadilloes. They were a special lot and she knew how to train them quickly and efficiently.

The flock moved gingerly toward the fence and began climbing over it in hopes of a romp in the lush green grass. One by one, they started the climb and were now all straddling the fence.

Almost instantaneously, each fell to the dirt and all writhed in agony. Their throats screamed horrified groans, painful shouts and even a few curses. They balled up their bodies in vain attempts to throw off the unrelenting torture of the electrical current inflicted on their balls and cocks. Finally Rhonda nodded to Control and the current ceased. The hapless chickens, still squirming on the dirt, looked up at her in shock.

"Ball collars are electrified," Rhonda said smugly.

Rhonda watched her chickens began to understand that no animal was free on the Farm. They were constrained to wherever their Trail Boss told them to be and sneaking off or running away was out of the question.

"Get up," she ordered and the chickens rose first to their knees and then to their bare feet in the dirt. "Girls, let's get them shod. We don't need any more dirty chicken toes," she said.

The trainees hurried into the coop to find the shoes that had been set out next to their chicken's identification number. It was one thing to dress them up, the Owner learned, but it was quite another to make sure their feet were cared for in well-fitting shoes. A tight pair of panties might leave only a visible line, but badly fitting shoes could injure chickens' claws.

As the trainees emerged into the sunlight carrying an array of both platform and stiletto pumps, the chickens were put their asses in in the dirt for fitting. The trainees shod their feet quickly in a variety of high-fashion shoes. When the trainee was happy with the fit, she locked the shoes' straps around the chicken's ankles and ordered each bird to stand. The trainees watched in amusement as the chickens sought to balance themselves in four or five inch heels on the dirt. With their soft cocks dangling limply from the crotchless panties, the chickens were afraid to flinch as they tried to balance in their footwear under the warm sun.

"A good chicken is a self-confident one," Rhonda reminded her trainees. "To give them confidence, they must learn to prance and preen properly." Her eyes twinkled as the trainees moved into action.

With no heel or wedge shorter than four inches, the chickens could barely stand without swinging their arms wildly to maintain a semblance of balance or worse, falling into the dirt. The thought of walking in a straight line seemed beyond their understanding and certainly outside their ability. Trembling in fear, the chickens felt the burn as their calves strained and the crunch of their toes suffering as their weight pushed them deeper into the dreaded shoes. It was the most unnatural position they had ever experienced.

"Parade them around the yard," Rhonda ordered.

Some pain produces understanding, she had learned. First Day requires as much of both as possible.

One by one, each trainee grabbed her chicken's scrotum and yanked it forward. The first steps a chicken took were always shuffling and unsure, Rhonda reminded her girls and cautioned them not to expect too swift a gait today. One after another, the chickens fell ignominiously to the dirt and were forced up by a trainee's swift caning on their asscheeks. On the Farm, all animals learned on First Day that it took all of their concentration to absorb the training and perform even close to expectations demanded of them. First Day training was consistent in teaching that rule before all others.

They also learned that their Trail Boss and trainees neither expected nor tolerated anything less than perfection.

At first, some of the chickens tried to hold onto the now-infamous fence rail for support as they hunched over and took tiny steps. As the trainees took the ball collar reins and moved them away from the fence, the chickens were forced to hobble in a circle, not yet able to put one foot successfully in front of another. They tried to learn from more successful chickens but all they saw was similar suffering throughout the flock. There was no sense of Pack yet, Rhonda knew, but soon her chickens would figure out that if they would simply hang on to each other, as they had hung onto the low fence, their success would increase. It was simply too soon.

After an hour of practicing in warm sunshine, the chickens moaned in pain with every step but it was obvious to Rhonda's practiced eye that they had made a modicum of improvement. They weren't nearly ready to be paraded among the packs, but their progress was measurable. It was time to begin Phase 2 of First Day training.

"Get me my roosters," Rhonda said. A few trainees scurried into the Coop.

Roosters had a special function on the Farm and Rhonda's training was designed to make them excel in their jobs. Even though the chickens wore the luxuries of wigs, lace and hose, the roosters were given one spectacular accoutrement and they had to learn its value. There was a good reason they would be called "The Cocks" during their Season on the Farm.

When the roosters were brought into the yard, it was obvious to the trainees that Processing and Intake had done an excellent job selecting them. Their penises hung between their legs and reached noticeably down their thighs. Rhonda and her trainees grinned at the five limp and lengthy cocks. They were sure that most of the chickens were drooling in jealousy and in fear.

Each cock had been costumed in a colorful collar and scrotal band that were the Farm's identification of each as a rooster. Similar to the chickens' disciplinary scrotal bands, the roosters' cock straps kept them safely incarcerated inside the Coop's training area. Given their evaluation and performance during Intake, each rooster sported not only a thick and lengthy shaft, but also managed to make sure it responded quickly when it was stimulated. That talent was important to the roosters' tasks and to the flock's needs during the Season. Quick erection separated the cocks from the chickens.

There's no time like the present, she had learned. Let the cocks perform and the chickens will fall into line.

Rhonda stepped toward a handy rooster and spoke to the flock as well as to the trainees that circled around them.

"A cock who services my chickens does its duty daily. Each cock will service at least five chickens per day so be sure to gauge the hardness reaction time of your assigned cock before setting up the schedules." The trainees nodded as Rhonda continued.

"Look at this one," she took a nearby rooster's shaft by the tip and pulled it toward her leather shorts.

The trainees gathered closer to inspect the rooter's shaft and its reaction. They knew that the chickens weren't going to escape from the fenced yard so they could be easily ignored. To their astonishment, the shaft in Rhonda's fingers elongated measurably and within seconds it stood straight up and out from the cock's body, proudly stiff within its pretty collar. A few of the trainees commented on its potential.

"That's a big one," Hester, a new trainee this Season said. Karin, also a new trainee to the Farm this Season completed the thought with, "It should fill a pig or pony nicely." Finally, Josie said, "I bet it could do two at once."

The trainees giggled at Josie's comment and Rhonda felt her own lips turn upward.

"Get yourself a chicken," Rhonda said to her girls, "and we'll use this one first to demo how it works. Permanent chickens will be assigned later today."

Several trainees dashed toward the first available chicken and Rhonda grabbed hold of the closest one by its scrotum and turned it around quickly as it struggled to maintain balance in the locked pumps strapped to its feet. "Bend over," she commanded and the chicken bent clumsily and grabbed its knees for balance.

"Prance over to the fence," Rhonda said and the unfortunate bird struggled to move its feet in tiny steps to comply.

"The fence has several purposes," Rhonda said to her trainees but her words carried to the ears of her flock struggling to reach the rail. "Straddle the fence near a post," she said and the chicken in her grip complied reluctantly while holding onto its knees for dear life.

"See how it knows what to do?" she said to her girls. They nodded with new understanding of how chickens seemed to take to the coop more easily than many of the other packs did to their own barns and sties.

"What are the two requirements for the cock and chicken flock?" Rhonda opened the question to the entire group. They shot back immediate answers.

"Lubrication!" Karin called loudly.

Hester yelled, "Sheaths!"

Rhonda smiled at her girls and pulled a wrapped chicken penis cover from her waistband and handed it to Josie, who stood to her left. "Cover the cock," she ordered.

"Where do we find lubrication in the Coop?" Rhonda quizzed them before Josie could move a muscle.

The trainees looked at each other and then at Rhonda. No one had told them where the lubrication was kept in the Coop or yard but every one of them knew they could not proceed without it. Their eyes looked over the area and one of them offered a reply.

"Could it be stored in the post containers?" she asked but her voice sounded sure.

"Good deduction," Rhonda said as the other girls nodded. "Remember that everything needed for the flock is always within reach and in a logical place. When you take your chicken to another pack for service, you'll find what you need close by. Use your eyes and your brains and you will figure it out," Ronda advised the nodding trainees.

As she stepped toward the chicken that was now straddling the low fence and holding onto the post for dear life, Rhonda pressed its head to the rail and raised its ass in a single motion. "What is the best way to spread chicken tail feathers and asscheeks?" she tested the group again.

"Kick its feet apart," Karin suggested. But another added, "That might throw it off balance and injure an ankle." Rhonda smiled at her trainees who weren't afraid to discuss possibilities in the open and always kept safety in mind.

There is never a reason to damage an animal carelessly, the Owner had taught every senior Farm staff member.

Hester suggested, "A finger? Couldn't we just stick in a finger and shake it?"

Rhonda contemplated her trainee's idea and waited for one of the girl's comrades to point out the problem with that suggestion. She didn't have to wait long.

"A dry finger doesn't work," Josie replied as Rhonda smiled at her group.

Wait for them to get it, she had learned. Don't ask twice. Make them come to it on their own. That's how they learn.

As the trainees and their Trail Boss stood in the warm sunlight and the chickens tried to balance on their tall shoes as the cocks stood aimlessly in the yard, Rhonda waited for the right answer. Oblivious to the fence-straddling bird, Rhonda looked over her trainees to see which girl would figure out the right choice. The air grew thick with anticipation.

Karin began hesitantly, "What if we trained it to spread its legs all the time? Wouldn't that solve the problem for the whole Season?"

There's always one, Rhonda thought. One with huge potential.

"Yes!" Rhonda said happily. "How would you accomplish that?" She stared directly at the girl who offered the key response to test her ability to think under pressure.

"May I, Ma'am?" the trainee looked expectantly at her Trail Boss.

Rhonda stepped away from the straddling chicken and invited the trainee to test her theory. She approached the chicken and put a glove on before opening the post container and taking a large dollop of lubrication. She spread the oozing gel well inside the chicken's dry hole. Finally she reached for her prod and touched it once to the lubricated orifice.

The chicken screamed and its legs shot far apart.

That should take care of the rest of the Season, Rhonda knew as she surveyed the flock's horrified faces staring in bewilderment at the hapless chicken's reaction to the prod's kiss.

"Good girl," Rhonda said, "I think your chicken lesson was very educational." The girls giggled as the chickens trembled atop their shoes. Turning her attention to the trainees, Rhonda asked, "You know that gel is an excellent conductor, right?"

Everyone except the chickens and the five cocks understood that Rhonda's was definitely a rhetorical question.

"Hand me a rooster," Rhonda said and a trainee dragged one by its shaft it toward her Trail Boss.

Inspecting the rooster's dangling organ, Rhonda grabbed the tip between her fingers and pressed her nails into it. Within seconds, the cock sprang to life and elongated in her hand. Fishing a condom out of her waistband, Rhonda had the entire penis covered quickly. She positioned the rooster behind the quivering, lubricated chicken whose legs still straddled the fence. There was no question in anyone's mind what that rooster was supposed to do.

"Each bird in our flock has a strong bisexual orientation and some more than others," Rhonda explained as the chickens and roosters' faces filled with a bright red hue. "If they didn't have strong attraction to same-sex partners, would this cock be so eager?" She held the rapidly-hardening shaft for them to observe and the trainees nodded. "We don't break limits on the Farm," she reminded them and added, "but we sure as heck stretch them."

As she pressed the rooster's cock into the well-lubricated chicken anus, the chicken grunted first in pain and then added the clear sound of delight. As the cock was driven deeper, the chicken clucked louder and louder with each thrust Rhonda forced by punishing the cock's asscheeks with her small whip. The chicken's noises increased in both intensity and volume. When the rooster's hands reached for the chicken's saddle, Rhonda flicked them away with her whip and insisted it perform without touching.

It was obvious to the trainees that the chicken and rooster enjoyed this task even though they were both trying to show outward signs of discomfort.

Rhonda stepped around them and beckoned a trainee to follow her. "They sound like they're close to orgasm, don't they?" Rhonda said as the girl nodded. "Glance your prod on the chicken's scrotum when I tell you," she instructed. The girl nodded again and readied her prod into position as Rhonda stepped closer to the thrusting chicken. Both chicken and rooster were clucking and panting as the finale drew near.

"Now," she said as the two birds reached close to what she knew would be a fairly synchronous conclusion.

With Rhonda's prod on the rooster's shaft and the trainee's on the chicken's scrotum, the animals began a wild dance that captivated the trainees as well as the flock. Their throats screamed in pain and shock and their bodies flew wildly in the air. They each sought frantically for something to hold onto but within seconds, the two birds fell onto the dirt and merely quivered.

Rhonda turned her attention to her trainees as she stepped over their carcasses.

"Service on the Farm is not simple wanton copulation. It serves a purpose – my Owner's purpose," Rhonda concluded and wrapped up the First Day's lesson.

Every trainee nodded as most of the flock tried to protect their own testicles and penises with their hands.

"One last chore," Rhonda added, knowing that her point had been made to everyone in the coop. "It's time to castrate the chickens."

Each trainee ran for the chicken's specially-designed codpiece and wrapped it around her chicken's cock and testicles. The rough fabric covered each set of genitals completely and when they drew the strings through the holes and tied them off, the codpieces castrated every chicken visually. When Rhonda inspected the flock for the last time on First Day training before they would be returned to their nests to recover, she was delighted to see a bevy of lacy naked chickens with no visible genitals to distract from the next step in their training.

"Run the cocks," she said, "and then nest the birds."

It wouldn't be too long before the chickens were sent out to service the packs, Rhonda noted with an approving nod. Then she turned her attention to the rooster and chicken still entangled on the dirt at her feet. She kicked them once with her black leather boot to make them separate and then Rhonda forced both to crawl in the dirt back to their roosts. She perched them there where they would remain until she was ready to send them out to entertain the Farm animals. Rhonda was certain their use with the packs would make great footage at the First Day Dessert.

They are perfect for the pigs to use later. She grinned as she walked into the coop to oversee her flock's morning nesting.

Chapter 26: The Pig Sty

When a Trail Boss drew the Sty as her training pack for any Season, she knew was in for a test of her skills but also provided a lot of fun. Paula saw no reason that her Season with the pigs would not be as memorable as prior ones on the Farm. Pigs were always entertaining.

She wasn't sure the pigs ever felt the same way, especially on First Day, but a surprising percentage of them tried to re-enroll for an advanced Season. Paula always took that as a sign that the ones selected by Assessment to live in the Sty realized that the Farm staff knew what was best for them. Even though it took a few of them a long time to come to that understanding, every pig in her Sty eventually came around.

> *When they realize that you provide what's best for them better than they do themselves, only then do they become truly yours.*

After their run from the exercise field back to the Sty, the pigs were lined up behind a filled trough. The day's schedule included a rare time for their Trail Boss to address them directly before their training began. First Day was one of the only times the pigs were spoken to while they were allowed to remain upright. On the Farm, pigs crawled and grunted. The Sty was always noisy and messy.

Paula looked over the pack that stood in sloppy states of attention. She then eyeballed her trainees who were standing in a loose circle at her side. The girls were tall and proud; their breasts jutted out from their chests and their well-oiled leather shorts glistened in the morning sunshine.

They almost look pristine, Paula thought. Not in the Sty. No one can stay clean and work with the pigs. Teach them that early.

"You are *my* pigs," Paula said proudly to the naked pigs whose faces stared blankly back. "This Season, you will think, act and perform like the pigs you are." She allowed her words to sink in as her trainees grinned at the pigs' reaction.

"Pigs grunt," she said. "And so do you."

The pigs' faces were stricken with horror and their eyes darted nervously around the confines of the Sty. A large fenced-in area sported muddy pits and each pig experienced a sense of dread as each finally understood their Trail Boss's implication. A few were calculating methods of escape, but Paula was one step ahead of them.

"Collar them," she said.

The trainees approached the pack and without a word grasped their genitals and fastened a plastic strip behind their testicles. After sliding one end through the loop, pulling and snapping, the trainees had each pig banded for the entire Season. The process took only a few seconds.

"Georgia, take your pig to the fence and spread its leg over the rail," Paula said to one of her trainees. Dutifully, the trainee led her pig by a handful of its genitals toward the fence and slapped its asscheeks so it would perform as it had been instructed. The reluctant animal, its mind confused from having witnessed the effects of one too many punishment prods and whimpered in confusion.

Paula stared at her trainee, hoping that she would handle the situation without direct instruction. Georgia allowed the animal a moment of vacillation before she reached for her cane and swished it through the air landing a solid blow to the pig's soft backside. With a yelp, the pig raised a leg over the fence as it had been instructed.

Fear ran through the pack and Paula enjoyed their anguish. The Owner loved the conflicted tension the animals lived through on First Day and often showed outtakes of them trembling during the First Day dinner to amuse the staff. Paula hoped this pig's faltering would entertain the trainees and Trail Bosses tonight.

As soon as the pig lifted his leg and draped it over the rail, its throat emitted a horrifying shriek as its hips collapsed and its torso plunked down onto the fence post. Unable to move from its pain, the pig wailed as the security fence did its job. The pigs always required special lessons, Paula learned through her Farm Seasons, and the staff constructed a magnetic fence that would slam pigs' genitals onto the thick wooden posts if their cock bands got too close. Once a single pig learned the lesson, the rest of the pack did as well. There was no escape over the fence.

"Bring it back to the pack," Paula said as Georgia punched a code into the fence post's keypad and released the wretch from its painful perch. Sobbing from humiliation and with aching testicles, the pig limped to the pack as the rest of the group focused on Paula. They now were paying strict attention to every word she said.

"You are pigs," she repeated. "Your Season will be training suitable for pigs. In fact, your Season will contain hard work that will entertain everyone on the Farm," she said as she watched their eyes grow wide. But she knew that they would get over their shock with more training. "You will be the Farm's punishment pack as well as the Farm's show," she finished with panache.

"You will learn to grunt," Paula threw the order at them and leaned against the fence where she propped her leathers against a low rail and waited for the trainees to start. With her eyes keenly aware of every pig's movements and every trainee's performance, she relaxed against the rail to oversee the pack's progress. Pig training could be laborious.

They are pigs in their other lives outside the Farm, the Owner taught. Let them learn to be pigs for this Season.

"On your knees," Paula said as the pack sank slowly toward the ground.

"Hooves on the ground," she said and one by one, the pigs' fingers and toes gripped the dirt.

"You are pigs!" she said again with a slight sneer that froze their hearts. "Girls, take over."

Each trainee bent down and faced a kneeling pig. Taking the pigs' scalps in their fingers, each trainee approached her animal's wet eyes and pressed her face as close as possible without touching. On all fours and scared to its core, the pack trembled visibly from the trainees' closeness. From her vantage point, Paula smiled as pig asscheeks jiggled from their increasing levels of panic.

Then the noise was birthed.

Donna, first in the trainee line, grunted directly into her pig's snout and demanded silently that it return the sound. Afraid either to grunt into her face or worse, to be silent, the pig in her grip cried as its eyes dropped toward the dirt in defeat. Whatever its lifestyle it was used to a mere 48 hours ago, this pig was simply unable to force its voice grunt in reply. Dissatisfied with the pig's silence, Donna reached for her prod and the sight of her movement drew a whispered groan from the pig's lips.

She grunted into its snout again. Louder this time.

The pig tried to back away but Donna's grip was too strong. Unable to escape, the pig tried one more time to force a grunt from its throat, but none emerged. Tears fell from the pig's eyes onto the dry dirt in defeat. Donna grunted again, even louder, this time with her lips pressed against his snout.

*Three tries the first time in pig training, Paula had
taught her girls. The we use punishment.*

Donna glanced at Paula and saw a nod of approval. A single
pig-less trainee trotted behind Donna's reluctant pig as the rest of
the pack remained motionless with their heads still held firmly by
the trainee's grips. Within seconds, Alex, standing behind the
reluctant pig, lubricated its anus and plunged a plug deep inside.
Then Donna grunted loudly in the pig's face again.

This time, her grunt was returned.

The intensity of its anus being violated drove the pig past any
reluctance and its guttural grunt hailed the entire sty. Each time
Alex plunged the plug deep in the pig's rectum, it grunted louder
and louder until its noise shattered the Farm's silent scenery with a
primal sound. Over and over again, Alex pressed in the plug and
with each plunge the pig's grunt shrieked from its snout. With
Paula's nod, the rest of the trainees grunted into their pigs' snouts
and one by one, the pigs returned the noise with increasing
volume.

*Make an unforgettable example of the right one and
the rest always follow.*

Each time a trainee looked at Paula to alert her that her pig
wasn't performing loudly enough, Alex, standing behind the
pack's raised asses, donned a new glove, lubricated a new anus and
inserted a new plug until that particular pig learned as required.
Even though it was usually very messy, the Sty had high standards
and the pigs would perform up to or exceed them. It was the Farm
way.

The cacophony of grunting and squealing was the symphony of
the Sty and music to Paula's ears.

She walked the length of the kneeling pack and assessed their
faces and body language from several angles. With half of the pack
of pigs plugged and grunting, the remainder, still unaware of what
was happening behind them that caused the others to participate so

suddenly, began grunting simply to avoid whatever was happening to the others in the pack as she paused for a moment near each pig's head. She walked the line several times before approving this lesson for First Day training.

It was time to move on to teach the pigs their second First Day lesson.

"You are pigs. This is the only sound you will make during this Season," Paula said. Her words hung over the Sty like a thundercloud ready to explode in fury. "This pack entertains during Farm Shows," she said ominously. "Pigs are also the punishment for the other Farm creatures that dare to disobey."

She watched their eyes as a few dared to meet hers, encouraged by Donna and the other trainees' firm grasps on their scalps. Their Season as pigs in the Sty would find them looking up at all times from their season-long crawling and now, Paula knew, was the time they should learn what their status really meant. Their eyes were filled with uncertainty and fear. Paula smiled. It was time to teach them just what punishment meant on the Farm.

> *Always use discipline first, the Owner taught them. Save punishment as a final resort but never be afraid to use it to change unacceptable behavior. The goal is always to change behavior.*

"Gather them in Pit 1," Paula said as her girls released their pigs and led them toward a large rectangular fenced area. Walking behind the line of crawling pigs, Paula touched her prod briefly on one set of handy asscheeks and ordered the group to proceed without speaking a word. When the first one in line moves, she knew, the rest would follow.

The pigs lined up around the pit and the only sound was the gurgle of water running through hoses and filling the pit. Jeanne, another new trainee that caught Paula's eye in training, used a paddle to stir the muddy concoction. Every pig focused on the thick muddy slop that was brewing in the pit. As more and more water ran in, Jeanne's paddle met moved more easily and the brown mixture coalesced. When she was satisfied with the thickness, she offered the paddle to Paula to test it for approval. Taking it happily in her hands, Paula tested the brew and pronounced it ready. She tossed a small approving smile to the beaming Jeanne.

"Fasten their belts," Paula said to her trainees and each girl approached a pig with a length of black twine and each pig's personal plug dangled from each trainee's grip. After each pig was lubricated and the plugs were inserted unceremoniously and were greeted with grunts of pig surprise, the trainees lassoed their animals around their waists and ran the twine through their crotches so that the wide flanged end of every plug was secured with several loops of thick black twine. After having their knots approved by their Trail Boss, the girls tugged the pigs' belts to make sure that no plug would fall out and that no belt would loosen.

For their part, the pigs were ordered to lower their snouts to the dirt in humiliation. Having been forced to crawl to the pit was difficult enough to maintain any remnants of their pride; however, being plugged and roped was almost too much indignity for some in the pack to endure. Paula smiled at their distress and surveyed her girls, most of whom were unaware of one of Paula's favorite surprises. It was one of her most anticipated pleasures training in the Sty and she savored the moment that was now at hand.

"Pigs play in the mud and require supervision," she said. The girls looked at her questioningly as Paula reveled in their confusion. She answered that question that they dared not ask aloud. "Strip your leathers," she said.

The trainees, most of whom were new to the Farm and many in their first season, stared at their Trail Boss in shock.

"Now!" Paula said more loudly.

With only a moment's hesitation, the trainees shed their boots and dropped their leather shorts to comply with her order. The Owner insisted that every set of trainees be stripped of their leathers at one time during the Season both as a test of their obedience as well as a personal lesson in what separated the staff from the animals. In their nudity, the trainees shared a unique experience of feeling like one of their animals. That lesson taught them to appreciate why being on the all-women Farm staff was an honor and a privilege.

They just never liked learning it.

With their toned bodies gleaming under the late morning sun, the trainees dug deep into their well of obedience and finally stood naked behind the pigs. Paula looked up and down the array of firm breasts, strong legs, and glistening labia that always displayed so nicely in sunlight. Walking in front of the line, she touched an occasional trainee's breast and patted a hip or briefly fondled labia as if to accept them fully as her trainees.

"Drop the first one in," Paula said to no one in particular and Jill, whose breasts were in Paula's fingers at the moment, decided that she would own the 'first one' this Season. Tugging her pig firmly by its thick twine belt, she threw the animal forward and dumped it head first into the deep mud. Then she lowered herself in behind him. Her pig's head emerged from the slop and its mouth sputtered for air. Jill pushed the pig under the slop again and held it there until Paula's nod instructed her to yank its hairless head upright.

The pig sputtered incomprehensible syllables. Jill's sharp grunt directly into its snout reminded the pig what the only proper response was to be. As the pack listened to pig squeal from mud-drenched lips, they all learned quickly the horror that was expected of them in the pit.

"Toss the rest in," Paula said and trainees grabbed their pigs' belts and threw them haphazardly into the slime. Each trainee followed her pig into the pit and stayed with it as each dunked its head, lifted it and demanded a grunt each time. The Sty had become a muddy collection of naked bodies, half of which led the grunting and the other half that grunted and squealed back on command.

When Paula was satisfied that the pigs were accustomed to the mud hole, she issued her next training instruction.

"Push the pigs toward the edges," she ordered. "Choose two and put them in the center."

Let them figure it out, Paula remembered from her earlier Seasons. Never give too many orders. Don't be completely specific. Make them learn how to do it together.

She was pleased with their teamwork as the girls' bodies slopped through the mud while positioning the pack around the edge. Not knowing what the next step was in the training process, the girls could never be sure if they wanted to be observers on the edge or participants in the middle when Paula offered them a choice as unknown as this one would certainly be. Jockeying around in the mud was physically demanding and Paula noted the time it was taking. She decided that her girls had performed adequately in the first task, although a few minutes would have to be shaved actual from performance time. She made a mental note to repeat the exercise several more times.

"Here," she said as she tossed a hook into the pit, knowing that a hand would reach up and catch it. "Attach them front to front."

Lifting the pigs by their rope belts and listening to them squeal as the thick black rope cut into their genitals, Donna and Jeanne attached the short double hook and locked it to their pigs' cock locks. The two pigs were forced to face each other, their bodies plastered together by thick mud. Whether their visible discomfort was caused by wet slime or physical closeness, Paula ignored it and moved to the next step in pit training.

"The winner is the pig who lifts the other out of the mud," she said and leaned against the railing to watch the action. It didn't take long for it to begin. It never did for First Day Contest.

Slippery from the gooey mud that coated them from snout to tail, the pigs flew into each other with only one thought in their minds – to win. The Assessment team chose only the most competitive during Intake for a Season in the Corral, but the overflow of talent with that trait were consistently sent to the Sty. Paula enjoyed watching the two pigs vie for the win, no matter there was no prize beyond pleasing her. Pigs were like that, competitive to the core.

It was always amusing watching them splash and splatter in the mud pits and Pit 1 was the deepest one in the Sty. Grunting and squealing to please their individual trainees as well as the Trail Boss, the pigs grappled in combat trying to lift its opponent above the mud's surface. Paula allowed the contest to continue for a few minutes before she caught the attention two of her trainees. Once they met her eyes, she shook her head from side to side.

The girls caught on immediately and whispered down the line. Soon all the trainees figured out what Paula already knew: the pit was too deep and neither pig would win because it was impossible to lift a pig if it couldn't plant its feet on semi-solid ground. The trainees giggled softly and Paula allowed them to enjoy First Day Contest.

"I want all the pigs paired off and then get out," she said above the trainees' giggling. Paula tossed hooks into the pit for the girls to fetch and apply to their pigs. In just a few minutes the pigs were coupled at the waist and the girls emerged from the deep mud and hosed themselves off. The struggling pigs in the center of the pit continued their useless expenditure of energy trying to succeed in a no-win situation while the girls enjoyed the sunshine and dressed in their leathers.

"Stop!" Paula said and ordered the pigs to end their useless struggling and crawl out of the pit to assemble on all fours before her.

As the hooked pairs of pigs labored to climb out of the deep mud pit and arrange themselves in a semblance of kneeling on all fours while hooked to the waist of another pig, the trainees pulled wider hoses and got ready for the next step. They waited for the command to hose off the pack and make them presentable for the

Trail Boss. Paula had one more training order to issue before the water was turned on.

"Roll in the dirt," she said and walked through the pack of filthy, stunned pigs. She held her prod threateningly close to several of them. She had used it merely twice before the entire beefy pack of pigs figured out what the prod could do and they were soon rolling in the dirt, adding insult to the injury just inflicted on their pride. Only when Paula was satisfied that they could get no grimier, she ordered the hoses on.

Frigid water spurted from the hoses and the trainees scrubbed the pigs with stiff brushes that scoured every inch of their skin. Pair by pair, the pigs' freshly sheared bodies shined in the sun as the trainees turned their attention to their heads, faces, groins, feet, and every crease between. The pigs grunted at being hosed and scrubbed while they remained on their hands and knees on the Sty's dirt floor

When they were clean, it was time for the final session of First Day training.

"Grab your partner's scrotum," Paula said to the pairs of pigs. "My trainees need to see your ID numbers." Reluctant hands rested on their sides as the pigs hesitated to touch each other's belted privates. A few whacks of solid rattan canes against their fleshy asscheeks encouraged the group to perform as ordered. As the girls called out numbers and then unhooked the pairs, they were separated into two groups. But not before Paula enjoyed each pig's discomfort gripping another pig's penis and balls.

Paula moved to the last phase of First Day training.

"Put the higher numbers over here," she pointed to the right, "and the lower ones over there." It was soon obvious that one group outnumbered the other by at least three-to-one. "The small group are the mommy pigs and the larger group is this Season's litter." The trainees grinned at the thought of the exercise and the pigs shuddered that there could be no more ultimate degradation they could imagine this Season. Until now.

"Get the mommies ready," she said and the small group was separated and placed into stalls around the sty.

"Move three piglets apiece to their mommies," she said.

Donna was the first who used her cane to prod a few piglets toward their Season's assigned mommy. She made them duck underneath the mommy pig and slither into position on their sides. The Sty was filled with pig terror and it imbued Paula with a sense of accomplishment. Training the pigs was a complicated job and the few moments like this one was a welcome respite to the Trail Boss's work. She relished her job.

When the piglets were pronounced ready, Paula issued First Day's final training order.

"Suck your mommy's teats," she said solemnly. The trainees peeked in to make sure the piglets heard and understood the command. Some even offered bits of advice for the reluctant.

"Take it in your mouth and suck," Donna whispered to a frozen-in-fear piglet. "Open your mouth wider," Alex cajoled her own little piglet. "Yes, the whole thing!" Jill encouraged hers.

One by reluctant one, the piglets parted their lips and closed the inches between their faces and what Paula now called their mommy's teats. One by one, prodded by whistling canes and a few prod shocks, the piglets eventually performed as Paula had ordered. The mother pigs, larger and beefier than the piglets underneath, knelt unmoving with tears of mortification spilling to the dirt. Their own legs driven apart by the sting of canes and prods, the mommy pigs were stationed to kneel and be sucked by those huddling together underneath them.

Paula drank in the sight as tears, runny snouts and quiet sucking noises filled the Sty.

It was time to savor the moment before hustling the pigs to their watering hole and training them to use it when ordered. After session-ending cold water hosing, she would send them into the shed where the babies would nestle next to their mommies and suckle themselves to sleep for a short rest.

Chapter 27: Training the Ponies to Dance

Every Season on the Farm produced highlights that fed the Owner's love for watching her Herds and Coops and Sties full of new flesh for the Season. She often had her staff organize the best of them to provide education for her staff and entertainment for her occasional guests. Replayed events generated good humor as the Farm staff knew how to treat its visitors with aplomb. Both trainers and trainees learned from highlight reels and video outtakes. Even First Day competitions could become spectacles and the Owner had the staff prepare to make sure that each training session was filled with pageantry, high-quality events, Farm-style decorum and seasonal protocol. After all, First Competition took place during the auspicious day when the Farm's herds first met their Owner for the Season.

It had to be special.

After their successful initial training, the ponies were taught advanced skills that were always a hallmark of each of the Farm's competitions. They were worked long hours by their specially-chosen Trail Boss so they could perfect each set of skills and perform at every event for later review. Every morning before sunup, Sharon had the pony teams chained to fence posts by their collars to begin competition-worthy conditioning. Each pony jogged in place for at least 30 minutes before any was allowed its watering. Ponies with full bladders and rectums worked harder, learned faster and with better concentration, she had learned during her Seasons. After all, when one or two who had accidents were disciplined in front of the herd, none of the others wanted to be the pony on his hands and knees sucking up wet dirt or worse and carrying it to a disposal area mouthful by mouthful.

Sharon relished the sound of pony hooves plopping on the corral's dirt. She loved the sight of the herd lifting their hind legs high as she demanded more forceful practice. With their genitals thumping against their thighs and bellies as they lifted their forelegs higher and higher to her pounding rhythm, they provided a delightful early morning spectacle, especially for their Trail Boss and her Owner. Sharon sipped coffee and watched them run with precision toward nowhere. She enjoyed their perspiring bodies and bobbling penises and flapping ball sacs immensely.

High-stepping ponies were an honored Farm tradition.

With the first Competition coming up in less than two days, the herd's training took on even more intensity. Leading the sweaty group to the watering shed herself, Sharon spoke to the crawling ponies as they lifted their legs to guide their streams down and try not to soil themselves.

"Attention!" she said in a loud voice. "Continue watering and listen carefully." She loved knowing that they were peeing into community holes yet were paying attention to every syllable she spoke. The ponies, in the midst of peeing on command training, had learned to follow her instructions to the letter no matter what else they were ordered to do. Sharon loved training the ponies.

"Your Owner has scheduled the first pony competition for the day after tomorrow," she said. "You have a tremendous amount of work to finish by then so you are absolutely ready to perform to my expectations." Allowing her words to sink in for a few seconds, she continued. "The winners will enjoy a reward. The losers are to be punished. In addition, there will be a high-step show that precedes the Competition. Every pony is entered and must be trained perfectly."

The ponies whinnied as they had been instructed as hoses were inserted into their lubricated rectums and the morning cleaning gel was pumped deep inside each of them. The floor tilted and they held onto the handrails as they were shown on First Day but with an increasing sense of terror even though Sharon continued talking as if their daily enemas were a normal occurrence. It would soon become their daily routine.

"I have selected ten ponies: five each for two teams. The others will serve as backup in case of injury," her voice trailed off. Then she added, "Or for other reasons that will soon become obvious." She was silent and forced them to wonder what those 'other reasons' might mean. Not one pony imagined 'other things' could be *good* things.

The pack's overnight collection of feces fell from their rectums into a community hole and Sharon continued giving instructions as if nothing unusual was happening to the ponies in the pack.

"Riders will now saddle the ponies." She was done issuing instructions and walked out of the fetid watering barn stench.

Her exit handed silent control of the ponies to the trainees who would finish their morning watering and hose the herd off quickly. Competition always brought out the highest level of trainees' skills, Sharon recalled from her own early days. Now, with only two days remaining to practice, time was truly of the essence. The trainees knew that putting on anything less than a spectacular performance was intolerable and no trainee wanted to meet the Owner in her private studio being guilty of having demonstrated a less-than-perfect exhibition of Farm talent.

The ponies were hosed off, oiled and gleaming, and their feedbags were locked across their snouts while nutrition was pumped in. They learned how to eat quickly during First Day training so training could commence. After morning feeding, the ponies were lined up in a perfect circle around the perimeter of the corral. They stood in strict attention for Sharon's daily inspection. She recited their ID numbers and as each pony's number was called, each pranced forward and joined one of the two opposing teams that would engage during the initial event of the Season's first Competition. Ten apprehensive ponies stepped into the center and the rest were positioned on all fours around the corral to learn from the training. Their trainers knew that the unselected ponies would be trained as the high-stepping entertainment team and would begin learning the choreography shortly after the actual competitors were announced.

Sharon wasted no time getting started. "Saddle your ponies!" she announced.

The girls ran to the fence to grab their saddles after learning which ponies had been chosen to compete. Many felt smug with delight at being given the opportunity to compete. The selection of each of their ponies for Competition told the new trainees that their training so far had been evaluated as superior by their Trail Boss. Sharon knew those self-satisfied grin her girls wore and allowed them a few moments of that small pleasure. Given that her trainees were as naked as the ponies for the Season, she could afford them a momentary sense of contentment because Competition training would take its toll on both the girls and the ponies. Besides, their self-satisfaction even in their nakedness reminded the other trainees how much they wanted to be selected for future competitions.

After checking their saddling techniques and making sure each pony's straps were tight and locked, Sharon finally instructed each girl how to pad the straps so that the pony's skin would not be rubbed raw and suffer unnecessary chafing. Only then was Sharon was ready to start. Her next instruction surprised and thrilled ten of her trainees.

"Riders, dress in your leathers!" she said and ten delighted trainees quickly donned their leather shorts and open vests for the first time since they were stripped naked in the corral. The faces of unselected trainees who remained naked behind their kneeling ponies revealed their envy that Sharon expected and encouraged. They would take their high-stepping training more seriously in the future, she knew, in an attempt to gain her favor to be selected for the next competition.

A little jealousy is acceptable, the Owner reminded them. It makes them work harder and we will always reward accomplishment.

She turned her attention to the main ring where the competitive ponies and their riders were assembled. Sharon addressed them with specific instructions. "First, the trainers will mount their ponies," Sharon said. "Ponies, you will kneel to accept your riders as they mount into the saddle. Don't move a muscle. Do not try to assist. Remain absolutely still until your rider commands your movement."

As each trainee positioned her leather-clad bottom into each saddle and adjusted the stirrups to accommodate her legs, the ponies struggled with their unexpected weight but remained keeling on all fours in accepting silence. A groan finally escaped from one pony's snout as its rider bounced into position. The crack of Sharon's singletail whip near its bit silenced the pony quickly and the rest of the team learned vividly just what 'silence' meant when Sharon commanded it.

After the girls were in the saddles and she checked every rider and pony, Sharon ordered the ponies to stand. First standing with a rider in the saddle was always a memorable Competition training event.

Every pony labored heroically trying to stand upright with the weight of a rider on its back. The saddles, designed specifically for each pony's body, held them perfectly. The ten ponies selected for First Competition finally appreciated the daily running and training Sharon required as their legs screamed in agony in their struggle to stand while carrying the saddle and rider on their backs. For their part, the trainees atop the ponies shrieked with delight as their animals stood. There was something exhilarating about being up so high on a strong pony's back that Sharon remembered from her long-ago days as a trainee. First lift was always special.

Preliminary pony steps were always challenging for new packs. More than one pony in prior Seasons had proved unable to step properly with a rider and Sharon was always on the lookout for any subtle signs of imminent failure.

"Take one step toward me," she said to the wobbly group. With her eyes watching each pony's legs, Sharon evaluated their gait, shaky posture and tentative steps. Some seemed to take to their role more easily than others; it was those ponies she was looking for to enter into the more complicated phases of Farm Competition. Only two ponies were needed for the grand finale and she was always careful to select them after season-long improvement. The quality of the ponies' performance in Final Competition was critical to satisfying the Owner.

"Another step," she called out and urged them forward again. "Another!" Her voice was as confident as their steps were tentative.

After 30 minutes of mounted walking practice, the ponies managed to step around the corral with increasing confidence and their riders, still sitting silently, were deemed ready by Sharon to begin individual work.

"Trainees, take your reins and hold them tightly. Direct your ponies into a single circle and walk the perimeter."

Her nod was all they needed to issue their own commands to the ponies.

The trainees worked the reins and led their ponies into a semblance of a circle. The ponies who would be selected for Competition had to walk with more confidence under the control of their trainers. To Sharon, they would have to work as if this was the role each of them had been bred for all their lives. Most ponies walked more assertively with each step. They turned to the side as the trainers tugged their reins this way or that. With all of their concentration focused on their feet and legs, the ponies were oblivious to how they might appear to others.

Sharon was pleased and smiled for the first time that Season.

In the side corral, the high-steppers were led through their paces by Nadia, a trainee who served as Sharon's main assistant this Season. Each shorn pony was saddled with its naked rider, one of Sharon's long-time training preferences that she believed enabled a rider to control her pony's movements better. As a trainer, Nadia was direct and issued brusque orders.

"Step," she said to Teri, Sara and Marie who were on the left of the long row. "ONE step!" she added clearly.

The lineup of high-steppers was awkward and Nadia was intent that they would perform as a fluid dance troupe at the First Competition. With each step taken apprehensively on the smaller corral's dirt floor, the ponies gained a small level of confidence in how to handle their riders' weight while plodding across the ground. When she was satisfied they could take five steps without falling, Nadia added the first dance move.

"Raise your right hoof and hold," she said.

Fifteen ponies tried to obey but teetered gracelessly around the corral. Frowning, Nadia repeated her instruction.

"Raise your right hoof and HOLD!" she said more loudly with a trainer's aplomb. Fifteen ponies again struggled into position as their riders held the reins loosely in their hands. Fifteen sweaty ponies with one hoof aloft held fifteen naked riders should make a beautiful snapshot of Farm life but this group was appalling. Nadia felt tension in the herd and used it to her advantage.

"Drop the right hoof. Raise the left," she instructed. Watching them carefully, Nadia noted which of the ponies hesitated between commands where she wanted an instant exchange of hooves that were raised in the air. Taking her singletail and whipping one pony's ass after another down the line, she repeated her command in a voice loud enough to be heard over their shrieks of pain.

"One hoof. Then the other. Listen to the beat. No stopping," she said plainly, drowning out their chorus of pain. She repeated the instruction, "One hoof. Then the other. Perfect motion. No stopping," and the ponies wailed softly as their hooves moved up and down and their pace quickened. Within 15 minutes, she had 15 high-stepping ponies performing together in a single line with their riders becoming more comfortable balancing in rhythm to each simple movement.

It was time for the trainees to take more control of their animals.

"Marie, lead them in a circle," Nadia said. "Sara, crop its left flank if your pony doesn't raise that hoof higher!

Nadia was cautious about allowing trainees to crop the ponies; after all, her singletail landed on the right flank today so the trainees would have to use the left. That way, any marks inflicted by trainees would be distinguishable and they could be retrained in proper crop use on a new pony's ass.

The riders cheered when they were given their animals' heads. The corral buzzed with the excitement of high-stepping ponies working under the hot sun learning their riders' commands and responding to every pull on their reins. As their legs tired and their steps' height lowered, the trainees' effective cropping on the ponies' left flanks reenergized the herd. Within an hour, the performance ponies were dancing closer to Nadia's vision. Sharon noticed that the hour produced remarkable progress.

"Dismount!" she ordered.

As the girls jumped down and ran to the side rail to share their experiences in their own gaggle, Nadia took the ponies' reins and walked them to the trough so they could slurp up vitamin enriched water that was designed to sustain them through the entire morning's training. No pony was allowed to leave the trough without drinking and two food service trainees who oversaw the process held their snouts under water until they were quite certain that the ponies had their required fill.

After only a few sputters and three snouts held underwater, the ponies finished their required allotments.

Nadia restarted their training immediately after watering. Her pace increased and the ponies struggled to match her rhythm. They first performed the required stepping without their riders, and then with them in the saddles. They danced to the crack of their rider's whip and turned as they tugged the reins. Their hooves raised and lowered on cue and as the morning wore on, they resembled a fledgling dance troupe's first rehearsal. Even with their awkward mistakes, Nadia grew more assured that when the brutal workout was through, she would present a herd to Sharon that had the makings of a performance team.

While she trained, Nadia thought about Sharon and what she was probably accomplishing with the competition team in the main corral. Her experience was only three seasons' Competitions, but the thrill had left her longing to become a Trail Boss whose teams would perform for the entertainment of the Owner and her guests at the First Competition. She hoped that honor would be hers one day.

> *First Competition training always brings out trainees' deepest desires. They will never fail to astonish you, the Owner taught. Watch them and use them to train your trainees.*

Ponies selected for the corral were hand-picked by the Assessment Team. They had to meet a complex physical and emotional profile. Their psyches were explored and their bodies inspected and tested. Yet in spite of the well-tested process, each Season's ponies managed to bring a few surprises to their Trail Boss that made excellent viewing at pre-competition dinners in the Manor House. With all her Seasons on the Farm, Sharon knew that at least one pony every Season would astound her with something unexpected. That's what she loved most – the unpredictable displays that the Farm animals brought to her and to the Farm each Season.

Today's Competition training was unrelenting and the ponies were eventually led to the trough for a second time by their riders. This time, they were forced to kneel with the riders' full weight, drink and then to stand. Nadia thought some of the Competition ponies were probably exhausted but she trusted Sharon's insight. With the morning almost gone, Sharon ran them around the perimeter of the main corral one more time before interrupting training just long enough for feeding. She slowed the line with short overhead cracks of her whip and finally had the ponies kneel to dismount their riders.

Her trainees removed and oiled the saddles prior to replacing them in the storage area. While her trainers attended to equipment, Sharon assembled the ponies in a circle at her feet. Their glazed eyes and sweaty faces told her volumes. First morning of Competition training can push ponies beyond exhaustion. A pony in that state can no longer be trained effectively. It can merely be ordered through paces and little long-term education is ever accomplished. It's a fine line.

> *Hold their minds with your words first, the Owner said. Then with your silence. Only then will you own their spirits. They will work harder for you than they have ever worked before. They will work beyond their capacity. That is Ownership.*

While they panted, Sharon spoke to them as a group, but each pony heard the words as if she were speaking only into its own ears.

"After feeding, we train on balance techniques. You must be confident and proud when you compete so you honor your Owner and the Farm. When you enter the ring, posture and gait will be scrutinized. When you carry your rider, self-esteem will be measured. When you win, you will be recognized as the pride of the Farm. Serve the Farm well." Sharon let her words fill their brains before she added a final comment.

"The winning pony team receives a prize directly from me." She could feel them drink in her words as their imaginations ran wild. Then she added ominously, "And so do the losers."

Fear filled the corral and Sharon luxuriated in their anxiety. She knew that when her ponies were pushed to their edge, they would work harder for her. After feeding, she was certain they would push themselves cruelly to gain her favor. During that workout, she would evaluate each of them and determine the two who might represent the Corral for the Final Competition.

In the small corral, Nadia worked her ponies and Sharon could hear their hooves plopping as their legs stepped higher and higher to meet her demanding cadence. The riders were most certainly on a rough ride; after all, the first high-step training was brutal for even the best-trained ponies' legs. It was the Farm custom to feed the competitors first and during their feeding, Sharon was sure to wander to the small corral and evaluate her head trainee's progress.

Teri appeared and Sharon turned her attention to her. She dismissed the ponies to her for the brief trot to the feeding shed. The feedbags would be strapped to their faces to be certain their nutritional intake was measured. The Farm Staff was well trained in the special feeding needs of working ponies. As they crawled to the barn, Sharon swatted a hind flank or two just to assess their reactions.

Find the ones who bristle from your whip. They are feisty and make good competitors.

After whip's third kiss on a pony's flank, Sharon noticed one crawler twist its head and stare at her with rebellion in its eyes. "I didn't do anything wrong!" The pony seemed defiant.

Its look transfixed her for a moment and Sharon hoped the cameras recorded it so she could review it after dinner. An offended pony bode well for Final Competition's intensity. Finding a proud pony was a Trail Boss's dream. She noted its brand on her tablet.

Once she had the herd in the shed and their feedbags were attached, Sharon walked to the small corral to review the choreography that Nadia had selected for the show. This Season was Nadia's first show as a Competition-level trainer and the Sharon knew she would work tirelessly to make it memorable. Sometimes that passion produced a magnificent spectacle; at other times, it simply wore out the ponies and produced a lifeless event. The Owner's distaste for a routine that was merely ordinary was well-known and Sharon had no desire to be called to her salon to re-learn that fact. Nadia's success or failure carried implications for Sharon so she was careful to oversee her head trainee with a keen eye.

What she saw as she first approached the corral was a mishmash of clumsy ponies jostling their riders in a routine that was as unattractive as it was inept. Yet Sharon knew that the first morning's choreography session would produce very few artistic results. Rather, the fact that the ponies were all upright and no rider seemed to have been thrown today spoke loudly about Nadia's skill and growing expertise. Leaning against a fencepost, Sharon watched the ponies try to dance.

Their performance was laughable. The sweaty ponies wearing training saddles with naked trainee riders filled the corral with only a mere semblance of a circle. The rhythm that Nadia stomped with her boot in the dirt had no relationship to the ponies' cadence as they tried to stand erect and not throw their riders. Her long hair was thrown back over her shoulders and Sharon laughed out loud.

The herd froze at the sound.

"Ponies can be so... amusing!" Sharon said loudly and watched every pony's snout turn beet red from her ridicule even after all their backbreaking work. Even Nadia's face fell when she heard her mentor's words but she recovered and to her credit lifted her whip to restart the session once again. The unexpected crack of her singletail above their heads set the troupe back to the beginning of the routine and Sharon noted how their intensity had returned. This group had the makings of a fine performance pack and they were responding well to Nadia's training methods. She just would never tell her that on just the second day of training.

It was feeding time for the dancing ponies and Sharon nodded at Nadia to give her permission. After disembarking, the riders saw to the training saddles and only then led their ponies by the reins to the trough to oversee their proper drinking. It didn't take much encouragement for these ponies to stick their snouts deep into the liquid and suck it up eagerly. With a second nod, Sharon turned over the ponies' care to the Feeding Staff and had them sent into the shed so their feedbags could be strapped on.

Lunch feeding would be a routine high-calorie paste but dinner on the day before a competition would be more filling. Fiber, vitamins, and simple calories were not enough. Later that evening the ponies would taste the Chickens for the first time.

Chapter 28: Bull Games

The ten bulls selected for Competition had shown remarkable progress under Tara's tutelage. Their training was intense, as it always was with the herd that sported the Farm's best-sized cocks, and now it was time to prepare them for the Season's competition. After all, training bulls simply to erect on specific commands was merely one phase of more complex bull training. According to Tara's schedule and the Farm's expectations, it was time to move the bulls to the next phase of their schooling so they would be fully prepared for the upcoming Grand Show.

The Farm's prize bulls, a small but elite herd, were presented to the Owner and her guests during the Season's competitive games. For the first time during the Season, their prowess, size and control were to be components of the exhibition. A big cock was a juicy attribute; however, the Owner demanded that her bulls exhibit controlled restraint in addition to powerful ejaculation on command.

> *One without the other was meaningless, Tara had been taught. The Owner enjoyed the power of bull ejaculation when it was at Her command. Anything else was not tolerated.*

After repeated sessions of training to ejaculate on demand, not one of the bulls had been allowed to climax for more than a week. Tara was certain that with proper orgasm denial training they might approach setting a Farm record when the trainees began the bulls' intense penis workouts. With only two days left until the Competition, today would be their last opportunity to have ejaculation stream length measured and output weighed. Assessing the bulls' production was as scientific as it could be entertaining.

Tara's job was to ensure that her girls measured output accurately; the trainees' enjoyment was simply a perk of working in this pen.

With bulls that could stiffen their cocks with just a trainer's look and harden to bursting with the proper application of advanced tools, Tara was ready for the herd to learn the rest of the rules of Competition. Only then would she select the best to perform for the Owner and her guests. The onus of choosing what would become the cream of the pack was squarely on Tara's shoulders. Her trainees' jobs were focused at this moment on encouraging each animal to quick stiffness and spurting as much and far as possible only when commanded.

It was as simple a task as it was complicated.

By their nature, bulls were an aggressive pack. Their penises, by far the longest and best-performing of all the herds on the Farm, seemed to generate bloodthirstiness among them that during Competition always percolated to the surface. Controlling their cocks was always the Trail Boss' first job; after that, everything usually fell into line. After only a week of training, every bull's penis was responsive to her commands and each felt a sense of pride when they saw her eyes focus on their successfully engorged shafts.

Tara rarely looked at them in the eye. They were simply cocks to her and each penis was now identifiable with a simple look. If she needed an ID number, she instructed a trainee to lift the bull's sac and verify its brand. The bulls had been reduced to animals who simply wore cocks with ID numbers for her to train and that suited Tara just fine.

The order of Competition followed strict Farm guidelines. The bulls opened the spectacle right after the introductory Parade of the Herds. Just before Competition, the Owner's guests were treated to a private showing of the bulls' prowess. Each of the trainees proudly erected her bull so each stiff penis was measured in the Owner's private viewing area. When they were dressed in their Competition leathers, the bulls' appearance could be daunting. Only Tara fully understood that in spite of their magnificent appearance, each of the bulls was simply a cock worn by a muscular body that suffered, and sometimes enjoyed a rare moment of bliss, but only at her choosing. Bliss on the Farm, as always, was what she defined it to be.

The first thing the herd had to learn today was how to be shown.

The lineup of naked bulls in their barn was enhanced by spotlights that the control room focused on bull genitals. Various roving lights picked up and highlighted chests, shoulders and necks; others spotlighted powerful legs. But the lights that shined on their dangling cocks and smooth sacs would never move. The Owner's guests found their attention focused on the animals' penises and several would smile while they laughed at the slightest movements that the bulls were able to make by jiggling limp penises. Making their cocks dance for the Owner was the bulls' first skill learned each Season.

Teaching a bull to make its cock dance was a painstaking process that Tara began on First Day.

The dance of delight is required to entertain my guests, the Owner repeatedly instructed, but the dance of passion is what I demand.

Tara learned over the Seasons that a well-practiced dance of passion was the only bull ballet that the Owner accepted. Every bull was trained to perform it; but only those who conveyed enough intensity that Tara approved could be selected for Competition. Rejected bulls were sent for discipline because failure in the bull pen – more than any other Farm pen, coop, or barn – was not tolerated. Tara's decision on First Day morning had Season-long results for each of the bulls in her charge.

With her tools fastened to her vest's bright red waistband, Tara marched down the line of eager bulls. They didn't understand what Competition involved, but to an animal, each understood that something significant was happening right now that would impact their future this Season on the Farm.

Tara walked back and forth, her eyes focused on the bulls' sagging shafts.

"Now!" she demanded and stared at the ten cocks shining under hot lights. One by one, their bodies tensed to make their cocks jiggle. One by one, they waggled their hips as their wearers grunted to stiffen at her command. One by one, their cocks pulsed with growing energy and obedience. Tara walked back and forth in front of them.

"Down!" she said and ten bulls struggled to reverse the direction of their cocks that she had just started. Cocks flopped and wriggled as the bulls tried to force them into their former soft states. When she found one that pleased her, she called out to the trainee working with that particular penis. "Number! Fourth from the left!"

Dutifully, the trainee lifted the bull's sac and announced the ID number to her Trail Boss. A small grin of pride filled the trainee's face.

"Take it to the training stall," Tara said, satisfied she had her first Competition bull selected. She needed four more.

As Ana led the chosen bull into its training stall so its cock could be fully trained and its output measured, Tara turned her attention to the nine remaining bulls. Although they were incapable of understanding the full extent of Tara's plans, each of the bulls knew that it wanted to be selected. Within moments, a growing sense of rivalry filled the pack. Tara felt it and used it.

"Wag the cocks!" Tara said without fanfare.

Nine spotlighted bulls responded and nine brightly lit cocks began to magically wiggle and wag for her. With her eyes focused on their hips while she searched for even the slightest movement, Tara inspected her herd to determine which bulls showed greater cock control and which were merely shaking their hips to improvise a dancing cock. Unless their groin exercises had produced effective muscle control, Tara would order the hip-shakers to the punishment area and dazzle the Owner and her guests with the real thing.

Her eyes scrutinized the lineup of wiggling genitals. Suddenly, a single cock bobbed. It caught her attention as if a cymbal had clanged.

"THAT cock!" she demanded and pointed. A trainee scurried to lift its sac and read the numbers to Tara.

"One-seventy-two," Elise announced.

"Get it in its training stall," Tara shot back as her eyes dawdled on the meaty cock that was being led away by a cock leash. Three more to go, she calculated.

The lights focused on the remaining bulls' cocks and ball sacs. Tara inspected the hopeful eight to find which three would qualify for training for Competition. Her choice, discovering the bulls that would please her Owner and stand up for Competition, was always gut wrenching. Tara approached the task scientifically. Yet she always experienced the task with a single and primal understanding.

> *Go with your gut feeling, she had been taught. Don't live inside your head and don't over-think it. The answer is usually clear. Simply recognize it.*

"The rest of you," Tara said to the remnants of the herd, "make those cocks jump! Now!" The tone of her voice left no room for misunderstanding. Each bull struggled ferociously to force its cock to perform and dance for Tara. Their grunting and groaning spoke to the seriousness of their effort. By now, the bulls learned that it didn't matter which woman gave an order on the Farm; their job was to obey it. Yet each of them to a bull, understood that when this particular woman stood in front of them and issued a direct command, the pressure to obey increased multifold.

The bulls' faces drew into grimaces and their hips tensed. Within a few seconds of her order, Tara watched a few cocks jerk and bounce and she ordered those particular bulls to the training stalls. What stood under the hot lights now were five useless bulls whose disobedient cocks hung motionless from their groins.

Those penises are useless to me or my Owner, she thought. As she had been taught, uselessness on the Farm was unacceptable and must be corrected so every animal is useful in some way each Season.

"Punishment stalls," she said over her shoulder toward Monique as she strode toward her prize-winning bulls to get them ready for intense individual training.

Monique, one of her recently-promoted trainees, led the other trainees as the women jerked their bulls' reins and hauled them to the punishment stalls. After all, what trainee wanted a discarded or rejected animal to have to call her own and work with all Season? Each girl decided right then that her bull would never again fail as miserably as it just had. The humiliation of Tara's rejection meant that they would be unable to wear their Competition leathers and would be relegated to the sidelines to watch. No trainee wanted to be sent to the incidental parade of the Farm's first Competition of the Season.

That insult was almost too much for several of the young trainees to bear.

Their pointed breasts leading the way as they followed Monique, the girls hauled their discarded bulls toward several sets of metallic bars and pressed them down on their knees on the scratchy straw. After locking their heads in place and wrapping a padded metal bar around their midsections, the girls spread the bulls' legs and fastened their hooves to the floor bolts. Although they had never participated in bull pen punishment, the trainees had been instructed how to secure their animals for the possibility. And now it was everyone's reality.

It was up to the Trail Boss to oversee the punishment of the animals in her herd. They knew Tara would join them when she was finished with the first round of Competition training for her chosen bulls. Every moment they waited for her to arrive was like pouring salt into a raw wound that chafed between their breasts. The girls knew that their bulls would be punished but they also understood that the bulls' failures weighed heavy on how they had trained their members of the herd and how they would be evaluated.

Tara's attention focused on the five bulls that were selected to perform in first Competition. The trainees, whose fingers were busily fastening their animals into place for distance training, beamed with pride when their Trail Boss inspected their work and pronounced it satisfactory. Because the girls rarely interacted with the Owner, what their Trail Boss said next constituted their line of communication with the Farm's Owner through the staff.

"We'll take an initial distance measurement," Tara said. "Then we'll judge recovery time to determine how quickly each bull can re-erect. Finally, you'll perform a secondary distance evaluation." Tara's voice trailed off for a few minutes as she watched her excited trainees plan the morning's workout. "Remember," she finished, "any bull that is unable to perform up to my standards will be rejected and sent to punishment. Be certain that your animal is fully trained. Make sure that the penis is properly primed. Be sure that its attention is fully focused. Finally, and most of all, be sure that it performs exactly as I instruct."

Then she added ominously, "I will reject any animal that fails to meet my criteria and will punish both the animal and its trainer."

The girls nodded in a mixture of fear and excitement.

"I have five others to replace them," Tara threatened and the girls took a collective gulp. They made a mental note that their select position was tenuous at best.

Never allow them to relax. Keep them dancing on the edge. Push them off-balance while they are dancing.

"Start with these two," Tara pointed arbitrarily as Ana and Elise hauled their animals to their feet, lifted their bulls' heads and snapped a metal collar around their foreheads and another one around their chests. Two semi-limp cocks hung from their groins and Tara evaluated their potential.

"Let's see how well you've done with their training," she said as she strode toward the bound pair. The trainees felt the challenge wash over them.

Taking a two-pronged bull prod from her belt, Tara zapped it lightly against the tips of the two dangling cocks and waited for the bulls to react to her simple but clear demand. Within seconds, the dangling shafts thickened and bobbed with juices. She nodded, ignoring the bulls' grunts. Their bodies were rigid and occasionally wrenched uselessly against the strong metal bands that held them securely in place. Their cocks began dancing for the Trail Boss.

Next!" she pointed at two particular bulls in nearby training pens. Their trainees immediately hoisted them up and locked them just like the first pair and Tara, who believed that repetition was good for animals in training, repeated the electrical prod. She was greeted with the sight of four mostly erect bulls whose cocks were engorging nicely. It was time to get the fifth ready.

She had saved that one for last because, as Trail Boss, she was privy to certain information that was parsed directly from the Assessment and Intake teams and shared only with the highest-level staff. Now was the right time for Tara to use a valuable tidbit to her advantage and to make a point with the trainees and their training bulls. Pointing her prod toward the quivering animal, she pointed up for it to stand for her. Monique, the trainee assigned to that particular bull, stood silently in place, having been given no instruction to complete.

Tara stepped toward the trembling animal.

Tara pointed her prod toward the bull's midsection and drew a sharp line from its navel toward the shaft's tip. The bull screamed in agony yet didn't move an inch from its assigned spot. To Monique's amazement that was buoyed by the other trainees' ogling, the tortured bull's penis shot up straight and it pointed in a perfect 90-degree line from its body.

All of their eyes stared at Tara.

"A few special bulls enjoy and react to pain," she explained." The girls nodded, only beginning to understand. This particular bull's secret was now common knowledge and the trainees learned that the Trail Boss knew things that they hadn't yet been told.

Tara said, "You will learn that pain is the appropriate training method for some special animals on the Farm. Agony," her voice was strong, "is better."

> *Tara loved pain training, which is why her Owner often gave her the bulls. Her work with new trainees was a Farm legend. Only a select few on the Farm staff knew of Tara's private Blue Studio sessions with her Owner that left them both smiling afterward.*

The bull struggled to gather its wits as it succumbed to the Trail Boss's accuracy. Its huge cock still stood firm and affirmed Tara's correct use of its former secret. By the time that Competition training was in full swing, there would be no secrets left in the bull pen and every bull's secret proclivities would be common knowledge.

"Let the cocks drop and go limp while I tend to the other bulls," Tara said. "This group will be fed only after 15 consecutive successful erections on command." Tara walked toward the punishment stalls at the other end of the pen to focus on the animals she recently rejected. In the competition training stalls, her trainees ordered the bulls' cocks down. A few tried to command them to rise again. There was glee as one or another of the animals performed to the young trainees' instructions.

Failure is unacceptable and the goal is to educate and improve both the animals and the staff. Use punishment only when training and discipline do not succeed. Use punishment to make a point that is made best with creative agony.

The five rejected bulls knelt silently in the punishment stalls as their dejected trainees stood motionless while awaiting their Trail Boss's entrance. Their humiliation in having failed at trained successful animals was written all over their faces and in their crestfallen posture. Sad breasts pointed down from the girls' slumped shoulders. Tara knew exactly how much time she should allow them to wallow in self-pity yet her goal was to teach them how to accept failure and at the same time to improve their skills so that this result would never happen to them again.

The bulls were not the only ones who were about to benefit from Tara's skill with creative punishment.

Silently, Tara walked up and down the line, occasionally touching a bull's chin to lift its head uncomfortably against the limitations of its neck collar. The animals' eyes continuously failed to meet her own; they wore their embarrassment throughout their bodies. When she stepped behind the line to inspect their spread legs, locked hooves and open asses, Tara pressed her prod lightly on one ball sac after another to educate the imprisoned animals further that their pain was completely at her whim.

"Trainees, strip your leathers."

Her command surprised the five crestfallen girls and Tara noted that there was at least an eight-second pause before the first trainee pulled down her leather shorts and kicked them aside. Soon, five trainees' naked bodies stood in embarrassment behind their bulls. The girls' eyes could not meet Tara's and she smiled as she assessed that both her bulls and trainees were suffering equivalent states of shame.

Tara suppressed a smile as her fingers gripped the nearest pair of nipples and had one of two girls' breasts pressed tightly in each hand. Tara dragged two humiliated trainees to the front of the punishment area. The bulls, whose heads hung low in their own degradation, were ordered to stare at the barn floor. Given Tara's handy electric prod, they did exactly that.

The two naked trainees glistened under the spotlights as their nipples tightened in the cool morning air.

"Spread your legs," Tara ordered the amazed pair who squirmed a little before obeying. Then she added a further insult with a single word: "Squat!"

With only a two-second hesitation, the two trainees lowered their asses toward the floor, their spread cheeks only a few inches from the dirty straw. Because they were facing the bulls, they presented their open labia toward the animals' faces. Tara walked behind the lineup of bull flesh and poked her prod firmly into each set of spread cheeks as she moved down the line. With a growl of pain and an involuntary reaction they could not physically suppress, each bull lifted its own neck and was greeted by the sight of the trainees' dripping pussies only a few inches from their eyes.

Tara said to the three remaining trainees, "Measure them NOW!"

It became clear in that instant. The trainees had failed to command their animals; instead, they had never risen above the rank of "female" to assume the more respected rank of "trainer" to the bulls and consequently, the animals neither respected their commands nor fulfilled their orders. One of the hardest lessons for the trainees to learn was that they had to discard their gender to become accomplished trainers.

Tara's punishing them was the trainees' first real life lesson in learning how to separate themselves from 'girl' and become 'trainee.' Although a harsh example, Tara usually found the punishment to be helpful with her girls.

"Exchange positions," she ordered and the three trainees moved from behind the bulls and squatted in front of them while the other two took their places behind the bulls' asses. Tara walked the line again, this time reaching between each bull's legs and feeling every cock condition. When she was certain that the bulls' shafts were limp, she repeated the command. Each bull growled in pain from her prod's kiss yet was greeted with a glimpse of three pair of spread labia when their heads jerked up in reflex to Tara's expertly placed prod that kissed the outer rim hidden deep inside their beefy cheeks.

Tara walked the line silently again and evaluated each bull's hard cock by grabbing it in her hand. Smiling now, she turned to her girls.

"All of you, up front and squat!" she ordered. The five girls jumped into place and Tara inspected them. Wielding her leather crop expertly, she duck-walked a few trainees closer to their bulls' snouts by whipping the girls' asscheeks one-by-one. Almost hopping into place, all of the trainees were now crouched only a few inches from their animals.

"Inhale your trainer," Tara ordered and the bulls gulped air through their noses. For their part, the trainees, who felt like they could not be humiliated any further, experienced an even deeper sense of shame. Naked and being sniffed by their animals was their most degrading experience they had suffered to date on the Farm.

"Our instruction today will conclude with one additional lesson," Tara said casually. "Your bull is reacting to your scent," Tara explained as she grasped each bull's shaft again and noted its steadily increasing hardness. "You will learn to use your scent to train your bull."

Tara watched the girls' faces and smiled without moving her lips.

"Inch closer," Tara ordered, and the squatting trainees struggled forward until their spread labia nestled around their bulls' snouts. "Their cocks are hard," Tara commented as she walked behind the bulls and manipulated their shafts again.

"Closer!" she ordered and the girls legs, now screaming with the stress of squatting, pressed themselves fully against the bulls' snouts, effectively cutting off their animal's oxygen. Behind the bulls, Tara cracked her whip on one ass after another. As the bulls suffered their whipping, their snouts were driven deeper into their trainees. When the whipping ceased, they withdrew their snouts slowly.

Over and over, Tara whipped the bulls and each, in turn, pressed its nose deeper into its trainer. She withdrew the whip only when she turned her attention to another bull's ass. As Tara continued the lesson, the pressure on the girls' spread lips from plunging bull snouts provided an odd sort of pleasure that made them almost forget the pain in their hamstrings. Again and again, the process was repeated and soon Tara saw the well-known look of impending orgasm on her trainees' faces.

The lesson had been successful. She lowered her whip suddenly and ordered the girls to stand.

With juices dripping down their legs, the trainees stood totally humiliated before their Trail Boss and the bulls. Tara inspected them, touched their wet thighs, drove a finger or two into them to measure their wetness and clucked at the results.

"Learn my lesson," Tara said quietly. "Unless you separate and elevate yourselves from the animals, you are no different from them and you will be treated like them."

She turned and walked toward the Competition training stalls to continue her work with the chosen bulls as the trainees slinked behind their own rejected animals. They took a collective deep breath and began training their bulls with new determination and with new skills.

They will give me five good bulls to use as backup, Tara thought and smiled. And my Owner will be pleased.

Chapter 29: Cow Milking

With only two days left until the Farm's First Competition of the Season, Ursula worked the herd of cows urgently. Wearing bits held tightly between their teeth with reins hanging limply from each end, the cows were secured in their stalls and the herd was ready to begin morning's training. Most of the cows were needy; after several days of constant milking, their udders had been untouched for at least two days. Given the complexity of the program and the level of success required for their training, Ursula was certain that their production today would be enormous.

Her trainees taught the cows' udders to respond to a variety of stimuli and by now, the cows could each produce quantitatively larger amounts of pre-ejaculate, or what Ursula called "cow milk" on command. With the Farm's careful measuring system, she had accurate data from which to select her choicest cows for Competition. Only the most productive in the herd would satisfy her needs.

A cow that hadn't been milked for a few days always produced ear-splitting mooing, a testament of its new understanding of how a trainee's fingers or a milking machine had become its only comfort. Without a trainee's touch, a cow felt lonely and neglected, but worst of all, endured an unending burning to empty itself. The mooing that resulted from a cow's full udder that was desperate for relief grew into the barn's special symphony. Ursula loved that music. Making the cows moo for her pleasure was a skill she worked hard to teach her trainees.

The trainees had heard the song of contented cow moo throughout their training and even the new trainees missed the music during the past two days. Even though they had worked the cows to create an acceptable line of marching-in-step bovines, each tied by its udder to the one behind, the girls missed the daily milking routine. It was increasingly noticeable that the cows were tense and growing more agitated without their daily milking routine.

Ursula woke the cow barn with her familiar greeting. A horn blasted over the barn's loudspeaker and every cow scurried to rise to all fours, spread its legs and allow its udder to dangle between them. Once they were all in position to her satisfaction, Ursula addressed the herd.

"Competition is in two days. I will select the most productive cows to compete. Each cow's production and rebound capability will be measured today. Only then will I take the Competition cows for enhanced training." She let her words sink in as the cows shook sleep out of their brains and tried to understand.

"Those who fail to produce to my specifications will be sent to discipline. That course of remedial work will focus on teaching the herd to increase production on command for future Competitions."

The cows were jerked to alertness and grew alarmed. Each wanted to be selected for Competition training and the sound of 'discipline' didn't sit well in any cow's ears. Their distress was doubled by the growing discomfort of their full bladders so early in the morning.

The trainers bustled about their animals, tapped hooves to spread their legs farther apart, and ensured that each udder dangled free. Even though they knew that the cows had to be watered pretty soon, the girls were more eager to begin production measurement. Ursula inspected her trainees and noted expectant glimmers in their eyes. Getting your animal ready for testing was a procedure that the trainees practiced over and over until it met with their Trail Boss's approval, which gained a successful trainee one of Ursula's nods.

Cows never noticed those nods; instead, they were always fully immersed in their training, setting their legs just far enough apart, responding to swats from their trainers' crops, and anticipating every move to avoid having to repeat the exercise, or worse, being taken for discipline.

During their Season on the Farm, the cows had become accustomed to their daily milking under the hands of various milkers. It surprised all of them that the milkers' hands varied so much. Even though they learned not to expect any favorable treatment, some of the cows seemed to ejaculate more milk with more force when certain trainees' hands squeezed the final drops out of their udders than when others tried the same thing.

Ursula knew it; after all, cows and trainees had no secrets in her barn. Every milliliter of milk was measured by Assessment and Ursula read their reports daily on her tablet. Whenever a cow suddenly produced more milk, she researched the causes until she was satisfied that she had the most likely answer. Every Season produced both good and *great* milkers. It was Ursula's task to find the best ones for Competition and retrain the weaker ones with extra cows while she readied the herd for Competition.

By now, the herd needed watering and Ursula decided to ready the lot of them for their first milking after their multi-day abstinence. Rather than take the herd to the watering shed, she instructed the trainees to empty them.

"Get the hoses," she said to her girls.

As the trainees scurried to secure rubber hoses to the cows' udders, Ursula continued issuing instructions.

"Apply the hoses. Tighten the clamps," she said. "Then press the yellow button. After the whirring stops, check for tension and tightness." By now, she knew her girls and was confident with their ability to follow multiple instructions.

The trainees complied with her instructions quickly. They each pulled a large clear tube to their cows' udder and tightened the bolts at the top. Each hose fit snugly around the base of each udder's shaft and a clear plastic band wrapped around its testicles.

As they finished hooking the bands, the trainees pressed the yellow buttons on their tablets and the barn was filled with the sound of electronic vacuuming. Barn-filling cow moo followed quickly.

Ursula used her master control to adjust the contracting speed so the suction increased. She smiled when the mooing amplified nicely. Surge after surge of suction sucked the cows' bladders dry and also served to engorge their udders until they were all chubby and firm. Ursula perfected this technique in prior Seasons, yet most of the trainees were just now seeing their first electronically-enlarged udder. She enjoyed watching her girls' faces when the vacuum tubes were released.

> *Make it long enough to serve its purpose and use it to make the point. Their surprise is one of your best weapons.*

As she adjusted the intensity again, first lower and then higher just to watch the herd's faces struggle to remain composed during their watering, Ursula issued additional instructions to the trainees.

"Caryn, wrap your hand around that udder," she said. "Get to know its tensile strength. Girls, notice that each udder is now full and thick." The trainees obeyed and felt and measured. "Cows react to vacuum stimulation," she added. As Caryn felt the cow's sheathed shaft, Ursula watched her eyes widen in awe of the size that her cow had achieved.

"Do the same to your cows," she ordered the rest of the trainees. "Feel each one carefully."

The cows mooed in a delightful melody when the girls' fingers wrapped around their raging cocks.

"Control!" Ursula said as she glanced toward the control area. "Display the measurements on my monitor!"

With that order, the control room staff uploaded the report and Ursula determined which cows might qualify for Competition and which would be cast as supporting animals that would merely march in the parade but not be entered into the first Competition.

Using today's measurements alongside their season-long performance records, Ursula was content that the right cows were about to be chosen. This close to Competition, she knew it was time to separate the herd into the Show cows and those destined for punishment and retraining.

"Press your blue buttons," she said as the girls complied and the whirring ceased.

The whole herd seemed to teeter on the verge of hysteria. Their udders were bloated and they had an urgent need to expel their contents. Some were in a near frenzy from need but the hoses' tightened bands prevented even simple urination. The mooing song changed dramatically into one of primal need.

First things first, Ursula decided.

"Girls, some of you will take the rejected cows to the discipline area so that we can focus on training the show cows. Look at your screens."

The girls' eyes stared at their tablets.

"Red lights will be taken to the side pen for discipline. The green lights will follow me to the corral for Competition training. I don't need all of you for advanced training so most of you will tend to the rejects in the pen. I think we'll have better discipline retraining with a lot of trainers," she said.

Don't make them feel inferior unnecessarily. There's plenty of time for that. But if their work is inferior, make sure they know that or they'll never improve.

Every trainee knew that being sent to the small pen was an inglorious rejection of both her training capability and her cow's performance. Those tapped for the coveted Competition training corral understood that they had performed better so far this Season. Many of the green-light trainees struggled to keep serious faces as they followed their Trail Boss proudly to the corral. The procession of Trail Boss, prize cows and selected trainees was one of Ursula's Season highlights. She wanted her chosen girls to bask in the pride that went along with successful work and her cows could, at least for a few moments, crawl with self-respect and the envy of the rest of the herd.

As the prize herd plodded forward, Ursula instructed the rejected batch of trainees to spend their morning exploring additional ways to increase each cow's milk output. She suggested that they work together to form a plan to accomplish those results. The trainees were aggravated with the busy work they had been assigned while the prize herd and the trainees were working for Competition. None of them liked feeling second-rate at all. Ursula was certain that the superfluous cows could expect a particularly arduous morning. Smiling, she led the prize herd toward the training corral.

"Each cow will be milked," Ursula said with a smile directed to both her small group of swollen cows as well as to their trainers. "The prize herd will be worked today and rested tomorrow to be in the best possible shape for Competition. First, we milk them."

She look at the swollen size of their udders, she knew the girls had to take them to the head rails immediately."

As the trainees led their animals by their reins to the far size of the corral, Ursula watched the herd's erect shafts and dangling balls bob painfully up and down as they plodded on all fours across the dirt. Once their heads were locked in the padded rails, she ordered them up to their hind hooves and directed their front hooves to grasp the handrails. Positioned this way, the herd was almost standing up straight but their spread legs afforded the trainees complete access to their udders. With their heads locked into place, not one of them could fall.

Ursula stepped behind one cow and took its swollen udder in her leather glove. "Watch this particular technique," she said as the group circled around her.

With expert moves, she manipulated the cow's udder so that its hips jerked repeatedly with each stroke. Her black leather glove tugged and pulled, circled and fondled, and finally stretched the udder so that the cow was both shrieking in pain and mooing from its gut for relief.

"Pay attention," she said to her enrapt trainees.

She pinched the tip of the udder with two fingers. The cow's mooing grew into a desperate cry of pain. The udder, to every trainee's astonishment, shrank visibly in front of their eyes.

"You control the timing of a cow's every moment," she said. "Never allow it to expel prematurely or you'll lose quantity. And worse," she looked each trainee in the eyes, "it won't be any use to you for at least an hour."

The girls nodded. They all knew what happened when a cow exploded before it was their time.

"For Competition, we want every cow to be at its level of full potency. After all, Caryn, how would it look if yours could not produce as much as, say, Carrie's?" She looked down the line of her trainees and watched them nod in agreement.

> *A prematurely exploding cow would disappoint the Owner. That was something that got you a special invitation to the Owner's Green Salon the next morning. Everyone on the Farm knew it was to be avoided at all costs.*

"We stimulate the udder, get it ready, move it to its highest state, and then when it looks like your cow can't endure one more second, you stop it immediately. You must control your cow." She looked at each of them as her leather-clad hands manipulated the cow's udder again and its mooing reverberated throughout the corral. The cow's noise got louder as her hands worked the udder and then suddenly, an ear-piercing scream filled the air. For the one trainee who had the managed to get best view of this training, the udder relaxed visibly.

Ursula saw Colleen recognize the change in size. As if just for that one trainee who she believed would rate high on the promotion list for her power of observation, Ursula worked the cow again and again as she watched Colleen watching the cow's hind legs tremble trying to hold itself upright. Having had many Seasons' experience with cows, Ursula was tuned into each one's mooing and could tell without looking at its face exactly when it was ready to burst. The pinch usually worked and she demonstrated it repeatedly to her trainees and especially to Colleen. For its part, the cow continued to moo frantically.

"Work your cow exactly as I demonstrated. They must inflate and deflate at your command and you must control everything your cow does. If your cow sheds any milk before I order it, you will be sent for punishment and be excluded from Competition."

Ursula knew that she had selected more cows than were to be shown. Experience on the Farm taught her that at least one or two would fail to meet her standards during the Final Competition training. She expected a few to fail and she would push each trainee almost beyond her limits to winnow the select herd and trainees down to an appropriate number.

"I'm going to check the discipline pen," she said over her shoulder as she walked away. "Train your cows."

The mooing that started by the time she had taken her third step toward the discipline pen convinced her that her girls took her words seriously and were engrossed in their work. The prize herd was in for a long morning and she chuckled while walking to the small pen's discipline area.

The pen was gloomy with unhappy trainees and sullen cows.

Ursula understood their feelings of dejection yet the reality of the Farm was that only the best of the best would be selected for any Competition. The cows and the trainees would learn that fact during the Season – that the ineffective would be disciplined and the best trained were the trophies. In the meantime, as much as she knew that a few of the prized herd would join the rejects in the discipline pen soon enough, she understood that an occasional jewel might have been cast too soon as a failure. Once in a while, she discovered a pearl in the rejects and moved that cow up to the show herd. After all, if three cows failed in the corral, she'd need one to fill its place. Otherwise, there were only two extras.

Her eyes were fixated on the cows and her morose trainees.

"This will not do," she said and snapped the prod from her belt. Walking to the line, she touched its evil bite to every cow's udder and elicited one painful moo after another. Then she marched down the line and set the prod on every trainee's nipple and enjoyed their screeches of pain.

"We do NOT act like calves in this barn!" she admonished the trainees. "Selection is based solely on production and yours was inadequate," she said. "I want every cow in this pen brought to full milking potential!"

> *Punish your girls when they lose sight of the bigger goal, she knew well from experience.*

No one dared argue with Ursula's raised voice. Her orders were clear.

"UP!" she commanded and every cow rose to its hind quarters.

"STROKE!" she ordered and the trainees moved in front of their cows and manipulated their udders to erection. The cows' mooing rose in volume and urgency.

"PINCH!" she said and each trainee took the udder's tip in two fingers as they had been instructed and practically tore it off the cow's shaft as the animals screamed in pain.

"REPEAT!" she said and the girls returned to manipulating the cows' udders.

The exercise was repeated until Ursula was satisfied that every participant had relearned the first training technique, that is, utter obedience to her commands.

"Now we begin *cow* training," she said to the flabbergasted group who just realized that *they* had just been trained and not their animals.

For the next hour, the melody of the prize herd's mooing filled her ears. Ursula took the pen participants on a fast tour of preparing for Competition. She taught the trainees how to maneuver the cows' ball sacs and showed them stretching techniques that were sure to stimulate even an exhausted cow. Then she demonstrated several advanced tricks that slowed down any impending explosion, which meant that each cow was taken to the edge orgasm and pushed farther than the last time before its milk production was suddenly shut off by the trainees' newly-learned techniques. To Ursula, it was like a water spigot being turned off suddenly in midstream.

The trainees' moods elevated with each new procedure Ursula showed them and the cows, for their part, were treated like mere physical and breathing extensions of the girls' training.

Build them back up after you have brought them down,
Ursula learned. Then they are yours for all Seasons.

"You have 45 minutes before I return," she said. "When I come back to this pen, I want to see every cow teetering on its brink. I want each one of them to moo for relief and I want you to show no compassion. They are merely cows and you own them. Perhaps one might even qualify for Competition training." She watched their shining faces before issuing a single parting comment.

"No mercy," she said as she left them on her way to the corral.

Her prize herd had been worked for more than an hour and Ursula was certain they would be teetering on the brink. It was always fun to see her prizes mooing in a desperate attempt to be allowed to spill milk for her. Her ears enjoyed their frantic sounds; her eyes loved watching their fervent dance of need; and her hands took pleasure in fingering each udder to feel its stiffness and readiness. Competition always brought out the best in her.

She wasn't disappointed when she drank in the scene in the corral. The cows, their heads still locked in the rails, gyrated desperately for relief while the trainers grew expert with the skills needed for a great event at Competition. Ursula reveled in imagining what they had endured while she was busy in the punishment pen. But based on the scenario she saw, she was convinced that a single correct touch would cause rapid-fire explosions worthy of her Owner's expectation of an exciting milking contest.

But then a single cow caught her attention.

Unless Carrie, its trainer, acted quickly, Ursula was sure that it was going to expel prematurely, partly due to how it noticed her return and its trainer's split-second distraction. That combination was fatal, she recalled from an earlier competition when the crowd's cheering momentarily distracted a trainer. Her cow humiliated itself and worse, its trainer, by launching a projectile of milk that spilled on the dirt of the Competition ring. A chill ran through her as she recalled how the Owner paused the Competition and personally escorted the trainer and errant cow to the punishment area and administered the sentence herself. Both her guests and combatants were forced to wait for her return and could only imagine what punishment befell the trainer and her animal. For the only time she could ever recall, Ursula saw the Owner's temper show itself and she was determined that neither her cows nor her trainees would be the cause of that ever happening on her watch.

Before she could warn Carrie to pay closer attention to what was happening within her fingers, the cow's eyes filled with tears and its hips humped wildly. Its udder shot a stream of wasted milk onto the dirt.

Shaking her head from side to side, she marched toward the chagrined trainee. Grabbing a handful of her long hair, Ursula jerked Carrie's head upward and stared into her fearful face.

"Just WHAT were you doing?" she demanded as she forced her head farther backward.

Too humiliated to respond, Carrie tried in vain to avoid her Trail Boss's eyes that were piercing into her own. Ursula would not allow silence in the face of such a huge transgression of training protocol. She demanded a response.

"Answer me!" she said more loudly into the trembling trainee's face.

"I... I... don't know what happened," Carrie hesitated. She struggled to get each syllable past her lips.

"*I* know what happened!" Ursula exploded into her face. "You violated my first rule – you did not pay complete attention to your animal!" Her voice shook with anger that an animal was, even for a moment, unsupervised. "Intolerable!" she spat into the girl's face.

The corral was silent during the exchange. Ursula's stare bore down on the mortified trainee and the cow, for its part, sobbed into the dirt as the rest of the show herd snapped back into cadence by Ursula's single command.

"TRAIN THEM!" she barked at the rest of her girls, who dove directly into milking training and tried to ignore the spectacle that was unfolding across the corral.

Dragging the spent cow and its trainer toward the punishment pen, Ursula's anger was accompanied by the sound of her stomping boots. Each pair of rejected cow and trainee in the small pen stared at their Trail Boss dragging a sobbing trainee by the hair and noticed that Ursula's hand gripped the cow's reins so tightly that the animal could hardly keep pace behind her. Without knowing the specifics of the situation, each trainee knew that there had been a serious breach. Watching that scene in astonishment and fear, none of them wanted to know more at that moment. Whatever occurred, they knew it had been horrible.

> Never explain failures to trainees. Just make your point so they never forget it and they know not to let it happen to them.

In one motion, Ursula dropped Carrie ingloriously onto the pen's dirt floor, alerted Control, and stomped back to the

Competition corral. One down and only one more expendable cow to go, she counted silently as she left them on the pen's dirt floor.

Let them fear their punishment as they consider their transgression. And never punish out of anger. Punish only to teach the lesson.

For the rest of the morning, the prize cows were driven to their threshold and then brought down again. Ursula shared more training techniques with her trainees and showed them methods that tortured the animals into frenzy yet controlled every hump and thrust. From her experience with past competitions, Ursula was confident that the prize herd would serve her well and put on a good show for the Owner and her guests.

There was only one more task to accomplish.

With First Competition a mere 48 hours from now, Ursula wanted her girls to understand what her training with the prize herd had accomplished. She knew as a result of the incompetent trainee experience they had seen that they must know by now the pitfalls of over-stimulation of any animal. Even with all her Seasons on the Farm, Ursula was still amazed at the reaction that some cows had to enhanced training and being pushed beyond the edge of it limits. Inexplicably, some animals simply failed to ejaculate after aggressive training while some bordered on setting new Farm distance and quantity records. The girls had to know that potential result so they would not be overwhelmed with a sense of personal failure if their animal failed.

However, failing during Competition was unacceptable so they needed to learn the warning signs now.

"It's time to finish them off before feeding," Ursula said to the sweaty group. "Control will take measurements of both force and quantity so let's get the herd hooked up to the tubes before we conclude this part of training."

The trainees, whose arms were almost worn out from their morning's udder stroking, were grateful for Ursula's order. Once the cows' udders were attached to measurement hoses, their Trail Boss undertook the task of illustrating methods of forcing completion from over-worked cows. The first animal she selected did not yet suffer from that syndrome.

Lead with success, the Owner taught them. Make sure the first one performs to expectations.

A single electrical tap to the tip of the cow's udder elicited both a fierce moo and torrid humping that culminated in the cow's accomplishing its task. Its stream was measured carefully. Control recorded both the quantity and speed with which it was released. With time to study the results after lunch, Ursula moved to the second prize cow in line.

"Prods work well," she said, "but there are more presentation-worthy ways to get the job done." Her hands drew an object from her belt and after covering and lubricating it, Ursula pressed the oval object between the cow's asscheeks and pushed it firmly inside. When only the handle protruded from between its asscheeks, Ursula used it to pry around inside the animal. When her forefinger flicked a button on the handle, the device emitted a low sound. The cow's lips released a moo of gigantic volume in response.

"It's a prostate stimulator," Ursula said. "Watch this." She spoke as much to Colleen as she did to the rest of the trainees. Everyone's eyes were glued to her hands.

The cow's reaction to prostate stimulation resulted in a flurry of hip and ass gyrations that amused the Trail Boss. Its frenzy also fascinated the trainees lucky enough to witness it. The animal's hips rocketed from side to side and its hooves stamped in the dirt. In just a few seconds after Ursula increased the speed and pushed the object deeper inside, the cow expelled so much milk that it almost fell to the ground in exhaustion. Only the head rails kept the animal upright but its wild eyes told the true story.

The girls were fascinated after seeing their first prostate milking. Colleen let out a soft whistle of admiration.

Ursula handed the tool to a trainee for placement in the sterilization bath and faced her girls.

"Finish and measure each one," she said. "I will study the results after feeding. Then I'll make my final decision which cows will be entered into Competition and which will serve merely for the procession."

Each girl listened carefully for a hint or innuendo that her cow might be selected, but Ursula offered none.

"I'll be in the pen," she concluded. "This is your final chance to get your cow chosen."

Walking toward the pen to see to the rejected cows' sweat, mud, and milk hosed off, Ursula heard the sweet mooing of one prize cow after another being forced to finish. That song was accompanied by her girls' giggling as they followed her orders to the letter and the cows' mooing was music to Ursula's ears.

Chapter 30: Chicken Feathers

The morning just before Competition made for one of Rhonda's favorite times in the Coops. While the other Trail Bosses struggled to select which animals they would show in the upcoming Competition, Rhonda knew that every one of the chickens in her charge would be part of the parade. Most of all, she knew that each chicken would carry out its orders in full-feathered finery. The Coops were a special barn on the Farm and their inhabitants fulfilled a unique function. Both the chickens and the roosters made up the decoration on the Competition's cake and Rhonda was the dessert chef. Her birds were the frosted cupcakes.

Rhonda's first task was to awaken the chickens from their nests and ready them for the intense two-day preparation period prior to First Competition. She knew that the Owner expected the flock to be adorned in spectacle-worthy finery. As an added bonus, the flock of chickens were required to entertain the Owner's guests with a combined persona of dignity and gaiety. That combination allowed the chickens to open the ceremonies with memorable flourish. As each event began, the roosters and chickens were used as a part of the rewards claimed by deserving herd members who made their Trail Bosses proud.

Only the winners received what the fowl had been trained to give. That's why these two days before Competition took on an air of critical mass for the coop's Trail Boss. A prize worth winning had to look good and act splendidly. To be a prize, a chicken or rooster had to be splendid.

With her boots' pounding on the coop's wooden floor, Rhonda rang the morning bell herself. Then she marched up and down the tiers of nests to inspect the initial moment of her animals' day.

Beginning with the instant their eyes fluttered open, she injected herself into every minute of the 48 hours that were left before the chickens and roosters would become the Competition's trophies. As the flock groggily greeted daylight, Rhonda issued orders designed to upset their focus.

"Up! Get UP!" she said loudly as she walked the length of the coop's tiers of nests and then back again. "Release their ankles and get the flock watered. There's not very much time to whip this bunch of birds into prize shape!" She continued stomping up and down the rows of nests to get their full attention as well as to produce her own audible cacophony that served to confound the still-sleepy birds.

The trainees trotted with the flock to the watering shed. They cleaned their birds inside and out while Rhonda continued stomping on the shed's floor in a successful attempt to be as distracting and disconcerting as possible. Rushing the group to their initial feeding, she urged the handlers to strap on the feedbags as fast as they could and then open the valves wider than normal to force feed the flock like geese selected for paté. Finally, the trainees returned the flock to the Coop so real training could start. Each chicken and rooster became alarmingly aware of the number of times Rhonda used the word "real" training so far in this day's instructions.

"Now that they are finally clean," Rhonda said in a voice so loud that it shook the fowl's ears, "it's time to dress them up. I want the ones who will be prizes for the first-place finishers in the regular events over here," she pointed to the far corner. "The second-place prizes go over there," her finger indicated the closest corner. "And I want the grand prize right here next to me."

The chickens perched motionless as they waited for their handlers to let them know which were to become the first, second or grand prizes for the Farm's Competition winners. Each bird hoped silently that it would – and at the same time prayed that it would not – become the 'grand prize.' Each trainer looked forward to her bird being selected for the top honor, no matter how much extra training that entailed. Rhonda called out the brands so the trainees could lift each scrotal sac and confirm every bird's identification.

The groups sorted themselves out as Rhonda read the list of which birds would become the first and second-place prizes. Soon the coop was divided into two clusters of chickens, with each assigned two roosters. The birds would need the roosters' services and Rhonda's experience taught her that two could serve the needs of at least seven chickens, albeit with a little prompting from her own bag of tricks. She grinned when she thought of the electrical stimulators that had a long and successful history with the Coop's denizens.

It was time to announce which chicken would receive grand-prize honors.

Rhonda looked over her flock and checked out their trainees in the short time it took her to clear her throat. The effect wasn't lost on either the birds or the trainees. She used her sternest voice to make the announcement.

"Listen carefully!" her voice reverberated throughout the coop and every pair of ears in the structure attended to her words. "The lucky bird is," she smirked in a pause designed to produce the desired effect, "number 210."

All the birds stared at one another and each trainee lifted her chicken's scrotum to double-check its identification number. Even though the trainees had the numbers memorized by now, one last check was a good idea and a hope that her bird had been identified for this special honor. As each trainer dejectedly uncovered her bird's unworthy ID, she tossed the useless scrotum down with enough force to make her bird wince.

One voice rang out through the coop.

"Mine!" the voice called with unhidden glee. "Mine is 210!"

All eyes turned toward the voice attached to the arm whose fingers were holding a large scrotum aloft. Although the particular bird's eyes evidenced the pain of her tight grip, there was noticeable glee that glowed from its face. Even its beak smiled through its pain.

"Bring it here," Rhonda said to the lucky trainee who hauled her bird by its scrotum to the Trail Boss and deposited it unceremoniously at her feet. Rhonda's boot prodded the bird this way and that, turned it on its side, its back, and flipped it over to its stomach. Finally resting her leather boot on its ass, Rhonda turned her attention to the waiting flock.

"Every chicken will need two outfits," she said. "The first is full-feather finery for the Parade of Colors. The second," her voice took on a stronger tenor, "will be its prize outfit." She allowed her instructions to sink in while the trainees' faces beamed with anticipation of the outfits in which her bird might be dressed for the parade and another for the awards ceremony. Allowing them a few moments of reverie, Rhonda brought them back to the reality of the mere 48 hours they had left to dress the chickens.

"Parade dress choices are on the back wall," Rhonda pointed. "As for the awards, you'll find treasures in the wardrobe area behind Control. Outfit your birds for the parade and I'll inspect them during our first walk through."

When she stopped talking, her trainees knew they were dismissed and leapt toward the treasure trove of parade finery. Each trainee dragged her collared bird absentmindedly behind her as she fingered the possibilities. Just as chickens' bodies were in various shapes and sizes, the perfect parade dress for skinny or fattened chickens had to be selected from among enormous choices. Trainees' hands flew through racks, rejected many and secured a few, and finally held each outfit against her animal's frame to eyeball the fit and weigh the appearance.

More rejections, more hands reaching deep into the garments to find those as yet unearthed, the girls' bustling brought a smile to Rhonda's lips. She recalled her first Competition and how she dressed her first chicken.

Make it resplendent, she recalled being taught. Make yours stand out as a reflection of you. An under-dressed chicken is a disappointment. So is its trainee.

The control room filmed the wardrobe selection process and Rhonda was certain the frenzied selection process would make a lovely after-dinner viewing session. With her finger on the bell, Rhonda waited for it to be the perfect time to bring the mass of motion to an end. She wanted the flock outfitted for the parade run-through as quickly as possible. It was at that moment that one trainee's chicken caught her eye. Quietly, she removed her finger from the bell while she inspected her trainee's actions from across the Coop.

Even with the commotion that surrounded her, this particular trainee seemed focused on her first-prize chicken's adornment and not on the upheaval going on around her. Rhonda appreciated that level of single-mindedness and watched her actions. As the girl placed one crown after another atop her bird's head, she shook her head side-to-side. Then she reached for another until finally, when Rhonda could feel the perfect fit even from her distance, the trainee nodded and her selection was made. It was time for her to inspect the feather choices.

Rhonda was pleased with the girl's top-down approach to the costume quandary. Making a mental note to get the girl's name for later promotion consideration, she surveyed the disorderly group and contrasted all of them to the new trainee's top-to-bottom more sensible approach. Finally, she rang the bell and followed up the clang with her own voice. Every movement in the Coop stopped immediately.

"Finished!" she said and brought the Coop to order. "Line up the flock with the first prizes in the front, followed by the seconds," she ordered. "The grand prize will lead them out."

One after another, birds were yanked by their collars and scrotums into an orderly procession that wound through the coop's tiers of nests. Rhonda walked to the front while dragging the grand prize chicken behind her by its collar. She saw the bird's trainee scurrying to keep up with her pace. When she was satisfied that the chickens and roosters were in order, Rhonda had Control ring the bell for the first walk-through rehearsal of the opening parade.

The grand prize's crown shined brightly in the morning sun when its wearer emerged from the coop's double doors to the outside pen. With her finger wrapped tightly in its collar ring, Rhonda dragged the lead chicken on a winding path around the perimeter of the yard until the entire flock created a circle along the edge of the fence.

Striding to the center of the makeshift circle, Rhonda surveyed her flock and frowned.

"What a mess!" she rebuked them in a single syllable, "Look at this! This is *not* how I want to open the parade!"

The trainees' eyes looked around the circle and their lips began to turn upward at the ludicrous sight they saw. The birds, each resplendent in Farm finery, complimented only itself and not each other. Each bird had its own color scheme, its own frocks, feathers, and jewels. It was obvious that they didn't coalesce into a display that would please the Owner and open the Farm's first parade with dignity.

Rhonda thought that looked hilarious. She laughed so hard that the trainees joined in. "This will never do," Rhonda said between chortles.

As the trainees giggled with their Trail Boss, the chickens tried to carry themselves with a shred of dignity, but the task was beyond them just like it was beyond their ability to walk in platform heels on dirt.

"What is our message?" Rhonda asked of the group.

At first, silence greeted her question but then a single trainee's voice attempted to answer. "We are the first in the parade. We are the best. We set the tone," the trainee said.

With her eye on the trainee whose answer summed up the coop's role in the Farm's parade, Rhonda called for the second place trophies to be returned to the coop for re-outfitting. Now she could attend to the first place awards and their trainees to discuss what that group tone would be for this Season.

Give them the theme, Rhonda was taught. They had to understand that the theme was integral to the Spectacle. The theme is their Season.

"What IS our theme?" Rhonda asked the trainees.

"I think," a trainee voice started, "that if our birds are the prizes, then they are the best. Our theme is 'the best,'" she said. Rhonda nodded and listened to a second and surprisingly stronger trainee answer.

"When they are awarded to the other packs, what they are wearing makes them a more worthwhile reward," the voice said. Again, Rhonda nodded and waited for more. Surely, they realized that response just wasn't enough.

Finally, a third voice offered both a question and answer. "The animals who win Competition? They are prizes that have to be outstanding. Our birds will be their well-earned reward to ejaculate. For most, their first after weeks of training. Our birds are whores and sluts and are the trophies for the animals who win."

Rhonda's face drew into a grin. It was especially rewarding when one of the trainees finally got it. *Whores and sluts*, indeed, she thought. The chickens and cocks were just that – they were the Farm's whores and sluts that were given to animals who performed the heavy work and needed relief. They were prizes for the herds that trained and fought during Competitions. Rhonda knew that even though their value was prized on the Farm, their function was more important.

They were there to provide physical relief for the working herds. That was their bottom line; their function; it was all of what they were meant to be. Their costumes, plumage, feathers, and finery were showy effects to showcase their primary job.

Animals are happiest when they are doing what they have been bred for and trained to do, Rhonda was taught. Chickens are merely receptacles for my Owner's herd.

Smiling at her trainee, Rhonda sent the first-place trophies back to the coop where they would be outfitted in feathers and finery that drew them into a single theme. Only with them dressed to present properly could the procession be orchestrated to keep rhythm with the Competition's precise schedule. Leaving her girls to their best judgment, Rhonda turned her full attention to the grand prize, a rooster with muscular legs and a thick neck. The animal sported a chest so broad that she wished briefly it had a mat of hair in which to lose her fingers, but of course, like the rest of the Farm animals, he was kept hairless for the Season.

The rooster's demeanor was almost regal, like a king that clucked around the dirt and reigned over all the chickens in the coop with a sense of privilege and ownership. It displayed a sense of possession that made the chickens realize they were subordinate to it. The king of its dominion, at least until it was given as the competition's grand prize, the tanned and well-built specimen at her feet filled Rhonda with pride. Only Rhonda knew what the rooster would face after being handed over to a winning animal as the grand prize. She allowed it to relish its false sense of pomp for a few moments.

It would learn soon enough what being the grand prize on the Farm meant.

Whispering into a trainee's ear, Rhonda outlined her idea of its parade-leading costume. She sent the trainee into the coop to fetch the appropriate paraphernalia required for a grand entrance. With a quick about face, the trainee disappeared into the coop. One by one the flock reappeared; this time each with a chicken that was regaled in a well-coordinated stream of plumage that approached Rhonda's expectations. The flock presented harmony and she was amused as the chickens struggled in their stiletto heels on the pen's choppy dirt floor. One or two would topple over before today's training was completed, she knew.

"Let's get moving," Rhonda said as she dragged her grand prize by its collar for a quick spin around the corral. The others quickly followed her lead. First prizes fell into line and the second prizes were relegated to the rear of the line. With her finger still looped tightly in the o-ring of her grand prize's collar, Rhonda picked up the pace to force the group to move faster. With their legs straining to keep them upright in spite of their high heels, Rhonda glanced at the straggling lineup of prizes and chuckled as they lurched across the yard.

"They will prance perfectly in an hour," she said. Rhonda turned, her grand prize still in tow, and led it, along with its trainer, back into the Coop for resplendent dressing. She oversaw this ritual every Season; it was her right. Because the parade was one of the Farm's most unforgettable spectacles, Rhonda took the grand prize's plumage as her personal challenge and knew she would have to work carefully to get this prize dressed up to the Farm's high standards. As she hauled it into the coop for dressing, Rhonda saw the trainees' prods tap the open-toed shoes that barely covered the chickens' feet. She lingered for a moment to watch them dance to painful electrical jolts on their toes. When the third chicken fell unceremoniously to the dirt, she towed her prize to the catacombs of the wardrobe closet and hoisted it onto a high perch.

If her leather vest had any sleeves, she would have pushed them up. It was time to get down to business.

The prize's physical appearance didn't hurt its presentation, Ronda thought as she looked over the hidden outfits that were secreted for the grand prize's outfitting. She realized that Control was recording this session for the Owner's after-dinner amusement so Rhonda pulled her shoulders back, forced her breasts up and out and set to work with enthusiasm. She eyeballed the unfortunate grand prize that was going to face her full fury in concocting the perfect regalia for the parade.

Every year, the staff provided something dazzling for the grand prize to set it apart during the parade. Rhonda was eager to discover what they had included in her special wardrobe choices. As her fingers sorted through the hangars and lifted flounce from their hooks, she searched for the perfect grand-prize outfit that would honor the Owner. It would also set the tone for the Farm's first-of-the-Season parade. Surely there was something outstanding hiding behind ...

That's when Rhonda's fingers touched it. In that moment, she knew it was exactly what she wanted.

Without even have to see it, Rhonda's fingers luxuriated in the shimmering fabric. She grasped a small corner to draw the rest of what was surely a fabulous garment into the light of day. As she squeezed it carefully, her hand emerged from the clutter of silk, satin and sheers. Then Rhonda discovered that it felt nothing short of the most sensuous fabric her fingers had ever handled.

Pure gold lame. Her grand prize would sparkle in a dazzling golden aura under the dome's bright spotlights. When the trophy rooster was presented to the Owner for her approval and she slid the golden garment from its shoulders, Rhonda knew that the prize cowering at her feet would astound the Farm's guests and staff with matching gold lingerie. Surely there had to be golden lingerie in the wardrobe, Rhonda knew.

"I have it!" she said almost breathlessly as her fingers seemed unable to let go of the golden cloth lest it disappear back into the wardrobe's mass of choices. Then she dictated her choices to the trainee. "Get a gold open lace bra, crotchless panties and sparkling hose with seams," she added in a hoarse whisper as her trainee watched Rhonda's excitement grow. "And a golden lace garter belt – it has to be lace!" Rhonda finished with a throaty voice.

Knowing that her Trail Boss was in a moment of personal exhilaration, the trainee bolted for the lingerie chest to secure the list of items without needing an additional reminder that time was at certainly short. She leapt into the lingerie with excitement. Flinging red, silver and ivory lingerie every which way, she leaned deeper into the massive chest to discover how the Farm staff could manage to create amazing pageantry as well as entertain themselves with little fun moments, like this struggle to find the right garments which was certainly going to be recorded and replayed for after-dinner fun.

She was certain they would enjoy the tape of her backside twisting and turning as the rest of her body was immersed in the chest's deep cavity.

With her Trail Boss's instructions seared in her brain, the girl reinserted herself into the chest until her fingers felt the gleaming gold. One after another, she felt for the cloth's quality and without even needing to see it, she pulled one required item after another from the chest. When she emerged, she saw the sparkles from the golden fabric shimmer in the sunlight.

Open bra, panties without a crotch, seamed hose and a lace garter belt – her shopping list was complete. She drew herself from the depths of the chest and stood victoriously with the golden lingerie held high above her head. Walking triumphantly back to her Trail Boss, the girl stopped in her tracks, transfixed by the sight in front of her.

Rhonda was decorating the grand prize rooster by herself.

With the spotlights blazing brilliantly on the trembling subject, Rhonda had a magnifying glass and used pointed surgical tweezers over every inch of its skin. Her feather removal skill was legendary among the trainees. Given the grand prize's tears, the trainee knew that Rhonda was leaving no feather to mar its smooth skin. This bird would be denuded to Rhonda's standards. It would be her crowning contribution to the Farm's First Competition parade of the Season.

One wayward pubic hair after another was removed with precision. The pitiful subject of Rhonda's attention, chained and dangling spread-eagle between ceiling beams and floor bolts, screamed as if its lungs would burst when her tweezers plucked out yet another feather. Each pluck aimed directly at a single strand

and Rhonda used the tweezers expertly. She held them directly in front of the terrorized chicken's horrified eyes before she searched for yet another unruly feather that was ready for her ministrations.

The trainee watched in awe as the macabre ballet unfolded.

Rhonda called in her direction, "Bolt its wings to the floor!"

Shedding her armful of golden lingerie on the nearest nest, the trainee dashed for the rooster's cuffed wings and drew the chains down to the same bolts that held its feet. With the chicken now bent in half and with only a few inches of slack in the chains, Rhonda focused the spotlights on its naked ass. She beckoned the trainee with a crooked finger.

"One cheek in each hand," she instructed the trainee, "Pull wide apart. I need a better view."

Without considering the chicken's humiliation at having its asscheeks spread wide for the Trail Boss's work, she reached around the bent bird and grasped its buttocks. Pulling the cheeks wide apart, she heard Rhonda order that she wanted even more egress into the bird's ass.

"Wider!" Rhonda said and the trainee pressed her fingers deeper between the cheeks. She pulled hard to spread them as far apart as possible.

"Now I can finally see," Rhonda muttered and continued her work.

Punctuated by the rooster's screams, Rhonda plucked hidden feathers one by one from her bird's ass to assure that even the closest inspection would not reveal even a single one. For what seemed like hours, the hot lights shined into the rooster's dark hole as she continued to work. Rhonda scrutinized every follicle to insure that all were perfectly smooth. For its part, the rooster's throat greeted the Trail Boss's torture with screams that were music to Rhonda's ears.

Finally, she seemed to be done, at least with its ass.

"Check it *all* over," Rhonda said to her trainee as she drew yet another pair of sterilized tweezers from a plastic pouch. "I want to know if there's a single feather left anywhere on its body."

The girl didn't need any urging. Throwing herself fully into the inspection, the trainee rearranged the lights, held the magnifying glass and moved the bird this way and that to look over its skin with the utmost care. When she thought a feather might have been overlooked, she took a flat scalpel and drew it horizontally across the bird's skin to see if one might pop up against the steel blade. Her inspection skills were admirable. Finally she suspended the spent bird by its feet so she could begin her final round of scrutiny.

Its toes had to be as clean as the rest of the bird and that deserved an up-close look.

Using the flat scalpel edge and her forehead magnifier together, Rhonda inspected the bird's toes with attention to detail that surprised her trainee. Every toe was separated from the next, and each was inspected for any telltale sign of a loose feather. Finding one filled Rhonda with a strange sense of glee. Plucking it out to the strains of the bird's shrieks made Rhonda smile and that made her trainee glad.

> *Let them see your enjoyment in your work, Rhonda was taught, so they will always know the Farm is a joyful place and they will want to be the best so they can share in the fun.*

Toe after toe was checked, plucked and rechecked before the trainee finally pronounced it done. Rhonda hoisted the bird and began her own final scrutiny for feathers and studied the bird bent and dangling above its perch. Rhonda examined every detail, both inside and out, pulling one missed feather here and there with the razor-sharp tweezers. With each pluck, the bird screeched again. It was easy for Rhonda to ignore its protestations as she continued the search for her next target. Its legs and asscheeks were pulled apart. Its crotch bore the brunt of her scrutiny before she moved to yet another spot and began plucking again.

Finally, the bird had been hoisted head-high and its face was close to Rhonda's own. The tears that streamed from its eyes filled her with a sense of accomplishment. She knew that her grand prize would now make a suitable entry in the parade.

Featherless, the bird was ready for basting.

"You," Rhonda said to her trainee, "Get it prepped for the golden lingerie." She never turned her head toward the girl. Rhonda knew that her orders would be carried out without hesitation – that's what being the Trail Boss meant. Keeping her attention focused on the dangling bird, Rhonda took the proffered hose from her trainee's hand and squirted gleaming oil onto it from its toes to its nose. The bird glowed brilliantly under the spotlights and Rhonda pronounced it done.

"Set it down on its feet," she instructed the trainee, "Then outfit it. I want to see how the rest of the flock is doing."

Leaving the de-feathered bird to its trainee for dressing, Rhonda smiled at the control room and breathed a sigh of happiness. For the first time today, she felt a sense of relief.

When the grand prize is truly exceptional, the rest of the flock falls into line.

She marched into the late morning sun and inspected the circle of chickens and roosters as they pranced around the perimeter of the yard. One by one, they passed by her and one by one she watched them quicken their pace. All of them lifted their stiletto heels higher and sucked in their stomachs to push out their chests as they approached Rhonda's vantage point. Their plumage made the otherwise drab dirt come alive with splendor.

The Season's first parade was always a grand pageant and this one promised to rival other years pomp. Yet Rhonda wanted something more; something that would make this parade stand out in the Owner's memory as the penultimate parade that the Farm had ever experienced. Her mind raced as she sifted ideas through her head. Finally, one leaped out and fairly shouted at her, '*This is it!*'

"On your knees!" Rhonda ordered the flock and watched as every bird fell to the dirt floor. "You too," she commanded the trainees who, after only a moment's hesitation, obeyed their Trail Boss's command.

When the group was appropriately supplicated, Rhonda called to her grand prize and ordered it to be led toward the kneeling circle. Leashed to its trainer by the o-ring on its cock collar, the golden trophy appeared on the dirt circle and walked on unsure legs to the middle of the pen. Once in place, its leash was given to Rhonda who led the bird in a walk-around and showed off the grand prize to every runner up in the flock.

> *Let them know what they could have been, the Owner taught. Make sure they know what to strive for next time. That's how they will better themselves and try harder.*

The kneeling chickens and roosters were transfixed with the prize bird's grandeur. They envied its golden plumage and Rhonda broke their jealous silence with her announcement.

"This is the grand prize," she said. "It leads you all in the parade. If every bird performs to make me proud, I will pass it around as a prize to each of you," she told the stunned group of birds and trainees

"You may share it if you perform well enough." She let her words sink in before adding, "On the Farm, every animal must learn from the best. The golden rooster will be your teacher."

The trainees giggled as the flock drank in Rhonda's promise. All they had to do was to create the perfect parade, then service the contest winners and that might be given a turn with the golden trophy. It was all up to the flock and it would measure their training.

Rhonda smiled as she looked forward to the video that would certainly become the centerpiece of the post-Competition review.

Chapter 31: Pigs in the Mud

The sounds of pigs grunting in the sty filled Paula's ears when she stepped inside the building. She flipped on the bright overhead lights and yanked the drove out of their sloppy slumber. Each piglet slept entwined with its mommy pig that been assigned to it and by now, they all had become accustomed to close male proximity. When a piglet was disciplined, it was punished by making it sleep alone.

With Competition approaching and only two short days left for training, Paula realized that the drove needed specialized training to serve the Owner's needs during the first event this Season. She was responsible for a putting on a grand piglet show. Some of the pigs would be included in the procession but the rest of the drove would participate in actual competitive events. Her first task was to select those for training only for the grand parade. Her second was to make the drove build animal pleasure to entertain the Owner and her guests, the most important responsibility of each Trail Boss during each Season on the Farm.

The Owner's guests enjoyed watching male-on-male animal contact. There was something special about it that created a thin red thread that connected all the women on the Farm.

A Trail Boss worked all Season to make sure that her pack performed spectacularly so that the Owner was pleased with the performance and her work. The Owner always wanted the guests to be entertained with the sight of the piglets and their mommy pigs parading and competing. The pigs' job, like rodeo clowns, was to enter a contest midway to break up some of the fiercer competition that the other packs performed. They added a delightful sense of comedy to the proceedings while also defusing potential over-competitiveness that some packs displayed. In spite of the seriousness of Farm life, the Owner had a sharp sense of humor. She looked for a similar one in her staff.

A humorless staff member never saw her name on the promotion list.

After watering the pigs, Paula led the crawling drove to the training pit, already filled with icy water and a few toys for training and play. One by one, she planted her boot on another set of asscheeks and sent one more pig face-first into the muddy goop. She smiled as they sputtered from the frigid water and the ignominy of their ass-kicked entrance. To a pig, they had learned how to tread in the mud even in the deepest end of the pit; nevertheless, Paula stationed three trainees there as overseers. She issued each one a winch hook that could easily yank a drowning pig from the muck. Safety was always first on the Farm.

As the pigs flopped frantically in the icy mud, Paula drew her trainees into an small circle for today's training directions.

"Every pig will perform in two days," she said. "I want each one trained well enough to win every event; I will tolerate no 'losers' in Competition. That's unacceptable to me." Her words reached every ear and the trainees nodded.

"We have new games this Season for First Competition." Paula's voice rose slightly with her own excitement and the trainees picked up on her enthusiasm. "Let's get started with the first new event."

Standing near the edge of the pit, Paula's boots ground the dirt with each step. The pigs' ears were attuned to her whereabouts; the pigs' snouts turned toward her boot stomping and watched closely. The cadre of trainees formed a line behind her. As she stood on the wooden platform that bridged the wide mud hole, Paula smiled at its inhabitants.

"First Competition will be challenging," she informed the shivering group matter-of-factly. "My trainees will guide you through the steps of the race with their whips. The winner will be displayed to the Owner." The pigs' ears perked at the idea of being presented after winning whatever race was in store for them and it seemed to be a highly desirable outcome. "This race will be a..." her voice trailed off. "A challenge," she drifted off and the pigs shivered again.

"Girls, strip your leathers and get in the pit with your pig," Paula tossed the comment toward the line of trainees huddled in the cold morning air. Having spent a few weeks training with Paula in the sties, the girls were no longer shocked at her command to strip and wallow in the mud with their animals.

Sometimes there is only one way to train an animal, and that is in their natural habitat, the Owner taught them. All animals value their home for comfort and safety. Make them know that you own their home.

One after another, the girls stripped their leathers and plunged feet-first into the arctic mud.

"We reward fast ejaculation in *this* game," Paula explained the single rule. She added ominously, "But not the way you think."

Immersed in the mud pit up to their necks, the pigs and the trainees stared at her for instructions. They waited, shivering and expectant, until she deigned to explain the rest of the rules. Cold wet mud didn't matter to Paula and every pig and trainee treading furiously in the pit knew it.

"These are pigs!" Paula said loudly to her trainees. "These animals are filthy, sloppy, and create a bigger mess than any other pack on the Farm. How you achieve fast ejaculation should fit the way they live." As she stood on the pit bridge, Paula waited until every head beneath her feet nodded.

"The contest has three levels," Paula said. "The first uses mud as lubricant and the second explores trainee expertise." Heads nodded in understanding and Paula finally explained the third level.

"There is a diving competition this Season." Paula watched the heads stop bobbing and saw the quizzical looks that replaced them. "We'll get to the last one when you master the first two."

With that final statement, Paula turned to make sure her observers were stationed at the deepest ends of the pit. When she saw them in place, she had them test the three winches to which every pig was attached by its waist harness. "Up!" she said and the winches whirred in unison. Soon every pig, dripping mud, was hoisted a few feet above the deep mud hole. Dangling from their harnesses, their kicking, flailing and grunting reminded Paula of the reason she enjoyed working the pigs Season after Season on the Farm.

She allowed herself a few moments to enjoy the scene. One pig after another kicked fearfully while dangling in the morning sunshine. She watched as they kicked from fear of falling as well as from panic at being hanged so high above the cold mud pit. They could see the hard earth that surrounded the pit. Their forelegs grabbed vainly in the air in a useless effort to stop twirling as they hung from the hoist bar. The macabre exhibition made Paula laugh as she saw globs of mud rain indecorously onto the trainees in the pit below.

"Grunt!" Paula said and every pig grunted loudly. Their noises filled the sty with a chorus of submissive compliance that pleased her. She liked obedient pigs.

As they hung and grunted, more and more slop fell and landed on trainees' faces until the girls realized that turning their eyes away from the spectacle was more prudent. Paula ordered them to lower the pigs and then raise them forcefully. The Control team repeated the process until Paula was satisfied. With each jerk of the hoist, the pigs threw off more and more dark mud onto the trainees, and the smile across Paula's face grew wider.

She nodded toward Control and the pigs were dropped into the cold mud. Their forceful grunts were music to Paula's ears. Once they were settled in the pit, she ordered practice to begin.

"The pigs' ejaculatory speed will be measured at the moment they are dunked," she said. "That means that when they are in the air, they are to masturbate. When they are in the pit, you are to do it for them. Does everyone understand the sequence?"

The trainees nodded and the pigs' faces showed their failure to comprehend her instructions and they really meant for them.

"Let's start," Paula said. The hoists whirred and the pigs were hauled again from the safety of the cold mud hole.

"Now!" she ordered and a few of the flopping pigs flailed their arms in the air as they tried to reach under their bellies and clutch their cocks. They grabbed at themselves over and over in an effort to comply with her order but failed repeatedly as they hung uselessly from their harnesses high above the pit. A few managed to touch their organs just as Paula issued the 'drop' command.

They were suddenly immersed again in the pool of cold mud. The trainees swam through the muck toward their pigs, grabbed their shriveling cocks, and started manual masturbation. When Paula was sure that every pig's shaft had been sufficiently stimulated by its trainer, she ordered the beasts hoisted again. That was followed by her single command to masturbate. A few more pigs managed to clench their own cocks in mid-air. Paula noticed that one or two actually managed to begin decent self-stroking.

She knew that only a few successes just wouldn't do. Until every pig had both of its front hooves wrapped around its organ and was working it properly, they were going nowhere, certainly not to Competition.

She kept them hanging from the hoist as she ordered each pig to grab its cock between its forelegs. She wanted each to grip itself tightly or she would force the entire pack to hang there until dark. Knowing that she never gave up on perfecting a training skill, the trainees swam around in the cold pit in an attempt to warm themselves with body heat while the dangling pigs learned how to follow the simple instruction.

Paula waited and watched. Everyone in the sty knew she would wait as long as it took for even the clumsiest pig to obey her instruction. One after another of the pigs managed to grasp its organ with its forelegs as instructed. Finally, a single pig dangled overhead that was unable to reach its penis. It was situations like this that forged Paula's reputation as a superior trainer who always achieved her goal, no matter how merciless she had to be to secure it. There would be no assistance – the pig had to overcome whatever its challenges were and perform her instruction.

They could dangle there all night, she thought, until everyone of them had obeyed. And every pig and every trainee knew that she would do exactly that.

> *Make them into a team by separating them first, she was taught. Make them perform and use them as a model to the rest.*

With a pack this large hanging from the hoists, Paula knew that one pig would eventually bump into another and the impetus from that collision would start one or both pigs on a swinging odyssey through a domino effect. Paula timed them to see how long it would take and which pigs would finally find the solution to their group puzzle. Those might be her real competitors.

The pigs humped their hips while stroking and the motion made them swing and bump into each other. They swung more forcefully as they masturbated harder, bumping into dangling pigs on both sides. They kept masturbating to fulfill her requirement and swung as they did. In short order, the entire pack was swaying, bumping hips and asses, and pressing the pack together. But they were swinging with no goal.

> *One always rises to the challenge, Paula learned in her own training. Look for the animal who figures it out.*

As they swung on the hoist, shed more mud and masturbated, Paula waited, tapping her boot against the wooden bridge impatiently while the group continued to fail to realize the teamwork that was needed. To a pig, each knew that the whole pack was in danger of strict punishment but none seemed to be able to produce a solution. They hung there until one of the cubby mommy pigs adjusted its intermittent swing in a way that appeared to Paula to be intentional.

Its actions caught Paula's eye. She watched it pump its body toward the incompetent runt until, with one of its forelegs masturbating its own cock as ordered, it used its other to grip the soft shaft hanging beneath the hapless runt. On the next swing, it gripped the shaft again and stroked it before its swing's arc pushed it away.

Finally, as if a huge light bulb had been turned on over the rest of the pack, the pigs began pumping their bodies toward the runt and each took a foreleg's swipe at the runt's cock. Smiling but without allowing her lips to curl upward, Paula watched the drove with the kind of pride that only a Trail Boss knew how to enjoy. By now, the runt's cock was stiffening and Paula ordered the pack dropped into the cold mud pit as a reward.

The trainees swam for their pigs in order to masturbate each pig's cock. The girls vied to be the first to force pig ejaculation that Paula would approve. Given the freezing temperature of the mud and the now-frosty air, Paula knew that the process could take a long time. Time after time, she had the pigs hoisted, watched them struggle to masturbate, and then had them dunked into pit and into the eager hands of their trainees.

Finally, Paula issued her final command for this task.

"The only ejaculation that counts is one that I see," she cautioned them. "If your pig ejaculates outside my sight, then you are both eliminated," she said.

You are the judge and jury, Paula had been taught.
Use that power frequently and wisely. Make them know
that you are the arbiter of their fate.

Paula squatted on the observation platform and watched in delight as the pigs masturbatory drill was performed. Staring into their eyes while they self-stroked always delighted her; most male animals displayed personal pride of their masturbation techniques through their eyes. Their humiliation grew from being forced to masturbate for show not just for a Pack Leader but also for the lower-ranking trainees. Each pig knew that in two days' time, the gallery at Competition would be their audience, and their masturbation would be a public exhibition. Paula set up this particular training exercise to show them what their future had in store and let them wallow in their shame.

"Now!" she said loudly.

Their overhead squeals filled her ears and were muffled quickly by frosty mud as they were dunked one more time into the muck. The trainees picked up on Paula's impatience and shouted at their pigs to grunt louder and fill the sty with the noise of obedient masturbation performance. Nothing would ever be hidden from Paula, or for that matter, from the Owner and her guests at Competition. Pigs on the Farm were allowed nothing to hide and had no right to hide anything.

After almost ninety minutes of extreme physical exertion, a trainee motioned for Paula's attention to her pig in the pit.

"Here!" she called, "Mine is ready to shoot!"

Paula turned her head casually toward the excited voice and watched from the observation platform. The pig's deep-set eyes were black with intensity. For her part, the trainee was celebrating her potential first-place finish. There's nothing quite as exciting for trainees than to win a ribbon at the Competition, especially in their first year.

Paula surveyed the pit carefully before deciding which step to take.

Agonizingly slowly, she moved her eyes toward the pit, and then toward the litter of squealing pigs mired in the mud, struggling to allow their trainers to masturbate them successfully before the hoist yanked them one more time from their muddy home. Paula enjoyed the show and knew that the Owner's guests would be equally entertained with this physical competition. The same trainee called again and yanked Paula's thoughts back to the reality of the pit.

"Ma'am," the voice implored, "My pig is ready!"

Paula turned her head leisurely toward the voice and examined the masturbating pig's eyes. She wanted to ensure that it was truly ready to ejaculate and only then, and with a single nod, had every pig in the group hoisted higher than before so she could get a close look at each one's cock status. Paula always kept a close eye on the pigs when the finale approached. She didn't care how long it took and no neophyte trainee would dissuade her from that practice.

> *They are yours to train, use, and enjoy but most of all,*
> *to make ready for the Owner's desires. She owns their*
> *ejaculation, Paula knew, and I own giving it to her.*

She had wanted the contest to be a little closer. Competition was good for Farm animals, she had learned, but especially for pigs. The sty was special because they were used to living in sloppy conditions and were often denied use of the watering shed for days at a time. That's when they were required to pee and defecate in the shit pit and then sanitize it. That's when they learned their true role on the Farm. Paula always brought a shit pit experience to her pigs early in the Season.

As the pigs whose cocks had shrunk from the cold air dangled from the hoist and started masturbating again, Paula's mind wandered back to their first day in the pit this Season.

It was a warm morning. When the pack was ordered outside on all fours, the surprised drove of pigs was led in a line across the sty's fenced yard. Not yet used to having to lift their heads to see where they were going, the pigs followed the asscheeks of the pig in front and slavishly trailed along in a single unthinking line. When Paula stopped them, only one pig had the temerity to look up.

And what that pig saw almost hit it in its snout.

There was no question what the pit it was staring at was for just like there was no question what was expected of the pigs in the shallow trench in front of them. The fact that water was already soaking into the straw that lined the trough's bottom left no doubt in the first pig's mind as to what act it was going to be forced to do there.

One by one, the pigs looked up and their eyes took in the trench's length. Requiring them to perform this primal function in the pit washed through their brains. After only a few days on the Farm, the pigs were now face-to-face with any animal's worst nightmare. Their horror made for one of their Trail Boss's greatest delights. Making new pigs feel and act like real pigs was the first lesson she taught them, and that lesson was always joyful for Paula to teach. She adored the impression it made on the pigs and the trainees at the same time.

Her spoke evenly to them.

"Crawl into the trough and pee on the straw," she said.

The beleaguered drove of pigs was perplexed by her order yet they all knew they would be forced to obey it. The thought of using the outdoor pit to relieve themselves was incomprehensible. Some pigs hesitated, but the trainees' swift kicks to their asscheeks made the decision to scurry into the trough for them. Hesitation vanished when the first pig crawled into the gully and heard the straw crunch under its hooves and knees.

One by one, the pigs followed the lead pig and soon the entire sty was lined up in the pit in uncomfortably close quarters. Their moment of horror would soon become their daily morning watering routine.

"Quickly," Paula said. Each understood that if it didn't perform at this very moment, its next opportunity for relief would be in the uncomfortably distant future. They had no choice and as they fathomed their predicament, Paula grinned at her trainees.

She explained to the trainees as the pigs struggled to lift a leg and in a few cases, even to squat. The trench's close quarters prevented them from retaining any shred of dignity. Privacy was a long-forgotten privilege and did not exist for animals on the Farm.

"They are pigs," Paula began teaching the trainees' most important lesson. "They are filthy and wallow in their own slop. Every Season, the Farm requires that pigs in the sty learn what they are by performing morning watering." She watched their eyes shift back and forth between the spectacle of pigs trying to pee in the outdoor pit and their Trail Boss.

"You see they are still trying to maintain some personal space," she pointed at a few of the pigs to illustrate her point. "But on the Farm, no animal has personal space or privacy. During the Season, the pigs will learn that pee is just pee and it doesn't matter whose it is." Her words dripped with confidence gained from experience. The eager trainees drank in every syllable.

"When it comes to defecation," Paula continued, "you'll see them exhibit a higher degree of anxiety. On the Farm, we break that down quickly. That feeling may not linger." she concluded and their eyes refocused on the pigs.

"Watch this," Paula said.

She walked to the pit and listened to the grunts and squeals of humiliation emanating from her pigs' snouts. Their embarrassment overwhelmed them but no shred of self-respect would remain after this exercise. Their egos and psyches were being reshaped by

Paula in one life-altering exercise. Absolute debasement was a requirement of sty cohesion and Paula taught the new Season's pigs that lesson every Season. This Season would be no different.

Paula reached between the hind legs of handiest pig and inserted a lubricated gel tube deep into its ass. She pressed the plunger in a single motion. The pig squealed in surprise mingled with humiliation but its protests were lost on Paula's unhearing ears.

"Wait for it," she informed the trainees.

Within seconds, the pig grunted louder and thrashed its hind quarters wildly over the narrow trough. Its squeals told the trainees that Paula inserted something powerful into its rectum. Without knowing what the gel actually did, they learned that its effects were fast and effective. The pig's legs bucked as it tried to dislodge the painful intruder. Paula smiled at the effects of the new concentrate that Assessment had tested and supplied. The trainees watched in amazement as the pig screamed in wasted protest and its body humped and bucked in a useless effort to force it out.

Only Paula knew what was going to happen next. Her steely stare caught the trainees' attention as the rest of the sty's eyes focused on the single bucking pig.

Pulling its lips back, the pig gritted its teeth and spread its hind legs wider than Paula thought it was capable. Squatting in the trough, the pig emptied its rectum onto the straw in front of Paula, the trainees, and rest of the sty's inhabitants. The fetid aroma wafted into the pack's nostrils and then shifted toward the trainees. After several Seasons on the Farm, Paula knew where to stand to mostly avoid the odor, but it was good for her trainees to learn that trick for themselves.

There was no escaping the stench as it wafted through the sty before it eventually dissipated enough that the trainees could again focus on Paula's instructions. A few girls wiped their eyes with sweaty forearms.

Finally, she had both the trainees and the pack crowd around the trench and stare into it. What greeted their eyes was amazing. The pigs were helping their sty-mate cover its mess with straw. Paula's grin was worth more than an hour's lecture could ever produce for lifelong learning for her girls.

> *Break them down one by one, she had been taught.*
> *Only then can you mold them into a pack and you will*
> *own them.*

Shifting back to the moment, Paula watched the pigs dangle and masturbate more fiercely. It was obvious that each wanted to be first, to win, to gain her approval and certainly to avoid punishment. Pleasing her was the totality of what each pig wanted right now. They had been taught – and now finally demonstrated – their ability to respond and not to think separately or even plan beyond the moment. After all, that's what pigs do on the Farm. They follow the herd.

Paula tilted her head back and smiled at the sight of a sty full of dangling pigs masturbating overhead in frenzied attempts to be the first to complete its task. The trainees, treading in the cold muddy slime, stared up and dodged the turd-like clumps that fell from the pigs. All in all, Paula was pleased with the training session. She knew that the Owner would enjoy the show and she rarely cared about the winner.

Sooner or later, one of them would ejaculate and Paula would then move the pigs to the next practice session for the second new event in the Farm's first Competition of the Season.

Chapter 32: First Show

Under the comfortable blush of summer sun, anticipation of the Competition parade filled the stadium with happy excitement. It was always a moment that the Trail Bosses, Pack Leaders and even Control enjoyed. Pre-parade was a tense time for the herd because all the training this Season on the Farm would culminate in this upcoming show. For many of them, it was the first time they were allowed to see the Owner. Their curiosity grew as much as their fear increased.

Each pack was regaled in its finery. Every animal-in-training had been groomed specially for Competition. Every Trail Boss was dressed in her full leathers that shined brightly under the warm sun. Everyone's mood was elevated and every heart pumped in its chest. No one talked about their excitement because this feeling that they shared needed no words. The shared anticipation linked everyone on the Farm.

When the music began, Olivia, as overseer of all the packs, led the procession into the arena. Carefully choreographed, the animals arrived pack by pack and soon created a circle along the track's perimeter. The pack leaders stood proudly in front of their animals and readied them for showing to the Owner and her special guests. Black leather outfits dotted the audience seated in the grandstand as the women in attendance ooh'ed audibly at the spectacle. Parades at the Farm always filled the guests with tingling emotions that crept up from their toes and rose higher and higher until some were almost overcome with thoughts of a slave satisfying the women's growing needs. This parade lived up to Farm standards and for the first time all day, the Owner smiled.

Leda, always at her side, finally exhaled.

The Farm's women were seated in a circle surrounding their Owner by order of rank. They wore their official colors and watched with increasing anticipation as the first event began. The pony Trainers wore their green pompously, as the Processing staff sported neon blue as their badge of honor. The red-striped Technicians sat closer to the field so they could monitor the events and ensure safety while the trainees, donning vests with colors for the first time this Season, filed into the main ring.

The Owner eyed them with pride. Only the strongest women survived a Season on the Farm and she enjoyed the best of her best.

The music faded and drumbeats piped throughout the assembly. Ursula, Tara, Sharon, Ronda, and Paula stepped forward and fell regally to their knees, in supplication to their Owner. The ceremony for Pack Leaders was performed every Season at the start of Competition. In this magical moment, there were no others in the gallery, no audience, no cheering, no special guests, and no thoughts in their heads except their focus on their Owner. The packs of animals watched as their trainers knelt in homage to the woman who had perfected The Farm.

One at a time, almost in synchrony, each pack turned its eyes toward the box in which the Owner, circled by her staff, sat silently. They could feel her drink in the adoration paid to her by her women. No voice uttered a sound and no throat grunted. The stillness was infectious.

The stadium was silent until a starter pistol's bang broke the hush. Leda handed the microphone to her Owner and waited for the words heard only once each Season on The Farm.

"Let Competition begin," the Owner's surprisingly low voice resounded throughout the stadium.

As if on fire, the Pack Leaders bolted to their booted feet and swung their whips over the packs' heads. Their shouting was heard above the din of cracking whips because the animals had been trained to discern their leaders' instructions no matter what distractions might try to interfere. Whether they were standing or kneeling, bound or tethered, afoot or suspended, every slave animal tuned to the single voice that held its fate all Season. The roar of the crowd would not hinder their obedience.

The trainees, their breasts flying as they ran to the perimeter track, rushed to divide themselves among the packs and follow their Pack Leaders. Each secretly hoped that one day, pack leadership would be theirs, but for today, they pushed that thought aside. Today they were fully involved in their first show, the day that their Owner could see for herself just how accomplished each trainee had become and which had developed enough skills to be kept on next Season. Only the best could even hope for promotion. The Pack Leaders would certainly use today's results when they filled out the trainees' evaluations and submitted recommendations.

Each of the stadium's three performance rings held a single pack. The cows were sent to the north ring, the ponies to the south, and the bulls to center stage. The packs were showcased first as the chickens and pigs were moved to an outside track, out of the way, to be used later. The chickens, regaled in their finery of stiletto heels, full makeup and glittery costumes, knew from their Season in the Coop that they were to become the prizes for the winning pack. But the pigs, naked and collared, knew that they were to be in the grand finale, the festive offering to a stadium packed with sex-filled women who would enjoy the mirth of their ejaculations-on-command. What the pigs didn't yet know was how heavy the betting on some of their performances would be.

With her whip cracking above their heads, the ponies were saddled expertly by the trainees. As the Owner watched their skill and speed, the trainees, sporting the corral's vests, pushed leather bits into the ponies' jaws. They harnessed and saddled them with gleaming leather tack. Stirrups were adjusted and reins knotted professionally before the final headpieces were locked in place. After their Pack Leaders tugged every connection one last time, the ponies were ordered to kneel in front of their riders as their Competition feathers were placed atop their bald heads. Each pony took on an additional air of dignity when its top feathers' chin straps were secured. One by one, the riders stood next to their mounts and held their reins tightly in their perspiring fists.

Sharon walked up and down the line and inspected each trainee's work. There would be no wobbly straps, no unfinished knots and no loose buckles during Competition. A single nod was Sharon's sign of approval for each. Proud of her trainees, Sharon did not need to adjust a single pony's fit. The pack was ready and Sharon proudly indicated the status by turning her head toward her Owner.

Meanwhile, Ursula scrutinized her cows in the northern ring. The success of their training would speak for itself soon enough and although she was confident in her work with her trainees, every Pack Leader had a moment's hesitation before the opening bell. Would her cows' long penises produce enough milk to satisfy the Owner this Season? Would she compare them to the group from two Seasons ago whose output was so extraordinary? Would Ursula's animals measure up and entertain the crowd with length, amaze them with durability, and thrill them with the ever-important final explosion? Shaking any worry out of her mind, Ursula re-focused on the pack. Every eye in the grandstand must be evaluating her pack's penises, she imagined, and with a firm hand, gave each dangling shaft a final tug before the show began.

With her eyes on the Owner's box, Ursula signaled that her beefy cows were ready for Competition.

Center stage always belonged to the bulls. With meaty genitals caged in metal that shined under the bright sun, the bulls were the Farm's prize herd. Only the chunkiest were selected by Assessment to be the bulls and Tara knew her pack sported some of the thickest shafts that had ever been brought to the Farm. Even though size mattered, Tara was at the mercy of Victoria's Processing team that selected which animals would be handed over to her for the Season. Olivia's Processing team was careful to measure every animal during Intake and supplied her with the thickest cocks that Season. Then it became Tara's job to make the pack learn how to use them for Competition.

Too often, the biggest were the most difficult to train. That was one reason that the bull Pack Leader was so carefully selected by the Owner.

Their body harnesses were strapped snugly on their oiled skin so that each bull's meat stood out and was showcased. The gallery stared at her bulls as they did every Season, oozing with jealousy or desire, hoping that a prize bull would be awarded to their own stables when the show was over and the betting settled. When the Owner decided to give away a prize bull, the betting was even faster and more furious. Tara hoped that this Season's crop would match the previous record high wager, and if she was lucky enough to force the betting higher, she was sure to move up in the Owner's promotion list. Her work this Season was meticulous and her bulls, with the trainees wearing her colors lined up in front of them, were the center of attention.

Tara patted and tugged each set of bull organs, as if to say to the women in attendance, "These could be yours."

All eyes focused on her fingers as they dawdled for a split second on each bull's meat and fondled their testicles. Then she turned her head toward her Owner to signal her pack's readiness.

Competition was ready to begin.

Chapter 33: The Northern Ring

Ursula was fidgeting while waiting for her pack to start. Anticipating the starter's pistol drove her wild with eagerness every Season. With no ejaculations allowed for the entire week prior to Competition, each cow was bursting with milk. Every trainee was ready to pump her animal instead on the practice rubber udders she had used for the past seven days. The cows were familiar with being bought to the edge of explosion but each time the trainees brought them down, one way or another, so they didn't ruin their chances to win their main event.

Today was the day for Competition milking.

As the cows crawled into their tethers, their hind legs were spread by a metal rod that was adjusted for each animal's breadth. One after another they moaned in pain as their hind quarters were stretched wider than they had ever experienced before. After she was certain they were spread properly, Ursula nodded to Control and the metal waist locks hummed into place around their cows' midsections. In short order, the whirring got louder as the entire herd of cows was raised from the dirt by their waist locks. With their legs forced apart and their arms flailing for balance, the tethers tightened and the cows were spread fully open in mid-air. An appreciative *aaahhh* escaped from the stadium as the audience waited breathlessly for the milking exhibition to get underway.

The trainees took their places between their cows' legs and slapped the cow udders that hung at hand-height in front of them. With that single touch, the cows the mooed in unison and made the Owner's guests smile.

The girls' fingers moved expertly. No cow would be allowed to finish its milking until its trainee was convinced that the milk it would produce was sufficient to win the quantity measurement event. The ripened cows would suffer under each trainee's hands until the last possible moment. Ursula taught them how to prolong a cow's ejaculation and this was the time that their expertise was highlighted. The crowd watched the young women's hands move and their fingers work and not just a few of the guests were soon sporting the same perspiration that beaded on the trainees' skin.

The leather vests and the balmy sun combined with their labor and make the girls glow. After only 10 minutes, one of the trainees uttered a slow, low moan. She was focused only on controlling her cow and Competition's pomp took a back seat as she melded her mind to her work. Fully involved with her cow's udder, the trainee sang a silent song of her love of her work.

Leda supplied the missing information for the Owner without being prompted.

"Hailey," she said quietly and the Owner nodded.

Scribbling notes, Leda made sure that Hailey's name was moved up a notch on the watch list. A trainee who could block out the distractions of First Competition on the Farm and throw herself into the task so completely was one that the Owner would keep her eye on for possible promotion. Remembering her from the First Day luncheon at the Manor House, the Owner smiled slightly. She could always pick them out early on and this Season was no exception.

The girls worked on their suspended cows as Marla fixated on her control panel. Each cow was wired to her computer so that winning quantity could be measured carefully. For safety, every cow was monitored for heart rate and respiration. This Season, the Owner added trainee monitoring as well. As soon as Hailey's moan grew loud enough to be heard throughout the stadium, Marla quickly glanced at her monitor. The girl, she assessed, was working extremely hard. Her nod reassured Leda, who saw no reason to translate the gesture to the Owner. Leda was adept at knowing when to bother the Owner with details and when to handle a situation by herself.

Milking competition continued and the cows' reactions grew as time moved forward. Not only did their mooing reverberate throughout the stadium, but their hindquarters began to dance in rhythm to the trainees' manipulations. Hips gyrated, abdomens heaved and hindquarters quivered as the girls worked without pause. A suddenly-humping cow caught everyone's attention and after a hard slap to one bulging udder or another, a cow finally calmed down.

After another ten to fifteen minutes of good hard milking, several of the cows were thrashing comically in mid-air. Ursula had taught the girls how to differentiate between an over-stimulated cow and one that simply had reached its limit. She glanced at the sun and knew from experience that the event would culminate soon. In all the Seasons she worked on the Farm, the most any competitive cow had endured was thirty minutes of milking. It had been almost twenty five already.

One by one, cows' moos became increasingly hysterical. One by one, they began shooting milk into the air as the trainees pumped every drop out of them. The audience smiled as the cows, suspended and wriggling, suddenly stiffened and spasmed for them to enjoy. Some of the cows spurted several times and those were the cows most carefully watched by the crowd. If you had been to only one Competition at the Farm, you knew that an occasional cow might spurt twice. The second one always drew gales of laughter from the audience and brought the cow a seriously reddened ass from its trainee's whip.

The beakers below caught their milk and it was capped and sent to Marla's monitor for scoring. No one wants to see her cow spill anything that didn't get counted in judging.

Hanging cows shot hot ejaculate into the air as the women watched. The trainees stepped away after each one was sure that her cow shot every drop into the beaker. She then turned her attention to her pack leader for her next instruction. No one moved away from an animal until all of them were finished. The pack always moved together.

They finished one by one. As a group, they waited anxiously for Marla's score. It was only Ursula who saw a lone struggling cow, gyrating and floundering, trying desperately to finish. After the herd was done and the cheering subsided, its twirling body drew the crowd's attention. Ursula moved toward the cow and studied her trainee's efforts. She nodded and glanced at the sun as Leda whispered to the Owner.

The girl was performing expertly and not holding the cow back. The cow had learned its lessons well. Ursula didn't have a poorly-trained cow; rather, she had a perfectly seasoned one. A new Farm record was happening and Competition was the perfect time that event.

The Owner glanced at Marla, whose eyes were trained on her monitors. Marla raised one finger and the crowd began cheering. A record was about to be set if the cow could make it a single minute longer. Seconds were disregarded and only full minutes were rewarded in Competition. Leda beamed as Ursula pushed her chest out and her big breasts shimmered. Setting a record at the Farm was a mark of high distinction and Ursula coveted one of her own for many ss. She studied the girl's hands, arms and how she involved her body into the effort. From now on, no move she made would go unnoticed. The crowd was focused on her technique and was roaring approval.

A moo began from deep inside the cow's gut. It started slowly, grew and finally flew out of its mouth. The primal sound filled the warm stadium air. It came from nowhere but seeped into every space in the stadium. Its eventual scream of jubilation was heard by everyone in the stadium. The cow's humping, thrashing body was merely secondary. The trainee's efforts to make the cow shoot the final drop into the beaker went almost unnoticed. Only the scream remained.

Taking a deep breath, the trainee studied the line and realized that her cow was the last to finish. She turned, faced the crowd, and led her line of trainees to kneel and offer respect to the Owner and her guests.

Wild applause greeted the girls while everyone waited for Marla's verdict. Control lowered the cows to the dirt where they were unstrapped and herded to the outer ring. It was there that they would be watered while the next event began.

But the audience was wild with anticipation for the final score. Leda received the scores from Marla and after showing them to the Owner, flashed them on the stadium screen. The green lights showed respectable numbers, but two red lights were the brightest of all.

In an incredible display, two Farm Competition records had just been set; one for quantity and the other for duration.

Ursula beamed and the Owner smiled right at her. She knelt and bowed, and then headed off to tend to her trainees and the herd.

"Bring her to me," the Owner said to the ever-present Leda, who delivered the demand via radio to Control.

Minutes later, Hailey fell to her knees in front of her Owner's seat. The Owner lifted the trainees' breasts that jutted from the confines of her leather vest's new colors. Pinching the nipples just to her liking, she smiled at the young girl and kept her in that position as the southern ring's show began.

Chapter 34: The Southern Ring

The ponies were a much-anticipated event in Competition every Season on the Farm and this year was no exception. Sharon had worked her herd and trainees to perfection. They knew how to do their jobs, had honed their skills and showed talent. She watched them prance for the first part of the Season and was satisfied that at the worst, their performance might rival last year's pony show.

The women in the audience were there to be entertained and show ponies were traditionally the most fun event to watch. Cracking her dressage whip high above their heads, Sharon captured the crowd's attention and began the routine – the prancing ponies ridden by their trainees made a spectacular entrance event for the herd with the pack literally on their toes. The Owner's audience always loved it and Sharon chose the maneuver on purpose to begin the Season's pony show. She was rewarded with a shared gasp from the gallery.

This dance was especially taxing on the ponies' hooves. Prancing and high stepping while wearing stiletto heels was difficult enough but raising and lowering their legs in perfect sync made the audience sit up and take notice. Even though the shoes were locked around the ponies' ankles, standing upright was chore even for prize ponies. Winning Competition was Sharon's goal this Season and she liked leading with nothing short of an extravaganza.

That's exactly what she trained her pack to do.

With the thunder of drums growing louder and faster, the ponies paraded in a circle around the southern ring and knelt in the dirt dramatically to accept their riders. The trainees, for the first time this Season, were dressed in their splendid black leathers adorned with a brilliant splash of color between their breasts. Each mounted her steed and in a vivid move and the herd stood as one. The audience cheered as the ponies pranced with their riders and Sharon could hardly suppress a smile at how their weeks of training and discipline coalesced into that move. The ponies, too burdened with saddles and riders to bask in their success, never witnessed her lips turn slightly upward in approval.

But the Owner saw it. She nodded almost imperceptibly toward Sharon in congratulations of a job well done. Leda tapped more notes into her tablet.

The show grew into a furious tempo. The ponies danced in choreographed lines and crossed the center of the southern ring almost perfectly. So far, there had not been one misstep. Not one of them wanted to face their Pack Leader over a miscue at the Farm's First Competition. Sharon knew that fear was an effective training tool.

Finally, the pack retreated to a circle around the southern ring. It was time for the real pony contest to begin.

Two riders gathered the reins and pressed their ponies to center ring. The young horses pranced proudly and showed off their physiques to the crowd. Each sported royal plumage from the top of its headgear and both sets of pony and rider were on target to receive the Season's first pony tails from their trainers. Only the best of the show ponies were awarded tails. It was a Farm tradition and a trainee honor to select the most promising trainee from the pony corral to insert the first tails. Sharon had struggled over her selection. The one she selected to present tails must also be approved after the Owner's inspection, so it was doubly difficult for Sharon to make a choice knowing that her Owner would evaluate her in part based on that nomination. Honors on the Farm were always double-edged swords. As splendid as it was to take center stage and insert the ponies' tails, all trainees were reluctant to face the Owner in private and endure personal inspection in her Green Studio.

But one had to be chosen; it was a Farm tradition.

Leda focused on the ring to see which trainee Sharon had elected to receive this Season's honor. The Owner had evaluated two finalists in her Green Studio just prior to the Show. She used them both for a relatively long time, Leda remembered, and when they emerged, both naked girls had to be helped into their leathers and ushered back to the corral.

The Owner always used time efficiently and having the two girls demonstrate their skills on other trainees' asses seemed an effective way to determine who would receive this year's pony-tailing honor. As she instructed them on lubrication techniques and the merits of various gels and liquids, the two candidates knelt on all fours, raised their asses, spread their cheeks, and accepted the Owner's intrusion into their rectums as part of the Farm learning process that made the Farmhands the best trained in the world. Leda watched as the Owner positioned the girls and then filled their asses with various – and occasionally unpleasant – herbal salves. The Owner made them feel deep inside each other with their fingers and then their noses to determine the merits of each type of gel. Finally, she showed them the benefits of adding a drop of warming oil to each jar of lubrication. Her oils were special recipes and the clenched teeth and low moans she watched again and again on the video proved that the hot oil worked wonders for gaining any animal's attention.

Then the two girls started to scream.

That's when the tape stopped. For the time that the Owner turned off the cameras until she restarted them, Leda could only wonder what mysterious assessments she had inflicted on them.

She would never have guessed that the chosen girls were first forced to insert pony tails into each other and then into a lineup of first-year trainees specifically chosen for discipline for training infractions. It was rare that Farmhands, no matter what position they held or what level they had risen to, were allowed to watch direct discipline of one trainee by another. The Owner loved trainee-on-trainee discipline. It brought cohesion to the corps.

When the girls emerged, Leda knew they understood the value of creating their own herbal tools. That would push them ahead on the promotion list for sure.

Georgia stepped into the middle of the ring and was presented with two beautiful long pony tails by her Pack Leader. Sharon smiled and remembered the Season she had received this same honor. With a trembling hand, Georgia accepted the tails and in a show of joy, held them victoriously above her head.

The crowd erupted into cheers. Inserting the first pony tails of the Season was always a thrilling part of the Farm's southern ring's display.

Covering her leather glove, Georgia coated her hand with the special oil she had prepared for the Tailing. In a short time, the audience would figure out exactly what properties of the oil she used would inflict upon the two show horses. What they would not learn was exactly what Sharon had added to the mixture to bring out the best in the show ponies in the southern ring. That was her secret and a gift from her Owner.

The best-of-season ponies whipped solidly to present their hindquarters to the grandstand. A few simple crop directions later, they were bent and spread, ready to accept the Tailing. Throughout their training this Season, Sharon alluded to the show tails. She hanged them high above the ponies' heads in the barn so they could see them every morning when they were awoken and every night when they were put to bed, some sucking the teats of others to calm down as they got used to Farm life. Each pony was desperate to win this best-of-season honors and be awarded one of the coveted tails. Now that the moment had arrived, the ponies were almost beside themselves with anticipation.

The moment would be short-lived. Sharon had a gleam in her eye that only her Owner fully appreciated. She leaned forward as Leda tapped more notes into her tablet and anticipated a memorable moment in this Season's pony show. She would not be disappointed. She never was, not by her pack leaders or her trainees.

Georgia lubricated the first pony and with a grand gesture, while holding the tail high above her head. Then she pressed the molded end firmly into the animal's rectum. The young trainee beamed with pride as she raised her arms aloft in victory. She repeated the process with the second show pony with measured precision. With both deliriously happy ponies wagging their tails for the crowd's delight, Sharon's lips curved slightly and she glanced toward the Owner's box. It was her special signal, meant – and seen – only by her Owner. Soon, she promised silently.

She leaned forward just enough for Leda to see her body twitch a fraction of an inch. Georgia had captured the attention of the two most important people in the stadium.

That's when the chaos began. With Leda searching the Owner's face for a clue about the secret spice in the oil, the two newly-tailed ponies felt their rectums light on fire as just the right amount of heated oil tested them to their limits. A well-trained pony could handle that level of fire and Sharon believed hers were at least that well trained. She certainly hoped so. Having a prize pony throw a rider was unheard of and was certainly not an acceptable occurrence at any Season's First Competition.

Her concoction was meant to challenge them and see if they were truly worthy of their tails.

The two ponies' riders knew something was upsetting their animals and couldn't believe the awarding of the tails would wreak mayhem on the animals' self-control. No, the tails were special gifts – coveted awards – and the ponies should be thrilled to be wearing them. It must be something else, they thought, and struggled to rein in their beasts. It was a terrible time for ponies to misbehave. The first Pony Competition was just about to begin.

Leading their steeds to opposite sides of the ring, the two prancing ponies' asses wriggled with each step. Their elegance was shaken and their gait unsteady. Atop their mounts, the riders tried to crop some discipline back into the animals. With each stroke of their whips, the ponies fought to demonstrate what took precedence above all: their appearance, their gait, their promenade, their high-stepping. They had been trained to perform and at the moment, they were more desperate to soothe their burning asses. But their riders would allow none of that.

With each stroke of the crop, the ponies seemed to regain a little of what they had momentarily lost. Yet every step challenged their self-control and made Georgia smile, Leda smirk and the Owner lean forward in her chair. The object of the show was to entertain and Georgia had certainly accomplished that. Leda thought the Farm hands would likely see more of Georgia next Season, perhaps via a promotion or another special appointment. Watching her Owner's focused gaze, she sniffed success.

The two ponies faced each other as their riders struggled to regain control.

Olivia watched the spectacle with professional interest. As Overseer of the Trainees, she was evaluating not just the riders' capabilities in regaining power over their animals, but also she was measuring Georgia's cleverness and skill. If the oil were too hot, the show would be ruined. Too little and it would be unnoticeable. But just the right amount? It would be a fine addition to the show and a positive mark on Georgia's chances for promotion.

With a nod, Olivia signaled her satisfaction with the surprisingly accurate trainee.

The drumbeat boomed as the ponies readied themselves for the first pass. With the crowd's cheering to prod them on, the ponies faced off. They charged across the ring directly in each other's path – the first one to veer off would lose points. If a pony threw its rider, it would also lose points. Only the mount left standing with its rider in place could win the points needed to be the victor.

They closed in at high speed and the women in the gallery inhaled so much air it felt like the stadium trembled. If the ponies collided, it would be a defeat for both teams. A tie would dishearten the crowd and was vigorously discouraged by the Owner.

Who would yield? Who would fight to the end? The climax broiled under the sunny sky.

The music grew louder and louder as the ponies ran closer to each other. They were so well-trained that they didn't stare at the opposing rider and pony; instead, they focused only on their riders' whip and commands. By now, their asses were bright red from the riders' pounding but the horses' spirits remained determined as they followed their training and fought for the win.

The space between them narrowed to just a few yards when a sudden jerk of the reins pulled one pony out of the path of the other charging animal. First, the crowd was hushed, and then a roar broke out as the on-target pony's points were recorded on the scoreboard. For her fine work, the charging trainee was awarded five points – a sizeable lead. It would take a full press to triumph over a lead that big.

No one knew if the pony that was pulled out was up to the challenge. Sharon considered her trainee's options and what she might be consider doing in a similar situation. All trainees understood the second pass was more difficult than the first because the animals were weary from carrying their loads and from the first go-round. Watching the second pass was always entertaining and the audience could see if either trainee had lost her nerve or worse, had gained too much confidence from the first outcome.

Sharon raised her whip and the riders moved their ponies to line at opposite ends of the stadium. The second pass would begin when the two contenders were in place. First Competition rules allowed for just three passes before the winner had to be declared.

The young rider with five points on the scoreboard cropped her pony's hindquarters quickly and urged on her steed. It knew what it was supposed to do and readied itself for the challenge. Digging its hooves into the dirt, the pony began what would be the most important pass of the Competition. A win would put it so far ahead of the other rider that no pony or rider could likely overcome it.

Sharon signaled and the ponies, with their riders digging their heels deep into their midsections, charged toward one another.

The grandstand was silent as they ran. Then the audience broke into loud cheers as they neared one another and got even louder as the gap closed. The pass had to be as straight as possible. No deviations were allowed. Rather than risk disqualification, the riders focused on driving their steeds nose-to-nose. With the decibel level of the cheering growing by the second, the trainees pushed their mounts even harder. By now, the two ponies' hindquarters were bloody purple and welted.

The horses ran true. Sharon was proud of her work in the corral this Season.

They were ridden closer and closer. As if in slow motion, the gallery inhaled and watched as the distance shortened. A collision could be dangerous but the riders' pride and ponies' obedience often overrode good sense or fear.

Suddenly, the Owner realized there would be no veering off in this pass. She leaned in as a smile graced her lips. Leda's eyes stayed on her Owner and she took satisfaction that her Owner was entertained. When her Owner was happy, Leda was contented.

Shoulders and chests smashed together and soft neighing grew into screams. When the audience caught their collective breaths enough and shifted their focus to the center of the ring, it was clear to everyone. One pony had fallen to its knees and the other remained upright. The pony in the dirt was on all fours with its rider dangling from the saddle but her feet stuck into the stirrups so she was not quite thrown. One swift kick to its groin drew a shriek of agony from the animal – it's rider still attached – fell to the dirt in a useless effort to overcome its pain.

When the points were posted by the judges, the 8-0 tally was now an insurmountable lead. It seemed almost pointless to go to the third pass, Sharon thought, but rules were rules and the event would continue.

The women in the audience rearranged themselves under the brilliant sun. Readjusting was required because so many of them had leaned so far forward during the prior pass that their hands hurt from gripping the rails. Many were out of their seats, standing and cheering. With the outcome all but sealed, they were more relaxed and could enjoy the sunshine and chat. The events today were living up – and surpassing – the Farm's reputation as one of the most grueling competitions of all the Season's shows in the North Country. It was a shame that it was almost over, they sighed, because now they'd have to wait another Season to enjoy the Farm's next First Competition.

With everyone settled into their seats, Sharon raised her whip to signal the riders who dragged their exhausted steeds into position one final time. One pony had bruised knees that were covered in dirt from its earlier fall and was covered in brown mud from its dirt roll after its rider kicked it a few minutes earlier. The winner of round two was soaked with sweat yet had no free hoof to wipe its eyes. Both riders were focused on winning the competition and everyone hoped that the leader wanted to conclude the event with more than a win – with a flourish. The Owner, with her years of experience in building her Farm's reputation, knew better.

It's not over till I say it is.

She knew that no rider on her Farm would ever allow its pony or herself to be humiliated. In the eyes of the Owner, the rider on the wrong side of the huge lead would now make what was going to be the most exciting pass of the day. Leda watched her Owner's eyes carefully and struggled to decipher what she was thinking. To Leda, the competition seemed all but finished and the results foretold. The Owner's face told her that something unusual was in the works and Leda was eager to see what the surprise ending would be.

When Sharon's whip was raised above their heads one last time, the two riders cropped their ponies' well-beaten hindquarters and drove their mounts forward. What few in the audience saw – but the Owner noticed immediately – was the young rider's hand reach over and touch her pony's tear-stained face in a simple gesture of reassurance. The Owner drank in that small movement and smiled.

"Her name," the Owner said to Leda, who entered the answer on her tablet. "Watch this," she added, and Leda's eyes refocused on the event unfolding in the ring.

The drumbeat screamed from the speakers as the ponies charged. The rider in the lead drove her steed straight ahead with a solid gait but her opponent slowed her pony and readied for what was to become a majestic spectacle that would become a Farm legend.

The horse slowed in response to its rider's command and stepped solidly forward, one high-stepping hoof at a time. Its feet hit the dirt hard with each step as the charging rival galloped directly toward it.

"Attack," the Owner whispered.

As the lead pony was whipped faster by its rider toward the challenger, the high-stepping mount braced itself as its rider's hand reached to fondle its snout again. It took two quick steps and leaned in to defend against the charging steed's attack. Instead of bracing to absorb the impending violence, the pony threw itself forward on two hooves and the surprised challenger's rider jerked her reins up in disbelief. Her pony had no choice; it lost its balance and the two tumbled awkwardly to the stadium's dirt floor.

There was no question about it: a thrown rider was immediately defeated.

The Owner smiled as Leda marveled at her foreknowledge with new appreciation. Women in the grandstand erupted in cheers. The drumbeats grew into victorious strands as the rest of pack began their well-choreographed celebration circle around the winning rider, who was still seated atop her mount. As their colors overtook the ring, Sharon knelt and bowed toward her Owner.

The Owner greeted her with a single approving nod that filled her with joy. A new legend had just been birthed on the Farm.

Chapter 35: Center Ring

After the surprise ending of the pony show, onlookers were treated to cold drinks and hors d'oeuvres delivered by this Season's well-plumed flock of chickens. As they enjoyed the food and company, the bulls were herded into the center ring. Tara wore an air of confidence as she led the procession. Pack Leaders gained that level of confidence only after working several Seasons with the Farm's biggest beasts.

A group of Trail Bosses and most of the Assessment team gathered to watch Tara's animals perform. The bulls were the most difficult herd to train and their performance was always a sweat-filled experience that no one wanted to miss. The bulls' prize was the most sought-after reward the Farm offered. A winning bull could hope to become the Owner's property and be invited for another Season on the Farm where it would graze, water, and be caged in the Owner's pen just outside the Manor House. A bull could wish for no higher honor than being the Owner's prize.

Bull Competition was the always the fiercest during First Competition.

Dangling between the bulls legs were the meatiest cocks on the Farm. Each woman wanted to see for herself just how such a huge penis might be useful to her and her household. On some occasions, the Owner might sell a bull to a willing buyer if the proper paperwork had been signed. On other occasions, the Owner held an invitation-only auction of best-of-show animals. During some Seasons, she might even offer some of the more disappointing members of the herd to willing buyers who knew they might be getting animals in need of training and severe discipline.

For those reasons, the bulls' event drew the noisiest crowd. They always performed in the center ring.

Today's spectacle had been playing out for hours. Many women were eager to stretch their legs and visit with once-a-season friends. The Owner scheduled a break before the bull competition because many of the audience found their attention drawn toward the penises that were on display in the center ring. As the chickens clucked and offered drinks and snacks to the women, several onlookers responded to the invitation Marla offered over the loudspeaker to come to the center ring to inspect the herd more closely. There they could see for themselves what the Farm's merchandise offered this Season.

Throughout the Season's training, Tara kept detailed records and she, as well as the control room staff, knew how much the each bull's size had grown. The Farm workers grew the bulls' ejaculation time dramatically during the Season, effectively lengthening the pleasure process for the bulls' future Owners. The ability to hold off ejaculation and focus on their Owners' desires made the bulls' lives hell but highlight reels of that training entertained their potential new Owners.

Some of the bulls had gained almost a half-inch in length and most had garnered an extra inch in width when their cocks were bursting full. One noteworthy bull gained an astounding combined three-and-a-half inches in length and girth and that came very close to setting a Farm record.

The Owner spent the break sipping lemonade while evaluating the bulls' cocks and balls from her prime seat. One lucky herd stud might become hers to keep at the end of the Season and she considered her choice well. As she inspected them and commented, the ever-present Leda tapped her thoughts onto her tablet.

"That one is big – long enough for sure," the Owner said with a hint of dissatisfaction in her voice as she pointed to one big bull in the ring. "I need sufficient width as well," she said. Nothing was as boring to her as a long thin cock. It rarely did her much good.

A few moments later, a second bull caught her eye. "It seems big enough," she said, "but does it have the staying power I require?" Leda knew that question called for no answer and remained silent. It would soon be apparent just how much staying power that particular bull, and for that matter, all of them, could muster.

The Owner's remarks were as sharp as an icepick. "Not enough meat on that one," she said in the beginning of a series of rapid-fire comments that Leda typed as she struggled to figure out which bull she was evaluating with each remark. "Big enough balls," she said and added, "but ball size isn't a direct predictor of knowing how to *use* its meat properly." Leda nodded as she typed more notes. "That one over there," she pointed, "bring it closer," the Owner said and Leda transcribed her words before she realized action was required.

She had been given a direct order.

"Yes, Ma'am," she said as soon as she regained her wits. Leda escorted her Owner toward the center ring.

Her presence on the field was rare and Tara directed the trainees to clear a path for her. The bulls were hers to use as she saw fit and although no one knew just what she wanted, they made it effortless for her to have it.

Ten bulls were ordered to their knees.

Their chins were bowed to their chests. The trainees gripped their collars and yanked their heads so their steel and leather muzzles gleamed against the afternoon sun.

She walked the line and studied each bull. None of them had seen her before and certainly didn't know what the secret prize was that she held out for a lucky one of them. Only a stupid bull wouldn't understand that she was important and one by one, a glimmer of recognition crept into their brains. As a rule, bulls could be notoriously slow learners but the trainees' tight grips help speed up their learning process.

"Ma'am?" Tara asked quietly.

Let them wonder. Let them ponder. Let them conjecture. Let them fret. The more they worry, the easier it is for you to own them.

She walked silently to the end of the line, turned on the high heels of her black boots and inspected each of them one more time. Suddenly, she stopped.

Tara looked at the bull that captured the Owner's attention. She envied her uncanny sense of knowing on sight which bull was the biggest or had grown the most.

She kicked the bull's thick penis with the toe of her boot. It emitted a fierce bellow that made the Owner smile. Then she planted her leather sole atop its organs and stepped down hard. The meat beneath her foot was squashed mercilessly onto the ring's dirt floor. The bull's throat screamed brutally and drew many onlookers stares as they looked up from their drinks and snacks toward the center ring. Several rose from their seats and moved toward the ring for a closer look at what was happening between the Owner and one special bull in her herd.

Her boot expertly pinned the skin of one testicle to the dirt. Without a word spoken, the bull knew the Owner could squash its balls as flat as she wanted and it would offer no resistance. With the trainee holding her bull's head still, it couldn't help but meet the Owner's eyes with its own. Her stare pierced its brain.

The torturous process was the Owner's way of evaluating her animals and its screams were ineffective. The animal struggled for a while and then resigned itself to the torture she was inflicting on its organs. The ultimate test she had in store would be played out in front of the entire audience.

When its shoulders sagged, the Owner felt the always-new joy of an animal in complete surrender. She smiled in elegant victory. Tara saw her lips turn up, Leda noted the time and Marla identified the ball sac brand to research the animal's training history. They knew – the Farmhands understood – that the Owner was close to making a decision. Her announcement as to which bull she would keep was always the grand finale of First Competition. If this particular bull lived up to her demands during the Competition, it could be hers for a full Season before she released it and sent it on its way.

That possibility was worth the price that the bull and the rest of the herd was going to pay.

It was time to get the bulls ready for the final event.

Tara glanced at the crowd of trainers and Farmhands who were circling the center ring and chatting along the rails. Their eyes were fixated on the herd. While the crowd stared at the animals, they waited almost impatiently for the most exciting event of the show to commence and while waiting, kept feasting on the bulls' size and potential. Tara felt the herd's combined strength as she cracked her whip over their heads. The bulls stood up instantly and then dropped to all fours, just as they had been trained. Tara smiled.

Demand silently that the pack live up your expectations. They will rise to your demands. Worthy animals would exceed them.

"Pair off!" she commanded as the trainees led their prize bulls into position, one facing another. While the animals worried about the impending event, the Owner nodded as Tara cracked her whip and said, "Begin!"

Almost instantaneously, the beasts lunged at one another. Using every part of their bodies, the bulls launched into one-on-one combat. Strength was rarely the deciding factor in the bullring; instead, it was cleverness, practice and above all else, their endurance that mattered. The bulls trained for an entire Season just to reach the center ring. Not one of them could imagine their own defeat. Ten bulls each believed that it would be the Season's prize.

It was stunning to see them in combat.

One pair was engaged in a brawl so brutal that it drew growls from the participants and shouts of delight from the audience. As the pair wrestled and rolled in the ring's dirt, their sweat glistened under the hot sun. With each growl and every gasp, the Owner's attention was drawn to a different pair. The spectacle of the five pairs of bulls fighting throughout the center ring distracted her. Eyes darted from one struggling duo to the next and each guttural growl drew their focus back again. The best part of bull fighting was the screams and grunts mixing with the commotion of five pair of sweaty animals grappling in the dirt.

Tara cracked her whip twice. The loud snap increased the excitement infecting the already charged atmosphere. The fighting bulls reacted to the crowd's pleasure with renewed ferocity.

Make them perform beyond their capabilities; only then will they transcend their last vestige of humanity and become the real animals they were meant to be. And you will own them.

Tara marched around the corral with her whip cracking the air. She noticed one pair that she knew from the Season's training were close to the end of their struggle. With their gut-wrenching gasps, Tara knew that the crowd had just learned it as well.

One bull gripped the other's cock in its teeth and began sliding its lips along the shaft. The bottom bull was pinned to the dirt and its organ was being carefully stroked by the top bull's fierce lips, tongue and teeth. Tara knew it would be only a few seconds before its limits were reached and the bull's cock would burst in front of the entire crowd of cheering women. The bull snarled through its humiliation and anguished at its impending defeat but the top animal's strength overcame any fight it had left.

The audience giggled as a stream of white juices exploded from the bull's thick cock and flew into the air. The creamy explosion landed all over and decorated the bottom bull's belly as well as made little puddles in the dirt, where it was quickly turned into a black paste as it mixed into the loose soil that flew around the struggling pair. But the bull knew there was no escaping its loss.

Tara pointed at the bull's trainee and she ran over, scooped the liquid from its stomach and legs with her hands, and brought the slime to the bull's mouth. With a groan of defeat and wearing a face sporting its humiliation, the bull was force-fed its own discharge and then crawled red-faced toward the ring's outer fence where it was forced to witness the remaining bulls fight longer than it could manage. Sorrowfully, it knelt and watched as the herd fought on.

The remaining four teams barely noticed their comrade's defeat and continued their own battles. Their focus had to be on their own challengers. As they guarded their highly-trained penises from the lips, of their opponents, they grunted and wrestled to the entertainment of the crowd. But one by one, four bulls had to taste defeat and feel their own explosions. One by one, they were forced to ingest the telltale signs of their losses with distaste and dejection frozen on their faces. Finally five defeated bulls were positioned around the corral while five more enjoyed the cool water from Tara's hose as it rinsed dirt from their bodies.

The stream of cold water served a second purpose: it created a sizeable mud hole in the center of the ring. The Owner leaned in for a better look.

When Tara's trainees reeled up the hose, the first-round winners bulls were summoned to the mud pit. Crawling through the slime, they wore black dirt with pride. All the herds' attention was focused squarely on the center ring. The audience knew that every First Competition at the Farm concluded with a fierce muddy bull fight and this Season's bull finale was about to begin. The women, herds, trainers, Farm hands, trainees, and Owner were transfixed on the mess in the center ring.

With a single crack from her whip and Tara's monosyllabic order of "Now!" the bulls charged.

It was a free-for-all worthy of the finest Season on the Farm. Bulls raged one against another, two on one, and pair against pair. They found herd-mates to form teams and attacked unprotected animals ferociously. Bull after bull spurted and just as quickly, its trainee fed the loser its just desserts before leading the vanquished animal to the edge of the ring.

When the dust settled , there were just two bulls left.

Muddy and grimy, the two beasts faced off against each other. Leda noted that one of them was the bull that had caught the Owner's attention at the onset of the match and she was pleased at having made a good choice. She relaxed for a moment when she saw her Owner's smile.

It was time for the finale.

Tara added sprayed them off with more cold water and added to the goo in the mud hole, but the bulls' eyes stared only at each other with thoughts focused solely on winning. By now there was nothing else for the two bulls – *winning* was the only thing that mattered. Winning would show the bull's and its trainer's success. Too exhausted to care about rules, dignity, or presence, the two bulls could taste victory.

No holds were barred at this point. Nothing would be held back.

Tara cracked her whip and they lunged at each other. The bulls struggled and used every part of their bodies – their hands and feet, arms and legs, mouths and tongues and lips. Every attack drew a loud reaction from the crowd as every lunge propelled a counter-attack. The audience was gripped in the spectacle of flailing arms and battling legs that foretold the beginning of the finale of the First Competition this Season on the Farm.

Only the Owner knew that for one lucky bull, if it pleased her, the Season's end was really its personal beginning. No bull could know exactly what was in store for it if the Owner chose to keep it as her own for an extra Season. The bulls fought for the win and the Owner took home the prize.

Suddenly, the crowd inhaled at what was happening in the center ring's mud hole. The bulls managed to twist themselves into a mangled pair with one's mouth approaching the other's organ as the second's fingers drove into the first's crotch. Sucking and stroking with its teeth and lips, one bull brought the other to the edge of climax but had to fight against its own impending finish. The two seemed like a single intertwined carcass and their humping bodies slogged in the mud performing a rhythmic dance of infectious titillation. The crowd loved the spectacle and were sitting on the edge of their seats. The Owner grinned as she watched the demonstration of two huge organs struggling to rage against what was natural to them.

It couldn't last for much longer, she knew, and Competition would be over soon. She felt the tingle of the finale's coming to an end all over her skin.

If it holds out long enough and wins, I may just keep it.

Leda stole a glance at her Owner and was impressed by her intensity. As she studied the Pack Leaders around the rings, Leda saw Ursula, Sharon, Ronda, and Paula delighted that their Owner was pleased with this Season's First Competition. It was as if the entire Season so far was wrapped up in the fight-to-the-death that was unfolding right now in the muddy center ring. No two Seasons were ever be the same and yet no Season ever disappointed. This year's Competition was concluding on a high note as the two bulls slapped, stroked and sucked the other with no thought other than their own success.

Driven and charged, they were locked in mortal combat.

Drums screamed from the speakers and filled the sun-drenched air. Each bull wrestled with the other and against its own imminent ejaculation. The fierceness of their combat filled the corral's air. The herd was transfixed as one cock after another seemed to be on the verge of climax and then somehow, through all the work of its training and each bull's tenacity, managed to fall back into a safer level. When one bull pulled back to hold off its own finish, the other moved in to attack. Then it reversed. Over and over again, the two bulls struggled mightily and the crowd was now screaming in delight.

Shrieking soon replaced the screaming and that was soon followed by bull bellows that bordered on hysteria. The Owner was spellbound by the spectacle and the audience was overcome with sexual desire brought about by the sheer untamed penis power displayed in the center ring. The rest of the packs knelt in awe; the trainees stood behind their animals in respect for the savagery of Tara's show. The only sounds were those of pure animal instinct flowing through the bulls' vocal cords and released into the same air they were breathing.

With simultaneous bull cries of horror and triumph, a huge stream of yellowish-white liquid erupted, splattered onto one combatant's belly and testicles, and finally drooled toward the muddy ground.

Tara cracked her whip as the audience cheered wildly. The Farm hands stood straight and tall in silent ovation to Tara's achievement as Leda watched her Owner lean in to determine just which of the two bulls had actually won the event. Afraid of the potential of her Owner's wrath if the unanticipated bull had won, Leda held her breath and waited for Tara to inspect the bulls' penises one final time to end the Season's First Competition.

Almost too exhausted to raise themselves up, the two bulls struggled to their knees. And then the victor was clear.

One penis hung small and limp. The other stood proud and erect, as if in salute to its Pack Leader and through her, directly to the Owner. There was no noise, no cheering, no clamoring that entered this bull's ears; instead, all it heard was the strong voice of its Pack Leader.

"Well done," Tara commented and the bulled grinned from ear to grimy ear.

She raised her whip and pointed to the crowd, singling out her Owner with her eyes.

"I present to you the winner of the First Competition," Tara called to louder adulation. "I hope the event pleased you." Then she knelt and bowed her head in ultimate submission to her Owner.

Leda barely found the courage to turn her eyes toward her Owner. With a tiny movement, she glanced to her right and drank in the smile of happiness that filled her, along with the other Pack Leaders, staff, and trainees with pure joy. A nod. A solitary nod. The Owner was pleased. And all was right on the Farm.

The herd would continue its training till Season's end under the watchful eyes of their Pack Leaders, Trail Bosses, Assessment and Control teams, and most of all, their Owner.

But now it was time to celebrate.

Chapter 36: The Bus Ride

Zoe was frantic as she tried to complete a never-ending stream of orders that Willa and Yvonne were spouting in her direction. Counting, checking, double-checking and finally lining up the herds for their bus rides back to the city was an all-consuming task for a trainee. Because it was her first time as coordinator, Zoe was even more harried but Willa had confidence that when she boarded her bus for the return trip, each member of this Season's herd would be accounted for and in its proper seat. It was like that between the professional staff and the trainees – you had to count on your girl to do what she was supposed to do and be confident that she would rise to the occasion. Yvonne wasn't so sure. Her eyes triple-checked each list and performed the final count and testicle ID tag check to ensure that every Farm animal was in the correct seat on each bus.

That was one difference between being Leader and a trainee or mid-level hand on the Farm. As far as Transportation was concerned, Yvonne knew that the buck stopped directly with her. She would leave no animal's fate to chance.

This Season was like every other Season on the Farm in some ways. No two were ever identical and that was the only aspect that made them all the same.

Victoria stood at the center of the five circles of Farm packs, each with its Pack Leader in charge, and announced the final instructions.

"Seasons come and go," she said with a lilt in her voice. "You are no longer the same males who attended our introductory session many months ago," she said amid the pack's heads that were bobbing up and down in absolute agreement, "and you are no longer limited by those cumbersome male traits that prevented you from growing into the best animal slaves you had the potential to become." As she surveyed the herd, Victoria was pleased to see grins on the faces of the bobbing nods. "Remember everything you learned at the Farm, and take every lesson with you. Serve your new owners well."

Every lesson became part of their beings. They were changed. They were new. They had made the ultimate journey into submission.

She stopped for a moment and let her mind wander to the events that were surely unfolding in the Manor House so far away over the ridge she saw in the distance. Almost out of sight from the dusty road filled with five idling busses that would take this Season's herd back to the city, Victoria thought about what the Owner was likely doing right now.

Regaining her focus with a slight cough, Victoria continued.

"Most of all, remember your discipline!" she said firmly. "And pushing yourself – to new heights – to greatness – to perfection!" Her voice flared along with her nostrils. Willa grinned because she loved seeing Victoria's excitement displayed in her final charge to the herd.

"You will serve your new owner well," she said. And everyone knew that there was no more that needed saying.

Willa began herding the packs onto their busses and her breasts stuck out of her black leather vest while her blue colors peeked into the sunlight. The males seemed almost uncomfortable to be standing upright with real shoes and socks in contrast to their comforting nakedness that had become their new normal. No animal left the Farm wearing clothing, but each was always shod. Every testicle's brand was inspected by several staff members to ensure that it was appropriately classified and returned to the proper city in appropriate fashion. Clothing would come later, as the bus neared a more populated area.

For now, the animals were better off naked and shod displaying their hairlessness, newly-gained muscles, leaner physiques, and above all, their total acquiescence to the authority that now grouped, marched, and finally boarded them onto the buses that would return them to their old and very new lives. Their new owners were looking forward to their return and in some cases, to their new homes after bartering and purchasing were completed after Competition.

Willa glanced toward the ridge and toward the Manor House that stood just beyond it in the morning mist. She, like all the other Trail Bosses, Pack Leaders, Assessment and Control teams, wondered exactly how the final event of the Competition was unfolding at that very moment in the Owner's private salon. The staff would gather for dinner much later that night and learn a little more about the conclusion; however, only a select few were allowed to participate in the excitement that was sure to be transpiring within its darkened salons.

The real end of the Season at the Farm took place in the Owner's residence and only the top staff members were allowed to witness any part of it. Each Farm hand hoped for the day she might earn a high enough rank to participate.

With a Season-ending sigh, Willa boarded the bus after her last male was belted in. Nadia, her green colors brilliant between her breasts glowing in the sunshine that was just breaking through, accompanied her Transportation Coordinator and smiled bravely at Willa before disappearing into the confines of the bus's now-closed doors. Irena, one of the new trainees who worked the ponies this Season, climbed aboard the third bus and shortly each set of doors closed with a whoosh as the engines revved up. Another Season was ending and the staff felt a combination of utter relief mixed with anxious curiosity.

What was going on inside the Manor House was on all of their minds.

Red spots of fabric peeked out from the black leather vests pushing the full breasts of the Processing Staff up and out. They –

happily showing off their lofty bosoms – stood alongside the road and watched the caravan leave. They didn't wave; none showed any sign of recognition or sadness that the Season had ended. For them all the end of one Season signified the beginning of the next and each staff member knew that she would enjoy the end-of-season dinner only to wake up to the happy chore of readying the Farm for next Season's herd. The next flock would be another challenge. They always were.

Behind the Processing Techs, small glimpses of neon blue pressed between their trainees' tanned nipples. Their job was finished this Season but the next Season, which would begin so quickly the next morning, was already on their minds. It was finally time for each group to retire to their offices and complete the end-of-season reports that Victoria would analyze and compile for Leda to deliver to their Owner. The final report, which would be delivered that night at dinner, was one of many that helped the staff revisit the Season as they related highlights to the Owner so her reactions would be immortalized on Leda's omnipresent tablet.

Katrina nodded to Victoria and the two turned in step to signal to the rest of the Farm hands that each should take her staff and begin the data entry and evaluation that would turn into vivid reports delivered over a sumptuous meal. Finally they would enjoy video highlights from the Season. The video was their group treasure; after all, no one could see everything as it happened in a place as vast as the Farm. The video was always played in silence that was punctuated by laughter as the staff saw clips of what the Owner had viewed nightly during each Season. The episodes that she determined were in their best interests to view was what they saw. Now in her fifth Season on the Farm, Katrina looked forward to this year's celebration, even though her thoughts wandered inside the Manor House as she imagined what was happening inside. She wasn't focused solely on the next crop of animals right now. Her curiosity was in the secret details of the Owner's choices that were being made at this very moment.

Ursula walked with the other Leaders, Tara, Sharon, Ronda, and Paula, toward their offices. Their boots were black and shiny as if the Farm's dirt dared not impugn the luster they worked so hard to create. They chatted quietly until Sharon asked the question that was on all their minds.

"Who do you think she will choose this Season?" she asked.

The four other women smiled and let the awe of anticipation energize them to begin – and finish – their reports during the remainder of what daylight was afforded them. It was time to get to work. The Season started tomorrow.

Chapter 37: The Ride Home

The herd's silence filled the buses but didn't overshadow their distinct animal presence. Each male had grown in physical prowess during the Season as well as in understanding of what each one was always meant to be but needed to learn how to accept. The Farm was much more than a place that turned men into animals and on the bus ride home, the pack finally figured it out. Their Season on the Farm was a life-altering experience that reorganized their way of viewing themselves within the world they used to know. Each had been given a new reality. Each had been trained to become the slave they were meant to be. The Farm staff had also arranged for proper new ownership for many of them.

When they first arrived at the Farm, as was usual for new herds, it was difficult for each newcomer to realize that his power in the city meant nothing on the Farm. A male was simply an animal to train on the Farm, whether he formerly inhabited the C Suite or was a truck driver. Each survived only as well as his mind and body could endure; each was rewarded and punished in accordance with the way the entire herd performed. No male existed individually on the Farm. The first lesson, they all remembered so well, was that the way they had misunderstood their power and uniqueness just didn't matter.

A well-performing herd was the only goal their Pack Leaders wanted and it was the single achievement that mattered. There were no winners or losers on the Farm and the males had come to learn as they did in every Season, that the herd had a purpose that had to be discovered by each of them but performed as a group.

Naked men sat on tiny white towels that kept only their rectums – but not their asscheeks – from the seat fabric on five identical buses on their way back to the city. This trip would return them to the location of their old lives but not to their former experiences. The small towels barely covered the split in their asscheeks that were spread on each leather seat. Had they tried to shift their positions, each would have betrayed himself with the sound of a sweaty ass ripping off warm plastic. None moved. The bus drove in total silence.

In the lead bus, Willa stood in front of the anxious group and inhaled their scent.

"You have only a few hours to begin a difficult transition," she said. "Each of you has a lot to say. You want to relive the Season. You want to talk it over and hear what others experienced and what they feel. You're not even sure how you feel."

She waited for the nervous giggling to subside before continuing.

'I will tell you how you feel." She watched their faces like she did every Season when she said these exact words. They wanted to share, to talk, to commiserate and to bond. But Willa, like the others Trail Bosses on each bus, would never allow that. Males don't need to bond, she had learned.

They are meant to serve women and do not need each other. They serve. That is how they are truly fulfilled.

"You want to get back to your 'old life' but you have no idea how to do that or what that life is anymore. You want to share how you feel and no one wants to hear you because they have complicated feelings as well. You want to put on some clothes but you also want to be naked because that's what is normal to you now and it makes you feel comfortable. You have questions but I'm not going to answer them. Is that about right?" Willa waited for the nervous smiles to morph into silent frowns on tense lips.

"You are no longer who you were at the beginning of the Season," she said. "You are now trained enough to become proper slaves. That's all. You are trained. You are not more or less than you were but you are very different. You see the world – what used to be your world – differently. The only question that remains for you to think about is this one." Willa waited for them to pay even closer attention to her.

"What are you?" She stopped and waited for their blank stares to change into questioning looks.

"No one can answer that for you," she seemed to finish. "But I can show you."

Curious faces followed her as she walked the bus's center aisle. Her leather vest supported beautifully tanned breasts that had completely escaped from their confines and jiggled as she strode. The males didn't fixate on her breasts; instead, they listened to her words.

They will learn. They have to understand what they just learned this Season. It's not just their bodies that have changed.

"You don't own yourself anymore," her voice was somehow different. "There no more of a 'self' and there is only what you are to the women we have selected for you or the Mistresses who paid good money for some of you. You now have a new special *owner*."

Her words touched every herd member's heart individually and collectively. They understood that she had stated exactly what they feared and knew and that no words they could say would match the weight of what she had just confirmed.

Without a woman's ownership, they were – and always would be – incomplete.

Chapter 38: Season's End

The usual bustling that marked the end of a Season on the Farm had infiltrated the Manor House as each Pack Leader was busy wrapping up the Season's reports. Control finalized the Season's video that would be shown when the buses, emptied of all save the farmhands, had returned to its home on the Farm. A full dinner would begin shortly and the Owner and her staff would watch the Season's movie and laugh and learn. Leda was in a state of heightened anxiety as she coordinated every staff member's efforts amidst a cacophony of data entry and analysis that the flurry of trainers, technicians, maintenance women, trainees and Trail Bosses were finishing. They filled the Manor House with a whirl of controlled turmoil.

It was at times like this that Leda thought she would lose her mind. Coordinating the end of a Season was a perfected practice but she always felt that she might overlook something critical amidst the insanity that swirled around her.

As usual when a prize was taken by the Owner, she was secluded in her salon with her newest bull in another season-ending ritual: the taking of new property. The women tried to tamp down their curiosity in what was unfolding behind the locked door. They worked as quietly as possible to give their Owner privacy and possibly to overhear whatever sounds might escape from the darkened wing of the Manor House. During other post-season rituals, they occasionally overheard only the loudest shrieking. Normal screaming rarely escaped the confines of the Owner's soundproofed salons.

All heads snapped in the same direction when the women heard a poorly stifled giggle.

"Do you remember when the pigs first learned they had to eat out of the troughs?" Paula asked to no one in particular. All heads turned toward her and most smiled at the memory.

"Remember the vomit?" she said and laughed as others joined her merriment.

A second question was shared from behind a row of computers in which the Pack Leaders were entering data.

"Do you remember when they first figured out they were going to be dressed up in nylon and feathers?" Rhonda giggled at her own question and laughed at the memory.

Several trainees joined in, feeling for the first time that their voices had a right to be added. Rhonda smiled at them in reassurance that their participation was no longer out of line. Not tonight.

"Oh, sheesh," a third question rang out, "do you remember the first pony circle and how the long whip cracked against the big asscheeks of the fat boy with blond hair?"

The entire room burst into the laughter and gave the staff much-needed physical and emotional relief. The fat boy with blond hair had been a reluctant participant at first and needed special breaking. That pony's participation had been a frequent source of after-dinner amusement. Just remembering what that pony had achieved – the weight loss, bigger muscles, the ability to coordinate high-stepping without knocking down the rest of the herd – filled the women with a feeling of accomplishment. A pack leader who couldn't break an animal quickly enough was often demoted outright.

The loudest laughter came from Ursula as her accent grew when she relaxed from herd work. Several trainees waited for her memory so they could add to the oral history that was unfolding at that moment. It took a few seconds to control her amusement and the trainees were eager for her to share what she remembered so well.

"This one cow got milked so hard that it shot straight into Georgia's eye!" she blurted out and convulsed in her own laughter.

The room of women joined Ursula in laughter in what had to have been Georgia's most embarrassing moment, especially when it was replayed in slow motion after an otherwise stern dinner that the Owner arranged just to play the short piece and uplift her workers with a single effort.

> *You own their reality and you sculpt it to make it what you want them to be. They are yours. Build the image of what they should become and they will become it. And you own them.*

A parade of naked breasts marched throughout the Manor House as vests were turned down and colors shifted up between just-promoted trainees jiggling bosoms. Each wore the magnificent tanned hues of working in the sunshine for an entire Season. Keyboards were tapped, tablets were synchronized, video files were uploaded into cloud servers, and each hand's focus was riveted on her work, except for that small part that hoped to hear the slightest shriek emanate from the Owner's salon.

"Are we on schedule?" Leda asked with a hint of desperation. The nodding heads and jiggling breasts assured her that they were.

Chapter 39: Four Words

No one left a Season on the Farm without being changed from the inside out. The packs and the farmhands learned something new each Season. Leaving the Farm was a combined end and beginning for everyone but the one whose life would be forever transformed the most was currently kneeling at the feet of its new Owner in an uncluttered room with no outside light or sound seeping in to interfere with her interacting with her new property. Just a few moments ago it was a prize-winning bull and now it simply was a naked and filthy animal kneeling at the feet of a woman he had never seen before. His mind struggled to adjust to her words. Her simple sentence reverberated over and over in his head.

"I own your reality," she had said matter-of-factly. That was it. Just four words.

Her eyes bore into his and the prize bull felt his body tremble from her intensity. Naked and dirty, kneeling and vulnerable, alone and frightened, it struggled just to meet her eyes. In another world, he would be sitting behind a spotless desk that rose in three directions around him and he would stare at his staff with half of her intensity and reduce them to sputtering morons. Her glare tore through his skin and landed in his soul.

For the first time he didn't know what to say and couldn't manage to make his lips, tongue or teeth work together to form words.

"Muh?" was the only sound that fell from its parched lips. She smiled with lips that curled in an evil and triumphant grin.

Create their reality and make them live in it. When you own that, they are yours forever.

"Sit," she said and after a moment's hesitation, the bull sat at her feet. The plop of bare asscheeks against the wooden floors warmed her.

"Kneel," she said and a little more quickly this time, the bull complied.

"Flat," she said and first it flopped onto his back before rolling over onto his stomach. *Which way?* he wondered and wallowed in the increasing unhappiness that this one-sided monologue was bringing into its life.

"Up," she said with yet another single syllable and the bull struggled to its feet with its full nakedness and spent penis filling her eyes.

"Spread," she was unrelenting in her conflicting demands and the bull complied almost simultaneously with her syllable. Its legs were now shoulder width apart because the bull hadn't been instructed what to do with them.

"Turn," the Owner said next in her macabre ritual of claiming her property. The filthy bull complied from a trancelike state of complete obedience.

"Bend," she said but the animal still had no idea where her commands were going. Yet the naked bull felt unable to resist her orders so it bent in half and moved its hands toward its asscheeks to ready itself for what might be demanded next.

The surprise that registered on the bull's face when she cracked a sturdy whip against its asscheeks and scored its hands holding its cheeks apart was visible to her in the mirror. Its yelp of pain was sharp and the sound filled the room.

"Obey!" she raised her voice just enough for it to understand that anticipating her commands was not its best option. It needed to listen.

The Owner worked the bull for an hour and wore down whatever strength remained after the bullring performance at Competition. It didn't take long before it was performing in a silent dance of submission to the single words that she spoke in an increasingly quick tempo. For her, it was the dance of ultimate submission; to the bull it felt like sinking into insanity.

Own reality. She lived those words.

When the Owner was certain that her new bull had no will left to break or remaining strength to fight, she knew it was time to claim it fully as her property. Every Season that she took a prize bull from the herd, the legacy grew. Taking one as her own contained a built-in ritual that she enjoyed as the real Season spectacle on the Farm. This one would be no different.

Stuffing a black hood over her property, the Owner circled her naked prey as it struggled to figure out where she was. Like a cornered beast, it reacted with primal responses to her quiet movements. The hooded bull tried to hear her, feel her, smell her or somehow place her within its blind perimeter. When its hands reached out, a whip punished them. It jumped to the side and the whip kissed its hind legs. Hopping and dancing to her whip's kiss, the animal finally screamed in terror.

"What the hell is happening to me?" it cried. "Who are you and what do you want me to do?" it wailed.

The bull was just beginning to become her property, she knew from experience. Just a few more minutes and it would be on its knees, begging for her to own its body and soul completely. But first, there was an important step that the beast had to take in order to please her. When the bull accomplished her next demand, it would let her know that it had completely surrendered. Without that final giving of itself to her, she would not feel the Ownership she required from each brute she took as her own.

She called it exactly what it was. Reality ownership. When she owned its reality, it would surrender and become nothing more than her property.

"Never speak," she snapped at the nude figure huddled and trembling in the corner of the room. "Not a word," she dictated and waited a few seconds. "Obey."

There was no need for her to add any words. It had to accept the reality she created and then she would own all of it.

The animal's reality is what I want it to be. It exists only in relationship to me.

"Nooooo...." fell from its lips and escaped through tears that fell from under its hood. Several seconds later it was followed by, "Arrrrr," and then "nnnnnnnnn" finished its noises. The bull finally knelt and lowered its head in abject submission.

Her whip kissed its dirty skin over and over as it bawled louder and louder in incomprehensible syllables.

Outside the oak door, the gaggle of bare-breasted women snickered as they heard each screech until the ever-vigilant Leda saw the light on the wall shine. She scampered toward the Owner's office and knocked quietly.

The door swung open and her words reached every woman's eavesdropping ears.

"Take this thing out and scrub it. Then cage it."

Leda dragged the beaten bull out the back door and hosed it off and scrubbed it completely, inside and out. Knowing that the sting of disinfectant soap awaited its whipped skin, the women competed for vantage points to see more of the amusing ritual. The beast was filthy. The water was cold. And the soap would sting its wounds.

They all knew they wouldn't see the bull again until they were well into enjoying their dinner feast. With the show over for now, they returned to work and tabulated the Season's data so that evaluations could be finished and they could report that the Farm improved in every possible aspect. Anything less was simply unacceptable.

Chapter 40: The Feast

The final Feast of the Season was the only night when all Farm staff, from lowly trainees all the way up to the Manor House caretaker could relax. All Farm workers sat together and ate, chatted and visited with those outside their Season-long venues. While catching up, they relished in their own and each other's accomplishments. The time for them to work on improvements would come soon enough at first light. This special evening was for relaxing and it was often the most memorable night of the Season for the staff.

Feast was the only meal of the Season that was catered by outsiders so that the entire kitchen and maintenance staffs could dress up, join the others and eat leisurely. The Owner valued her entire staff and believed this special evening that celebrated another successful Season on the Farm belonged to everyone.

As was served every Season but was nonetheless stunning for the first-year trainees, was the quantity and elegance of the Feast. Food was displayed in a long table filled with sumptuous choices. Hungry women dived in without restraint till they were full of a particular course and then welcomed new foods to grace the table. Lobster tails were piled next to thickly sliced beef. Vegetables were fresh and roasted. Plates were large and returning for seconds was the norm. It was the one night that no one was shy about what or how much she ate, or for that manner, in what way she ate it. Farm work was more than enough for all of them to keep in excellent shape; the prepared meals gave them energy without fear of gaining weight. Tonight's meal was the Owner's offer to them to enjoy personal abandon.

They ate, chatted and ate more. Ursula's bowl that overflowed with shrimp shells was an ongoing Feast joke. Nadia went after the lobster tails with two hands and everyone watched Marla load up her plate with plenty of the rarest roast beef slices. Both Katrina and Victoria argued over who had eaten more scallops wrapped in bacon while Willa and her trainee, Zoe, found an unlimited supply of spareribs that they had no trouble eating with their bare hands while smearing their faces with barbecue sauce. Wine and beer flowed because Feast was the perfect night to enjoy every ounce of achievement and revel in satisfaction from jobs well done.

This year's meal shaped up to be yet another extraordinary Feast.

Finally, a gong sounded and the chatter in the room ceased. Hired staff whisked every plate and glass from the tables, removed food platters, handed out hot washrags and unveiled a centerpiece of desserts that drew a chorus of *oooohs* and *aaaahs* from the Farm hands. The tall ice sculpture that was a dead ringer for the Manor House in minute detail down to the shutters was placed between the legs of the now clean prize bull that had been the Feast table's centerpiece. If it moved even an inch, the penis and testicles would fall on top of the ice sculpture and its skin would taste frostbite. Warm sauces for ice cream filled heated fondue pots along its sides and every inch of its plastic-wrapped skin supported treats that dazzled the staff so much they forgot they were stuffed from dinner.

They lunged for the sweets and the prize bull was their target.

Forks pricked its skin. Knives cut cheese and sliced cake from its chest. Dollops of whipped cream fell from huge spoons and landed on its crotch. Hot sauces that spilled from serving spoons coated its penis into a swirl of chocolate, caramel and strawberry. Two cookies served to close its eyes and its mouth was held open by a small bowl of cherries to top whatever dessert the women concocted.

When it was determined that they had filled themselves in an orgy of calories topped with whipped cream, Leda rang the evening's final gong and the women stepped back from the dessert table.

It was time for their Owner's entrance.

Olivia nodded and the trainees fell to their knees, bent their heads to the floor and waited silently in their topless leathers for instructions. Higher-level staff formed their own group and knelt in a perfect semicircle so that the highest ranking among them were in the back, standing with their heads bowed. The entire Farm waited in perfect silence.

They heard her heels tap against the floors before they saw her. The clicking of her steps against wood filled their hearts with anticipation and each wanted but did not dare to steal a glance at the new outfit the Owner was certain to be wearing because every Feast demanded a stylish set of new leathers. The scent of her outfit filled their nostrils and confirmed what the seasoned veterans predicted. Brand new and polished, her leathers would outshine them all.

"The end of a Season for all of us to share," she said to their closed eyes. Focusing only on their Owner's voice, the staff listened in silence. "We celebrate the beginning of a new Season together!"

"Triumphs and accomplishments, victories and challenges, success and conquest – that is the story of our Season." Her voice was clear as the staff, from the most experienced overseers to the newest trainees, remained silent. Some of the new trainees had to remind themselves to breathe.

"I saw the reports." The group inhaled collectively. "I commend you all," she said.

Cheers and tears erupted from the staff as the Owner mingled among the lineup of trainees for the critical decision that impacted their young lives at the Farm. Would she keep them on? Would she send them away as unsuitable for her Farm? Their fear was palpable. Leda, with her ever-present tablet's screen glowing, recited the name of each one as the Owner touched every upraised ass with approval. Her touch determined their future.

> *Create and own their realities. Then they belong to you completely.*

As Leda recited names, shouts of joy erupted when each trainee realized she would be kept for another Season on the Farm. Only one new girl was rejected and she was led away quickly from the room. The mood never abated because the staff knew that some trainees were simply not suited for the Farm.

Excusing the trainees, Leda had the staff sit near their Owner so the promotions – or the dreaded demotions – could be announced. The staff's eager anticipation made several tremble with hope. The Owner smiled at her staff and recited the list.

"Willa," she said and watched the woman shake with expectancy. "You are my new transport chief." With a flip of her dark hair as she lifted her head in response to hearing her name, Willa stared at her Owner.

"You've done well on the Farm," the Owner said, "busing wild animals to the Farm and returning well-trained beasts to their new lives. Never lost one, did you?" The Owner's smile drew one out of Willa as she rose to complete the promotion ritual.

Stepping toward the Owner, Willa knelt in front of her and raised her head while pressing her neck back so far that every muscle in her body was rigid. She closed her eyes and waited. The Owner ripped the gray fabric from her chest and stuffed a lime green one in its place. Ehen the trainees stared at the drops of blood that coursed down Willa's chest did they realize that the staff's color markings had been sewn into their skin.

If Willa gasped, she did so silently. The room erupted in cheers and they ignored the drops of blood and instead cheered the ear-to-ear smile on Willa's face.

A few more staff changes were made. The Owner rarely made significant changes in front of the staff; instead, she and Leda created the new positions and informed the recipients individually. Complex changes upset the staff and were always handled in the Owner's salon. Announcements to the entire corps, except for a few at the feast, were rare.

Irena was selected to become First Assistant to next Season's Pony Pack Leader and Zoe was awarded red stripes for joining the Processing team. Yvonne, the former Transport Head that Willa replaced was promoted to become Leda's new assistant, a Manor House position that drew an envious gasp from many. Finally, the most-anticipated designations were shared: which staff members would become the Pack Leaders for the next Season.

The Owner took this announcement very seriously because her Pack Leaders set the tone for everything that happened on the Farm. Although they joked that it took five Control technicians to support one Pack Leader, everyone aspired to that role. Some Seasons saw a shuffling of Pack Leaders while occasional Seasons witnessed a new staff member be given that coveted job. It was the final breath-holding moment of every Feast.

Leda held the tablet against her hip because she knew that her Owner had memorized this Season's list of names. It was too important to simply read and she always spoke personally to each newly-appointed Pack Leader – directly into her ear – and left the others to wonder what special words were shared. Those who had experienced that honor never revealed what was said in that private conversation.

"Josie," the Owner said simply.

Josie crept from her place midway back in the semicircle and moved forward in slow motion. In addition to her shock, she wanted to savor every moment of this occasion. Finally, she arrived at her Owner's feet.

"You have remarkable organization skills," the Owner said. Then she bent toward Josie's ear and whispered private words meant for her alone to hear. Josie closed her eyes to concentrate on the special moment. Tears welled as she accepted her colors as they were ripped from her body and new ones stuffed into its place. When she turned toward her comrades, the unmistakable flame of orange jutted out from between her breasts. The new cow barn Pack Leader had been named and it was a joy they all shared. Ursula, they learned later, had been promoted to the auspicious position of running the Medical Intake unit.

One after another, positions were filled and staff members were named. Colors were plucked from the outgoing and new colors were stuffed in their place. The new colors mixed with drops of blood as if forming a lifelong bond between the newly-named Pack Leader and the Owner. Cheers erupted at each announcement, smiles dotted faces and nods greeted the newly promoted. No one paid attention to the Owner's newest bull as it suffered soundlessly on the dessert table amid a pool of melted ice and runny syrups. This was their night; the bull was merely a backdrop.

Finally, the Feast drew to a close. The exhausted staff was dismissed to their quarters and perky trainees, now looking forward to their first day as full staff, caroused happily on the Farm's lush fields before retiring into much-needed sleep.

Back in the Manor House, Leda waited for her Owner to retire so she could oversee the evening's cleaning and then supervise as the facility was returned to its appropriate pristine condition. There is little to say when a Season ends and for Leda, there was always a lot to do.

"Leda?" The voice was her Owner's. The inflection was new.

"Take the bull," she smiled at her closest assistant. "Enjoy the night. Hailey and Georgia will clean up." The Owner turned toward her private quarters to sleep the dreams of the victorious.

A good Season, she thought. A very good Season.

Leda smiled at the bull mired in its goo on the long Feast table and licked her lips. She knew that tonight would be very sweet.

Tomorrow was the first day of a new Season on the Farm.

Epilogue: Intake

Willa counted the buses. There were six. It was time to leave for the city and pick up this Season's herd.

ABOUT THE AUTHOR

Amity Harris is the author of the novels *Debbie's Gift* and *The Training Farm* and has written Femdom stories for decades that are available on her website, *Amityworld.com*. One of the community's best-known and original online writers of erotica, Amity Harris has made many of her stories and novellas available to the BDSM community on her website. Her plots are complex and her characters are compelling. In *Debbie's Gift*, Ron's story is that of strict training with male overseers and a mysterious Mistress whose facility for training is macabre and most importantly, successful for the women who want well-trained slaves and slave-husbands. In *The Training Farm*, Amity moves into a world where 245 males are converted into the animals they were meant to be and sent home to perform for their owners as perfectly-trained slaves. Amity Harris lives the life she writes about and that makes her tales all the more real for her readers who understand very quickly that they are reading the works of someone who lives the life of a slave-owning Mistress and enjoys the males and females she trains for her use.

Printed in Great Britain
by Amazon

22697914R00215